A
NECESSARY
BLESSING

SARAH HEAD

HERESY PUBLISHING

First Published in 2020
by HERESY PUBLISHING
Newbury RG14 5JG
www.heresypublishing.co.uk

Cover design by Charlie Farrow

This is a work of fiction. Names and characters are the product of the author's
imagination and any resemblance to actual persons, living or dead, is entirely
coincidental.

A CIP catalogue record for this book is available from the British Library.

ISBN 978-1-909237-02-5

INSCRIPTION FROM A WELSH HOLY WELL

Water is a necessary blessing,
which God has given us on Earth.
Let us remember 'The author of all goodness'
as we drink from Ffynnon Fawr.

Glossary & Dramatis Personae at back of Book

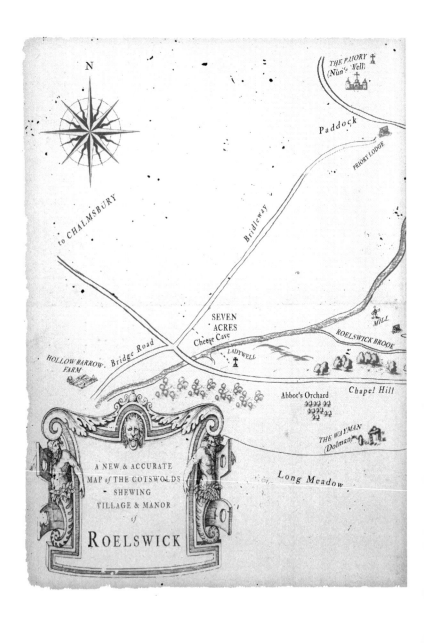

N

to CHALMSBURY

Bridleway

THE PRIORY
(Nun's Well)

Paddock

PRIORY LODGE

SEVEN
ACRES

Cheese Cave

LADYWELL

MILL

ROELSWICK BROOK

HOLLOW BARROW
FARM

Bridge Road

Abbot's Orchard

Chapel Hill

THE WAYMAN
(Dolmen)

Long Meadow

A NEW & ACCURATE
MAP of THE COTSWOLDS
- SHEWING
VILLAGE & MANOR
of
ROELSWICK

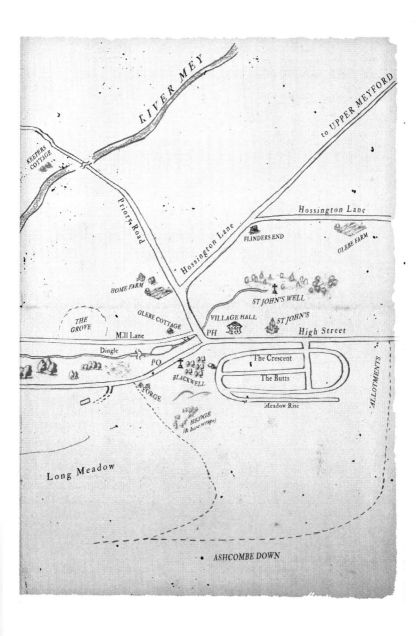

CHAPTER ONE

Ruth wished the woman in front of her would hurry up. How many stamps could she use, for goodness sake?

"Morning, Mrs Turner." The cheerful greeting from her neighbour was unnerving. She attempted a quick smile as she moved towards the counter. "Must be good having your husband home."

Ruth watched the letter in her hand flutter to the ground. It lay in a pool of light as the rest of the world grew dim. "What do you mean?"

"Robert. Back from abroad." The woman's words dripped like black rain onto the disappearing floor. "I saw him having lunch in town last week. Pretty little Chinese girl with him. I think she was expecting."

Ruth stooped to retrieve the errant letter, jabbing it under the Post Office window. She felt sick. A new man stood behind the grille, unkempt grey hair brushing his shoulders, his dark clothes leaching more light from the cubicle. If she peered too closely, the edges of his form broke away in shadowed wisps. His piercing eyes mocked her. His laughter filled her ears.

"You must be mistaken," she said moving to face the bearer of unwelcome news, her voice loud in the quiet shop. "Robert's still in Nanking. I spoke to him last Sunday. He told me they'd extended his contract."

The woman frowned then Ruth saw pity cross her pasty features.

She turned back towards the Postmaster now standing behind the grille, refusing to consider any possibilities or wonder when the dark stranger left.

"Airmail to China," she said, daring anyone to contradict her. While she searched for the correct money in her purse, she asked, "Do you know anyone who might prune my fruit trees. I haven't had time and I wouldn't know what I was doing." It wasn't what she intended to say but it stopped the noise in her head.

The Postmaster called over to another customer browsing the card section. The woman was in her late sixties wearing a plaid skirt and green, quilted jacket, her silver hair wrapped up in a knot at the back of her head.

"Your Zeb free, Granny?"

The woman put back the card she was considering. "Think so," she said. "He finished helping Colin with the Abbott's orchard last week." She turned towards Ruth, her face impassive. "You there today?"

"Yes. It's my week for home working. Part of a new efficiency drive." Ruth was very aware she was dribbling words. Why would Granny care how she worked?

"Pear Tree Cottage?"

"Yes," Ruth wondered how the woman knew where she lived. Apart from a few neighbours, she hardly knew anyone in the village despite living here for almost two years.

"He'll be up around three to see what needs doing."

Ruth smiled her thanks and left, the shop bell jangling as she closed the door. Dark clouds covered the February sky, a chill wind forcing her to pull her coat closed around her. She walked quickly along the footpath by the stream then crossed over the road before she reached the village green to start climbing the steep steps which led to the back of her cul de sac.

As she closed her front door and dropped her keys on the hall table, she heard the computer in her office signal an appointment. She filled the kettle and made herself a cup of tea before settling down in front of

2

her screen. The Skype button bleeped and she found herself connected to her manager far away in Leeds.

After exchanging pleasantries, he looked down at the papers in front of him.

"I'm really sorry, Ruth. I'm afraid the company is restructuring because of the current financial climate. You've been brilliant but your role isn't required in the new system. We're not renewing your contract."

Ruth watched the bobbing Adam's apple as he spoke. Everything made sense now. The lack of referrals, the change to hot-desking instead of her own office. The silence from other colleagues. She was unemployed.

"I know this must be a shock for you. I was going to come down and tell you in person but there wasn't time."

"When," she croaked and cleared her throat. "How long?"

"HR will go through all the details. Basically, you need to return your laptop and all our equipment by the end of next week. I'm sure you'll find something else in no time. You're a very skilled lady. Good luck."

She stared at the blank screen as he broke the connection. She didn't have a job. Robert wasn't there to give her advice. What was she going to do?

The mobile on her desk began to shrill, startling her. She picked it up. The woman from HR was calm and carefree. She had no idea her manner was making everything ten times worse. Ruth answered in monosyllables, scribbling a few notes as the woman went on and on.

"I'll confirm everything we've discussed in an email. Alright?"

"No," said Ruth, "It's not alright but there's nothing I can do."

She pressed the red button, silencing the irritation before the woman could say another word. She placed the phone carefully on the desk. She wanted to smash it against the wall, but it belonged to the firm and would be expensive to replace. She didn't have the money. She wouldn't have the money. What was she going to do? She needed to talk to Robert. What was the time in China?

Must be good having your husband home. The woman's comment rattled inside her head. What did it mean? Twelve long months since Robert left. He rang her faithfully every Sunday evening. They chatted about the sights he'd seen, how much he wanted to be back in the UK.

Replaying their conversations in her head, she realised the past few months had been different. He still talked enthusiastically about sightseeing but when she asked him about coming home, he was evasive, almost angry. There was still so much to do, the firm needed his expertise. He told her not to keep harping on about things he couldn't change.

With trembling fingers, she reached for the house phone and dialled Robert's old office in Metchley.

"Mr Turner's phone, Sadie speaking. How can I help?" The crisp tones of the legal secretary grated on her ear.

"Is Robert there?" Ruth felt her heart begin a war dance in her chest. She could hardly breathe.

"I'm afraid Mr Turner is with a client. Can I take a message or get him to call you when he's free?"

"No." she was about to end the call, but she had to know. "Just one thing. When did he get back from China?"

"I'm afraid I can't tell you. I've only been here six months. Who should I say called?"

"Don't worry, it's not important." She let the phone slide back into its cradle. It was true.

The doorbell rang. Ruth wondered who it might be. Robert fixed a sign telling cold callers to stay away. Very few people came to visit and never during the day. It rang again. She wondered if she could pretend not to be there but when it rang for the third time, she dragged herself to answer it.

A stranger stood on the driveway. He looked like a farm worker, his clothes covered by a pair of faded brown overalls and topped by an old green jacket. His beard was iron grey and neatly trimmed, and he wore an old, felt trilby pulled down on his head.

"Mrs Turner?"

She stared at him blankly. Why was he standing there? She tried to think of a reason, but her brain wasn't releasing any clues.

"You wanted help pruning your trees?"

"Oh," her mouth stumbled, refusing to work. No money, her brain shouted. No job, no money.

"You all right?" His enquiry was gently made but she wanted to scream.

"Yes, yes, fine. I'll show you the orchard." She went to move past him, but he put a hand out to stop her.

"Boots?" he suggested, pointing at her fluffy socks. "Grass is sopping wet after last night's rain."

She closed her eyes, cursing inwardly. What must he think?

"Go round the side of the house, I'll meet you at the back door." She fled into the kitchen, banging the front door behind her. She grabbed her gardening coat from the hall closet. It took several minutes to find the house keys, unlock two sets of doors then wonder where she'd left her boots.

"I'm going mad," she told herself as she crawled under the patio table piled high with chairs in the conservatory to retrieve the errant footwear.

When she finally reached the garden, the man was nowhere to be seen. She caught sight of his hat on the other side of the hedge. He must have grown tired of waiting for her and made his own way into the orchard.

"Sorry for all the delay," she mumbled, following him from tree to tree.

"You kept these quiet," he said, running his fingers along a branch dotted with pale green lichen. "How long since anyone touched them?"

Ruth felt like a schoolgirl told off for forgetting her homework. "My husband liked the idea of an orchard when we moved in but was never here at the right time of year to prune them. They seemed to be all right. We never liked the small pears or those apple trees over there. The fruit was so sour we left them for the birds. The two cooking apples and three eaters were fine until last year. Must have been the frost or something but we had hardly any fruit. I've been meaning to get someone in to look at them all winter, but I kept forgetting."

He stood, looking at the trees for a while as if considering something. Ruth felt a knot begin to grow at the top of her stomach as she prepared for yet more bad news.

"Can you do something for them?" she asked at last, "or should we just get rid of them?" He swung round immediately; his expression so fierce she took two stumbling steps away from him.

"You want to get rid of them?"

"No, no, I love trees. I just wondered if we'd neglected them so much there was no hope."

"There's always hope," he said, the heavy grey cloud above lightening with his smile. "They need a bit of tough love, but they'll be fine. You've got some specials here. Mind if I gather some cuttings so we can graft a few?"

"No, take what you like." She was so relieved he was going to help, for a split second she would have agreed to anything.

"It'll be a few days and I'll need to bring my boys in with me."

Ruth waited while her insides tied another knot. It was going to be a lot of money. Time was money. People were money. Three people for several days would be seriously expensive. She didn't even know how much she had in the bank.

"You sure you're alright?" he asked again as she clutched her forehead in panic.

"Yes, it's just…" Ruth wanted to tell him. He reminded her of her grandfather, when he was fit enough to work his allotment, before the stroke took away his legs and his speech. "My contract's just been terminated. I don't have a job."

She waited for the pity, maybe for anger towards her for wasting his time, for him to walk away once he realised she couldn't pay. She was surprised when his expression never changed.

"Sorry to hear that," he said. "Mr Turner still working for that big law firm in the city?"

"Yes, but…" she wanted to tell him, to confide in someone but if she spoke the words, it would be real. It might not be real. She didn't know. She didn't know anything.

He looked thoughtful, first at her then back at the trees. "It's a big job but I'm sure we can come to some arrangement."

"How much will it cost?" She heard desperation in her voice, but she couldn't help it. Until she knew where she stood, she couldn't afford any extra expense.

"Don't you fret about money for now. These trees want pruning and that's what will happen. We'll see about payment later, when I've had a think. You get back inside and I'll tell the boys we've got a job for tomorrow. They'll be very happy. They like banana muffins if you've any to spare."

"Banana muffins," she repeated, suddenly seeing the three black bananas sitting on top of the fruit bowl in the kitchen. "I'll see you tomorrow then?"

"9.30am or thereabouts. We'll have to go up to the Abbott's and get the pruning gear first."

He walked with her to the back door then disappeared around the house. She waited for the sound of his car but heard nothing. He must have walked. She wondered where he lived. She'd never even asked his name. He'd given her a task. For the next two hours, she worked in the kitchen baking.

CHAPTER TWO

She woke in the darkest point of the night, her heart racing. In her dream, she could hear Robert laughing. He was sitting in their favourite pub beside the canal but when she asked for a drink, he ignored her. She asked again but he was too busy talking to someone else. She tried to shake his arm, to make him notice her but she couldn't reach him and when she tried to move closer, she realised she had no shoes on her feet and she was only wearing a shirt.

Everything felt uncomfortable. When she reached for the light, she found she wasn't in bed but sprawled across the sofa. She must have fallen asleep watching TV. The set was still muttering in the background.

It was too much trouble to find the remote in the tangled rug. She stumbled upstairs, leaving her clothes in a disordered heap on the bedroom floor. As she threw back the duvet, her neatly folded pyjamas stared back at her. She could hear her mother castigating her for coming to bed so late. This was stupid. There was no one else in the house. She was completely alone.

She hurled the offending nightwear at the nearest wardrobe where Robert kept his clothes. The top hung on the latch. She shivered. It was cold standing around naked. The pyjamas might be a hideous shade of pink tartan, but they were warm. As she pulled the top towards her, the door swung open.

She stood, staring at the emptiness inside. Burglars? She hadn't noticed any disturbance in the house. She opened her wardrobe. Everything was there. She checked her jewellery box on the dressing table. Nothing missing that she could tell at first glance. She pulled open the drawers where Robert kept his socks and cufflinks. Nothing. Where were Robert's possessions? They were all there last weekend when she dusted his shoes and polished his grandfather's silver tie pin.

Slowly, she pushed the drawers closed, pulled on the pyjamas and sat in the middle of the bed hugging her knees with the duvet cuddled around her. Robert had been here. He had taken all his clothes and he had gone.

She pushed her folded arms against her middle trying to quell the void. Beyond the window, owls were hunting. She slid down the bed, covering her head so they couldn't find her.

She didn't remember falling asleep, but she began to hear horses' hooves and men talking. Rubbing her eyes, she peered out into the road. A pony was walking up the street pulling a small cart. Inside was the tree man and two younger men.

Horrified, she realised they were coming to the house and she wasn't dressed. The hoof beats stopped and then the doorbell rang. She opened the window, hoping they couldn't see what she was wearing.

"Sorry, I overslept. You know where to go." She wondered what they would do with the pony. Surely it couldn't be left on its own. She noticed one of the smaller men was tying reins around the garage door handle. "Is it safe there?" He looked up at her and she realised he had Downs Syndrome.

"Flash is a good pony. We look after him. Don't worry." His face beamed.

"You know best," she stammered, retreating into the room to start dressing.

When she reached the orchard, the third man was already at the top of a ladder sawing carefully at a branch.

"I wondered if you wanted tea or coffee?"

The old man smiled at her as he stood on the bottom rung. Everything looked so normal it somehow brought her comfort. They looked at home amongst the trees.

"Coffee, one sugar for me. Patrick likes his with two sugars and Geordie prefers squash if you have some."

On hearing his name, the man she had seen with the pony came towards them holding a small pile of sticks in his arms.

"Yes, I like orange squash and blackcurrant. Do you have some?" Geordie asked her.

"I have peach squash."

"I like peaches. Does it taste of peaches?"

"Yes. I'll bring you some." She stopped for a moment; conscious how wet her shoes were. There hadn't been time to hunt for her boots as she couldn't remember where she'd left them. "I'm sorry, I don't know your name. I'm Ruth."

Still keeping his weight on the ladder, the old man held out his hand for her to shake. "Zeb Compson. You met my wife, Amy, in the Post Office."

Ruth remembered her gaze rather than the woman herself. She wondered what it must be like to be married to someone who looked as if she knew everything worth knowing. "The Postmaster called her Granny. Is he a relation?"

Zeb laughed. "No, we might look ancient but we're not that old. Amy and I went to school with John Richards. Everyone calls Amy, Granny."

His words implied everyone knew his wife and Ruth felt a pang of loneliness. Even after all this time, she knew so few people in the village and those she did wouldn't care if she lived or died. She needed to change the subject or she was going to embarrass herself.

"Do you always use a pony for transport? Is it safe with all the cars?"

"Blame, Geordie," Zeb grinned, "He worries Flash doesn't get enough exercise. It's quiet enough after the commuters leave. We'll go home for dinner at 12pm. Be back here around 1pm then we'll finish by 3.30pm so we can be outside the school when the bell rings. The children like to see Flash with the cart. We collect my grandchildren and take them home to the farm."

"You live on a farm." It seemed a stupid thing to say. Why couldn't she just talk normally?

"Not any more. Amy and I live in Glebe Cottage opposite the green. Henry's at Home Farm now."

"Henry's your son?"

"Yes. Our Emily's in town. She's a midwife at the hospital."

Ruth smiled. "It must be wonderful having your family so close. My son, Simon, lives in Switzerland." She excused herself and went to make the drinks.

The day passed in a blur of serving drinks and sounds of sawing. Geordie picked up every pruning and stacked them neatly in the cart. Ruth watched him talk to the pony and pat its neck every time he brought another load. He obviously had a close rapport with the animal.

It was afternoon before she remembered the muffins. Patrick thanked her as he studied the cake carefully before taking a bite. Geordie's face was a shaft of sunlight as he stuffed it into his mouth scattering crumbs all over the grass.

The house was silent after they left, the last clip clop echoing around the cul de sac. Ruth smiled as she cleared muffins back into their tin and put it into the cupboard. She went to check emails on the computer and found a form listing all the equipment she must return to the office by midday on Friday. This week, not next.

She would have to go into town. She would have to walk into her office and say goodbye. In the eight years she had worked for the firm, first in Metchley, then transferring to their Chalmsbury branch, she was always the outsider. Would anyone notice her absence? It was their pity for her jobless status, she feared most. Maybe they would ignore her all together, she wasn't part of their world any more. She wasn't part of anyone's world.

She needed to start looking for another job. Update her CV, register with agencies. Talk to Robert.

The empty wardrobe loomed in front of her. How was she going to do this?

Sitting here, staring into space wasn't going to help. There must be someone she could call, ask for advice. She thought about Clara. They'd been best friends at school, kept in touch all through university but Robert disapproved so they'd stopped. The same thing happened with all her friends. Robert found them boring; she felt embarrassed inviting them around.

He said she was busy enough entertaining his colleagues and attending all the social functions he was invited to and she agreed. She was busy. Looking after Simon, making sure he had everything, there wasn't any time left to follow her own interests. She'd forgotten she had any interests. She loved going to the theatre, but Robert fell asleep and said it was a waste of money. She used to draw funny pictures for Simon when he was little, but Robert laughed at them and Simon wasn't interested in her stories once he discovered football and then girls, so it all disappeared.

Simon's engineering firm sent him to Zurich five years ago. She wrote letters to him once a week, just as she did to Robert. In fact, all her spare time was spent writing letters, but they never replied. She thought back to the last time she'd heard from Simon. Did he know about his father? Was that why she hadn't heard from him? It was over a year since his last visit; not even a card for her birthday. She suggested going to visit him at Christmas, but he told her he would be on holiday with friends.

She got up from her desk. There was no use sitting around moping. She needed fresh air. She'd go for a walk; explore the village, maybe find something new she'd never seen before. She found her shoes and a short jacket, setting off towards the post office which was the route she always took.

The shop was closed when she got there. She stood in front of the locked door for several minutes wondering what she was doing. Eventually, she turned to her left and followed the road out of the village past the mill. She could see lights inside and hear the mill wheel chuntering as it turned.

She wondered if it still ground corn or whether it was kept going by a small army of volunteers. Her father used to be interested in mills, spending much of his retirement visiting different types across the country. He would have loved to have one so close to where he lived. The central wooden door looked firmly shut. Maybe she would find out more details and see what was going on another time.

Tall trees, still bare in their winter sleep, lined each side of the road. The sound of the wind made her look up into the branches. It felt strange, very different to be gazing at something other than her shoes on the pavement.

As she walked up the slight incline away from the water, she began to hear a repetitive noise coming from a small, low barn. The footpath ended just before the road curved to the right, forcing her to cross over to follow the lane in front of the building. Its walls were formed of large, square, white stones topped with a dark, tiled roof. It was in good repair, squatting against the landscape as if it had always been there. She wondered what it was. She remembered passing the building every morning on her way to work but had never noticed it properly before.

She stopped to look at the large wooden doors tightly shut against the winter weather, a red glow through the single, dusty window drawing her closer. She could see live coals glowing inside the forge. To the right, a man was pounding on a piece of glowing iron.

14

He couldn't see her watching him as his hammer struck, always in the same place, always with the same force. It was almost hypnotic watching him work. He stopped and straightened up before thrusting the metal back into the fire. Ruth couldn't remember seeing him before, yet he seemed familiar. He wasn't young, but she could tell from his arms he was powerful. His features were hidden by the dim light inside, but she could tell he was comfortable in his surroundings.

"He belongs here; you don't." She heard the voice in her ear and swung around looking for the speaker. The stranger from the Post Office was standing by the building's edge. His gaze bore through her, making her flinch.

She moved on, following a footpath sign pointing towards a field gate next door to the smithy. She climbed the stile beside the gate and began to walk down the hill. She didn't notice her shoes getting wet in the long grass or how rain was soaking through her thin jacket. When she looked back, the stranger was standing by the gate inside the field. All she could think about was how alone she felt and the yawning black hole where once her future lay. She felt him coming towards her, heard his mocking laughter dogging her footsteps.

She half ran, half slid down the bank, each step taking her deeper into emptiness and pain. Still the figure followed. How was she going to escape? Where the footpath turned at the bottom of the slope, she saw a clump of thorn trees. If she could reach them, she might be safe. Bending low underneath the branches, she crawled into a slight depression next to the wall. His laughter followed; she began to scream.

CHAPTER THREE

Greg straightened his back and smiled. The trivet he just finished was everything he imagined. It just needed a lick of paint to accentuate the leaf patterns and it would be done. He could take it in to town when Bessie was working in the café and present it to her. He knew she would be pleased.

Through the pounding rain on the roof, he heard a sound; a piercing scream. He frowned. Owls shouldn't be out this early in the day. Full night was their hunting time. A screech owl didn't belong this side of the village either, only tawnies here.

He opened the door and listened again. More cries. Someone was in trouble. He pulled on his oilskin and hat, making sure the fire was safe before running down the field towards the sounds.

He couldn't find her straight away. She was hidden behind a bank of young thorn bushes. He only realised someone was there because of the powder blue jacket she was wearing. She was curled up in a shallow depression between the wall and the bushes, her face covered by tangled hair. He could see where she crawled through an animal hole in the undergrowth, like a hare escaping pursuers to hide in her personal scrape.

He shook his head, scattering raindrops. He didn't recognise her as one of the village women. What was she doing lying out here?

Ramblers didn't hide when rain came. The trees didn't provide much shelter given the direction of the wind. Her shoes looked sodden and covered with mud, as were her jeans.

"You hurt?" he called. No answer.

"Can you move?" Silence, the only sound raindrops dripping from his hat onto the ground.

"Do you want me to come in and help you?" He thought he saw a slight head movement and studied the tree trunks considering where the best entry point might be. The way in was easy enough but he was flummoxed to know how to get her out.

Blackthorns were wicked. Folk could get nasty infections if thorns pierced the skin. The hole was far too small for him to reach her and without someone to pull her free on the outside, they'd both be torn to shreds. Now he'd found her, he didn't want to leave her here alone while he went to fetch tools to cut his way in. This was his village and he felt responsible for her, whoever she was.

He reached into his coat pocket to see if he had any string to maybe pull the branches back and tie them to create an opening. His fingers found the hard surface of his phone. He brought it out and punched in the number for Granny's cottage. It was late enough for them to be at home. Soon enough he heard a familiar voice answering his call.

"Zeb, can you bring the truck and your pruning gear? There's a woman trapped behind some blackthorn. Haven't got a clue how long she's been here. Need to get her out. Come through the gate by the smithy and turn left at the bottom. Bring blankets."

He put the phone away and crouched down to peer through the slim trunks.

"Don't fret now, help's on its way. We'll soon have you out." Silence. He couldn't tell whether she was unconscious, asleep or just refusing to talk.

The thought floated through his mind whether she might have taken something but there was no sour smell he could detect. If she'd been an animal, he'd have left her there. No point in prolonging things.

Humans were different, especially ones he didn't know, even though he felt a connection between the two of them.

He wondered about calling an ambulance, but it would take them more time to get here than Zeb and the truck. He couldn't see blood or limbs at odd angles and it was easier for everyone if they could deal with it themselves. Outsiders asked too many questions.

Soon he heard the rumble of Zeb's old diesel engine and saw him coming towards them. He stood up and waved his arms. The truck stopped and two men got out. Greg wasn't surprised to see young Colin Ackerley accompany his old friend. Every tree in the village was Colin's responsibility since he was made Allon, Keeper of Trees, just as Greg was Anvil, Keeper of Metal.

"What's going on?" Colin asked. "Zeb said you needed to take some blackthorn down?"

Greg pointed to the prone figure, curled up behind the trees. Colin whistled. "How'd she get in there?"

Greg shrugged. "Looks like she crawled in through the badger track. No point tearing her to shreds getting her out when these thorns need removing anyway."

"They've been on my list but haven't got round here yet. Too much charcoal to burn these past few weeks."

Zeb passed out heavy gloves and they each took a saw and some loppers and began to remove the small trees. Soon they had a pathway into the space, wide enough for Greg to move towards the woman.

"We need to get you home," he said, crouching beside her. She was trembling. When she opened her eyes, he saw unmasked fear.

"Is he gone?" Her voice was a whisper, but the words filled him with dread. What had she been through?

"Are you hurt?" A very faint shake of the head.

"Up you come then, you're safe now." He wrapped his arms around her and carefully guided her upright. She was wet through and shivering. "Can you walk?" He waited but nothing happened, so he picked her up and carried her to the passenger seat of the truck where

Zeb wrapped her in blankets.

"Should we take her to your place?" he asked Zeb as Colin clambered into the bed of the truck and he pulled himself up beside the silent woman, holding her limp body against him.

"She'd be better off at home, I think. I've told Amy to meet us there."

"Who is she?"

"Ruth Turner from Pear Tree Cottage at the end of The Crescent. The boys and I are working on her orchard."

It took him a moment to register who Zeb was talking about until he remembered Zeb and Granny often looked after two young men with learning disabilities as part of a shared care scheme. He didn't know there was an orchard behind the new houses.

"Why would she be out here?" he wondered as Zeb started the truck and began the slow, steep ascent out of the field.

"Who knows. She told me she'd lost her job, but Amy thinks there's more, something to do with her husband." Ruth groaned and Greg felt her move. He worried she might struggle and try to escape. He drew her closer, stroking her wet hair.

"Ssh now. We'll protect you, little hare. Whatever you were hiding from, you're not on your own."

CHAPTER FOUR

Granny opened the front door when the truck drew up. It was clear she had been keeping watch for their arrival.

"How'd you get in?" Greg asked, knowing how incomers liked to keep their doors locked.

"Back door was open," she said, peering into the cab. "How is she?"

Greg got out and eased the blanket wrapped bundle towards the open truck door. "Can you stand?"

He saw a faint nod and lifted her onto the ground. Her feet seemed firmer now as he guided her slowly into the house. Granny took over once they reached the stairs, her arm around the slender figure as they made their way into the bedroom and shut the door. He heard voices but not what they were saying.

"Cup of tea, Anvil?" Mattie stood in the light of the kitchen. Greg wondered why she would be here but then remembered she was now the Circle Maid since returning from up north and was supposed to make herself useful. There was always something to do around Granny. She didn't hold with folk being idle.

Greg unlaced his boots before stepping gingerly onto the hall carpet. Despite the obvious central heating, the house felt cold, impersonal. As he walked towards the kitchen, he saw a living room on the left with a shining leather armchair dominating the room. A pristine rug sat in front of the wood burner in the fire place, but he doubted a fire had ever been lit. To his right was a dining room, the large table surrounded by stylish modern chairs then a small study beyond that. Everything seemed perfectly positioned to welcome visitors or new owners. It didn't feel like a home.

"Uncle Zeb has taken Colin to see the orchard before it gets too dark," Mattie told him.

Greg looked at the footwear in his hand, thinking he would rather be outside with the men than caught in the kitchen with Mattie, but he wanted to be within call in case Granny or the little hare needed him. He knew she had a name, but he'd forgotten what it was. He still remembered his first sight of her and the overwhelming feeling he must protect her.

He dropped his boots behind the kitchen door where he saw others and came back to the table. He picked up the mug, blowing on it before he took his first mouthful. A plate of biscuits sat in the middle, so he took one, only realising how hungry he was when it was gone.

"I'd take a seat if I were you," said Mattie standing over a pot of something and stirring it with a long, wooden spoon. "Granny reckons we'll be here a while."

"She does, does she?" Greg pulled out a chair, wincing as it scraped along the floor.

"She reckons something bad's happened and Ruth isn't coping on her own, so we're here for support."

"And food?" Greg asked sniffing the aroma coming from the pot. "Stew?"

Mattie nodded, turning her attention to another pan sitting on the hob. "Bone broth too if Ruth's not up to stew."

"Granny's taking no chances if she's brought bone broth as well." He grinned and was pleased when Mattie reflected his smile.

He'd known the girl since she was a toddler but living in the outside world had changed her, given her confidence and maturity beyond her years. He knew her parents were finding it difficult having her back home. There just wasn't the room in their small cottage at Flinders End for another adult with three youngsters growing like weeds and only three bedrooms between the seven of them. He knew the boys resented giving up an entire room so Mattie could have a quiet place of her own.

He suspected Mattie wasn't too happy with the situation either. Being the only daughter could be a drawback when you had your own jobs to do. It was only a few weeks since she told everyone about her plan to investigate the history of the Abbott's Orchard as part of her studies.

"Come and run her bath, Mattie," Granny's voice had no trouble reaching them in the kitchen. "Bring my small basket up with you."

"Gotta go," Mattie grinned. "Keep an eye on the stew for me?" as she scooped up the container and ran up the stairs.

Soaking in the fragrant bath, Ruth let her mind float with the water. Her head throbbed and her throat was sore. She couldn't understand why these strangers were in her house doing all these things for her, but it was too hard to think of an answer and asking was out of the question. If she opened her mouth, all that came out was a croak so she didn't try.

Lying in lavender-scented water soothed her. She had nothing to do but keep everything submerged in the warm. Under normal circumstances she would be concerned to be naked around strangers but somehow nothing mattered, as if she were in hospital and she had nothing to show the staff hadn't seen many times before.

Every so often the old woman came in and held a steaming mug to her lips and told her to drink. The first time she sipped slowly, wondering if her throat would swallow without convulsing but the smooth liquid slid down easily and she continued because she was thirsty and she couldn't remember when she last drank.

The second time, they topped up the bath water when it started to

23

cool and held another mug out to her. She was able to hold it herself this time, sniffing the rich aroma and looking up with a question in her eyes.

"It's just a broth," the old woman said, "you need nourishing. You're nothing but skin and bone."

Ruth looked down at her legs beneath the water. They did seem thinner than usual. Sitting in the bath felt different too but then, she couldn't remember the last time she'd sat in a bath, let alone soaked in one. She knew she did eat, generally but when she tried to remember what food she might have cooked in the past few days her memory was blank. It was too difficult. The smell of the broth was enticing. She sipped and sipped until the bottom of the mug refused to give up another drop.

She sighed, holding out the mug to be taken away.

"Thank you," she whispered.

The old woman smiled and held out a bath towel she'd been warming against the radiator.

"Time to get out now and sleep in your own bed."

Ruth stood up and stepped out onto the mat, feeling the towel envelop her with warmth. She didn't know what she'd done to deserve such kindness from strangers. She'd never done anything for them. She felt tears leaking down her face as the old woman rubbed her briskly until she was dry. As she rubbed, she made soothing noises as you would to a young child in distress and Ruth found herself comforted.

"It'll all be better in the morning," the old woman held out a pair of clean pyjamas and Ruth put them on. They walked together into the bedroom. The old woman pulled back the duvet and Ruth found herself snuggled in the bed. She heard someone else in the bathroom, letting out the bath water but the person beside her was singing gently. Not exactly a lullaby but equally soothing. Ruth's eyelids closed without her noticing and she slept.

Down in the kitchen, Mattie was dishing out stew to the three men when Granny came down to join them.

"She's asleep. Let's hope she can stay there long enough to keep the demons at bay."

Mattie handed her a plate of stew. "Do you want me to stay with her?"

"Not tonight, but once she's feeling better, I'll ask if she wants a lodger. Would that suit you?"

Mattie beamed. "It's not that I don't love my family, but I'm used to my own space and its hard having everyone rifling through my things all the time. They don't mean any harm…" she shrugged her shoulders and returned to her own meal.

"I'm staying tonight." Greg's tone indicated he expected no discussion.

"You just being protective or something else?" Granny asked. He could tell she was curious about his decision. He wished he could explain what he felt inside. As Anvil, he was responsible for all the villagers, protecting the weak and vulnerable, teaching those who wished to learn but this was different, almost personal and he couldn't work out why.

"Bit of both," he said eventually. "Something scared her. Once she's able to tell us why she ended up in a hare scrape, I'll rest easier. Until then, I'll sleep on the sofa."

"There's plenty of beds," Mattie chimed in.

"No need to make a mess," Greg replied with, "Sofa's long enough."

"I'll watch her," Granny said. "She needs someone if she wakes. There's one of those daybed things by the window, I'll be fine. Zeb, you go on home after you drop Mattie. Dolly doesn't like it if you aren't in the house at night. She's used to me being out."

"Soppy bitch," Zeb smiled affectionately. "Been that way since we found her as a puppy. Always checks I'm in bed before she goes downstairs to her own basket by the kitchen fire."

They ate in silence until their plates were empty and Colin got up to help himself to seconds.

"This orchard is a strange one." He said as he resumed his seat. "I thought I knew every plantation in the village and its surroundings, but I've never been here before. It's like the Abbott's, it's been hiding for years."

"Not so many years," replied Granny as she unscrewed a bottle of plums and directed Mattie to make custard. "This is Miller's Orchard. It was split off when they built the road through the village. I remember coming here a few times when I was very tiny. This cottage stood on its own before the rest of the houses round here were built in the fifties. It belonged to Granny Blackwell's godmother. She never married but she opened the orchard to the village children at apple bobbing time. She must have been in her nineties then.

"Granny Blackwell should have lived here but her husband moved them into the old Gamekeeper's cottage on the estate, the one your grandparents had, Colin. This place was so small, nobody in the village wanted it, so Granny sold it to a builder after the second war and he extended it and sold it to incomers. I lost track of who lived here after that."

"It's a wonder the orchard wasn't built on," Mattie said pouring custard into a large jug she found in the cupboard.

Colin grinned as he waited to christen his pudding. "You've not been in there, have you?"

Mattie shook her head. "No, why?" She looked harder at the faces around her. "It's protected?"

Colin nodded, making Greg think he needed to visit the orchard before too long. "We need to wassail the trees once Uncle Zeb has finished pruning." Colin said as he scraped the last of the custard into his bowl.

"Should be done by Friday." Zeb spat a plum stone onto the table, ignoring his wife's disapproval.

"Wassail Friday night then?" Colin looked at Greg, who nodded. "Then we can graft the cuttings up at the Abbot's on Saturday and get them planted out next week."

"I'll help," Mattie said. "I remember your father teaching me how to graft."

Colin smiled at her and Greg noted he'd not seen him smile at a girl like that before. "Help's always welcome. You can make a record of the new varieties too. There are a few I've never seen before."

They continued to plan for the coming days until the washing up was done and everything cleared away. Zeb took Mattie and Colin home and Granny and Greg migrated to the living room until they both started yawning and settled down in their chosen places to sleep.

CHAPTER FIVE

Frantic barking woke Greg from a deep sleep. In his dreams, he'd been chasing a hare over fields and for a moment he thought the barking was coming from the pack of hounds he was hunting with. It took him a moment to realise where he was.

Through a gap in the bay window curtains he saw a large van pull up outside the house. The grandfather clock in the hallway struck twelve. It was far too late for any tradesmen. He wondered what they were planning and if he should call the police. Usually he was loathe to call in outsiders but he wasn't at the forge or in his own cottage; he felt defenceless.

Outside, moonlight was shining fiercely down on the close putting everything in clear perspective. Two men were climbing down from the cab, obviously arguing. One of them held a bunch of keys and was pointing towards the front door. The other man held his arm as if trying to dissuade him from whatever action he was contemplating.

Greg crept out to the kitchen and pulled on his boots, grabbing his coat from a hook in the conservatory. He didn't want to go through the front door. He would approach them from the side, only making an appearance if they tried to enter the house.

The barking grew louder. There were snarls coming from the orchard. He wondered where the animals might be. They sounded so fierce, he shivered, wondering if he might be attacked. He paused for a moment to glance behind the hedge, his mouth suddenly dry as he caught sight of something huge rearing up on its hind legs, the ear-splitting growls making his knees buckle. Every fibre of his being wanted to run away but from what? He scanned the orchard again but apart from leaves rustling in the breeze, he could see nothing.

A shape brushed past his leg. He heard nothing but the hairs on his arms rose as he felt a familiar coldness. He breathed heavily, clutching on to the clothesline post in relief. Now he knew what was happening. As long as he posed no threat, he was safe. Colin mentioned the orchard was protected. These shapes and sounds must be spirit animals guarding the property.

Turning towards the front of the house, if he didn't look directly, he could just see the shape of a large dog coming up on one side of the garden boundary. The howls continued and even though he knew what they were, the cries still unsettled him.

He crept into the shadow of the house and peered around the corner. The two men were still standing in front of the van. They were dressed in dark, workman's overalls and a short jacket with an embroidered logo on the front. The van had "Finchurch and Sons, Removal Specialists" stencilled on the side in large italic lettering.

"We can't go in now!" the smaller man was tugging at the other's sleeve. His shoulders were hunched from the cold and he kept glancing towards the clamour which seemed to get closer with every bark or growl

"Why not, we've got keys." The larger man was older, his lanky, unwashed hair spilling over his collar

"What if someone's home and thinks we're burglars?"

"If we stop messing around, we can be in and out before anyone notices" The taller man took two steps towards the front door but stopped as the barks became louder.

"What if they call the police?" The shorter man asked, his expression a picture of misery. As he said the words, a patrol car raced into the cul-de-sac and pulled up behind the van. Two policemen got out and walked towards them. Greg stayed where he was. Let someone else deal with this conundrum.

"Would one of you two gentlemen like to tell me what is going on?" asked the first policeman as his colleague talked into the radio on his shoulder.

"We've come to collect some furniture for Mr Turner." The taller removal man hastily returned the keys to his trouser pocket. "That's his house." He pointed towards the front door.

"I see. Do you always make house calls at midnight?"

"We should have been here this afternoon, but the traffic was terrible and we got lost going round the ring road. There's no signposts anywhere." The man tried to explain but Greg heard his voice trail off as the barking began again.

The policeman turned to the other man. "Is that right?"

The smaller removal man gulped. "Sort of. We are here to pick up some furniture. Mr Turner gave us special instructions and a special price if we picked it up after dark, but we can't do it."

The policeman looked a little bemused. "Why not?"

"These dogs. In the house. Mr Turner didn't say anything about dogs."

"I think you'd better come with us while we contact Mr Turner."

The taller man shook his head but neither of them protested as they were led away. Sometime later they emerged from the back of the police car and drove off in the van with the police following them.

As soon as the van disappeared the barking stopped.

Greg breathed a sigh of relief and turned to go back inside; whoever warded this land knew what they were doing and he was very grateful. Ruth needed all the help she could get.

Up in the bedroom, Granny let the curtain drop. Thanks to the open window she'd heard most of the exchange and no-one could fail to have heard the dogs. She wondered what kind of man planned such things. A coward, she decided; so selfish only his own desires could be considered. She heard Greg returning to the front room and knew the incident was over. They'd discuss it in the morning.

She turned towards the woman asleep in the bed, her face a picture of innocence; her trust in her husband shattered into lethal shards leaving her bleeding and helpless. She'd have to find strength from somewhere. They would support her for a while, but it would be up to her to learn and grow from these lessons.

Ruth stirred, opening her eyes.

"What's going on?"

"Nothing to worry about. Greg's sorted it."

"I heard dogs."

Granny nodded. "They've gone now."

"I've heard them before," Ruth said, reaching for the water glass by the side of her bed. "Soon after we moved in. Robert tried to chop down one of the trees in the orchard. They made such a din, he was scared and refused to go in there again. I told him there weren't any dogs, but he got himself into a such a state, blaming me for moving here, when it was his idea we should use Aunt Izzy's money to buy a house."

Granny took her empty glass and refilled it from the bathroom.

"You must think me such a fool," Ruth said as she returned.

Granny considered her words before she spoke. "I think you gave your trust to someone who didn't deserve it. I think you've been alone for far too long and now you've got a chance to make changes. You may not want to make them. You may want to continue living in a world of lies but I think you're stronger than that."

Ruth burrowed down into the bed clothes again.

"I don't know how you can say that after what I did. I don't even know why I ran away from a ghost. He couldn't harm me. I probably need locking up."

Granny humphed. This was part of the story she'd not heard before.

"What you need is rest. We'll talk in the morning." She settled herself back on the daybed and listened until she heard Ruth's breathing slow, then followed her into sleep.

CHAPTER SIX

When Ruth finally woke, sun was streaming through her bedroom windows. Someone had opened the curtains. The events of the previous day seemed like a bad dream. She could hear voices coming from downstairs. Pushing aside the covers she pulled on some clothes and went to investigate.

Granny and Greg were sitting in the kitchen eating breakfast. Ruth couldn't remember the last time anyone other than herself and Robert had been here. For a brief moment, she felt annoyed. They were acting as if they lived there and she were the visitor.

"Morning, Ruth. What would you like to eat?"

Ruth tried to think what she might have in the cupboards. There was rarely time for breakfast. She couldn't remember when she last went shopping. She looked at Greg's plate. He was cleaning the remains of egg and bacon with a piece of wholemeal bread. Where did all that come from, she wondered?

Granny placed a mug of tea in front of her then busied herself at the stove. Ruth heard the toaster pop up and the sound of butter being scraped then she was being presented with a plate of perfectly scrambled egg sitting on toast.

"There you are," said Granny and went off to wash the saucepan in the sink.

Ruth began to eat; aware Greg's eyes were following her every movement. It felt strange to have someone notice her. So many years spent hiding she sometimes thought she had disappeared from the real world. A smile flickered over his face.

"Good to see you looking better," he said, getting up from the table. "I'm going over to the forge now, but I'll call in tonight to make sure you're alright."

She swallowed the mouthful she was chewing, wondering what she could say that wouldn't sound ridiculous.

"Thank you for saving me," she murmured.

Greg smiled and before she could say anything else, he was gone.

Granny poured them both another mug of tea and sat down beside her.

"You feeling better?" Ruth nodded. This woman made her feel like a six-year-old, safe but slightly scared of what Granny might say if she did something wrong.

Granny leaned back in her chair and drank her tea.

"You up to a bit of planning?"

Ruth wondered what she meant. Yesterday it felt as if the future was behind a locked and bolted gate. Granny made it sound as if she were offering a grappling hook and some rope to climb over the gate and maybe look around.

"I'm not sure but I'll try."

"I'm not one to pry into other people's business," Granny began, "but seeing as we only met yesterday it might be helpful to go over a few things."

Ruth wasn't sure she was up to telling a stranger what was going on, even if she knew herself but she couldn't call Granny a stranger any more. Not after the way Granny had cared for her yesterday and last night.

"What do you want to know?"

"This house. You said it was bought with a legacy. Yours or does it belong to both of you?"

"Mine. Aunt Izzy set up a trust. It would go to Robert in my will if I die first."

"Mortgage?"

Ruth shook her head. "I pay the bills. Robert said it was only fair since he was paying for the flat in town." Ruth felt the panic bird begin to flutter in her chest. "How will I pay them without a job?"

"We'll come to that in a minute." Granny patted her hand. It was so long since anyone extended this kind of physical comfort to her, she wanted to flinch, to draw away but that would be like throwing away everything Granny was offering. Ruth knew without this lifeline to support her she could disappear into yesterday's black hole of despair. "You know how much you need for these utilities?"

Ruth tried to concentrate on Granny's words. "I have a spreadsheet on the computer. I'm fairly organised. It's just this week everything seems to have gone to pot."

"Do you have any savings?"

Ruth looked down at her lap. "I don't know. I've been too scared to look."

"Not to worry, we'll sort that out later. Now, how soon do you want to work again?"

Ruth tried to stop the tears, but it didn't work and they rolled down her face. "I don't know. I need to revise my CV and start registering with agencies. It could be weeks or months or never!"

"Do you want to keep doing what you've done before, or would you like a change?"

Ruth took a tissue from the box Granny held out to her and blew her nose. "I don't know."

"There are two jobs going in the village you could do. Only part time and probably a lot less than you were getting before, but they would tide you over until you found something else."

When Ruth looked at her, Granny continued, "Henry needs a secretary for Home farm two days a week. His last one decided to go travelling and Gillian is struggling to keep up, what with the cheese and yoghurt and three little ones. The Earl has been asking for someone to help catalogue his library and archives. I figured Mattie could do that, but you could help so she doesn't get tied up trying to do her studies and everything else.

"Then there's the Rector. He needs someone to take over the parish magazines and look after the accounts. He's a lovely man but his grasp of finance leaves a lot to be desired."

"You said two jobs, but you've mentioned three."

Granny smiled, then coughed to cover her amusement. "The Earl doesn't always do what I suggest. Sometimes he gets his own ideas. I've known him since he was a baby and he's usually fairly amenable."

"The other two? I've never been a secretary or a treasurer before. "

"Don't say that. You can handle a computer, you said yourself you do spreadsheets. You know about the internet. You have lots of skills." Granny got up and began to clear the table. Ruth wondered how she knew where everything went but decided it wasn't worth enquiring.

"Now, about this house. Does it ever feel too big for just one person?"

Ruth thought for a moment. She remembered all the times she longed for someone to talk to since they moved here, pouring out her frustration into her letters or her diary. Simon rarely visited since he left home to study engineering at university. Even in the early days of their time here, she recalled Robert reprimanding her for singing or interrupting his sport on television with "her endless chatter" as he called it, when she tried to ask him about his week or tell him something about hers. She wondered how far back she would have to go before she found some happy memories of their time together. At the moment, she couldn't find one.

"How would you feel about a lodger?"

Granny's question startled her. "What do you mean?"

"The girl who was here last night. She's just come home from university and needs somewhere to stay. Her parents have four boys and they've grown used to Mattie not being there. You have spare bedrooms. Mattie would only need one and use of the kitchen."

Ruth thought about it for several minutes. Did she really want someone else in the house? Could she get used to the noise, the mess? What if the girl brought back friends, a boyfriend? Would she trash the kitchen with takeaways?

"Mattie's a good girl, very sensible. She knows how to cook and clean and respect other people's property. I think you'd like her."

Ruth stretched and sighed. "I know I've been on my own too long. It might be nice to have some company. Is she working? Can she afford to pay rent?"

There was a knock on the back door and when Granny opened it, Mattie was standing in the conservatory. Her head was covered by a multi-coloured, hand-knitted beanie which matched the long scarf wound around her neck, her thick, dark, brown hair fell in ringlets down her back. Her woollen coat almost reached her heavy boots and she was pulling off her mittens as she walked in.

"It's really cold outside. Uncle Zeb brought me down in the pony cart. He's in the orchard with the boys. Did the police come by last night?"

Ruth saw Granny's frown, but the girl didn't notice.

"Dad was walking the dog and saw a removals van parked up the far side of the pond. The driver asked if he knew Pear Tree Cottage. When he came home and told mum, I realised they were headed here so I called the police. Did they arrive in time?"

Ruth saw Granny purse her lips as if she didn't want to say anything. She remembered waking in the night to the sound of barking but then it all went quiet.

"I don't know," she said giving Granny a worried glance.

"They must have done," said Granny eventually, "We certainly didn't get any visitors."

As she finished speaking the phone rang in the hall. Ruth went to answer it, her mind losing its ability to think as she heard the familiar voice.

"You stupid woman," Robert was in one of his foulest tempers.

"What do you mean by contacting my office and then phoning the police?"

Ruth was almost too stunned to speak. "I don't know what you're talking about," she stuttered. She wanted to crawl away somewhere to hide. She hated it when Robert told her off. He would never listen. As she moved the handset from one ear to the other, she caught sight of Granny and Mattie standing in the kitchen looking at her. She realised she had done nothing wrong. Nothing. Robert was in the wrong and he knew it; that was why he was trying to intimidate her. She took a deep breath and stood up straighter.

"Robert, what time is it in China?"

"How the hell should I know?"

"So, you're not in China. When did you get back?" There was silence on the other end of the line.

"That's not important," Robert blustered. "You haven't told me why you phoned the police. Waking me up at 1 o'clock in the morning with all the neighbours gawking."

"I didn't call the police, one of my friends from the village did. Would you like to talk to her?"

"No, I don't want to talk to your friend. If she hadn't put her oar in, everything would be complete, now it's a mess."

"Robert, you're not making any sense. When are you coming home?"

"I am home, you miserable excuse for a woman. If you weren't so pathetically stupid you'd have realised ages ago. It's over. I have my own life now. Why I ever wanted to live with such a boring matchstick, I've no idea."

Ruth sank down onto the carpet. She felt Granny beside her, gently removing the handset from her fingers.

"Mr Turner, Mr Turner," she heard Granny speaking firmly into the phone. "What a shame your mother never washed your mouth out with soap and water when she could. I think you should consider your behaviour very carefully. Good morning."

CHAPTER SEVEN

The only sound in the house was Ruth sobbing quietly. She was aware of Granny standing beside her like a sentinel. The phone rang again but no-one answered. The horrible truth hung over her like the thickest fog. Her marriage was over. Her husband lied, cheated and manipulated her until she didn't know what was real and what was false. It was over. Finished. She'd been thrown out with the rubbish not only by her employer but by her husband as well, the one person who should have been reliable in her hour of need.

She caught sight of Granny's legs. Straight, dependable. This woman was offering her something new. She felt like a wet rag but somewhere inside a spark of anger began to warm her. Robert expected her to fall apart. Robert didn't care if she lived or died. She wished a plague of boils might make his life hell.

She looked up and caught Granny's eye.

"Those jobs you mentioned," she whispered then cleared her throat and spoke more confidently. "Could we go and see someone today?"

Granny took a mobile phone from her pocket. "You go up and put some warm clothes on and let me make a few calls."

Within half an hour Ruth was dressed in woollen weave trousers with a long-sleeved cotton blouse and thick jumper and leather boots. She found her winter coat and gloves and took Granny and Mattie out to the car.

They dropped Mattie off at her house first to begin packing her belongings. Her mother gave Ruth some very long stares.

"Ruth has lots of space and you're bursting at the seams," Granny told her.

"I know," Mrs Cooper was not going to be placated, "but how much is it all going to cost?"

"I have my savings, Mum. I'll be able to pay." Ruth knew Mattie was trying to reassure her mother. It must be a shock to have your eldest child return home then come and say she was leaving again. "It won't be as much as I was paying in St Andrews."

"You wouldn't have paid anything here. I was looking forward to the two of us being at home together."

Mattie gave her mother a hug. "I won't be far away. I can still come back and help you with the washing. It's not as if I'll be across the border again."

"You're welcome to come and visit whenever you wish," said Ruth, trying her best to appear friendly. "I'm hoping to get to know my neighbours better now that I won't be working in town anymore."

They said their goodbyes and Granny directed her to Home Farm. It was only half a mile from the village centre on the narrow road leading up to Roelswick Priory, the home of Peter, Earl of Haverliegh, who owned most of the village and its surrounding farmland.

"You can park right next to the office," said Granny, pointing at a wooden building next to one of the barns. As they pulled up, a young woman carrying a child on her hip came out to meet them from the cowshed across the way.

"Henry won't be a minute. The vet's just come out to deal with a cow that's gone down with milk fever. She's never done well and I think this is the last straw. I should have taken Harry into nursery this morning, but he's been up most of the night mithering. If I didn't know better, I'd swear he knew there was something wrong with the cow before we did." The little boy was kicking his mother with his muddy boots and wriggling to go down until she released him and he ran off back into the shed closely followed by Granny. "He can't bear not knowing what's going on with the animals."

"How old is he?" asked Ruth.

"Three next month," sighed his mother. "The night he was born, Henry was tied up calving our herd leader. He was running backwards and forwards between the house and the barn, not knowing where to stay. I swear he took the baby out to show the cow while the midwife's back was turned. I'm just glad he didn't bring the calf back in with him."

She stuck out her hand towards Ruth.

"I'm so sorry, I'm Gill and you must be Ruth. Things aren't always as manic as today. The milk tanker's due any minute and we're expecting a feed delivery this morning. If I don't keep an eye out, the driver is liable to just dump it anywhere and we have a special place in the Dutch barn where it needs to go."

"Come in to the office and I'll show you a few things." She led the way into the building, removing her wellingtons at the top step. "You'll need a pair of these if you come to work here."

Ruth assured her she already owned some and listened intently as Gillian explained the basics of the farm management system on the computer and showed her the filing system set up by her predecessor. Beyond the desk was a whole wall filled with ledgers and huge black files. The remainder of the room housed a table with six chairs and on the opposite wall was a map showing the extent of the farm and all the field names.

"Henry prefers to hold his meetings out here rather than in the house. It protects any visitors from the kids if they're around and keeps the farm business separate. There's a kettle and mugs to make tea and coffee and a toilet through the door over there."

Ruth gave her a copy of the CV she'd hastily printed off before they left the house and waited while Gillian read it through. She asked about the number of hours and was surprised they could stretch to three mornings a week with the possibility of extra time if things were busy. There would be a three-week probationary period just in case things didn't work out.

"When can you start?" asked Gillian with a wistful look in her eyes as if she hoped the answer would be today.

"I have a few ends to tidy up," said Ruth trying to swallow the lump in her throat which suddenly appeared. "Would Monday be ok?"

Gillian agreed and they shook hands. As they walked outside, Granny was waiting by the car with a taller, younger version of Zeb while Harry raced around the farm yard splashing in any puddles he could find.

"You must be Henry," said Ruth, mustering up an air of confidence she didn't know she possessed. "Your wife has just hired me as your new farm secretary. I hope that's all right with you."

Henry grinned; she could see he possessed his father's easy-going manner. "As long as you can read, work a computer and keep your temper with all the idiots we get from DEFRA, you'll be fine and I'll be more than happy. If I never have to create another invoice, it will be too soon."

They made their farewells and were soon on their way.

"Turn left when you reach the road," Granny instructed. We might as well go and see Lord Peter while we're nearby.

"Shouldn't Mattie be with us?" If Mattie was counting on the Earl's project for extra income, Ruth didn't want to damage their relationship before it started.

"Can't be helped. He knows about Mattie's project. Might be good if you invite him down to the Wassailing on Friday night."

"Wassailing?"

"Bringing your orchard back into the fold. It's a month later than we normally do it but as you've just had everything pruned, it'll be fine."

Ruth gripped the steering wheel tightly. Something else was being presented as a fait accompli without bothering to discuss it with her.

"When, exactly, was someone going to tell me about it? Or was it meant to be a surprise?" She pulled the car up before the entrance to the big house and sat and glared at Granny.

Granny sighed. "I know it seems as if everything is being thrown at you at once but we're trying to help. I don't know if you remember Colin. He brought you back from Long Meadow with my Zeb and Greg. He's responsible for the welfare of all the trees in the village. He'd never seen your orchard until yesterday. It was his suggestion they do the Apple Howling on Friday night. There hasn't been a chance to discuss it with you before now."

Ruth took a deep breath; trying to calm down but it still niggled.

"What will it entail?"

"Colin will bring a group, probably dressed like Morris dancers, with musicians. They will sing to the trees and make lots of noise to drive the evil spirits out and the Wassail Queen, which may or may not be Andrea, the Rector's wife, depending on how she's feeling, will put a piece of toast soaked in the wassail drink into the branches of the largest tree."

"Do I have to do anything?"

"It would be nice if you offered the wassailers some food and drink. Nothing fancy, just baked potatoes and some fillings and soup and maybe some apple pies."

"How am I going to prepare all that?" Ruth wailed. The price of several dozen baked potatoes made her shiver, let alone everything else.

"Stop panicking," said Granny. "Mattie will help you make soup. Henry can drop you over a sack of potatoes and we'll bring the apple pies. This is an event for the community, you don't have to do everything yourself. You're part of the village now. Don't forget it."

Ruth wasn't happy but decided there were only so many battles she could engage in today.

CHAPTER EIGHT

They walked up to the imposing entrance and Granny pulled the bell hanging to the side of the ancient oak door. Within a short while a young woman appeared in an apron with floury hands.

"Good morning, Lily. Is Lord Peter available? I rang him earlier to let him know we were coming."

"He said to show you into the library, Granny. Can I take your coats?"

"Have you lit a fire in there today?" The young woman shook her head. "Best we keep our coats on, thank you."

Ruth looked up at the huge vaulted ceiling. Someone wanted to impress their guests and succeeded. Granny didn't spare a glance at the marble columns and beautiful statues situated in several carved niches. She followed Lily talking about the church flower roster and asking if Lord Peter would be providing the Easter displays as usual.

As they passed an empty fireplace, Ruth noticed a huge wolfhound sprawled in front of it. The dog ignored the first two women, or rather they appeared not to notice him. When Ruth drew level, he sat up, his head reaching out towards her. He wore a thick, leather collar with a gold coloured nametag. Finn, she read the engraved letters. She stopped and put out her hand for him to sniff, wondering why she felt a cold breeze across her fingers. She was about to stroke his head when Granny said something which drew her attention and when she looked back, the dog was gone.

Lily and Granny were standing in front of a faded door. Lily knocked, while Ruth tried to see where the dog might have gone. After a moment, Lily opened it and ushered them in saying, "I'm sure he'll be here in a minute."

Granny moved into the library, while Ruth stood spellbound just inside the doorway. This was the room she used to dream about as a child. To her left, large, leaded windows flanked by wooden shutters allowed the morning light to stream in. Dust particles hung suspended on sunbeams as if attracted to the faint warmth. Three walls were lined with oak shelving with fitted drawers in some of the lower sections.

Underneath the window were two leather armchairs accompanied by several large ottomans, giving the impression of adults reading to a collection of children. Antique standard lamps hung over each chair.

Opposite her, a large mirror hung above the fireplace, reflecting the central table piled with books and scattered documents. The click of a latch alerted them to a man wearing a green parka appearing through a hidden door in the bookshelves. As he strode towards them, Ruth thought she noticed his left leg seemed stiff. His forehead was furrowed even though he was attempting a smile and held his hand out in greeting.

Ruth had expected the Earl to be an old man, but she realised he was the same age or younger than her. She wondered how anyone could have such amazingly blue eyes and when he shook her hand, his touch was strong and warm.

"I'm so glad you could come," he said. His voice was deep. It reminded Ruth of a favourite radio actor she listened to as a child whose voice always made her feel special.

"I love your house," she said, the words flying out before she could think of something sensible to say.

Lord Peter gave her a rueful smile. "So do I but I'm not sure how much longer I can afford to keep it."

"Now what's happened?" Granny asked. "I know the harvests were down last year, but you've received all the Yule rents and the next instalments will be due shortly."

"It's so frustrating," Lord Peter sighed as he re-arranged books into neater piles on the table. "I've wasted four hours trying to get into Grainger's computer. I swear he's never passworded it before. This isn't the first time he's spent Christmas with his family in Australia. I've always been able to keep things ticking over while he's away. He should have returned by now. The ansaphone in my study chewed up a message he left last week. Something about storms and flooding causing delays. I've tried to look through his papers but there's no sign of anything useful."

"The Historic Buildings Commission people were here in January and they're threatening to withhold the grant to replace the roof over the West Wing if we don't get on with the work before April. I can't agree the contract if I don't know how much I've got in the bank. If I can't get the roof sorted and redecorate the bedrooms for paying guests, I may have to start talking to the National Trust about taking the place over."

"Can't you contact the bank yourself and explain?" Ruth was puzzled. It didn't seem right that someone couldn't look at their own accounts.

"I only returned from London last night. Mother's not been too well and Caroline wanted me to persuade her to get the doctor in. You know what she's like. I found the letter when I went through the post this morning and they want an answer by the end of today. Makes me look such a fool saying my steward's not here and I can't act without him."

Ruth could hear Granny tutting beside her. She wanted to protect him from Granny's wrath.

"Would you like me to take a look? I'm no financial wizard but I do know my way around computers."

"Would you?" Once again, the hopeful smile lit Lord Peter's face, making him look like a young boy relieved of a terrible burden.

He walked over to the bookcase on the left side of the fireplace and pushed a leaver. A small door swung open and he led them into a long, narrow corridor. The plain brown walls made Ruth wonder if they were now in the servants' quarters rather than the main part of the house. Before they reached an exit, they stopped beside a locked door labelled Estate Steward, the faded paintwork peeling off to reveal a green undercoat.

Lord Peter took out a key from his pocket and put his shoulder to the door when it threatened to stick. The large square room smelt musty. A high, v-shaped wooden counter blocked the way forward. Lord Peter pushed up the heavy top and opened the flap below so they could walk through. An ancient bookcase stood on the left wall, underneath a window, while the desk with the computer sat under the window on the wall opposite to the door next to an ancient green metal filing cabinet with four drawers.

"What a strange room," Ruth exclaimed, thinking how dusty the whole place was which wouldn't do the computer any good.

"The Steward's room always had its own entrance, so people could come in and pay their rent or bring up any maintenance issues without having to go through the kitchens." Lord Peter explained. "Any meetings or social events were normally held in the barn or the church."

"The church in the village?" Ruth asked.

"No, the Priory church was the centre of a small Benedictine double house founded by Fontevraut Abbey before the dissolution of the monasteries. We still hold services there occasionally."

"I do hope I'll be able to visit it." The excitement was evident in Ruth's voice. "I've always been fascinated by history."

Granny cleared her throat. Ruth came back to earth with a bump. It was so long since she'd felt excited about anything. She really wanted to work here and explore the ancient estate in all its incarnations.

"Sorry, Granny, Lord Peter," she muttered, sliding into the rickety chair behind the computer and pressed the power button.

This was obviously an older model as the machine took a while to come to life. As Ruth expected, the initial screen demanded a password.

"What passwords have you tried so far, Lord Peter?"

He pointed to a list of words and numbers on a notepad by the computer. Ruth thought for a moment.

"Do you know his birthday?"

Lord Peter started to rub the back of his head then walked over to a filing cabinet and pulled out a paper file.

"28th July 1967" he read out.

Ruth tried the numbers but with no success then something made her think of the original mother house. She wrote down "Fontevraut2867" but shook her head. This was not strong enough. On a whim, she tried F0nt3vr1ut. Immediately, the screen cleared and she could see the desktop in front of her.

"Good grief, why didn't I think of that!" exclaimed Lord Peter, the loud boom of his voice making her jump. She could see he was eager to get on, so she slid out of the chair to let him sit down.

"Would you like me to come back another day to discuss the archives?" Ruth asked, "Especially if funds are going to be tight."

"Come back?" He was so busy with the computer, she could tell he wasn't really taking in what she said. "I won't be long. Ask Mrs Williams to make you some coffee and I'll join you in the kitchen."

As they left the room, a ledger fell off the table. Ruth bent down to pick it up. She noticed it was open at a page which listed all the various farm rents.

"That's strange," she said, pointing to the amount listed for Home Farm. "That's not the amount on the invoice Gillian showed me. Do they vary each quarter?"

"Not usually." Lord Peter took the ledger from her and began to open files on the computer.

Granny took her arm and guided her out of the room.

CHAPTER NINE

Granny led the way through more brown corridors until they reached the kitchen. As she pushed open the door, they were assailed by wonderful smells of cooking. Pies were resting on the counter under the windows and Lily was busy rolling out more pastry at one end of the central wooden table.

Ruth was introduced to Lily's mother, Janet Williams, a plump, bustling woman, covered in a large floral apron, who was Lord Peter's cook and housekeeper. She was busy tasting a huge pan bubbling away on the stove.

"Busy day?" Granny asked, sitting herself at the table. Ruth wanted to explore the other doors leading out of the light, airy room, wondering what she might find but she pulled out a wooden chair next to Granny and sat quietly.

"Just trying to get ahead of ourselves," the cook replied, replacing the lid on the pot and collecting four mugs from the large dresser which covered the wall behind them.

"Coffee?" She pushed the kettle onto the back of the range after checking to see if there was enough water. "Lord Peter's got one of his corporate events this Saturday so we're making the fruit pies and stew fillings today while I've got Lily to help. She's got college on Friday so I'll be here by myself."

"Couldn't someone else lend a hand?" Granny asked, "I'm sure Lizzy Ackerley wouldn't mind an extra bob or two."

Mrs Williams sighed. "I did ask but his lordship said no. No slack in the budget this time, he said. Until he gets this money sorted out for the roof, he can't see the end of his nose for his glasses, if you know what I mean. I hope he was alright with you. He's been like a bear with a sore head since he got back from town. I know he must be worried about his mother but she's not going to live for ever. I'm always amazed she's lasted as long as she has, given all her little foibles."

"The Moorcrofts were always stronger than they looked," Granny said. She seemed to be looking for something and when she found the calendar hanging on the back of the door they'd entered by, she got up and peered at it closely.

"You know what the date is, don't you, Janet?"

"23rd?"

"24th"

Ruth heard the woman swear under her breath as she spooned coffee into the mugs and poured the now boiling water.

"I knew there must be a reason but I've been so busy I haven't known which day of the week it was." Ruth wondered if they would explain the significance of the date, but nothing further was said.

They sat at the table, sipping their drinks while Mrs Williams started browning another pan of meat on the cooker. Within a few minutes, Ruth found herself chopping vegetables, while Granny rolled up her sleeves and began making another batch of pastry. Lilly was busy glazing the finished pies before putting them into the oven for their final bake.

"No point sitting around when there's work to do," Granny said, her hands white with flour. Ruth smiled. The warmth of the kitchen was reflected in the obvious friendship between the two women. As they chatted, they were busy with well-known tasks and even managed to include Ruth in the conversation.

She would have been happy to just be there and listen, but they asked her opinion about recipes and seasonings until she felt comfortable sharing her own experiences of entertaining the many guests Robert brought home when he first became partner.

When the pastry was suitably chilled, Ruth took over stirring the meat while Granny and Mrs Williams lined the huge dishes. An open bottle of red wine was sitting on the table so she added it to the pan, smiling as she breathed in the rich aroma. She left the empty bottle where she found it.

She was standing facing the stove so didn't see Lord Peter enter the kitchen. The first she knew was a crash of broken glass on the flagstone floor which made her spin round to see what had happened.

"How many times do I have to tell you I will not have alcohol in my house; today of all days!" he shrieked, banging his fist on the table so the china rattled. Ruth stared at him. His face was white with red blotches on both cheeks. She felt herself cower over the pan, hoping he wouldn't notice she was there. She wanted to run but her feet were rooted to the spot. She waited for him to come towards her, to throw the pan on the floor like Robert.

"It's only a sauce for your guests," Mrs Williams said. Her voice was calm, but Ruth recognised the edge of fear.

"I won't have it," Lord Peter screamed, "You know what drink can do. How could you!"

Ruth didn't realise she was whimpering until Granny laid a hand on her shaking arm.

"Stop this, Peter. Stop it now. We know your pain but that doesn't mean you can hurt others." The power in Granny's words caught the Earl just as he was about to hurl a pie dish onto the floor. He lowered it carefully to the table and sank into a chair.

Silence. Ruth concentrated on stirring the pan, her knuckles white around the handle. She could hear Lily sweeping up the glass. Beside her, Granny found another mug and made Lord Peter some coffee. Ruth noticed it was mostly milk with two large spoonfuls of sugar stirred in. She wondered how anyone could drink something so sweet but when she could turn around to look at him, he was already draining the mug.

"I'm so sorry." He was sitting with his head in his hands. Ruth was shocked how haggard he looked. This wasn't Robert, she kept telling herself, this was a completely different man, a haunted man. She felt herself wanting to help him.

Granny patted his shoulder as she would a small child. "It's all right. We understand today is not a good day. Has anything else happened?"

"Grainger."

"What about Grainger?"

"He's taken half the rent money. I've called Moulton, my accountant. He's going to come over and check everything."

"If it's true you'll have to call the police." Ruth couldn't believe she was talking to him.

"I can't, he's been part of the estate since.."

"You let your employees steal from you?" Ruth's previous fear was bubbling into anger on his behalf. "You need the money for the roof. You can't let him get away with it. You said yourself if the roof isn't fixed then you could lose the manor then everyone would be put in jeopardy."

Lord Peter sighed. "I suppose you're right. I think there might just be enough to start the roof. Moulton said he'll be here this afternoon to go through the books and all the files. I'll decide then whether or not to inform the police."

Granny humphed, her lips a thin line. Ruth wondered what it was she wasn't saying but didn't feel brave enough to ask.

"Time we were going," Granny said suddenly as a clock began to chime the hour in another part of the house. "The men will be wanting their dinner before we get back."

Lord Peter got to his feet, apologising again for his actions and failing to discuss Ruth's place with the archives.

"Maybe we could talk about it tomorrow evening," Ruth said as they shook hands. "My orchard is being wassailed. I'd be very pleased if you could all join us. Would 6.30pm be convenient?"

She saw Lord Peter glance at Granny who nodded, before he accepted her invitation. It made her cross that Granny had to give permission for everything before anyone around here acted but there was nothing she could do about it.

As their feet crunched across the gravel in the watery midday sunlight, her gaze was drawn to a lonely weeping willow tree by the car. Underneath the burnished fronds was a group of stones. As she looked closer, she could see names carved on each one. On one was clearly marked, Finn. Ruth felt a shudder run through her body. It couldn't be, she told herself firmly, not after all these years. She turned towards the car, gripping the door handle tightly as she searched for the key.

She was aware Granny was looking at her strangely, a question forming in her eyes. To prevent the need for a response, she asked Granny why today's date would have affected Lord Peter so badly.

"It's the tenth anniversary of his wife's death." Granny said. Ruth shut her eyes. This was too much. She tried to think of something to say but the words wouldn't come.

"He still blames himself, even though there was nothing he could have done." Granny was oblivious to her discomfort. "Susannah liked her drink, especially on hunting days. They were beating a cover over by Roel's Gate and her new gelding bolted, throwing her off.

"The others thought she'd gone to change horses and when she didn't reappear, they assumed she'd gone home. It was a filthy day." Granny paused as Ruth started the car. "Lord Peter was in Surrey collecting the children from boarding school. No-one missed her until they got home. Took them two days to find her body."

"The poor man!" Ruth gasped, overcome with pity for the Earl.

"He usually keeps everything bottled up. Too many years in the army to let his emotions out. This money business has hit him hard. Not that I'm surprised about Grainger. He's always been a weasel. I hope they lock him up and throw away the key!"

Ruth kept her eyes on the road, surprised by the vehemence in Granny's voice. She wondered what else had gone on to earn him Granny's wrath, but she guessed now was not the time to ask.

CHAPTER TEN

Ruth dropped Granny at her cottage before she returned home. Zeb's pony and cart were standing in the driveway. She sat for a moment looking at the house. She could see the outline of the original cottage. Where the extensions had been tied in the new brickwork had almost faded to the original honey-coloured stone. It always looked different from the rest of the close, cosy, more welcoming, a real haven from the modern world.

Robert favoured one of the newer builds with a smaller garden, but something had drawn her to the very end of the cul de sac. It was quiet, almost secluded despite the houses to either side; so different from their original suburban house on a busy main road. She remembered the arguments when she refused to agree to Robert's choice. It was her money and she wanted to spend it on a house where she felt comfortable. The orchard was a wonderful bonus.

Robert tried to tell her any money belonged to them both but even he couldn't overcome the Trust set up by Ruth's Godmother. She must sign the deed and the house was registered in her name.

Was that when their marriage fell apart, she wondered? It was probably the first time in her life she went against Robert's wishes. Robert said it was too far to commute, yet she knew several neighbours who made the daily journey. He bought himself an expensive flat overlooking the canals near the city centre within walking distance of his office.

She realised now he'd taken the most valuable furniture from their previous home for the flat. She never quite understood why he insisted on buying himself a new leather recliner which overshadowed the lounge and an enormous modern designer drinks cabinet which took up the whole of one wall of the dining room. Maybe he was trying to stamp his presence in the house, even though he wasn't there to use them.

She realised how angry he was with her when they moved in.

"You want to live there, you pay the bills and you look after everything." She could still hear his icy words. "Don't ask me to change a lightbulb or help you pick fruit from those stupid trees. You'll be sorry, mark my words."

How those words hurt her. She tried everything she could to please him, to make him happy with her choice but nothing worked.

Thinking back over the year before he left for China, even when they spent weekends together it was never a comfortable time for either of them.

"No, I can't help you dig the garden. I'm too tired after the week I've had at work. Besides, it's the Japanese Grands Prix today. You know I like to watch the racing. You wanted this place, you pay for someone to help you." His complaints were incessant if she asked him to help in the garden or do any DIY in the house.

She remembered how exhausted she was shopping, washing, cleaning and ironing his clothes for the week ahead while he spent most of his time dozing in front of the TV.

It was almost a relief when he first mentioned his trip. Then he asked her to write to him; any spare time consumed by her daily reports.

The pony shook his head, rattling his harness and the garage door. The noise broke through her reverie. She got out of the car realising her life could be different now. She had choices. Robert didn't consume, wouldn't consume every waking thought. Was it only this morning he reduced her to another sobbing heap? She vowed he would never do that to her again.

Thinking too far ahead still made her chest tight, making it difficult to breathe. She needed to make a shopping list and decide a plan of campaign for tomorrow night. Although she grumbled about having the wassailing foisted upon her, helping in the Manor's kitchens reminded her how much she enjoyed entertaining. This time it would be on her terms, not Robert's.

As she stuck her key in the lock, Zeb appeared from the orchard closely followed by his two helpers.

"We've finished the pruning," he told her as the smaller lad untied the pony's reins and backed him carefully out onto the road. "I'll see you this afternoon with a few things for tomorrow."

"How much do I owe you?"

Zeb smiled and waved his hands as if dismissing her question. "Don't you worry about that for the time being. I've got an idea how you could help us out, but I need to talk to Henry before I discuss it with you and Mattie.

This talking in riddles annoyed her but she thanked them all for the work they'd done on the orchard and they trotted away for their lunch.

The mention of her new lodger got Ruth wondering which room she should offer Mattie, her son's or the smaller guest room and if she should make the bed up before Mattie arrived. She still wasn't sure if she wanted to share her home with someone else but the thought of extra money coming in did make the idea easier to contemplate. Having another woman to talk to would be a totally new experience.

As she walked into the kitchen, there was a note on the table in handwriting she didn't recognise.

"Soup for your lunch is on the stove. Granny said to remind you to eat."

Ruth didn't know whether to laugh or feel annoyed at being treated like a child. When she lifted the saucepan lid and saw the thick orange soup inside she realised how grateful she was someone was thinking of her. As she finished her meal, she decided it was time to start looking after herself.

She took a deep breath and went to the study. The blank screen took her back to the moment when she lost her job. She wanted to curl up in a ball and cry but instead, she gripped the back of the chair and when she felt calmer, she packed the laptop into its carry case ready to take back to the office tomorrow morning. The work mobile was also sitting on the desk so she put that and its charger away as well.

At least her personal computer was new and the village internet service was more reliable than some. She needed to check her online bank accounts and make sure the passwords were changed. She didn't want Robert trying to gain access to her savings accounts. She knew he couldn't but that didn't stop her being fearful.

Up until they moved house, he'd had access to all her accounts, supposedly so he could transfer money across for any housekeeping she needed and make sure she wasn't overdrawn. Once he bought the flat, she noticed there were no payments in, but he had taken out several small amounts. When she plucked up the courage to ask him about it, he flew into a rage.

"After all these years," he shouted, "I've managed your accounts for you, making sure you didn't go overdrawn with your stupid trips to the theatre and charity donations. Think what your credit rating would be if I hadn't kept you on the straight and narrow."

"But I've never taken out any loans," she tried to interject but he wasn't listening.

"Don't you trust me anymore, now you've got your own house and your own money?"

Re-running the scene in her head, she realised from that point onward, she didn't trust him. He never answered her questions, never offered to share his account details with her when she asked and strangely omitted to tell her what happened to the money left over from the sale of their original house; a house they jointly owned. Half of that money belonged to her.

A week after Robert's tantrum, she'd received a reminder from the bank to change her password on a regular basis, so she did. When Robert complained, she showed him the letter and promised to tell him the new password but kept forgetting to update him. She could be very forgetful. She put it down to spending so much time writing letters.

Who was she kidding? Writing letters stopped her thinking. When Robert first suggested they buy a holiday home with her legacy, she was surprised. Simon had just left home and she was excited at the thought they could go away together. She assumed he was thinking of Devon or Northumberland or even a villa on the Algarve.

It was then he started working late at the office. He was always tired and disinterested in doing things together. She remembered going up to town to drag him out for a meal, but his secretary said he'd flown to Paris on business. Then he insisted she buy a house in the country with the money. She guessed with hindsight he didn't want her checking up on him. If she were further away than a ten-minute train journey, she couldn't surprise him so easily.

The woman in the Post Office had seen him with a pregnant Chinese woman, presumably someone he brought back with him. She wondered how many others there had been during the two years they searched for a suitable location. She should have realised he was trying to get away from her without the inconvenience of a divorce. How could she have been so blind?

None so blind as those who will not see. She heard the words in her head with a wry smile.

It was so true but now her eyes were fully open and she was determined to take charge of what was left of her life.

She glanced at the packed laptop and retrieved the mobile from inside the case. She found the last call from HR and dialled it. It went straight to voicemail. Did she want to leave a message?

"This is Ruth Turner, I'm too busy to return your property tomorrow. If you want it back, send a courier. Goodbye."

She felt her face break into an unaccustomed smile as she replaced the mobile. She wasn't doing anything for anyone she didn't want to, anymore.

As she carried the laptop case to the hall cupboard and shut it away, she remembered what she had come to do in the study. How much money did she have? When she checked her accounts, she was surprised by both balances. There was certainly enough to pay the basics for the next year, maybe longer if she were careful. Her savings should deal with most emergencies and she knew all her insurances were up to date if anything major happened. Her new job at Home Farm would pay for food and heating and she could take her time searching for something she really wanted to do.

CHAPTER ELEVEN

G reg felt the pillory mock him as he walked past to meet others gathered in the village hall on Friday evening.

"Hide your face if you will," it said. *"I know what you do. I shall be waiting when they bring you down to serve your time."* It had been standing on the village green for as long as current villagers could remember. Now children played at putting their head and hands through the holes and tourists took their pictures.

The device always made Greg shiver. He wondered how many times in former lives he'd been made to stand inside the wooden yoke, battered by rotten food and sharp tongues, back aching and no way to relieve the pain in his legs and arms.

He wished he'd brought his coat. The heat from the forge always fooled him as he stepped out into the night air. The journey down into the village never took more than five minutes and he knew once they started to dance, he would warm up. He walked briskly up the hill towards the lights of the hall.

As he turned into the entrance, he heard a soft click, click of paws running up the pavement behind him. In the wide pool of yellow light underneath the streetlamp, he was sure he caught sight of his dog, Jet, trotting up the hill. He knew he'd left the wire-haired mongrel safely behind in the forge. When he looked again along the road, he saw not one dog but two, the second three times the size of his own companion. There was only one dog in the village who fitted the size and shape and Greg knew there was no way he could be roaming the streets tonight. He'd helped Lord Peter dig the wolfhound's grave only a month ago.

"Evening, Anvil."

Greetings rang out from the other members of the Morris side as he closed the door and began to tie strings of bells beneath his knees. Zeb and the other musicians were tuning up their instruments, while some of the younger members began to jump and stretch to make sure nothing was going to fall off once they were on their way.

The box of hazel sticks was taken round to complement the large white handkerchiefs tucked into their belts and Greg felt somehow comforted holding the smooth wood in his hands. It wasn't as if he would need a weapon tonight, their only foes were any malicious spirits hiding out in the orchard to be frightened away by song and dance, but he felt uneasy. Nothing he could put his finger on, but he wasn't sure everything was going to go smoothly.

"Line up, please." The order from Mark Lowtham, leader of the Morris side and Greg's oldest friend, rang through the hall and soon everyone was in place. Greg found himself in the middle of the group. "Music in a moment, maestros please. We'll walk up in formation and cross the road into the estate. Our first dance will be outside Pear Tree Cottage then we'll go into the orchard. We're meeting Allon and Madron there, so take your cues from them. Andrew, you'll be last one out so don't forget to lock the door."

As the fiddler began the familiar jigs, they filed out onto the pavement. The moon was just touching the church tower as they marched up the hill. A single car drove out of the village as they walked along. They crossed over into the housing estate; their boots and bells providing a lively percussion to the ancient tunes.

Ruth tasted the soup for the final time and pulled it over to the side of the hob to keep warm for later. Just the thing for a cold winter's evening. Potatoes were baking in the oven while chilli con carne and other toppings stood ready to serve.

Mattie was busy mulling cider. The aroma gave the kitchen a festive air. On a whim, Ruth went into the dining room to seek out tankards stored in the drinks cabinet. They were a motley collection, bought over several years. Robert never used them, preferring his glasses of wine and whisky. As she opened the cabinet doors, she was surprised by the large number of unopened bottles of spirits inside. She would never use them but perhaps she could offer them to her guests. She carried them through to the kitchen and set them out on the counter where fruit juice and other soft drinks were already displayed.

Ruth filled one of the tankards with cider and placed it on a small tray together with a loaf of bread and sharp knife. She put on her coat and boots and took it out to the orchard where she heard Colin and Andrea discussing the timetable for the evening.

When Granny first announced the event, it seemed ridiculous to hold a wassailing in the dark but now, with tea lights lit inside a multitude of lanterns hung from every tree, the enclosed space had become a twinkling fairyland. It filled Ruth's heart with such emotion, it took her breath away.

"You're sure the orchard has been protected?" she heard Andrea ask as she and Colin set up a trestle table between two large, flaming braziers. Tonight, was the first time Ruth had met the young Rector's wife. She looked to be in her mid-thirties, with a round face and long hair covered with a bobble hat, a scarf wound around her neck. She stood a little taller than Ruth, her long woollen coat loosely belted at the middle.

"Anvil was certain he saw guardian animals on Wednesday night," Colin told her. "Made him proper scared until he realised what they were."

"Why would they show themselves?" Andrea shook her head in disbelief. "Both Granny and I thought we knew all the special places in the village. This orchard's not one of them. The boundaries can't have been renewed for at least fifty years if not longer."

Ruth put her tray down on the table. She wasn't going to let anyone else decide something for her orchard.

"If you ask me," she said, "someone thought these trees and the cottage worth securing. It feels a very safe place and if anyone threatens that, the dogs bark."

Andrea chewed her lip. "We don't usually wassail within a circle. Not even at the Abbott's." Colin looked at his watch as the church clock on the main road struck the half hour.

"If we are going to do something, we don't have long. The Morris side will be here any minute. Dad said they were meeting at 6.30pm."

Just as he spoke, five dogs came bounding in through the orchard gate. Such a large number would normally have scared Ruth, but they moved quietly, tails wagging and mouths slightly open as if in a grin. Two of them, a golden retriever and a fox terrier ran over to Colin, who crouched down to fuss them.

"Gracie, Russ, what are you doing here? Jet, too and Tess. Is Henry here?" The border collie barked once but none of the other dogs made a sound. Ruth recognised the huge Irish wolfhound she'd seen at the Priory and suppressed a shiver. She knew Tess was one of Henry's farm dogs but the other three were strangers. She noticed how Colin and Andrea both drew away from the wolfhound, but she felt no such apprehension.

"Dogs smell fear." She could hear her father's voice. "Always stand firm and show them who's master." It seemed a lifetime since she had any contact with dogs. Robert didn't like animals and wouldn't have anything to do with them.

The wolfhound came up to her and nuzzled her open hand, his nametag clearly visible. She was surprised to see it reflecting the candles. There was no cold breeze this time when his nose touched her hand.

"Hello, Finn," she said, stroking down his long back. "Have you come to help with the wassailing?" As she patted his head, he began to slowly walk away. When she let her hand drop, he came back, placed his nose under her palm and whined. She could feel his coarse fur through her glove, but no warmth came through to her hand. She could see the white breath of the other dogs curling up into the air, but Finn's great mouth was shut.

"I think he wants you to go with him," Colin said, his voice strangely muffled.

Ruth laid her hand on the huge hound and together they slowly walked along the circular hedge line. The other dogs followed, tails high, panting slightly. Ruth was struck by how calm they all seemed. No jumping or barking, they seemed to know exactly what was happening, which was more than she did, but she felt a strange curiosity growing within her to see what would happen next.

At the eastern edge, she noticed a large silver birch tree, hung with tea lights, its flawless trunk glowing white in the soft illumination. It struck her how beautiful the tree would look with the sun rising behind it at the beginning of a new day, each dawn bringing with it new possibilities.

The Wolfhound yipped and one of the dogs following them, Colin's Golden Retriever, Gracie, positioned herself underneath the bare branches. They moved along the southern boundary until they came to a tall holly tree, again adorned with tiny lamps. Ruth could make out the sharp shapes of the waxy leaves, already bereft of their red berries.

Russ, the terrier, was left to guard this space as Finn continued their journey towards the hazel tree. As Ruth looked up, she could see the moon 's light beginning to spill out across the sky. Tess stopped here, curled up at the base just like a huge salmon. Ruth shook her head at such a strange image. Where had that come from?

Soon they were heading back to the trestle table, walking between the braziers to the point where one of the thorn trees had begun to grow out of the hedge. She could see the stunned looks of both Colin and Andrea as if they could not believe what they were seeing. They both seemed rooted to the spot, as if any movement might break the spell of what was happening.

If not for the flickering fire light, this would have been the darkest part of the garden. North always is, Ruth heard a voice in her head. She looked down to see Jet take his place, turning around three times before he was satisfied. This must be Greg's dog, she realised, he smelt of burning coal and pounded iron.

She would have stopped longer, but Finn wasn't finished. With Ruth's hand still resting on his head, he led them through the gate and along the garden path towards the front porch. Zeb's spaniel, Dolly, was lying inside on the mat. She thumped her tail as Ruth approached but did not get up. The wolfhound shook his magnificent head, dislodging Ruth's hand before sitting down in front of the porch, for all the world as if he were keeping guard.

Ruth wondered what it all meant. Andrea had been talking about boundaries, about the need to, what had she called it, define them? Surely this is what the dogs had just done. She had no idea what Andrea meant by saying they didn't normally dance within a circle, yet the dogs had just walked around in just such a shape, each one of the four now marking the compass points. Maybe they knew what was needed. Some strange, canine magic. Whatever it was, if it meant her cottage and land continued to be protected, she was happy.

CHAPTER TWELVE

As she stood there, a mud-spattered Range Rover drew up and parked in front of her neighbour's house. Lord Peter got out and she walked forward to welcome him. It was on the tip of her tongue to ask him about Finn, but the conversation steered away from any questions she wished to pose.

They could hear sounds of music and marching feet coming towards them, so they stood at the curb, waiting for the Morris side to arrive. Granny, Mattie's mother, and another tall woman emerged from the footpath, along with several others just as Colin and Andrea came out of the garden. Colin greeted his mother and the young girl who was holding her hand. Ruth surmised she must be his youngest sister. She knew Colin came from a large family comprising two younger sisters and twin brothers who, by all accounts, kept everyone on their toes.

"I want to join in the dances," the girl whined.

"You will in the summer, but I don't think you want to jump around in the mud on this cold night," said her mother

"I miss dancing, too," admitted Lord Peter softly so only Ruth could hear. "Dratted muscle damage in my back stops me doing anything too energetic. Mark always complained I had two left feet, but it was great fun being part of the Morris side."

The men arrived, forming themselves into two long lines of four in the road outside the house. Other people gathered around them, some from the neighbouring houses but most from the older parts of the village. First, they danced, then they sang what Ruth recognised as the Gloucestershire Wassail, something she'd learned as a child in primary school.

When they finished, Mattie came forward with the largest tankard, which she presented to the nearest Morris man. He gave a formal bow, took a swig then passed it to his fellows.

"Hey, don't we get a drink!" called Zeb, the other musicians nodding.

"Have patience, Zebadiah," replied Granny, with a grin, "all good things come to those who wait." Everyone laughed and Andrea led the way into the orchard. Lord Peter followed Ruth and they stood together close to the braziers, trying to keep warm in the cold night air.

"I expect you've been to lots of these events," Ruth said.

"Not really," Lord Peter stuffed his hands into his pockets. "There are only a couple of orchards in the village, one at Home Farm and one at Glebe Farm. We never did anything there until the Abbott's Orchard was rediscovered. When Colin became Allon; about five years ago. I believe it was Mark, who discovered there was a special Roelswick Wassail. He found the manuscript in an old folder belonging to his grandfather up in his attic. The date on it was 1836, so they must have been wassailing then.

"He worked out the new dances too, mostly Cotswold, rather than Border."

"Why did it die out?" Ruth wondered aloud.

"Why have so many of our local activities disappeared?" Lord Peter countered. "You know how it was. The Victorians simplified everything until it was just a pale shadow of the original and anything to do with strong drink and enjoying yourself was thoroughly frowned on unless it was the aristocracy enjoying themselves."

Ruth was about to ask him how the Abbott's Orchard had been found but the Morris men were lining up again. The dances this time were wilder, with jumps and crashing sticks, each man shouting as the batons came together. The sequences were repeated four times on each side of the orchard. More drinks were handed round while Andrea blessed the bread, before breaking it into chunks and dipping it in a flagon of cider.

One at a time, the men came forward to receive a piece of soaked bread, then each walked towards a fruit tree and lodged it in a suitable branch. Only half the trees were studded, so they returned to Andrea until all the trees had their own dripping nugget. After another invocation from Colin, the fiddler and drummer began to play and the men began to whirl between the trees, beating their sticks against the trunks and performing great leaps into the air, their bells ringing as they came to earth each time.

Ruth thought she had never seen such a sight. It reminded her of dances she saw once on holiday. Dark shapes encircled every tree, their shadows flickering long after they had passed to the next one. Percussion reverberated through the night air like ancient tribal drumming. No malevolent spirits would dare to linger after such a drubbing.

The men eventually returned to their original formation and the orchard was quiet.

"No sacred space can exist without acknowledging the Guardians," Andrea's words rang out in the stillness.

"Your turn now," Ruth heard Granny's voice in her ear as she was led forward with Granny on one side and Mattie on the other, towards the tray Andrea held up in front of her. For a fleeting moment, she felt uncertain but then she took a deep breath, realising she did want to be part of this ancient ceremony. Maybe next year she could take Andrea's place and lead the wassailing. She wondered what she would have to do to make it happen.

"We salute the Guardian trees, Birch, Holly, Hazel and Blackthorn with our offerings of bread and mead." Andrea intoned. She smiled at Ruth, "Thank you for returning this place to the village, Ruth. Which tree do you feel drawn to?"

Ruth looked around. The birch was stunning but just didn't feel right. The holly seemed covered in a green fire all its own. Underneath the shadow of the church tower, thin, straight hazel shoots waved at her while the blackthorn in front of her was positively frightening with its long, dark thorns.

"Hazel, yes, Hazel, please." Andrea dipped a piece of bread in the goblet of mead and passed it to her.

"You're after those nuts full of wisdom like the salmon," quipped Granny, moving forward to collect her own piece of bread.

Andrea put down the tray and together the four women walked over to their chosen trees. Mattie to the birch, Andrea the holly, Ruth to the hazel and Granny to the scary blackthorn.

Ruth knelt to place her bread in the base of the tree, leaning over the curled form of Tess, who raised her head to sniff Ruth's hand before going back to sleep.

"I hope you'll help me learn what I need to know," she murmured, her fingers stroking the smooth speckled bark. "In return, I promise to keep the orchard a place of living fruit for as long as I can."

It seemed strange talking to a tree, but it seemed to acknowledge her. Long, furred catkins trembled on every branch and when she stood up, she saw her coat was covered in yellow pollen.

"Looks like it accepted you," grinned Granny, pointing to the pollen on her shoulders when they all returned to the braziers. Ruth smiled, feeling her cheeks blush as if she'd been caught doing something slightly risqué.

The fiddler was tuning his violin again and the men formed up into their original rows. "Roelswick Wassail, lads," called the leader and the song began.

CHAPTER THIRTEEN

The evening progressed into a convivial gathering. The Morris men and their retinue accepted Ruth's invitation to eat inside. With the moon shining bright in a cloudless sky, the temperature was dropping by the minute. There would be a heavy frost before the night was over.

Five of the dogs were claimed by their owners and brought into the conservatory, only Finn remaining outside. No-one seemed to notice the shaggy-haired mountain on watch beside the front porch.

Lord Peter followed Ruth into the kitchen as she and Mattie began to serve the food. No sooner was he inside when she saw him stare at the bottles of drink on the work top then glance briefly at her. There was a brief, muttered apology then he turned against the entering throng. He was gone before she could say goodbye. She felt a pang of disappointment because she was looking forward to learning more about the Priory and hoped they would have time for a proper chat during the evening.

There was no time to ponder his behaviour as the kitchen was packed with hungry mouths and chilled bodies. The soup and filled, baked potatoes soon disappeared, followed by apple pies brought by Granny and several other women. There were many compliments and toasts to the cooks in mulled cider. Ruth was beginning to worry she wouldn't get any when Mattie brought out a second slow cooker from the dining room and began to ladle the contents into empty mugs.

Greg brought one over to her.

"This one's yours," he said. "You deserve it. It's been a good night, a very good night. You couldn't have done better."

Ruth felt her cheeks grow warm. It was a long time since anyone praised her. "Everyone helped. I couldn't have done it on my own."

As the first guests began to leave, all the dogs started to growl and soon there was a furious barking from the front of the house. Dolly had been lying at Zeb's feet in the kitchen but the minute she heard the others, she rushed to the front door whining and scrabbling to be let out.

"What's got into them?" Ruth could tell Zeb was bemused by the dogs' behaviour. She saw Greg stiffen.

"Round the front, lads, sticks in hand."

Ruth could only stand and stare. What was going on? It must be serious because none of the men asked questions, they just followed instructions and left.

Before she could wonder any more, the doorbell rang. Mattie was in the hall chatting to her mother, so she went to answer it, her hand on Dolly's collar so she didn't rush out.

"Where's Mrs Turner?"

Ruth felt a familiar wave of dread quickly followed by nausea as she heard those words. Her feet seemed nailed to the floor. Nothing wanted to move. The mug in her hand felt too heavy to hold any more. She knew if she didn't put it down somewhere, the contents would spill all over the kitchen floor. She felt someone take the mug from her.

"Don't let him frighten you," Granny said. "We're here. He can't hurt you."

You don't know what he's like! Ruth wanted to wail. Why did he have to come now? Why did he have to ruin everything?

"You need to go and see what he wants. The sooner you do that, the sooner he will leave. You've still got to try my apple pie."

Granny's words, spoken so softly, somehow freed her feet and put strength back into her muscles and bones, enabling her to walk to the door. Robert was standing in front of the porch. He couldn't come any closer because Finn was filling most of the space. His ears were back and his whole chest rumbled. Ruth stepped out beside the hound.

"Hello, Robert."

He stood in the glare of the security light. For a fleeting second, he reminded Ruth of the man she married, sleek black hair, black polo neck sweater, black trousers and shiny black shoes. The sheepskin coat broke the illusion.

He's put on weight, Ruth thought to herself, his face is rounder. I don't remember those dark rings under his eyes. He can't be sleeping properly. Maybe his new woman is taking too much of his nights. I could tell her he doesn't do well on too little sleep. She noticed his dark hair was receding and flecked with grey. He's growing old, that's why he's so angry.

Her eyes scanned the scene behind him. A large removal van was parked in front of the house together with a black Porsche.

So, that's where my share of the house sale went, she thought.

Greg was standing at the front of the group of Morris men, Jet by his side. Colin and his mother were holding Gracie and Russ while someone else held Tess. All the dogs were growling, teeth bared. It was as much as Colin's mother could do to stop Russ from attacking the two white-clothed men cowering in front of their vehicle.

"Having a fancy-dress party complete with circus tricks?" Robert's smile never left his lips.

"Nothing I do is your concern anymore." Ruth heard the words coming out of her mouth and found each one made her stronger. "Why are you here?"

She saw Robert's hand come up as if to slap her, but Finn lunged forward in front of her and he dropped his arm. Ruth stood quite still. This was something new. He'd never tried to hit her before in public. She was determined not to give him the gratification of seeing her flinch either from his words or actions.

"We're here to collect my furniture. After the debacle you caused on Wednesday, I thought I'd better come and supervise the removal myself."

Ruth felt red fire flowing through her veins. "Your furniture," she snapped. "You mean the ghastly things you forced me to buy with my money?"

Robert glared at her. She could see him biting back words he wanted to fling in her face. Only the audience was stopping him.

"My furniture. The leather recliner and the drinks cabinet. Now let us in so we can load it up and go."

Ruth watched as Greg and a couple of the other men walked closer behind Robert. The removal men hadn't stirred.

"If Mrs Turner paid for the items. I do believe the law will support her claim to ownership," said Greg. Robert whirled round to face him.

"Keep your nose out of this. It's none of your business. I know the law. Anything owned by husband and wife is held conjointly. I'm the lawyer. I should know."

"And I'm the blacksmith," Greg's voice was menacingly quiet. "I hear when iron rings sour and I use my hammer until it sings true again."

"Don't you threaten me!" Ruth could hear the bluster in Robert's voice. Looking at Greg's demeanour, she could understand why he was frightened. She didn't remember anyone ever challenging Robert before. "If you continue in this vein, I shall be forced to call the police."

One of the Morris men stepped forward around the rose bed. "I'm a special constable. I'm sure I can help."

"Not dressed in that clown's outfit, you can't," Robert snapped. He turned to Ruth. "Will you please call off your goons and let me get my furniture and go home. It's all I want. It's been a long day."

This should be your home, but you rejected it! Ruth wanted to cry. It's warm and comfortable and we could be surrounded by friends, but it wasn't good enough for you. You could rest here but you'd rather stay sleep deprived with your Chinese lover. It's your choice.

She knew any hope of a future together was impossible. Their home had been destroyed when he forced her to move here without him. He changed their lives with his lies and deceits and she had done nothing to stop him. He thought he could do what he liked, take what he wanted and no-one would call him to account.

That time was gone. She could not keep the veil over her eyes any longer.

"You can have it if you pay me."

"What?" She saw Robert jerk as if he'd been stung.

"£10,000 should do it. The drinks cabinet alone cost over £8,000. I never knew what you saw in it, standing there like an upturned suitcase taking up all that space!"

She heard an intake of breath from the audience. She wanted to groan. What must they think of her spending so much on such unimportant items. The chair she could almost forgive. It was very comfortable and would last forever but it fitted Robert, not her. He was welcome to it.

"Give me a minute." She pushed the door to and walked into the study, searching for the two original receipts in a drawer. She scribbled down her account number and sort code on a piece of paper before returning to the porch. On the way, she whispered to Granny, who disappeared into the dining room with Mattie and Zeb.

"There you are," she said holding the pieces of paper out to him. "You can see I've allowed for depreciation. "I'd like a bank transfer now, Robert. Once I can see it's gone through, your men can come and collect the two items. I take it there's nothing else you want?"

He shook his head. She could see surprise and pain in his eyes. She knew how much parting with money hurt him.

"Ring the bell again when it's done."

"Ruth, bloody hell, this is madness..." he began, but Ruth shut the front door and leant against it with her eyes closed. She had laid out her terms. If he didn't like it - tough!

CHAPTER FOURTEEN

Two hours later, the house was quiet. Ruth stood by the kitchen door, a cup of tea in her hand. She kept wandering down the hall to gaze at the lounge and dining room. Her lounge and dining room. She couldn't believe how different they looked and felt. Gone was the overpowering presence of Robert's furniture, the constant reminder of all her shortcomings.

The lounge felt inviting; now the room wanted you to come in and be comfortable. There was no leather recliner guarding the entrance, challenging her to account for all her daily actions before she sat down. In the space sat Aunt Izzy's antique rocking chair complete with cushions and crotcheted rug.

The chair had been languishing in the back bedroom until Mattie suggested it be brought downstairs. It seemed very fitting to Ruth that her godmother's favourite seat should now have pride of place in the home made possible by her legacy.

The dining room was so very different; much larger now the hideous drinks cabinet was gone. Granny and Mattie had removed all the cut crystal decanters, wine glasses and tumblers, inherited from her grandfather's estate, before the removal men took it away. Now they were safely stored inside the dresser where no-one could see them unless Ruth decided to bring them out.

With butterflies galloping around her stomach, Ruth stopped beside the doorway and glanced towards the empty wall. It really was sitting in the middle as if it had always been there. Where it was meant to be, where she had planned for it to be before Robert banished it to the garage. Her piano.

No-one could call it beautiful. It was relatively small made from slim-lined wooden veneer. There were no antique candlestick holders like her grandmother's piano, no wooden music stand hidden away under the top, just a folding shelf beneath the lid. A leather stool stood in front of the piano as if inviting her to play. Dare she?

The darkness outside made it feel later than it was. Mattie was upstairs unpacking her belongings. The neighbours wouldn't hear anything if she closed the door. No-one was going to shout at her if she made a mistake.

She walked towards the bay window and drew the curtains. Someone had removed the centre of the dining table, pushing the two ends together so it no longer felt intimidating.

She turned round. Her piano was still there. She kept expecting it to disappear. She never thought it would be possible to move it inside until she saw the trolley the removal men brought in for the drinks cabinet.

"Wish I had something like that to move the piano." She didn't realise she had spoken aloud.

"You got a piano?" Granny asked. Ruth told her it was exiled. She'd always wondered how many people it would take to push it into the house. She didn't notice Granny talk to Greg, but she did wonder why Greg was gesticulating with the removal men a few minutes later. Before she could think, the piano was being wheeled in through the front door and carefully manoeuvred by several Morris men exactly where she had always imagined it would stand. The trolley disappeared, soon returning with the bureau which held all her music.

She noticed Robert getting out of his car to protest at the delay, but he was blocked by another Morris man until everything was complete.

The trolley returned, the van rumbled off into the night, shadowed by Robert's Porsche.

"Anyone know a good divorce lawyer?" Ruth asked as she thanked everyone who had stayed to help.

The man she had seen talking to Robert came towards her holding out a small card. He was around six feet tall with a thin, narrow face framed by iron-grey hair.

"Give my secretary a ring on Monday morning," he said as Ruth shook his hand, feeling bewildered.

"Nigel will sort you out," she heard someone say amidst several other nodding heads.

"Yes, Nigel will look after you."

She plugged in the angle poise lamp and set it on top of the piano where it used to sit in their old house. She took out a book from the cabinet and placed it on the music stand. It fell open at a familiar piece, the notes dancing invitingly upon the page. As she clicked on the light, she pulled the card from her pocket and read it for the first time.

Lockhart Prew Solicitors, she read, *Nigel Milson, specialist in family law*. It wouldn't hurt to talk to someone, she decided. She didn't want to stay married to Robert and she was curious to discover the financial effect of their three decades together. She must be entitled to something for all her hard work.

Crash! The first few chords of Beethoven's Pathetique Sonata filled the room. Ruth let her fingers dance over remembered keys. She could still play. She wondered what else she would be able to do in her new future.

Saturday was a strange day. Ruth woke early to the sound of quiet singing. At first, she thought she must have left the TV on but footsteps pounding down the stairs reminded her she wasn't alone in the house anymore. She sighed, remembering how noisy young people could be.

Ten minutes later, there was a knock. Before she had a chance to say anything, the door was pushed slowly open and Mattie hovered in the doorway holding a mug. She was dressed in flowery flannel pyjamas covered with a thick cotton dressing gown.

"I brought you a cup of tea. I know I should have asked last night if you liked tea in the morning, but I was making a pot anyway, so I thought I'd just bring it up. I can make coffee if you prefer."

Ruth sat up, arranging her pillows behind her. A cup of tea in bed was luxury.

"Tea's fine," she said feeling a smile creep up her face like a forgotten friend as she sipped the tea. "Is the sun shining?"

Mattie pulled back the heavy curtains.

"Anvil said last night it would be fine this morning. Are you ok if I spend most of today up at the Abbott's?" At Ruth's puzzled expression she explained. "The Abbott's Orchard. It's the place Colin discovered when he became Allon five years ago. Lord Peter's great-grandfather, or was it great-great grandfather, forbade anyone to go there after his son was killed by a falling branch. The whole place was forgotten for nearly two hundred years but now Colin's working to make it productive again. You know, apple juice, pear juice, cider, perry, all kinds of things. Although, Lord Peter's getting funny about the cider. If he had his way, no-one would drink anything alcoholic."

"Has he always been like that?" Ruth wondered.

"He was pretty fanatical just after his wife died. Tried to get the pub closed down at one stage until Granny sorted him. He got better for a while but just lately he's been in a right state. Lilly said he's thrown some terrible fits up at the hall in recent weeks, reduced her mum to tears, which isn't like him."

"He must have a lot on his mind." Ruth thought back to last Wednesday, the smashed bottle, the fury in Lord Peter's face. The look he threw at her before disappearing yesterday evening. Did he think she drank? She felt like cowering underneath the covers, but Mattie would wonder. Luckily, the girl couldn't read her mind and prattled on.

"You sure you'll be alright on your own? There's soup left from last night for lunch. I can make you some breakfast before I go. I'll put some bread to rise tonight when we get back so we can bake it after church tomorrow."

"Church?"

"Yes, it's not till eleven."

"But..."

"Everyone goes to church on Sunday. Of course, if you want a quiet service, you can go at 6pm but I help with Sunday School, so I go in the morning."

"Everyone goes?" Ruth couldn't remember the last time she'd set foot inside a church. She loved the sound of the bells. Her grandfather had been a bell ringer in his local church. She'd always gone to carol services at Christmas, but she never felt like following other people in the close who walked to church on Sunday.

"All the villagers. It normally takes the newcomers a few years to find their way but they come eventually. I put it down to Mum's iced buns."

"Iced buns?" Ruth knew she must be sounding like a parrot, but this was turning into a very strange conversation.

"Once a month we have coffee in the crypt after the service. Mum always brings her special iced buns." She grinned at Ruth. "Don't worry. You'll like the Rector and there's a proper choir and everything."

Ruth blinked, wondering how she could find an excuse to stay at home tomorrow. Mattie seemed to assume she would fall in with everything she suggested. Ruth wasn't sure she wanted to become one of the village flock, no matter how strong the lure of promised iced buns.

"What are you going to do in the orchard?" she asked trying to change the subject.

"I promised to help Colin graft your cuttings and plant them in the new nursery beds. He finished ploughing them with Molly yesterday.

He was really proud of himself."

"And Molly is?"

"His shire horse. She does most of the heavy work in the woods. It's easier for horses going up and down the slopes. You'd never be able to take a tractor in there. He's got Dick as well if he needs more horsepower. He's a Clydesdale."

Ruth felt as if she'd stumbled upon a whole new language along with her tenant. Thankfully, Mattie turned towards the door.

"I'd better get a move on if I'm going to be up there for nine. Do you want me to make your breakfast? I've put porridge ready."

"I'm fine, really," Ruth protested. "Porridge would be great but I'm not an invalid, I can look after myself. If it's going to be a nice day, I'll get some washing on and then potter about in the garden. It's about time I sowed some seeds if I'm going to grow any veg this year."

Mattie raced off leaving Ruth exhausted by her energy. Was she ever that enthusiastic about life, she wondered? She lay back against her pillows watching trees in the close slowly move in the breeze. She could see tiny patches of white, mauve and orange in various front gardens where snowdrops and crocuses were busy flowering. She envied those who could grow orange varieties, birds always ate those in her back garden, leaving ragged stumps where flowers might have been.

She heard Mattie thunder down the stairs once more and decided to get up. Her pace was decidedly more sedate. When she finally emerged in the kitchen with a full washing basket, Mattie had finished her breakfast and was filling a basket with sandwiches, fruit and wedges of pie left over from the Wassail feast.

"You don't mind, do you? Colin's always hungry."

Ruth smiled and shook her head but inwardly she was perturbed by the amount of food in the basket. Would there be anything left from last night's celebrations?

She filled the washing machine, setting it going as Mattie left for the woodland. Porridge was waiting for her on the hob, along with some quince jelly and a jug of thick cream. Ruth ate, listening to a robin singing in the garden through the open door of the conservatory.

Afterwards, she found packets of vegetable seeds, old and new; bringing in a bag of potting mix in from the shed to begin planting. She sprinkled tiny particles over dry, earth-filled trays before floating them on a water bath. Once drained, she placed them on shelving for maximum light.

Next it was time to review the outdoor beds. Robert had moaned about the lack of lawn in the back garden. He wanted somewhere to sit and read his paper when the weather was fine. She wanted a productive garden. Slowly, she'd taken up turf; building six raised beds. She loved watching tiny shoots emerge then race to top of the poles.

This year she was determined to grow enough to store for the winter. Humming softly to herself she raked and planted the first row of beans. Every year she intended to plant before autumn left but something always happened to prevent her. Maybe this year would be different.

She was tired from her labours after lunch and took a nap, waking just in time to retrieve the washing before rain started. She draped it over the clothes horse in front of the range, wondering what to do next.

She had been playing for nearly an hour when the front doorbell rang.

"Sorry to disturb you," Zeb said, rain dripping from his hat onto the porch floor. "I tried knocking round the back, but you didn't hear. I brought someone with me who wants to ask a favour. I have one too."

Ruth ushered the two men into the hall, thankful they left their boots in the porch. Their coats were wet. Should she offer to dry them over the fire?

"Would you like a cup of tea?" At least they could drip over the kitchen floor rather than the carpet.

The smaller man shook his head. He looked younger than Ruth, but his brown hair was already thinning on top. He had the air of perpetual anxiety; his eyes darting from one item to another as if he were too shy for his gaze to stay anywhere for long.

"Zeb tells me you play the piano. We could hear you playing from outside. Schubert?" Ruth nodded. What was he going to ask? A familiar knot began to tighten her stomach. Whatever it was, she wasn't sure she wanted to do it.

"It's the church choir," he said, wiping his wet hands on his coat. "I'm Lawrence Graves, the organist and choir master. We've got two big services coming up soon. The Bishop is coming on Easter Sunday to carry out the confirmations and then we're having a special service on St. John's Day in June to re-consecrate the undercroft.

"The choir has quite a few new members and I'm finding it really difficult to conduct and accompany at the same time. Could you help us?" His eyes pleaded with her; his hands clutching the sides of his coat as if he were concerned they might fly off and do things of their own.

Ruth hesitated. Although she knew she would accept, she didn't want to seem to too eager. "How much time would it take up?"

"We meet on a Friday at 6pm. We're always finished by 8.30 at the latest because of the children. Please say you'll consider it. I don't know who else I could ask. There aren't many pianists in the local villages."

"I'll think about it." Ruth said. She knew she sounded reluctant, but the truth was she was thrilled to be asked. "I'm very rusty."

Zeb grinned at her. "You didn't sound that rusty when we were outside."

Ruth felt her cheeks growing warm. "It's different playing for yourself." She looked up at him. "You said you had a favour to ask as well?"

"Nothing pressing," he said. "It was just you wanted to know how much you owed for the pruning. I wondered if we could do a deal instead. Henry will need somewhere for the pet lambs once they come off the bottle. He has a small flock of Cotswold. There are two ewe lambs that will join the rest of the ewes but the three wethers will go for meat as soon as they make the weight.

"We wondered if they could stay in the orchard for a couple of months. It won't be until they're weaned so you won't have to worry about feeding them or anything. They'd help keep the grass down around the trees."

Her first instinct was to agree. It seemed a good way of repaying her debt, but she wasn't sure. She'd never been responsible for animals. She didn't know what it might entail. She needed to talk to someone about what she might have to do.

"I'll have to talk it over with Mattie," she said, deciding that if the young woman was going to be staying, any livestock would be a joint responsibility. Besides, didn't Granny say her father was a shepherd? She should know about sheep. At least she would know more than Ruth.

"As I said," She could tell Zeb was trying to reassure her, "There's no rush. It'll be another month before they need to move."

"Yes, yes," the other man joined in. Ruth realised she couldn't remember his name. "Please don't feel pressured. I can show you the music after church tomorrow if you like. I could be here about 12.30 perhaps?"

"No need," she told him. "I'll see you in church."

After the two men left, Ruth wandered into the kitchen and made herself a cup of tea. *It never rains but it pours*, she thought to herself.

CHAPTER FIFTEEN

To Ruth's surprise, she enjoyed the service the following morning. She joined Mattie's mother, halfway down the aisle. Mattie's younger brothers and their father were seated in the choir stalls. Mattie slid into the seat beside her mother halfway through the service when Sunday school was over.

Adrian Hope, the Rector, was very different from how Ruth imagined he would be. He was short, about 5' 8", with unruly dark hair tinged with grey. His face was chubby and full of smiles. He seemed to bounce gently on the balls of his feet whenever he stood up to sing and his voice rang clearly around the church as he led the prayers. His sermon was short but thoughtful. The first wave of laughter running through the congregation after a clever turn of phrase caught Ruth by surprise. Rectors weren't supposed to be funny, but she couldn't help but smile. She liked him.

The organist was hidden behind the choir. Ruth was impressed by his skills with the foot pedals and stops and the choir reflected his abilities.

As the Rector made his way down the nave after the final blessing, Ruth looked around wondering where refreshments would be served. She couldn't see anywhere set up with tables and there was no sign of the famous iced buns. Her throat was dry after all the singing. She could do with something to drink.

"Where's coffee?" she whispered to Mattie.

"Downstairs, the door's open."

Doors. The church was full of doors. South, west, north, chancel, vestry. All of them shut.

The organ thundered towards the end of the voluntary. Ruth's head ached. In front of her, behind the lectern, she caught sight of a narrow opening in the wall with a pointed archway. A dark hole in the wall but she could hear singing. The choir must be downstairs.

She stood up. She didn't want to be the first one through the opening. She never liked being first at anything, but the music drew her forward. It was plainsong, hauntingly beautiful, echoing through the doorway. So achingly lovely it made her shiver.

Behind her someone laughed. Not a mirthful sound; it sounded like Robert. He loved laughing at her discomfort. She whirled round to see who it was, but her headache was giving her tunnel vision. She saw an old man with long, grey hair curling in lank ringlets below his shoulders standing by the north door. He was clean shaven and wore a black cassock with two white preaching bands hanging down from his collar.

She realised this was the stranger from the Post office, the same presence who had scared her into the hare scrape in Long Meadow. Before he had been a shape with indistinct edges, now he was as real as everyone else. His piercing stare scared her. It was as if he could see inside her and despised everything about her. His contemptuous laughter made her feel sick. The pounding in her head was intensifying. The worse she felt, the louder he laughed.

Whoever he was, she wasn't going to look at him. She wouldn't give him the satisfaction of her fear. She turned back to the doorway behind the lectern letting the music soothe her. She must find out who was singing.

She took several steps forward breathing deeply. She recognised the smell of frankincense wafting towards her. Its scent renewed her courage. As she reached the opening, she saw stone steps leading downwards in a steep spiral. They were narrow and worn in the centre. She thought they must be very old compared with other stonework in the nave; with walls both sides blackened from centuries of pilgrims' hand prints as they passed this way. Light flickered in the stairwell. Shadows moved against the stone as if someone were walking down the stairs in front of her but as hard as she looked, she could see no-one.

Music still resonated in her ears. She could feel herself humming the simple tune. Where was everyone? Why was it dark around her when sun had been streaming through stained-glass windows during the service?

Her hand reached out towards the doorpost but instead of solid stone, water trickled over her fingers. She snatched it back, thrusting it inside her coat pocket. What was a basin full of water doing beside an internal doorway? Why would there be holy water in an Anglican church?

"Ruth, where are you going?" She could feel Mattie's hand on her arm, but her voice seemed a long way away. "The undercroft is this way."

Ruth turned around, the nave once more flooded with pale, winter sunlight. How could she have missed the open door between two pews immediately behind where she had been sitting. Light shone from the entrance and the congregation were descending the wooden staircase in a steady stream.

"I heard singing," she tried to explain, in response to Mattie's puzzled expression. "I came over to investigate. Who's the other Rector?"

"What other Rector?"

"The old man with the horrid laugh. He was standing over there a minute ago." She pointed towards the north door, except there wasn't a door, just a bricked-up archway. She stopped, feeling her heart begin to pound in her chest.

What was happening to her? Were all the years of silence, never hearing nor seeing anything not noticed by others finally over? All those muted, wasted years with Robert.

She remembered their first holiday together. How he scoffed when their landlady explained her father always talked to the spirit child who lived in their cellar to stop him throwing their store of potatoes up the steps. When Ruth glanced around, she saw the child sitting in the doorway playing cat's cradle while they finished their breakfast. She didn't dare tell Robert, even when he asked her why she was smiling. She didn't dare tell anyone. Soon there was nothing to tell until she came to Roelswick and heard the wolfhound howl every time Robert made her cry.

She knew the cleric was real. His vile emotions still crawled along her skin. The door behind him was so clear in her mind she could have counted how many iron nails were used to hold the wooden planks together. The iron latch was thick, heavy, larger than the one on the south door but now it wasn't there at all; the doorway packed with Victorian bricks.

She didn't imagine the vengeful distain in the old man's laugh. He was determined to destroy whatever joy she discovered in her new environment, just like Robert. She refused to allow him such power over her. Not again. Never again.

"Come on," said Mattie, pulling her towards the stairway as if anxious to move her away from the site of her strange experience. "If we don't get down soon all the buns will be gone."

The undercroft was large and airy. Whitewashed walls reflected light from six high windows augmented by electric lamps suspended from the barrel-vaulted ceiling. Tables set up against the west wall brimmed with mugs of tea and coffee flanked by plates piled high with iced buns fiercely guarded by Mattie's mother waving a large pair of tongs.

Ruth grabbed a mug of coffee, walking carefully away from the table. She could see Mattie talking to Granny. From the way they both kept glancing towards her, she was obviously the main subject of their conversation. She couldn't bear to be drawn into any questioning when she wasn't clear in her own mind what was going on, so she walked off in the opposite direction.

Ruth still heard echoes of the melody upstairs, yet no-one was singing. Glancing upwards, she saw blue smears of paint on the ceiling just beyond a small table covered with a white cloth adorned with a simple wooden cross. It was darker here, the only illumination coming from high windows on three sides. As she stood peering up into the gloom, she noticed silver stars on a faded blue painted ceiling.

"You've discovered our tiny fragment of medieval painting," A voice at her side made her jump. It was the Rector, his familiar smile disbursing her unease.

"Yes," she said, juggling her mug and plate to find a free hand to shake his. "I love history. You have a fascinating church."

Their conversation was interrupted as Lawrence Graves, the organist, came bustling towards them. "I'm hoping Mrs Turner is going to help me with the choir," he said, waving a sheaf of music. "I've managed to put together copies of all the choir solos and I found a spare copy of the Benedicite you can have. We'll need to practice that next Friday so we're ready for Lent. Are you familiar with sung psalms?"

Ruth smiled, "My grandmother used to play the organ for her village church. I think all her sisters played or sang in the choir. She taught me to sing my first hymns when I was four and I was in the choir at church and in school. After university, I was tired of Requiems, so I haven't done much since but I'm sure I'll remember."

"Wonderful, wonderful," said Adrian, scooping up a toddler who was trying to clean his sugar-crusted mouth on the Rector's black cape. "Now then, Arthur, are you ready for your dinner. Shall we go and find Mummy?"

He wandered off, greeting other parishioners before Andrea appeared from another small group, leaving Granny and Greg standing in the shadows by the base of a stone staircase in the outside wall. Ruth was surprised by the look Andrea threw in her direction. Her brow was furrowed as if something from her discussion with Granny and Greg disturbed her. Ruth saw her smile at her husband as she led the way out of the undercroft.

She sipped her coffee as Lawrence tried to show her the music. Pages fluttered about, finally ending up on the floor. She hid a smile as he scrabbled around trying to retrieve them from underneath the altar cloth.

Mattie appeared with a tray collecting empty cups and plates which gave Ruth the opportunity to look more closely at the pages Lawrence handed to her. One was written on thick manuscript paper with very few bar lines. The notes were scratched onto the paper with words printed underneath which were almost too faded to read.

"What's this?" she asked, trying to sight read the tune in her head. After a few notes, she realised it was the chant she was listening to in the church. The choir must have been singing as they came down for their coffee. This simple explanation made her feel much better, but her relief was short-lived as Lawrence took the page from her and studied it carefully, moving his glasses to the top of his head and peering at the manuscript as if he'd never seen it before.

"I've no idea," he said at last, returning it to her. "It looks like plainsong but it's not familiar. It must have been lying underneath the altar when I picked up the rest of the music."

"But the choir were singing it earlier. I heard them through the old stone stairwell. It's beautiful." She hummed the tune for him expecting him to recognise it but his face was blank. "You must know it," she insisted but he shook his head.

Now Ruth was thoroughly confused. Why didn't he know the music? He offered to take it from her, but she clutched everything tightly and said she needed it to practice. "I'll do some research if you like and try to find the origin of this chant. I'm sure there'll be something on the internet somewhere."

He reminded her about the times of choir-practice next Friday and she promised she would be there to accompany the choir. She told him how much she was looking forward to being part of a choir again. It had been too long.

As they wandered towards the entrance, Granny came up to Ruth and Lawrence said he needed to get home to cook dinner for his mother.

"Mattie's going back with her family. Would you like to come and have Sunday lunch with Zeb and me? I put a nice piece of beef to roast before we came out and there's gooseberry crumble for afters."

Granny's smile was warm and welcoming. Ruth decided she didn't want to return home to an empty house and think about cooking for herself.

"Should I go home and drop this music off first?" she asked.

"Bring it with you," Granny said, "I heard you asking Lawrence if he knew that old tune. You could show it to Zeb, he's the keeper of our village songs; he may know something."

CHAPTER SIXTEEN

They made their way up the stairs and out into the spring sunshine. Early daffodils lined the lychgate path waving their golden scent in the breeze. Ruth caught sight of a tiny bird darting into the ivy covering the stone wall, scolding them as they walked past.

It only took a few minutes to go down the hill to Glebe cottage where Granny and Zeb lived on the other side of the small village pond. Several other houses flanked the narrow lane which led down to the old mill nearly a mile away. She knew it was being renovated and the mill pond and leat dredged so water flowed freely once more.

Dolly greeted them exuberantly as soon as they opened the door, jumping up and wagging her tail as if Ruth were a long-lost friend of the family.

She patted her head and ruffled her long, feathery ears whilst trying not to lose the bundle of music she was carrying.

"Daft dog," Zeb rumbled, pushing the spaniel away so Ruth could take off her coat without further interference. She followed him into the kitchen where Granny was pouring boiling water into saucepans and putting them on the range. She waved Ruth away when she offered to help suggesting she showed Zeb the manuscript while the vegetables cooked.

"What do you think?" Ruth asked, putting the two sheets of paper on the small table by Zeb's chair. He pulled his spectacles out of his shirt pocket and peered at the music for a long time. He hummed to himself, then got up and fetched his guitar from its case, tuning the strings thoughtfully before picking out some notes.

"Never seen the words before," he said at last, putting the guitar back, "but I know the tune. We sing it at Christmas sometimes. Where did you find it?"

"It wasn't me. Lawrence found them under the altar when we were having coffee."

"Nice little tune," Zeb said, handing her back the sheets. She tucked them in with the other choir music. "You going to do anything with it?"

"I don't know. I hadn't thought about it." She realised he was looking at her just a shade too intently. She wanted to fidget.

"Must have come to you for a reason." His words were so softly spoken she could hardly hear what he said, especially as Granny called them to the table for lunch just at that moment.

It was a wonderful Sunday dinner. Roast beef and Yorkshire pudding were accompanied by a wide array of vegetables grown in the cottage garden and now stored in the shed. They talked about seeds and planting, planning for the new season. Gooseberry crumble with thick custard was a fitting end to the meal.

Ruth helped to clear the table then stood at the sink wiping dishes as Granny washed up and Zeb disappeared for his afternoon nap in the front room. Ruth could feel her eyes wanting to close and wished she could join him.

"How did you know he was a Rector?" Granny asked. Ruth almost dropped the plate she was drying. She wondered how she could pretend not to understand Granny's question. She was so used to hiding, it was second nature but part of her wanted to discuss what she'd seen; to tell her she wasn't mad.

"Mattie said you saw another Rector." Granny's voice was deceptively calm, but Ruth knew she wanted a complete description of everything she'd seen in the church.

"It was his laugh made me look at him," she said, laying the plate carefully on the growing pile on the table. "Robert's laugh sounded similar; especially when he wanted to show what a fool I was."

"And when you turned round?"

"He was standing in front of the north door as if the church were his. I know it isn't there now, but I could see the doorway so clearly and the red curtains either side were moving. He just stared at me. I could feel the hair on the back of my neck rising but I refused to be scared, I was angry. He was the man who chased me into the hare scrape where Greg found me. Today, he was trying to stop me listening to the music. I walked towards the steps leading down to the undercroft. I was going to discover who was singing but Mattie came and fetched me and took me down the wooden staircase."

"We don't use the old stairs anymore. They're very steep and can be slippery in damp weather." Granny pulled out the plug and watched the water swirl down the sink. "You see a lot of folk who walk between worlds?"

"You mean spirits?" Granny nodded as she picked up the dishes and put them back on their correct shelves in the cupboard. Ruth wondered what to say but a quick glance towards the older woman made her realise today was the time for telling the truth. Granny knew.

"I've always seen them," Ruth folded the tea towel and laid it over the back of a chair. Granny filled the kettle and set it to boil on the hob. Ruth knew she was waiting for her to continue.

"When I was a child, I didn't know what they were. They were just people I saw. There was an old man who sat in the front room of my grandmother's house. He didn't like children. I wouldn't stay in there on my own, I was too scared. One day, Nanna asked me why I kept running back to her in the kitchen. When I said I didn't like the old man, she took my hand and we both walked into the room. Nanna took me right up to his chair.

"'This is my granddaughter, Ruth Flint,' she said. 'She's as much right to be here as you. Don't you be mean to her, Fred Anderton, you hear me?'" Ruth giggled. "My Dad came in the room and asked Nanna why she was talking to an empty chair. I can't remember what she told him but ever afterwards I'd say, 'Hello, Mr Anderton' and he'd either go away or sit quietly while I played with my doll or with Nanna's special tea set." She smiled at the memory as Granny set three cups and saucers on a tray, then sighed.

"It all stopped when I met Robert. We were visiting somewhere on honeymoon which was supposed to be haunted. He said anyone who thought they saw ghosts should be locked up and the key thrown away. The way he said it frightened me. After that I stopped seeing anything until I moved here."

"Without Robert," Granny said putting the milk jug and a pretty sugar basin onto the tray."

"I suppose it was." Ruth agreed. "I felt safe in my cottage. If Robert hurt me, I'd hear the wolfhound barking. I know Robert heard it too. He didn't like the sound. When I saw Finn up at the Priory, I thought he was real, the way he looked at me."

"When did you realise he wasn't?" Granny picked up the kettle to pour boiling water into the teapot.

"I saw a grave marker underneath one of the shrubs beside the car park. It said Finn and last month's date. Even then I wasn't sure until the night of the Wassailing. He nudged my hand with his head and he was as solid as anything but both Colin and Andrea looked so shocked, I knew he was spirit."

"It didn't bother you?"

"No, should it?"

"Not if you're a Blackwell." Granny picked up the tea tray and led the way into the front room.

"Who's a Blackwell?" asked Zeb, shaking out the Sunday paper as he turned a page.

"I am," said Ruth as she chose a seat on the sofa near to Zeb. "Or rather my Grandmother was. It was her maiden name." Granny set the tray down on the small table in front of them and sat down in the rocking chair, picking up her knitting.

Zeb regarded her over the top of his paper. "I thought Granny didn't have any children. She was on her own once Ernie died. Looking after her was enough to send anyone to an early grave."

Granny finished her row and considered the pattern growing on the tiny garment as if it were a picture of family relationships only just revealing themselves. Ruth thought she was trying to decide whether or not to say anything. When she spoke, her voice was thoughtful, teasing out memories as she would complicated stitches.

"There was talk of a child up at the big house but not a whisper in the village. No-one knew anything for certain and Granny wasn't someone who would answer questions she didn't like, no matter how you phrased them. It happened before she married Ernie. They said she was sent away to visit a cousin in the city on account of her 'weak lungs'. They said she was never the same after she returned which makes sense if you've just lost your child to another. It wasn't her fault she went senile when she did. As much as she and I had our differences, I don't begrudge the time spent looking after her."

Zeb humphed and rattled his papers while Granny started another row. Ruth stared at her teacup. She felt tired and miserable and longed to go home. For a moment, she was so excited to think she might truly belong here, but it was hardly likely she had any connection to anyone.

"What was your Dad's name?" Granny asked.

"Roger. At least, that was what everyone called him but there was a different name on his birth certificate, Beynon, I think it was."

"You know what it means?"

Ruth shook her head. "No idea."

Granny counted her stitches, then laid her needles down on her lap and looked at Ruth. "It's an old, Welsh name meaning 'son of Anvil'. It's been used in the village for centuries for children fathered by Anvil."

"Any child born out of wedlock was attributed to the blacksmith?" Ruth was confused.

"No, it meant he was the son of the Anvil and his surname tied him to the village just as Granny was tied. She was a Robin's child."

"Granny, you're talking in riddles. I think I'd better go home." Ruth stood up. This was ridiculous. Her head was beginning to ache again and the milk must be off because she had a sour taste in her mouth. What was worse, she heard that dreadful laughter again. She needed to go home and have a nap then everything would be better.

"You alright, Ruth? You've gone as white as a sheet. Sit down before you fall down." She heard the concern in Zeb's voice, but it seemed to be coming from a long way away.

She slid back onto the sofa. Zeb leaned over and patted her hand. As he touched her, she felt better. This was so strange. What was going on?

Granny appeared at her side with a glass of water, encouraging her to take small sips. With each swallow, her headache lessened until she felt herself again.

"That was weird," she said at last.

"Tell us what happened," she saw the worried glances pass between Zeb and Granny.

"I heard the same laughter I heard in the church. My head hurt and I thought I was going to be sick. I didn't see anything."

"That's a good thing. We don't want him in here," said Granny

"Who is he?"

"What did she see in church?" She and Zeb spoke together, both of them looking at Granny.

"Isaac Graves."

Zeb leaped from his seat shouting "No! It can't be. Not here. Not now."

"Don't upset yourself, Zeb. It doesn't have to mean anything." Zeb stalked out of the room, followed by Dolly and then the front door slammed.

Ruth didn't know what to feel. What on earth had made Zeb so angry?

"I'm sorry." The words stumbled out of her mouth more by force of habit than any other emotion.

"It's not your fault." Granny soothed her. "Maybe this time won't be like the others."

CHAPTER SEVENTEEN

As Ruth opened Granny's front door, mist was swirling up from the river making it difficult to see the way home. In her hand, she carried a bag with her choir music plus some scones and cake Granny insisted she take with her.

The fog muted everything. Pulling up her hood against the cold and damp, she followed the narrow path across the green, stopping for a moment on the bridge listening to the water rushing into the pond beneath her feet. It unnerved her not being able to see around her. Familiar spaces appeared strange and unworldly. The sound of water normally soothed her but now it seemed angry, swirling beneath her feet as if it would carry her away if she tripped and fell into the pond.

She paused at the roadside, listening for vehicles but all she heard was drips from the chestnut tree beside the stocks hitting blades of winter grass below. As she stared across the road, she saw a thin shape sitting at the bottom of the steep flight of steps which led to her house. For a moment, she was too scared to move, wondering what on earth it could be but then it stood up and she could see a tail wagging.

"Hello Finn," she said, reaching out to stroke his shaggy head without thinking. "Have you come to see me safely home?"

The wolfhound made no sound, padding silently beside her as she climbed the steps. When she reached the top and stood for a moment, catching her breath, he trotted on towards the front door. As he turned round to wait for her to catch up, she thought she heard mocking laughter behind her. She was furious. It was one thing to be accompanied by her own protective spirit dog, but she was fed up with some nasty cleric following her around the village. She'd done nothing to him, why couldn't he leave her alone?

"Go away!" she shouted, pointing towards the sounds she heard. "Not in my house, not on my land will your footsteps pass this day or any day while I have breath to say, 'Be Gone!'"

She heard a door slam from a house across the road. What on earth was she doing shouting at nothing. The neighbours would think she'd finally flipped! Even so, she didn't rush towards her own porch, she could feel something had changed. The fog seemed less dense although it was almost dark. She could see the light from the streetlamp, which hadn't been visible before and the ominous pressure she'd felt from the steps was gone.

What had she said? She'd just opened her mouth and words had sprung from them and they had worked. Well, they made her feel better. It was probably all her own imagination in the first place. She felt for her key and walked towards the front door. Finn was nowhere to be seen.

As she opened the door, she was assailed by the smell of newly baked bread. Lights were on in the kitchen and she could hear Mattie talking to someone. She hung up her coat and went to join them.

"Dad brought me home," Mattie greeted her. "He wondered if you could help him out."

Inwardly Ruth groaned, now what was she going to be asked to do? She smiled at George Cooper, who was sitting at the table with a mug of tea in his hands, hoping he wouldn't notice the irritation she was feeling.

"What's the problem?"

"Our Gerry brought four rescue hens home with him last week. He's been helping out over at Temple Northcote. They've got a barn full of seven hundred and they cull so many every year. Some of them hide away and he brings home the ones he finds and we either add them to ours or give them to folk who want hens. It's useful when the fox 'as been through and decimated a flock."

Ruth frowned. "I don't see where I come in."

"We were going to keep these four, but Dan, he's the little-un, he hatched four Marans last year he got from Jack Ackerley."

"Colin's Dad," explained Mattie.

"Well you know how vicious Marans can be," continued George, "even though we tried to introduce the newcomers over a week, they're laying-in to them something terrible. We've had to shut them up in a small coop for the time being until we can find them somewhere else."

"Dad thought they could come here, in the orchard." Mattie said, jumping across her father's measured speech. "We've got a spare hen house. We can get some flour from the farm like Dad does and they'll eat all our food scraps and old veg. I can look after them. They wouldn't be any trouble and we'd get our own eggs." Mattie's face beamed. Ruth wasn't so sure.

"But what about the lambs Zeb wants to bring us? I was going to talk to you about those tonight."

"Mattie knows lambs," said George. "She's been around them all her life. As long as they don't get out you won't know they're there."

"Is the orchard big enough?"

George laughed. "You've got plenty of room for four lambs and a flock of twenty fowl if you wanted. If you wanted pigs, that might be a different matter and of course horses wouldn't be good because they nibble bark and fallen fruit upsets their insides. The lambs'll be gone before you can turn round."

Ruth felt foolish. For all her desire to blend into country life, she knew so little. She did have choices. She could continue Robert's conditioning and believe she was a worthless idiot, or she could learn and move forward. George wasn't mocking her with his laughter, he was genuinely amused. She suspected he laughed at many things judging by the lines around his eyes.

"Seems like I'm going to learn a lot from my orchard," she said at last.

The conversation went on for a while, but once George's mug was empty, he made his farewells and left to go and check on the ewes in the field behind the church.

"I walk round 'em every night," he said. "Don't matter so much if they only drop a single, but doubles need taking inside before the fox find 'em."

Ruth wanted to ask him if he ever came across the ghostly cleric on his travels but decided it wouldn't be a good idea. If she hadn't heard the words of banishment coming from her own mouth, she could quite easily have convinced herself she imagined the whole scenario. Perhaps what surprised her the most was how calm she felt about the whole affair now she was inside. She settled herself in the lounge in front of the television and Mattie went upstairs to finish her unpacking.

CHAPTER EIGHTEEN

The fog was gone next morning when Ruth drew back the curtains. A pale sky waited for sunrise. Mattie was off helping Colin graft more trees from the cuttings Zeb had taken from her orchard and wasn't expected back before dark. She left while Ruth was finishing her breakfast, her basket filled again with food for their lunch.

"Mum gave me more pies when I was home yesterday," she told Ruth. "There's one in the fridge if you want some."

She still had time before she needed to leave for Home Farm, so Ruth pulled on her boots and went to check the mysterious gate at the bottom of the orchard. As she walked down the left-hand hedge, she realised why she hadn't noticed it before. The land sloped gently at first but then fell away more steeply as she neared the road. A hazel tree grew directly in front of the dip, making it appear the lower boundary hedge continued in a straight line concealing a large space behind it.

The ground was covered with debris; fallen leaves, dead plants and chunks of wood blown off or dropped from dead branches. Even so, there was a clear path leading down to a five-barred gate overgrown with brambles and ivy. It would be impossible for anyone to enter without getting ripped to shreds.

As she peered into the road, she was surprised to see Greg walking past towards the village. She called out a greeting, but he didn't stop, even though she was sure he heard her.

"Must have other things on his mind," she thought as she turned to walk back to the house. A patch of dark earth caught her attention. She thought it strange but there was no time to investigate further, she needed to decide what to do about the gate. Did she want to make it easy for strangers to enter the orchard unseen? It would be useful for livestock to enter here rather than bringing them all the way through the garden.

The phone was ringing as she entered the kitchen.

"Sorry about yesterday," Zeb sounded embarrassed.

"I've forgotten all about it." Ruth said, not wanting to revisit the previous afternoon. "I'm glad you rang. Would it be possible to make my gate on the bottom road open but still look impassable?"

"Don't see why not."

"George has some hens he wants to rehome. It would be easier if he could bring the henhouse that way." She was glad Zeb sounded more like his cheerful self.

"Have you thought about the lambs?"

"Yes. Mattie said she'd be responsible for them."

"Good. We'll make sure the boundary is secure. When does George want to bring the hens?"

"He said tonight. Is that too soon?"

There was a pause as Zeb shouted something to Granny. "No, that's ok. I'll do it this afternoon."

Ruth felt a sense of relief as she left a message for George before setting off for Home Farm. New things were starting to happen. The possibility of excitement warred with apprehension in the pit of her stomach.

As she drove down the hill, she saw movement in the small copse behind the church. She slowed down to see if she could make out who it might be. Someone was hiding behind a tree, watching the village hall. The figure leaned forward and Ruth caught sight of a familiar face. It was Greg. Whatever was he doing?

Gillian met her at the office and went through various tasks which needed sorting that morning before she left to take Harry to playgroup. Ruth was surprised when Henry popped his head around the door to see how she was doing and asked if he could scrounge a coffee. She couldn't believe two hours had gone already.

She made their drinks while she checked convenient times with him for various appointments and let him know a delivery of feedstuff was on its way.

"I'll tell Tom," Henry said, snagging a couple of biscuits as he made his way down the steps. "Just hope they get here before he starts the afternoon milking."

As she sipped her coffee, she realised she hadn't contacted Nigel's secretary to make an appointment to talk about her divorce. She knew if she let things slide for much longer, she would never be able to make the fresh start she needed.

She dialled the number and introduced herself.

"Mr Milsom told me you would be in touch." The secretary's tone was just the proper shade of friendly professionalism. "He has a cancellation this afternoon. Would three o'clock be too soon for you to come in?"

Ruth assured her she would be able to get there in time and thanked her for directions.

At one o'clock, Ruth tidied her desk and made her way out into the yard. She ventured into the kitchen where Gillian was serving lunch and told her she'd be back in the morning.

"Has it been ok?" Gillian looked anxious as she spooned pudding into Harry's bowl. "It can get lonely up there, but I've been too busy rushing around to come and see you."

"It's fine, "Ruth reassured her, "I'm used to working alone."

It seemed strange driving into town halfway through the day, the bag of diaries and notebooks she'd brought with her sitting like a resentful lump in the passenger seat. Despite the rain dripping from her umbrella, she felt almost cheerful as she made her way to Nigel's office. He joined her in the meeting room almost before she had time to sip the drink his secretary proffered.

After the usual greeting and enquiries, he sat back in his chair, his hands steepled against his chin. He was a tall man with streaks of grey running through his dark hair. He wore a well-fitting dark suit which hugged his slim frame. He looked so different from the Morris man of the previous week except for the calm face and searching grey eyes.

"What's the best you hope for from this divorce?" he asked.

Ruth took a moment to reflect, surprised by the anger and resentment she felt bubbling to the surface.

"I've had enough. I want him to suffer as he's made me suffer. I refuse to give him the satisfaction of simply ending our marriage. I want you to file for divorce on the grounds of serial infidelity beginning fifteen years ago and culminating with him living openly with a woman he brought back from China."

"Do you have any names or dates?" Nigel asked.

Ruth removed the books from her bag and pushed them across the desk so hard, several fell on the floor beside Nigel's chair. She couldn't meet his shocked glance as he leant down to retrieve them. What was the matter with her? Nigel was trying to help.

"I started keeping a diary of late working, unexplained conferences and trips abroad," she said. "At the time, I didn't know what to do with it. Divorce never entered my head. I learned never to confront him, it just provoked something more terrible for me."

"Was he violent?"

"Nothing I could show anyone else. He screamed and shouted and sometimes he'd shake me. The silences were worse. He found ways to destroy anything I valued. He kept everything from the sale of our previous home. I never saw a penny."

"Who owned that house?" She could see Nigel's pad was full of notes.

"Both names were on the mortgage and we both contributed to repayments for fifteen years. Money from the sale went into our joint account but when I tried to access it two years ago it was in his name. I asked the bank, but they refused to discuss it. Robert said I had my house and he needed the money to buy himself something nearer his office."

"What made you move to Roelswick?"

"Robert said we should move to the country, using my godmother's legacy. He chose the village and the road, but I fell in love with the house and orchard. For the first time in my life, I defied him. I love it there."

"The house belongs to you?"

Ruth explained the financial Trust set up by her godmother which owned the property, preventing Robert from benefitting from her will. Nigel asked many probing questions until they ran out of time. She was exhausted from such a thorough grilling and wandered back towards her car in a daze.

She was passing a small café when she saw Greg inside talking to a waitress at the counter. He gave her a package and Ruth saw her kiss his cheek and run to show the other staff. Ruth was just about to walk on when Greg beckoned her inside.

It seemed churlish to ignore his friendly smile. He ordered a pot of tea and asked her to choose cake from the wide variety on the counter. They sat down at a small circular table in the centre laid for two people. She wondered if Robert would hear of her sitting in a public place with another man then decided she didn't care, biting hard into her chocolate éclair as if she could emasculate her former husband.

The waitress brought the package back to the table, along with their drinks, eager to show Ruth her present. It was the delicate filigree trivet, Ruth glimpsed through the blacksmith's window.

"Bessie were my Maid," Greg explained, pointing at the trivet.

"She's promised herself to a good village lad and I wanted to show my blessing."

Ruth admired the sinuous curves and beautiful enamelling while Bessie giggled with embarrassment by her ear.

"Anvil is so good to all us women," Bessie simpered. "No-one need fear when he's around."

Ruth grabbed her teacup, feeling her cheeks grow warmer. She'd never really thanked Greg properly for rescuing her that dreadful night. Words seemed so inadequate. She was glad when another table required Bessie's attention and she went to take their order, leaving them alone.

Greg munched through his fruit cake in measured bites, glancing at her as he poured them both a second cup of tea.

"How are you, little hare?" he asked, tipping a heaped spoon of sugar into his cup.

"Much better now, thank you." She wiped her mouth with the serviette, hoping there were no chocolate smears evading her touch. "I've just come from Nigel's office. He's going to handle my divorce."

Greg stirred his tea for several long seconds. Silence lengthened until she couldn't stop the question bursting from her.

"Why were you watching the village hall this morning?"

The teaspoon clattered on the wooden table.

"It was you, wasn't it?"

Greg's mouth was a thin, angry line. She flinched, thinking he was going to shout at her. Instead, he sighed, his broad shoulders slumping.

"You ain't the only one fighting secrets," he whispered, a single drop of tea falling from his moustache.

"Sorry?"

Greg shifted uncomfortably in his seat; his large frame suddenly shrunk inside itself. Ruth was shocked by the change in him.

"I can't say and nor must you, promise me?" His hand gripped her wrist so hard he frightened her.

"You're hurting me," she hissed.

"Promise!"

"I can't promise something I don't understand."

"Nor would you understand even if I spent the day explaining." He loosened his grip, stroking his finger along the red mark. His brown eyes flickered around her face with such hopelessness, Ruth found herself feeling sorry for him.

"I can try," she said at last, watching his lips quiver with a ghostly smile.

"I'm sure you would but my fear's too great to speak what isn't mine. Who sent you, little hare? Have you come to jump the flames for me? Trick me into revealing what should be hidden? Who are you?"

Ruth found herself transfixed as the rest of the coffee shop slid away into a silent world. There was no way to avoid his question. She felt it burning inside her like a twisting arrow.

"Flesh of your flesh," she whispered, using words which came to her unbidden. "Granny knows. I was born Ruth Flint, daughter of Roger, son of Anvil and Granny Blackwell. Pear Tree Cottage is mine; Miller's orchard is mine and I keep the black well clear. I see what can't be seen. I am the shape in the moon bringing light to shadows. I leap the fire to burn away the old and restore the new. I know all and I know nothing. I am the hare."

She felt his hand slip from hers. Gradually they were subsumed by sounds floating around them. Snippets of conversation from other tables danced about her ears. Bessie passed new orders over the counter and the cash register rang up another bill. The doorbell clanged drawing in cold air from outside.

She grasped her teacup, draining the last drops into her parched throat. Like her namesake, she longed to run away but another fear held her in place.

"I'm so sorry," she said, hoping he would accept her apology and not be angry with her. "I've no idea why I said those things."

Greg grinned; his face suddenly clear of its previous emotion.

"Maybe it's too close to March." He spread his hand lightly over hers. This time she felt only reassurance. "I guess Granny was right to say you'd come home. You'll know soon enough why you're here."

CHAPTER NINETEEN

Weeks passed and Ruth began to enjoy the new rhythm of her life. From Monday to Wednesday, she worked at Home Farm and looked forward to the Women's Circle in the village hall on Thursday evening and choir practice on Friday. The hens settled in their new home just inside the orchard and spent their days exploring grass and undergrowth. She was getting used to feeding them first thing in the morning and again when she returned home at lunchtime. When she went to shut them up as darkness fell, they were usually inside on their perch, settling down to sleep.

One Thursday, the day was unusually dry and bright after a long spell of dismal gloom and frequent, heavy rain. Ruth decided she would take another walk around the village. Ally Tulliver had spoken about the need for a cleaning roster in the Ladywell chapel at the last Circle meeting. Ruth volunteered to help, not knowing exactly what it might entail. A visit might show her how much work would be needed.

This time she went prepared with stout walking boots and layers of warm clothes, a spare waterproof in her backpack in case of further rain. Mattie even drew her a map, so she could come home across the fields rather than follow the road all the way.

She could hear voices and saw the forge doors were open, but she didn't go up to see what might be going on. She was still embarrassed by their meeting in the coffee shop and tried to avoid Greg whenever she could. She crossed the road and walked up the hill, turning right at the entrance to the Abbott's orchard to follow the footpath which meandered down to the well.

She crossed a stile into a small enclosure sheltered on three sides by ancient trees. The well was straight in front of her consisting of a large, square stone basin filled from a spring gushing out of a curved brick wall built into the bank. The overflow trickled down the contours of the hillside as a tiny stream, meeting the river somewhere below.

The chapel stood to her left. The walls were stone with a thatched roof. It was a simple, rectangular structure with no windows and a single wooden doorway at the far end. As she reached the door, she was sure she could hear singing, looking around to see if Mattie or Colin were working nearby.

The wooden latch lifted easily. She pulled the door towards her, releasing a smell of incense. Surely, it couldn't be safe to leave an unattended thurible alight in a thatched building.

She stood for a moment, letting her eyes adjust to the gloom. Two large candles burned on the stone altar either side of a simple, wooden cross; two iron candleholders further forward held other tapers, giving out a soft yellow light.

Five figures in dark, woollen habits were kneeling towards the altar, heads bowed so candlelight flickered off tonsures as prayers were recited in Latin. She realised one man's head was not shaved and she wondered what status he held within the brotherhood.

None of them turned to see who was interrupting their devotions as she slipped towards the darkest corner. One of the monks began another prayer and when that finished, they all began to sing. Ruth wondered where they were from, wracking her brain to think of the nearest monastery. She knew there was one close to her previous home, but it was at least an hour away by car and there was no sign of any vehicle parked on the roadside. Maybe they were on pilgrimage, but no-one had mentioned this well being part of a pilgrim's way.

As the tune repeated, Ruth realised they were singing the same chant she'd heard in the church, the first time she'd been accosted by the spirit of the renegade clergyman. This time the words were clear and she scrabbled inside her backpack to find a piece of paper and pencil to write down as much as she could.

When the chant ended, the monks got to their feet and began to snuff out the candles. One came to open the door so there would still be light inside. Ruth shrank back, thinking he would be sure to see her and ask what she was doing but nothing happened. He didn't even glance in her direction. He looked to be in his early twenties with a round face, long brown hair and thickset features. His hands were rough and calloused as if he were used to manual labour rather than the dedication of the scriptorium.

Their tasks complete, the monks filed out of the chapel. Left alone in the silence and pitch black, the peace she had been feeling quickly evaporated. She noticed there was still a sliver of light around the door and when she pushed against it, found it had not been latched. She was curious to see where they would go next and if she would be able to find them again.

The group must know the area well as they were halfway down the footpath leading through the top fields of Home Farm before she shut the heavy door. She could hear them chatting to each other but couldn't make out which language they spoke. She understood some of the words, but others sounded more German than English.

The footpath was wide and well-used, unlike the one which had brought her to the sanctuary. She kept her distance, trying not to make too much noise as she walked but not once did any of them turn to see who was following them.

As they reached the field which led down to Home Farm buildings, one of the monks, Ruth thought it might be the same one who had opened the chapel door, left the group and walked towards a hollowed-out structure in the hillside. Ruth was intrigued, wondering what he might be doing. He pulled aside a wooden door and walked into a cave.

"How strange," Ruth thought, "I've never heard of any natural caves around here."

When Ruth caught up and peered into the gloom, she could see him turning huge cheeses which were stacked on wooden shelves. She wondered how long it had taken to excavate. She daren't look too closely in case the monk saw her. She thought she could see stones behind the shelves rather than bricks but she wasn't sure. She was so engrossed in the construction, she didn't sense the man looking straight at her until he spoke.

"*Gif ðu hleowunge frigest, þonne me folga hraðe.*"

She froze, staring at him. What was he trying to tell her? There was no anger in his voice, but he wanted her to do something. He pointed along the track and when she turned to look, the other brothers were disappearing into the next field.

"*Folga hraðe.*" He said again, the two words slow and clear as if he knew she did not understand but wanted to help her if he could. Understanding dawned. He must want her to follow them.

Ruth nodded. "Thank you."

The words stumbled out of her mouth. She couldn't tell whether he could hear them, let alone grasp what she was saying but the smile he gave her, warmed her. She trotted over the wet winter grass until she had them in sight again, then slowed to a walk, keeping a respectful distance behind. They seemed to be heading towards the Priory belonging to Lord Peter. She thought she could see the road leading towards the main entrance but there was no sign of the two cottages where Colin's family and Lord Peter's housekeeper lived. She must be further away from the road than she thought.

The monks went into the Priory through a small wooden door within a large gate, propped open with a short stake. Ruth followed them across a muddy courtyard and into a stone archway. It was dark and she couldn't see the men anymore. The passage curled left ending in a familiar door with frosted glass panes. She knocked, realising she was standing in front of the modern Priory kitchen. A shadow moved towards her from the other side.

"Hello, Ruth," said Mrs Williams, wiping floury hands on her apron. "Come in and warm yourself by the stove, you look perished."

Ruth took off her hat and coat and found a seat next to the Aga, rubbing her hands.

"I thought I'd do some exploring as the weather was so much better today," she said. "I followed some monks here from the Ladywell. Is Lord Peter entertaining five brothers from a monastic house? They came in this way but I lost them."

Mrs Williams frowned as she stirred a mug of coffee before bringing to it Ruth.

"No monks here. I don't think any holy brothers would approve of Lord Peter's houseguests. They're more interested in shooting things rather than praying for them. Are you sure they weren't ramblers of some description?"

Ruth curled her fingers around the hot cup, letting the steam touch her chilled face. Until she entered the kitchen she hadn't felt the cold but now she was chilled to the bone. It was hard work to stop her teeth chattering as she spoke.

"I don't think so. Unless you often get ramblers around here who wear hooded woollen habits and go barefoot in sandals in the depths of winter. They knew their way around." Ruth sipped her coffee, glad to be safe in the warmth of the kitchen.

"You say you followed them from the Ladywell?" Mrs Williams asked, her hands busy turning flour and margarine into breadcrumbs in a huge mixing bowl. Ruth nodded.

"He told me to," she said with her cup held halfway to her mouth as she realised what she was saying. "One of the monks talked to me. He said if I wanted shelter, I should follow the brothers coming here." She felt cold and clammy as if she were about to be sick. How did she know what the young brother was saying now when she didn't understand it before? In front of her she could see her coffee cup shaking but she had

123

no energy to either put it down or stop the movement.

To her great relief she found Mrs Williams in front of her, steadying the cup. She touched the back of Ruth's hand. "You're so cold, if I didn't know better, I'd say you'd been walking one of the spirit roads alongside our predecessors. You might want to tell Granny what you saw and see what she says."

Ruth felt shivers consume her. The brothers had been so real. She didn't want to think of them as ghosts, yet the housekeeper's words changed everything. Mrs Williams took her cup away and heated it up again, adding sugar and encouraging her to drink it down to get some warmth inside her. She pulled a rug from one of the blanket boxes underneath the window and wrapped it round her. As the warmth spread, the shivering slowly stopped. Ruth found herself able to talk again.

"Why did he speak to me?" she said.

Mrs Williams chuckled. "Have you looked at yourself in the mirror recently?" she said, her warm smile taking the sting out of her words. "You're still nothing but skin and bones. The monk probably thought you were a waif who needed shelter for the night. Lord Peter told me the Priory was responsible for the Ladywell Chapel, saying mass, greeting visitors and receiving their offerings; bringing them back here to the Visitor's Quarters if they needed a place to stay. He was just doing his duty, whoever he was."

Doing his duty. The words echoed around her head. A medieval monk tried to do his duty to a twenty-first century woman. It made no sense. She felt sick again. She couldn't think about it, she needed a distraction. She glanced around the kitchen trying to think of something mundane she could ask the housekeeper, who had gone back to the kitchen table where she was preparing food for the next meal.

"Have you always lived here?" Ruth asked her.

"Yes. My grandmother was the Old Duchess' lady's maid before she married Grandad. He was the Chief Ostler. My mother started out in the kitchens but also became a maid until she married Dad. I started here and never left. My Ralph is the gardener."

As Mrs Williams talked, a series of further questions began to niggle at the back of Ruth's mind. What was it Granny said? Something about Granny Blackwell and a possible pregnancy, here at the Priory. Maybe the cook could answer the mystery of her father's parentage.

"Did your mother know Granny Blackwell when she worked here?" Ruth said.

"They were close friends when they were girls. Before the accident."

Ruth felt her mouth began to dry. No-one had mentioned an accident before. Was this what changed Granny Blackwell into the spiteful old woman she became. Granny hadn't mentioned anything, but it was clear neither she nor Zeb really liked the old woman. Did she really want to know any more, but she couldn't help herself?

"Accident?" she echoed.

Mrs Williams sighed and looked out of the window. "Granny Blackwell, Miriam Blackwell she was then, was engaged to Roger Iles. He was farrier for the village and had just become Anvil. He was young for Anvil, only twenty-five but he knew the lore and all the villagers respected him. Mum said they were a lovely couple. So happy together. Their wedding banns had been posted twice in the church when it happened."

Ruth took another sip of coffee and let the rug fall off her shoulders. The heat was beginning to consume her. "When what happened?" she prompted.

"Miriam told my Mum she saw the old Reverend standing in the church, laughing at her, all the time the Rector was reading the banns. No-one else saw or heard anything but Miriam was terribly upset."

Ruth felt the hand holding her coffee mug begin to shake again and clutched it tight with her other one. If Rev Graves was involved, this story was only going to end in tragedy, but she needed to hear everything. Mrs Williams went to the cupboard and brought out a bottle of stewed plums which she poured into a large pudding dish.

She didn't seem to notice Ruth's reaction and carried on.

"A week later, Roger was up here to shoe the Earl's stallion. Great big chestnut hunter he was but quiet as a lamb normally. Something spooked him and he reared up, kicking Roger in the head. Miriam and Mum were passing one of the upstairs windows and saw it happen. Mum said Miriam flew down the back stairs and out into the yard screaming blue murder, yelling that it was all the old Reverend's fault and she'd see his soul rot in hell.

Mrs Williams started to pour the crumble topping over the fruit, staring down sadly into the bowl.

"Of course, there was nothing she could do. Poor Roger never regained consciousness. They sent for the doctor, but he said even if he did recover, he'd never be the same again. Took him a whole week to die. They buried him on what should have been their wedding day. Miriam was out of her mind with grief. She was sent away soon afterwards. Most people thought she'd been locked up in the Asylum, but Mum said she went to stay with her sister, Harriet, who married a chain maker, the other side of the city."

Ruth felt her heart beating against her chest bone. Her grandfather and his father had been chain makers, even working on the anchor cable for the doomed Titanic. Mrs Williams fetched another bottle of fruit and repeated the process as she continued.

"Over a year it was before she came back. Mum said she looked like a shadow, compared with how she'd been before. Wore black every day of her life, even when she married Ernest Compson, Zeb's uncle. He was gamekeeper here. They never had any children." She lifted her head and looked straight at Ruth as if really seeing her for the first time. Her next words seemed to bore down into Ruth's skull as if they were important information she needed to remember.

"Rob Trantor took over as Anvil, but he didn't last long, then Roger's younger brother, Frank, then George Bennett, the cartwright, until Greg was strong enough to make the challenge. He's been a real chip off the old block, thankfully, unlike his father." Mrs Williams gently shook the crumble she was filling until it was evenly spread then returned her gaze to Ruth. "Why did you ask about poor Roger Iles."

Ruth didn't answer immediately. She wasn't sure how much she should reveal. She didn't want to lie. Janet Williams was a good friend of Granny's and she trusted Granny.

"My grandmother's name was Harriet," she said at last. "She took my father in when he was a baby after his mother died. The name on his birth certificate was Beynon Roger Flint. Granny told me a few weeks ago that Beynon means "son of Anvil". I didn't think anything of it at the time but after what you've told me, I'm wondering if my father was Roger Iles' illegitimate son and his mother didn't die but returned here to become Granny Blackwell."

Mrs Williams came over to the stove and put the crumbles in the oven as Ruth stood up and folded the rug.

"Whose idea was it to call you, Ruth, I wonder?"

"Dad always said it was Nanna's. She said it was her favourite name and if she had had a little girl instead of four boys, she would have called her Ruth." She heard Mrs Williams suck in her breath.

"That were Granny Blackwell's name, Miriam Ruth. You have her look about you, too. I knew there was something when Granny brought you to meet Lord Peter. Did he ever give you the job of sorting the archives?"

Ruth shook her head. "I haven't seen him since the wassailing of my orchard. I thought we'd talk about it then, but he left early and I haven't seen him since." She almost missed the look Mrs Williams gave her, but she felt the atmosphere in the kitchen subtly change.

"He's got a lot on his mind." The older woman said. Ruth thanked her profusely and made her way back home.

CHAPTER TWENTY

The talk at the Circle meeting that night was all about the forthcoming ceremony for Spring Equinox. Ruth had never been to an outdoor ritual before. The mention of robes and cloaks made her apprehensive, as did the need for torches, bread and mead. It sounded too much like a secret society. Who knew what she might be asked to perform.

"You will join us, won't you, Ruth?" Mattie said. "You're part of the village now."

Ruth frowned, trying to think of a plausible excuse which wouldn't sound too ungracious. "I'm not sure I've got the right clothes."

Mattie giggled. "You only need to dress warmly. No-one will notice what you're wearing. It can get muddy, so I'd bring your walking boots."

No-one she asked would give her a clear answer where the meeting would be held. Someone said it was behind Granny's house; another mentioned the field beside the mill while a third said they might be in the Priory church if it rained.

Ruth sighed and picked up the lap blanket she was crocheting for one of the elderly residents of the village. Most of the women were engaged in some form of needlework as they talked about the significance of the season and how it affected their own lives.

"Why do you do this?" she asked. "You all go to church, why the need for something extra?"

In the long silence which followed her question, everyone looked at Granny, who was trying to undo a tangle of stitches brought to her by Colin's younger sister, Lucy. To Ruth's surprise, it was Andrea's quiet shadow, Ally Tulliver, who replied.

"It's about the land," she said, her face reflecting deep, far away thoughts. "We need to maintain the connections between seasons and growing cycles; to understand why and when and how, as much as we are able." She gave Ruth a brief smile. "It's hard to put into words but you'll understand once you take part. The church came from the East, from a dry land. They've absorbed some of our customs, but their stories are not our stories. If we neglect our ways, we lose our connection to who we really are."

When they paused for tea and home-made biscuits, Ruth took a cup over to where Granny was sitting, hoping for an opportunity to discuss the strange monks she'd seen. Granny thanked her for the tea and held out a printed leaflet towards her.

"I don't usually give a copy of the ritual to undecided guests," she said, "but Granny Blackwell would never forgive me if I didn't include you. Read this before Saturday night and hopefully it will help you understand what you see and hear."

Ruth decided to ask about the monks while she could.

"I went to the Ladywell this morning," she began. "I saw something strange and when I mentioned it to Mrs Williams at the Priory, she suggested I tell you about it."

Granny called Ally Tulliver over to join them, saying Ally needed to know anything concerning the Ladywell. Ruth wasn't sure she wanted the other woman to hear. Ally would think she was hallucinating. They both sat looking at her expectantly, so she told them what had happened.

"You're sure they were monks?" Ally asked, dunking her biscuit vigorously. Mattie was walking past and when she heard Ally's question, she pulled up a chair and tugged a notepad and pencil from the pocket of her skirt.

"Tell me what you saw in the chapel and I'll try and draw them." Mattie suggested.

Ruth described the four monks kneeling in front of the altar dressed in long woollen habits with the hoods thrown back. "The candlelight reflected off the tops of their heads. It made me think they were monks" she explained.

"You said there were five men?" Granny queried.

"Yes," Ruth pointed to the sketch, "The fifth man was kneeling just behind them. His hair was long and it wasn't shaved like the others."

"Were they all dressed the same?" Mattie asked.

Ruth saw the scene again in her mind. "Four of them wore sandals fastened with strips of leather. They had two twisted chords around their waist. When they left the chapel, one of the monks had a leather satchel which he slung over his shoulder."

Ally leaned forward to see the sketch, anxious not to miss anything. Ruth thought she could hardly contain her excitement.

"What about the other man? Did he look the same?" Granny asked.

Ruth found herself smiling as she remembered the look on the young man's face. Even though she didn't understand the words he used, she believed he truly cared about her.

"No, the fifth man was younger. He had a short beard and his hair was dark brown, like his habit." The memory of him standing inside the cheese cave, with his hand tucked into his belt as he'd pointed towards his companions was clear in her mind. "He wore a leather belt, not a knotted one, with a plain metal buckle and there was a leather pouch on it over towards his right hip. His hands were large, with long, sturdy fingers as if he were used to working outside. One of the other monks had long, thin fingers. I think I saw flecks of colour on them."

The women studied the sketches for several minutes before everyone agreed they were monks.

"You heard them speak to each other but not in English?" Granny asked Mattie to recite something. "Did it sound like that?" Ruth shook her head. Mattie rattled off another quotation.

"That was closer. I recognised some words, but others seemed completely foreign."

"Old English," said Mattie. "This one's a lay brother." She pointed to the outline she'd drawn of the man standing up. "Did he have boots?"

Ruth nodded, staring at the paper. Mattie had captured the images in her head. She shivered, remembering Mrs Williams' phrase, 'walking the spirit roads'. It seemed such an apt description, following thirteenth century brothers from the Ladywell chapel to their Priory. No wonder they disappeared when she knocked on the kitchen door.

"You say you recognised what they were singing?" Granny's question snapped her back to the present.

"It was the same chant I heard drifting up from the church sacristy last month." She pulled a piece of paper from her jacket pocket. "This time I could make out the words. I scribbled down as much as I could. I'm not sure what it says, my Latin isn't very good."

Mattie took the paper from her and started writing underneath each word in pencil. When she finished, her face was beaming.

"You're going to love this, Ally. I think it's a blessing for the well. I'm not absolutely sure of a few words but I can ask a friend of mine who specialises in medieval Latin. Pity we don't have the tune."

"We do," said Ruth. "Lawrence picked up a sheet of manuscript from underneath the altar in the undercroft the first time I heard it. I thought it was part of the music he was giving me to practice for the choir, but he said he'd never seen it before. It's been sitting on my piano ever since. I'll bet he'll be excited to find it has words as well. Maybe the choir can sing it some time."

"No!" said Granny so firmly, Ruth stared at her.

"But Lawrence is the choirmaster."

"No!" said Granny again. "I know Lawrence is devoted to his mother and to the church, but he wouldn't understand the importance of this piece of music. It's been given to you for a reason. We may not understand its significance now but until we do, we keep it between ourselves. Do you agree, ladies?"

"Yes, Granny," came the chorus but Ruth kept silent. She didn't like excluding Lawrence. He was extremely courteous during choir practice and always expressed his gratitude for her help but now she thought about it, there was something which made her keep her distance. Maybe Granny was right.

When the meeting was over, Granny asked Ruth to help her carry some boxes to her house. Mattie was talking to her mother, so Ruth said she would see her later.

Zeb had the kettle on when they arrived and took the boxes from Ruth to store in the sewing room.

"Stay for a few minutes. I think there are some other things we need to discuss before you go."

"I shouldn't be too long," Ruth began.

"I'll walk you home," Zeb said as he entered the room. "It's not foggy but we don't want to risk you having another encounter with Old Isaac Graves."

Ruth flashed him a grateful smile. She really didn't want to walk back alone this late at night, although she did wonder who had told them about her previous experience.

"Is that why you don't like Lawrence?" she asked Granny who was busy making cocoa for the three of them, "because the Old Rector has the same name as him? Are they related?"

Granny passed out the cups and they all sat down at the kitchen table.

"I don't dislike the boy," she said after taking her first sip and stirring the cup again. "If his father had stayed, maybe I'd feel differently, but Geoffrey saw his opportunity to escape from his past and took it. Joyce wouldn't go with him and Lawrence was too young to make his own decisions; now he's trapped. I keep hoping he'll find the strength to make the break, but I don't think it's going to happen any time soon.

"Anyhow, I didn't ask you to come here to talk about Lawrence. Greg tells me you ran into each other at Bessie's café a few weeks ago. He was a bit perturbed by what you said to him. He said he's been trying to talk to you about it, but you've been avoiding him."

Ruth blew on her cocoa as she took a drink. She studied the pattern on the tablecloth, so she didn't have to return Granny's gaze.

"I said something. It was embarrassing. It was as if someone else was speaking to him. It didn't make sense."

"Can you remember what it was?" Zeb asked. Ruth told him as much as she could. "If I asked you to explain it to me now, could you?"

She considered for a moment, thinking back to the conversation with Janet Williams earlier.

"I don't understand what I said about the hare and I can't fathom how I can keep the black well clear when I don't know what the black well is or what I'm supposed to do with it. The only thing which does make sense is the bit about 'flesh of my flesh'. Greg is my cousin, isn't he? He has the same name as my grandfather, Roger Iles, the one who was killed by the Earl's horse. Roger was Anvil and Mrs Williams said his younger brother also held same position as Greg." She looked at Granny then back to Zeb. "Am I right?"

Granny nodded. "Are you going to tell Greg or keep it a secret for the time being?"

"I don't know," replied Ruth. "How do villagers feel about illegitimate children. Is it going to hurt Granny Blackwell's reputation if people know she had a child out of wedlock?"

Granny smiled and for the first time Ruth felt warmed by more than her hot drink. "Once folk know you're a Blackwell, they'll realise who you are. You look just like her. Remind me to show you some old photos of her some time. She must want you to share your legacy or she wouldn't be putting words into your mouth."

"She's speaking through me?" The ticking of the kitchen clock was loud in Ruth's ears as her racing heart slowed down to the familiar rhythm. Granny's words were shocking yet in a strange way, she felt comforted her grandmother was trying to help her.

"Granny Blackwell could walk the spirit roads to different times and so can you. Those monks spoke to you, didn't they?" said Granny.

"Only one of them," Ruth said before she realised what she was admitting. "He thought I needed shelter." Every time she spoke about her encounters it felt less strange. Rev Graves made her angry, but she liked the monks. Their singing brought her peace; their actions thoughtful rather than threatening. Walking the spirit roads was not such a difficult gift.

Granny nodded. Ruth hoped she was satisfied with the answer. What Granny said next startled her.

"Granny Blackwell wasn't able to stop Isaac Graves from his foul ways but maybe you can try with her help."

CHAPTER TWENTY-ONE

Ruth was both intrigued and terrified at the thought she must take on and possibly defeat the ghost of Reverend Graves. She tried not to dwell on it and spent most of Friday preparing for choir practice and learning the well blessing as best she could.

From the quick translation Mattie provided, Ruth experimented with the tune found under the altar to see which set of words would produce a better fit, even composing a new poem based on Mattie's. The written tune seemed more modern than medieval plainsong. She decided she needed to write down what she originally heard.

She took herself into the orchard with some manuscript paper and a pencil and began to hum the wandering tune she remembered from both the chapel and the undercroft. As each phrase came together, she jotted it down. The more she meandered between the trees, the more the tune became fixed in her mind until she was able to add the words she'd written down from the monks and sing the whole Latin chant out loud.

The hens were cackling behind the lower hedge, whether in accompaniment or protest, she couldn't make out. She went to see what they were doing and gave a surprised cry when she saw what their scratching had unearthed. Instead of a sandy incline with a single dark stain, a steady stream of water flowed out of the bank just below the hazel bush. There was a shallow depression where water was pooling until it ran down under the gate and disappeared into the ditch on the side of the road.

"What on earth?"

Ruth couldn't believe what she was seeing. There was no mention of a spring in the orchard in any papers she'd read. Only last week Zeb was talking about bringing in a water bowser to provide a supply for the lambs. She wondered whether the constant weeks of torrential rain had caused the egress and whether it dried up over the summer, so people forgot it was there.

A piece of manuscript paper fluttered to the ground and she snatched it up before it became damp.

"Through rain and shine, this spring is mine" a new melody tickled her brain. She ran to the house, leaving the music on the kitchen table. She was eager to discover more about the water gushing out of the ground. She opened the shed and rummaged through the garden tools until she found a small spade and trowel. She carried them down through the orchard. Carefully, she began to dig around the depression, wondering if there might be a trough for the water underneath.

"For man and beast, this water sweet," she sang, throwing the wet earth into a heap beside her.

Sure enough, after she'd dug down just over a foot, her spade struck something solid. She scrabbled with her fingers until she could feel a familiar roughness, then picked up the trowel, trying to find the limits of the stone. The more soil she removed; the more water began to fill the basin. After an hour or so she had uncovered a small rectangular trough nearly three-foot-long, two feet deep and eighteen inches wide which tapered slightly from left to right.

"Once a grave now water saves," she hummed to herself, noting the U-shaped notch about four inches deep, two-thirds of the way along the side opposite the spring. Through this slot, water now cascaded onto the ground.

She took up the spade and cut a new channel for the water to flow under the hedge, far beyond the gate.

"*I keep the black well clear,*" she sang, "*I keep the black well clear.*"

"*This is it,*" she thought. "*This is the Blackwell. This is what was meant when I spoke to Greg. I must tell him.*"

She was just turning to open the gate and run up to the forge when Mattie came around the hazel bush.

"What are you doing?" she asked

"I've found the Blackwell, I've found the Blackwell, look! Isn't it wonderful!"

Mattie didn't answer. She picked up the trowel and, kneeling beside the basin on a patch of dry soil, she began to carefully prick out the soil around the spring mouth. She worked in silence until she uncovered two large vertical stones supporting a horizontal, carved plinth.

"Oh," breathed Ruth, "It's beautiful."

Mattie frowned, pulling a small brush from her pocket and clearing away any small particles until the individual bricks of the well back were exposed. She sat back on her heels and looked up at Ruth.

"It's a good job I arrived when I did. Whatever possessed you to try and excavate all this on your own? There's no telling what damage you could have done. This is original medieval stonework and if I'm not mistaken, the trough could be a burial kist, possibly bronze age by the size of it."

Ruth felt the excitement leach out of her and flow under the gate with the water. She hated being the subject of anyone's disapproval. She washed her hands at the slit in the trough, before cupping them underneath the spring and taking a drink.

It was so cold! She swallowed again and tasted the sweetness of the water. Her water, her Blackwell. She stood up and shook the remaining drops from her fingers.

"I'm not sorry," she said. "I did what had to be done. I'm sure you'll be able to record what's been found appropriately. Can you lock up the shed when you've finished?"

She brushed soil off her knees and walked up to the house leaving Mattie staring after her.

CHAPTER TWENTY-TWO

Light was beginning to fade when she made her way back to the house. The hens followed her hoping for an extra feed and decided to go to bed early, so she shut them in.

It was almost time for choir practice so Ruth grabbed a quick sandwich. Rain was beginning to fall as she scurried over to the church trying to keep her umbrella from turning inside out in the wind. She dropped her books by the organ and since none of the choristers had arrived, decided to take a stroll around the church to see if she could find any memorials to the infamous Rev Graves.

Lawrence was standing on a pew in the middle of the north aisle, rubbing away at a wall plaque with a rag.

"The cleaners never touch this memorial," he complained, running his fingertips over the surface in case he'd missed something. "He was an amazing clergyman, an inspiration to us all, yet no-one values him. They can hardly bring themselves to utter his name when they should be singing praises for all his achievements."

"Who are you talking about?" Ruth asked, not able see any name on the inscription.

"The Very Reverend Isaac Graves, my ancestor. He was Rector here for forty years at the end of the eighteenth century. He was so strong in his faith, he held the village together against attacks from all sides."

"Attacks, what kind of attacks?" Ruth tried to recall some major events from those times. All she could think about was America's war of independence which wasn't exactly local.

"It's hard to imagine now." Lawrence gave the marble a final, careful wipe and stepped down onto the floor. Ruth expected him to come towards her but instead he stood, staring out into space as he spoke, pulling the rag through one hand and then the other.

"The Church of England spends so much of its time trying to be all things to all people and pleasing everyone and no-one. We've lost so much allowing anyone and everyone to believe whatever they want and do whatever they want so we don't offend our friends and neighbours who may follow different beliefs. These days hardly any of the villagers come to church. In his time, every pew was full."

Ruth wondered why Lawrence was talking like this. She'd been surprised how many people of all ages came to the Sunday services. He took a step forwards and fixed her with his gaze.

"Rev. Graves knew what was right and what was wrong. He wouldn't tolerate any of the lily-livered dissenters in his parish. There are no Methodist or Baptist chapels in the village, thanks to him. He made sure any family who thought they could talk directly to God without the intercession of a member of the clergy lost their job and had to find work elsewhere. He stopped the poison before it started."

"A formidable man," Ruth said, feeling her mouth dry up and her stomach protest at the diatribe.

"That wasn't all," Lawrence said, his eyes shining as he stepped away from the pew and began to accompany her back to the organ. "He also put a stop to the Devil-worship in the village."

"Devil worship?" Ruth echoed, covering her surprise with a cough. She wondered if he would consider the Spring Equinox ritual she'd decided to attend the following evening to be something similar.

"Roelswick has always had witches." Laurence's tone had an air of certainty which brooked no questions. "Old women with cats or hares as familiars, who cavort naked in the woods with the Devil. He gives them special powers to cast spells."

Ruth had to turn away and shuffle her hymn books around to stop herself from laughing.

"Lord Peter's ancestor was a sorcerer." This time, Ruth couldn't hide the shock on her face. Lawrence nodded. "It's true. There used to be a holy well here at St John's. People used to travel hundreds of miles to take the waters. The sorcerer cast a spell so the well dried up and disappeared. He and my ancestor fought a terrible battle and Rev Graves won. He killed the Earl and saved the village. Unfortunately, he paid the ultimate price and died shortly afterwards. It was a terrible loss."

Ruth's mind was a whirl of questions. It was a powerful story and Ruth had no doubt Lawrence believed every word. The idea of a righteous religious warrior just didn't fit with the thoroughly nasty apparition she had encountered. There must be a true story somewhere. She just had to search in the right place.

"Anybody got a towel, we're soaked." Two bedraggled choir members trotted up the nave, shaking water out of their hair. Ruth went to find something from the vestry. Any further discussion would have to wait for another time.

On her way out of church, Ruth stumbled, dropping her Psalter. Everyone else disappeared once Lawrence dismissed them, but she stayed behind to lock up the organ and return the key to its hiding place. She looked on the floor for her copy of the Benedicite which she always kept inside the front cover; it wasn't there. It wasn't inside any of her other books. She turned back to the organ, thinking it must have fallen on the floor underneath the long, narrow seat but no matter how hard she looked, there was no sign of it.

She needed the music to practice. Lawrence said her phrasing was not what he used and demanded she put it right by the following week.

"I'll have to go and ask him if he picked it up by mistake," she thought.

The rain had stopped but it was very wet underfoot. She was glad she remembered to bring her torch as she wasn't sure if there were any streetlamps near the Mill once the road curved past The Dingle.

Lawrence and his mother lived at Mill Lodge, a small, single storey, brick house at the entrance to Roelswick Mill. The large 18th century house next to the mill was empty while the new owner completed his renovations. Henry was in negotiation to sell him some of last year's wheat crop for bread flour once the waterwheel was working again.

Lawrence's red mini cooper was parked beside the Lodge. The front door was partially open, light streaming into the lane. Ruth could hear two people shouting at each other as she got closer, stopping for a moment behind the entrance pillar in the hope they would finish before she had to make herself known.

As she listened more carefully, it was clear the old woman was deaf, as Lawrence repeated what he was saying several times with increasing volume before she grasped the content. This must be Lawrence's mother, Joyce Graves.

"It should be us at the mill house," grumbled the woman, her voice bitter-tinged from a lifetime of complaining. "Why don't you get a proper job with a decent wage instead of the pittance you get from the school. I told you not to rely on music. Musicians are always paupers."

"This place is quite big enough for the two of us, Mother," shouted Lawrence

"It wouldn't be if you found yourself a wife and started a family. If you don't do something soon, the Graves name will be lost forever."

"I'm working on it, mother. There will always be Graves in Roelswick. I'll never let Rev Isaac be forgotten, he's too important to the village. When everything comes together, the church will be back with its rightful incumbent. It won't be long now."

"I don't believe you. If you're seeing someone, why haven't you brought her here?"

"I will soon."

"Why haven't you told me before?"

"It's complicated."

Ruth pressed her back against the pillar as Lawrence screamed his response for the final time. What she was hearing, confused her. It was difficult to imagine Lawrence with a girlfriend. His exasperated tone scared her. Did she really want to make herself known?

"This isn't another of your little schemes, is it Lawrence?" said Joyce Graves. "They never work. You haven't got the gumption to see things through. You're just like your father, all pipe dreams and hot air. He never got anywhere, nor will you. You wouldn't still be teaching worthless brats if you had an ounce of ambition and drive."

Now it wasn't just words Ruth could hear, but a constant series of grunts, thumps and thwacks as if she were taking out her frustration on things around her.

"Why couldn't you take after your cousin, Derek? (Thwack!) He runs his own business and bought his mother her own granny flat with staff beside his latest mansion. (Thwack) I have to make do with one pokey room and no proper heating, not to mention this wallpaper hasn't been changed since we moved here. (Thwack!)"

She heard Lawrence yelp followed by further shouts. Ruth decided she couldn't eavesdrop any longer and made her way to the front door, knocking loudly. The sounds stopped but she had to knock again before Lawrence emerged, panting, with his hair askew, his tie pulled to one side and his cardigan hanging loose from a lost top button.

"I'm sorry to trouble you," Ruth began, wilting under his glare. "I couldn't find my Benedicite. Did you pick it up with your music by any chance?"

"You must have lost it. It's nothing to do with me," he said. In the harsh hall light, Ruth thought his face grew more flushed, guilt-ridden rather than mere exertion.

"If you want me to practice it before next week, is there another copy I could borrow?" she asked. He left her standing on the doorstep while he disappeared into another room, ignoring his mother's constant shouts of "Who's that?" He returned quickly, thrusting the slim paper into her hand.

"Don't lose this one."

She tried to thank him, but he shut the door and turned off the light before she finished speaking, leaving her shaking from the short encounter. It was like facing Robert on one of his bad days all over again. It must be her fault he was so angry. She wanted to cry, but a cold nose thrust into her left palm as she was about to start climbing the steps up to the Crescent, stopped her.

"Hello, Finn," she said, stroking the cold head. "Come to escort me home?" A soft woof was his answer. He was there to look after her. She wasn't on her own anymore.

She had done nothing wrong except witness an argument between mother and son. She guessed it wasn't the first-time words escalated to blows. She knew how hard it was living with the threat of violence and could almost feel sorry for Lawrence. She wondered if anyone else in the village knew. She would have to ask Granny.

CHAPTER TWENTY-THREE

Ruth enjoyed the ritual on Saturday evening, held in a clearing surrounded by trees near to the mill. Thankfully the weather stayed dry and a beautiful moon lit the proceedings. Most people wore cloaks, but she didn't feel out of place in her ordinary clothes. She noticed six people led most of the proceeding, realising after a while they represented the three stages of adulthood, young, middle years and elders. Colin and Mattie were the carefree youngsters, Andrea and Greg the responsible adults and Granny and Zeb the wise ones.

She recognised Janet Williams as the Memory Keeper who invoked the ancestors and Ally Tulliver held the West, where water was venerated. Colin played the part of the young god and Mattie the maid whose return heralded Spring.

Afterwards there was a shared meal in the village hall followed by songs and readings. She felt very much at home in the friendly atmosphere.

She was putting together a spreadsheet for the Home Farm accounts the following week when she heard voices coming towards the office. Henry opened the door and Lord Peter entered. He seemed taken aback to see her sitting at her desk and only gave a brief nod to acknowledge her presence. Henry asked her to make coffee while he led Lord Peter to the meeting table in the far corner.

"What's she doing here?" was the first thing she heard Lord Peter say. Henry responded but his words were lost in the roar of the boiling kettle. She poured out the drinks and took them over. She noticed how stiff Lord Peter seemed, still sitting to attention in an army barracks, rather than visiting well-known tenants.

Henry was standing at one of the bookcases, pulling several folders off the shelf then returning them. It was obvious he couldn't locate what he was looking for. Ruth could feel his frustration rising.

"Can you find the rent invoices for the past three years for Home Farm, please, Ruth," he said after pushing one folder back so hard, three more fell out onto the floor, scattering papers everywhere.

Ruth shooed him away while she cleared up the mess and found the documents where she had recently filed them. She set them on the table, trying to avoid spilt coffee and sugar grains before sliding back behind the computer. She didn't want to eavesdrop on what was becoming a heated conversation.

"I can't believe you're asking me to make up what your Steward stole from you. It's not our fault the rat fleeced you. Anyone could have told you he wasn't honest." Henry's voice became louder with each sentence. "When Mum and Dad were here, he tried all sorts of tricks to line his own pocket, but they told him exactly where to go. They mentioned what he was doing. Jack Ackerley informed you a dozen times in my presence he was selling birds left over from the shoots, but you always made some excuse for him. Why, I can't imagine. Now he's done a runner down under. Have you reported him to the police?"

Ruth stared at her computer screen, trying not to shake. She'd never heard Henry so angry. When she glanced towards the table, Lord Peter leaned down to retrieve one of the papers. A terrible grimace crossed his face as his body froze then he moved slowly back to his previous position. She heard him mumble something about accountants and solicitors. When he announced the total amount embezzled, all conversation stopped. Lord Peter was having difficulty speaking and Ruth couldn't decide whether it was from pain or the stress he must be under to try and make up the shortfall.

Ruth decided they needed another drink and put the kettle on again, then went to the table to collect their coffee mugs.

"I know it's none of my business," she said, "but do you have any extra events planned before the shooting season starts again in September which could be used as fund raisers? I was thinking about food or music festivals or historical events which could make use of the Priory."

Lord Peter looked at her, his face hard. "You're correct. It is none of your business."

"I know these things take time to get going, but we could start something this year, so it gets known then develop it further," she persisted.

"My financial issues are nothing to do with you, Mrs Turner. Nothing you could say would interest me. I don't have any time for people like you."

"She's not an incomer, Lord Peter," said Henry, coming to Ruth's defence. "She's Granny Blackwell's granddaughter."

"She's a liar." Lord Peter's words fell like chipped ice between them, each one clipped and precise. "No-one who drinks as much as she does could tell the truth."

Ruth and Henry looked at each other. She couldn't tell who was the more surprised and embarrassed by Lord Peter's outburst. Was he trying to discredit her in the presence of her employer. It was exactly what Robert would do.

"What makes you think I drink, Lord Peter?" she said, her voice dangerously calm and low.

"I saw all the bottles on the worktop in your kitchen the night of the wassail. No normal person would have so many on display. You must have a serious drink problem." He sat back in his chair, polishing his glasses as if the matter were closed.

"I must, must I?" Ruth edged closer to his seat. She wanted to shout at him, better still to shake him by the shoulders until his teeth rattled.

Instead, she gripped the tabletop with both hands. "Did it never occur to you, Lord Peter, perhaps the bottles were not mine? They belonged to my ex-husband who arrived later in the evening, after you left, to remove the drinks cabinet he forced me to purchase when I moved to Roelswick.

"If you were so concerned about my drinking habits, don't you think it might be courteous and polite to ask me about the bottles, rather than make assumptions?" Ruth watched the colour fade from Lord Peter's face. He wouldn't look at her. All his attention was on his hands, fingers interlaced on his lap, pushed together to keep them from moving.

"Do you know why those bottles were in the kitchen?" she continued softly. "I was going to offer them to friends who were helping me recover from the loss of my job and my husband's betrayal. A few of them drank cider which they'd brought with them. Most asked for tea or coffee. You know how I know? I made the hot drinks and served them myself. You would have known if you hadn't rushed away.

"To be absolutely clear, Lord Peter, I am not teetotal, but I can go months without drinking alcohol. I hope this will stop you repeating such misinformation to anyone else."

"I haven't said anything to anyone else," he said, his cheeks now red with obvious embarrassment.

"I'm pleased to hear it." She took a drink from her own cold coffee, daring him to speak. The only sound in the room was a cow lowing in the neighbouring cattle yard. Even though she was angry with him, she couldn't help noticing how blue his eyes were and how still he was keeping his body by sheer force of will. *He must be in terrible pain,* she thought to herself. Her anger slid away; she wanted to make things better for him.

"Do you know why Lawrence Graves is saying your ancestor was a sorcerer?"

The shock from both men was palpable, turning to face her with their mouths open in silent question.

"I understand several of my ancestors were not pleasant," Lord Peter said at last. Ruth thought she caught sight of his mouth twitching with a poorly suppressed smile. "Goodness knows my own father made everyone's life a misery, including mine but I've never heard any suggestion of sorcery in the family. That's more your domain, isn't it, Henry?"

Henry laughed. "Don't let Mum hear you say that unless you want a lecture on the philosophy of Druidry until both your ears are sore!" That made everyone smile. "What's Lawrence been saying?"

Ruth recounted Lawrence's glorification of Reverend Graves the previous Friday evening. "I thought his argument a little one-sided. I wondered if there were any documents in your archives which could shed more light on the matter."

Lord Peter hunched his shoulders and sighed. "Touché," he said. "I can't afford to pay anyone to collate the archives now. I know you were hoping for another day's work, but you're welcome to see what you can find."

Ruth smiled. Despite her previous emotion, all she wanted to do was hug him and tell him everything would be all right. He looked so vulnerable sitting there, he needed someone to protect him.

"Thank you," she said. "I'll be over as soon as I can."

CHAPTER TWENTY-FOUR

Despite Ruth's best intentions, the following week was busy and she had no time to visit the Priory library. Nigel called her in to go over the latest developments with her divorce and Gillian asked her to work extra hours in the Home Farm office to bring the accounts up to date.

"I'm really worried Lord Peter will hike the rent at the next review," Gillian told her. "We were intending to invest in a larger cheese store but I daren't ask Henry to risk our savings if we're going to be landed with a larger bill. The only trouble is, I can't age our hard cheeses as long as I'd like because there's nowhere to store them. I have to send them out immature which means the price we can ask is halved."

"Are there any other cheese producers in the neighbourhood you could rent storage from?" Ruth asked, not really knowing anything about cheese production but trying to look at problem solving from a practical viewpoint.

"That's the trouble. There are two other cheese makers in the village, one making goats cheese and the other organic ewes' milk and they've both been asking if they could rent space from us. If I could move our hard cheese out, there would be room in the cold dairy for them because they have a much shorter turnaround and it would bring in extra income."

Ruth thought back to the day she followed the monks from the Ladywell to the Priory. She was sure the brother who left the group had done so on Home Farm land. She got up to check the map of the farm pinned out on one of the noticeboards to the right hand side of the door opposite her desk.

"Have you considered using the medieval cheese cave at the top of Seven Acres?" She asked, pointing at the spot she thought the cave should be.

Gillian frowned. "No-one's ever mentioned a cave up there."

Ruth tried to think how best to describe her experience. She wasn't sure if Gillian would believe her if she told the whole truth.

"I was talking to Mrs Williams up at the Priory the other day and she described how the monks would make cheese." Ruth began. "She said they even dug their own cave not far from the Ladywell to age them. The place she described seemed to be where The Slopes rise up almost directly behind the field wall and there's that dip in Seven Acres as if someone quarried stone at one time."

Gillian thought for a moment. "There's nothing there now but a huge bramble patch."

Ruth shrugged. "I could investigate after I finish here. Would you mind if I took a slasher with me?"

Gillian looked at her watch. "Better still, why don't I ask Gus to go with you. You can show him where to hack the brambles away."

Gus, the assistant cowman, was more than amenable to follow Ruth across the fields carrying a slasher and pitchfork over his shoulder. He was a tall, lanky young man with an unruly mop of dirty brown hair underneath a Fair Isle cap. He didn't say anything as they walked, making Ruth wonder if he thought they were on a wild goose chase. After all, he'd been around the farm all his life and she was just a newcomer.

When they reached the corner of the field there was no sign of the cheese cave. Ruth was beginning to worry she would never find the spot until she retraced her steps coming down the bank and walked through the gate, remembering the point where the four men continued in a straight line towards the Priory while she turned right along the sunken path to the cave.

"Here," she said, pointing to a particularly dense patch of brambles. "Can you cut a section about four feet wide?"

"Don't want much, do you!" Gus grinned. "Better watch yourself, these briars can be vicious." He handed her the pitchfork and waited until she was well out of the way before he began to hack at the area she indicated. Very soon there was debris strewn all over the place, until Gus exchanged the slasher for the pitchfork and threw it all into a neat pile in the corner of the field.

As she walked towards the space, all Ruth could see was a wall of ivy growing up about twenty feet.

"Is there any way we can clear the same space in the ivy?" she asked. She could hear the tentative nature of her question, but Gus didn't blink an eye, setting to with a will to cut and pull away the great lengths of creeper. Ruth helped by dragging the rubbish onto the pile of brambles, expanding the heap until Gus suddenly exclaimed,

"Well blow me down with a feather, what do we have here?"

There in front of them was a large, stone doorframe about seven-foot-high and four-foot-wide with a pockmarked piece of wood in front of it. Gus fished around in his coat pocket and pulled out a mobile phone. Peering intently at the screen, his fingers found the number he was looking for and pressed the button. They both waited in silence until the call was answered.

"Boss, I think you and the missus need to come and see this. We're in the top left-hand corner of Seven Acres. Bring some torches and your camera. Your Dad might be interested too." He closed the connection and looked at Ruth. "Not right for us to go exploring without 'em."

Ruth agreed, although privately she suspected he might be slightly worried by what they might find. She thought she knew what was behind the decrepit door but anyone else was looking at a new discovery. Gus used the waiting time to hack away at more brambles while Ruth continued to pull at the ivy, to see if she could identify the extent of the building. It seemed to be a semi-circular stone wall filled in with some kind of daubed mud and painted with whitewash.

Before long they heard an engine coming across the field and soon a green Landrover came into view carrying three people. When it stopped, Henry, Zeb and Gillian got off and hurried towards them.

"Well I never!"

"I'll be..." exclaimed Henry and his father together.

"Is this what Mrs Williams told you about?" Gillian asked Ruth. Ruth saw Zeb give her a strange look. Presumably, Granny had already told him about her journey with the monks, but he didn't correct his daughter in law.

"I do hope so," replied Ruth. "Although it could just be a forgotten cow shed full of rubble after all this time."

"No point standing here gassing," said Zeb, moving forward to see if the door would open. Henry joined him. Nothing happened.

"Here, give me the slasher, Gus" said Zeb. He wedged the blade between the door and the frame and carefully pulled it towards him. The wood creaked. He tried a different spot and then repeated the action in two more locations before the wood finally released its grip on the doorframe and opened. The smell of fetid, damp air rushed out towards them. Henry propped the door back with the pitchfork so it wouldn't fall shut before they were ready.

Henry shone his torch towards the dark interior and was about to go inside when Zeb held him back.

"Wait a moment, lad. If that door's been sealed for over a hundred years, let some more fresh air into the place before you go searching. No telling what's been in there. It smells proper ripe from where I'm standing."

Henry stayed near the doorway, moving the torch beam around inside and whistling in surprise.

"I don't believe it. I don't believe it," he muttered under his breath. The others crowded around him until Zeb relented and let everyone into the strange chamber.

Ruth remembered a cold place with candlelight flickering on pale coloured walls. The light had not reached to the roof so she couldn't tell whether it was corbelled with interlocking stone or wooden beams. It seemed to go back quite a long way into the hillside from the sound of the brother's footsteps on the stone floor. On either side of the room were racks of shelving all covered in large cheeses.

The walls now were dark, from years of neglect, just as the floor was covered with a deep layer of detritus. There was a sudden flash as Gillian began to take photos, recording as much as she could. Zeb rubbed a low shelf with his sleeve.

"This is marble," he said, stroking it gently with his fingertips, his voice full of wonder. "Where did they get marble from to stick inside a hill?"

"We need brooms, scrubbing brushes and a load of water to clean this out so we can see what's really here," said Gillian, wiping cobwebs off her hands.

"It might be a good idea to ask Mattie to help you before you start anything," Ruth suggested apologetically.

Zeb chuckled, "I hear she gave you a right earful for uncovering the well without her."

Ruth's mouth twitched. "You could say that. She did have a point. It is a very old structure and if I'd have thought about it, it would have been better if I had waited to excavate it until an archaeologist was on site to advise." She coughed. "As it was, she did find some datable pottery in the soil I removed so I wasn't completely in the doghouse, even if it is my house and orchard." She grinned at Zeb to show there was no hard feelings. "I wouldn't want you to suffer in the same way."

Henry stepped outside to ring Mattie and before long, both she and Colin arrived on Molly, the shire horse. Mattie slid off and ran towards them.

"Don't touch anything!" she shouted. "We need to document everything, so we know the exact state it was left in." She stepped inside, swinging the torch in an arc backwards and forwards, at the same time taking a video with her phone as she went.

"What a strange place," she said when she finished and rejoined the others outside. "Any idea what it was used for? It reminds me of Tudor dairies except there is no ventilation."

"We don't know anything about it," said Zeb. "There was nothing on the deeds as far as I remember but I think Ruth has a good idea."

Ruth felt distinctly uncomfortable as everyone's eyes turned towards her. "I was up at the Ladywell a few weeks ago and heard some monks singing inside the chapel. They didn't seem to notice me, so when they finished, I followed them. One came here. I saw him turning cheeses. The rest went to the Priory."

Gillian frowned. "I thought you said it was Mrs Williams who told you about this place."

"She did. I mean we discussed it." Ruth didn't know what to say.

"You brought us to this place because you saw ghosts here or because you saw monks here in a dream or a vision?" Gillian persisted. Ruth couldn't make out whether she was angry or just incredulous.

"I was here, so were they. I don't know why our paths crossed." To her great surprise, Gillian broke out into a broad smile and Zeb came over and hugged her.

"It's amazing," Gillian said. "I don't care how you found this place, it's exactly what we need for the cheeses. We'll have our own maturing cave, just like Cheddar."

Henry and Mattie were talking at the entrance. They agreed it would be safer to shut the cave up again and conceal the entrance until they could return with stronger lights and other equipment the following day. Gus needed to get back to start the afternoon milking, so the five of them piled into the Landrover while Colin rode back to the stable.

Ruth decided she would retrace her path up to the Ladywell and make her way home from there. The excitement of the find was becoming overpowering and she wanted a few moments alone to restore her equilibrium.

The track the monks followed up to the chapel had completely disappeared. She could work out where the monks' path joined the bridleway since it led straight to the Priory. Ruth closed her eyes. She didn't know why it was important to find the old footpath, she only knew she must.

When she opened them again, the sun came out from behind a cloud and shone over her right shoulder illuminating patches of silver water droplets on the green grass. The areas bore the shape of a footprint. Ruth followed them diligently, afraid the sun would disappear before she could mark the new course.

She found wool fragments she'd cut from her lap blanket still in her pocket. Now she tied a different thread to several bushes and trees as she scrambled over the wall into The Slopes, then followed the contour of the hill until she came to a gap in the hedge which led her into the chapel grounds facing the unused north door.

To her left was the well and on her right, the west door, now the only entrance. She stared at the chapel. It was substantially larger than the building she had seen before. On her previous visit there were no windows. Now, as she walked slowly around, she could see two small openings, covered by wooden shutters, underneath the tiled roof on both the north and south walls while the end wall had a large stained-glass lancet window.

Above the entrance was a plaque, recording the restoration of the well and chapel in memory of Cedric Brazington, who perished during the Boer War. *His body may rest on foreign soil, but his spirit will remain here always.*

Ruth stood for a moment. The last thing she wanted was another spirit wandering around. She stooped to take a drink at the well and heard a blackbird begin his evening chorus. She took a deep breath. This was such a peaceful place. There was nothing to fear. Relieved she set off onto the road for home.

CHAPTER TWENTY-FIVE

It took several weeks for the new cheese store to be fully excavated to Mattie's professional satisfaction and cleaned to Gillian's exacting standards. As the building had once been part of the Priory, Henry asked Adrian and Andrea to perform a joint blessing as part of the Rogationtide beating of the bounds at the end of May. It would soon be Beltane and the whole village was busy preparing. The May Queen was chosen from the village school and all the children were practicing traditional maypole dances before the end of term so they would be ready for May Day. Anvil's Woodfolk practiced their dances on Tuesdays in the pub with the Morris side and the women danced theirs at the Thursday meetings in the village hall.

Easter was late this year, with only a week between Easter Sunday and Mayday. Lawrence was beside himself getting the anthems for the morning service perfected before the Bishop arrived to perform the annual confirmations. He insisted on so many extra rehearsals, Ruth didn't know whether she was coming or going. Mattie's youngest brother, Dan, was senior chorister this year. He was singing the solo, so was under added pressure.

The boy was normally a happy soul, much given to laughing and joking during rehearsals but the extra time with Lawrence saw him silent and pale, cringing when the choir master tapped his baton in exasperation for a wrong note or a hesitant entry.

"You need to lighten up a bit, Lawrence," Ruth suggested one evening after several children had been reduced to tears by his remarks. "No-one enjoys being harangued. They've worked so hard for you, the least you could do is praise them once in a while, especially Dan."

Lawrence continued to gather up his books. "I'm sure your motherly concern is to be commended, Ruth, but these young people need to be the best they possibly can be once the Bishop arrives. You may think me hard, but they will thank me when it's all over. No-one deserves praise for work which isn't perfect; tonight's efforts were nowhere near as good as they should be."

Ruth was appalled. As far as she was concerned, every youngster had tried their absolute best and the music they produced was stunning.

"If you're not careful, Lawrence, you won't have a choir after Easter." She didn't care how it sounded, someone needed to tell him the truth.

Lawrence merely sniffed loudly. She thought she saw his upper lip curling in distain before he flounced out of the church, banging the door behind him.

Ruth was about to follow him when she was gripped by a feeling of nausea and heard familiar laughter drifting down from the north aisle.

"This is my church," a deep, hollow voice whispered in her ear. He must be standing beside her. *"In my church things will be done my way. You can do nothing, Blackwell whore. Black your name and black your nature. You cannot prevail against me."*

Ruth clutched her music to her chest to stop herself shaking. In her head the voice sounded so much like Robert's she could almost smell his aftershave. She was instantly transported back to one dreadful evening before the firm's Christmas party. She knew Robert was carrying on with one of his trainees and hoped he wouldn't embarrass her during the party. She wanted to tell him but as he walked into their bedroom, he pointed at her, saying, "You women are all the same. Look at you, what are you wearing? Thinking of pulling tonight at the party? You're nothing but a common whore!"

His words stung harder than his hand ever could, leaving her a stuttering wraith. All she could remember of the party was cringing every time anyone spoke to her, then hiding in the toilet until it was time to go home.

Now this vile cleric trying the same tactics as her previous tormentor. She could see him standing by the north door, tall and thin, still dressed in the same black vestments and white collar she'd seen before but this time there was a cloak around his shoulders; the raised hood concealing his face and thin strands of hair. The lack of facial features made him ghoul-like; that and the closeness of his whisper made her shake even more.

What could she do to stop his evil influence? A single phrase from her strange conversation with Greg in the café came to mind. I keep the black well clear.

"Begone, foul spectre, away from here," she shouted, "Don't taunt me with your barefaced lies, I keep the black well clear."

A new verse of the monks' chant began to bubble into her mind. Without thinking what she was doing she sang the words, line after line, soft at first but gradually louder until the notes echoed from every pillar from the bell tower to the altar.

Hers was not the only voice raised in prayer. She watched in amazement, as a long line of hooded monks entered through the open north door and moved slowly up the aisle until they reached the steps down to the sacristy. The lead monk swung an incense burner in front of him, the sweet scent pervading the entire church.

Time trickled away, leaving only music. She could hear them singing in the undercroft before they emerged from the doorway behind the pulpit and processed down the nave, eventually returning through the same entryway.

As the final brother turned to shut the door behind him, his cowl slipped down to his shoulders and she saw the face of the man in the cheese cave. She would have recognised his smile anywhere.

163

In the silence which followed, Ruth said quietly, "Leave this place, Isaac Graves. You are neither wanted nor welcomed. Leave the darkness; go towards the light."

"You're wrong, Blackwell whore," the voice was much fainter now. "I'm tied here. When I'm called, I come. You cannot stop me."

A dark shadow flickered across the brickwork where the north door used to be just as the south door opened, letting in the late evening light.

"You still here, Ruth?" Ruth was never so pleased to hear Granny's voice. "I saw Lawrence leave a good half hour ago so I came to lock up."

When Granny heard what had happened, she insisted on accompanying Ruth home and making her a strong cup of tea. They went into the living room where Ruth curled up on the sofa and Granny sat thoughtfully rocking on Aunt Izzy's chair.

"I'm not a whore," Ruth protested at last, her voice quavering as she felt the shock of all her experiences suddenly crash on top of her. "I've never slept with anyone except Robert."

"You can't expect a ghost to be factual, especially when he's still living three hundred years ago." Granny's matter of fact tone was very reassuring. "I expect he believes all women are whores, whether you're married or not. He might even think you're Granny Blackwell, even though you're nearly thirty years older than she was when she saw him. He probably sees your essence and uses terms which mean something to him but should mean nothing to you. He's a puritan preacher with all the good from his life leached from him by the evil he's been called upon to perform. He's a stuck soul who needs moving on. That's what we've got to think about."

Ruth sipped her tea. "What did he mean that he's tied here?"

Granny pursed her lips. "This is the first time he's mentioned anything like that. We need to find out."

CHAPTER TWENTY-SIX

Ruth was glad she didn't have to go to work the following morning as she was still shaken by the events of the previous day. Mattie was in her room writing up the discoveries of the cheese cave. Ruth wondered if something was troubling her. It wasn't like Mattie not to sing as she worked.

Ruth was restless. None of her usual household tasks distracted her. She put it down to a troubled night's sleep, but she knew there was more to it than that. The house was too quiet; waiting for something to happen.

She tried to dispel the sense of foreboding by going out into the orchard. The hens would normally fly towards her with outstretched wings the minute she came through the gate but today, they were bathering underneath their shelter, as if determined to keep to the safety of the wooden structure.

Apple trees were just coming into flower. It soothed her to see pink buds full of promise thrusting towards the sky amidst the fading white flowers of the ancient pears. Zeb's pruning had made such a difference to the amount of blossom this year. She hoped there wouldn't be a late frost to destroy a plentiful harvest.

It always made her happy wandering through fruit trees then passing under hazel branches into hidden space to watch water flowing into the stone trough. Today was different, overcast and dull, cloud hanging just above the tallest trees and silence.

No bees buzzing through petals and no birdsong, no scolding wren or blackbird's alarm, not even a magpie's rattle, though Ruth was sure they would be looking out for newly hatched chicks or eggs to plunder. She kept away from the hedge where she knew there were several birds sitting on nests deep inside the green canopy.

When she looked into the stone trough, the white, headless carcass of a frog was floating in the water. She took a step back in dismay, wondering what creature would take the head and upper body and discard the long, elegant legs. She scooped it out with a twig and was just about to fling the remains into the hedge when she heard raised voices coming from the house. She hurried back to see what was happening.

"It's not my fault. I can't help you; I've got work to do." Mattie was standing at the kitchen door, dressed in a long brown skirt and matching cardigan embroidered with various coloured flowers although Ruth was sure she'd seen her in jeans and a college sweatshirt at breakfast. She was shouting at Colin who was standing in the conservatory running his hands through his hair.

"You've got to come, if we don't get them out now, there's no knowing how long the water will be contaminated."

"I've got to finish my work. Ask someone else." Mattie yelled.

"I have. They're all busy. I need you. The wood needs you."

"No, it doesn't, it's not my wood."

Colin stepped back as if Mattie had hit him, distress painted all over his face. "But you said…. I thought we…" he stammered as Ruth came through the open conservatory door.

"What's going on?" she asked, looking from one to the other. Mattie's face was flushed and Colin looked as if he were about to cry.

"Some cretin has dumped two dead sheep in the horse pond at the entrance to the Abbotts," Mattie said, only just managing to keep herself from shouting at Ruth as well.

Colin twisted his woollen cap between his hands so hard, Ruth thought he was going to tear it apart.

"If we don't get them out of there and the water emptied and the trough scrubbed, there's no telling how long it will be before the horses can go into the woods. They drink the water on the way in and the way out from work. Without it, I can't use them."

Ruth heard a rattle of harness from the front of the house and realised he'd arrived on one of the Shires. She tried to remember if the car was in the garage as she was worried the huge horse might cause damage if it were still on the drive.

"I'll come and help," said Ruth. They both stared at her.

"You'd never be able to lift the heavy weights," Colin dismissed her offer with a wave of his hand, his eyes focused on Mattie.

"I'm sorry, Colin," said Mattie, trying her best to stay calm. "I've promised to email my report to my supervisor by the end of today. If I don't, it won't count as part of my dissertation. I can't come with you now; I'm waiting for a phone call."

"Next thing you'll be telling me you're waiting for a visitor," Colin growled. Mattie's face turned a brilliant shade of crimson. "Who? Anvil?" She gave an imperceptible nod and he turned away, pushing past Ruth to get to the door. "I might have known he had his claws into you, like all his maids."

"It's not like that," Mattie called after him, trying to reach him before he went around the corner of the house. "We need to discuss what will happen at Beltane."

Colin stopped, looking back at her, disgust colouring his face. "I know what will happen, the same as always. I thought you were different."

"Colin, wait!" Mattie cried but he swung himself up onto Molly's back and turned her into the road, digging his heels into her side with such force she began to trot immediately, disappearing along the street as he turned towards the main road.

Ruth was shocked. Ever since she was introduced to the two, young people, over three months ago, she'd assumed they were a couple. The tension and hurt she'd just encountered took her breath away. She could see tears beginning to run down Mattie's face.

"Mattie…?"

"Go away, Ruth. You're not my mother. You don't understand." Mattie ran upstairs, slamming her bedroom door behind her.

Ruth wondered what had sparked this painful scenario, trying to recall what Mattie had told her. Putting dead animals down a well was a dreadful thing to do, the sign of a criminal act or maybe desperation. She couldn't believe anyone in the village would do such a thing with such a terrible outcome. She went to the study and started to phone all the people she knew. Colin was right, no-one was at home. She left messages on Granny's, Ally Tulliver's and the Home Farm ansaphones and in a moment of desperation, contacted Mrs Williams at the Priory.

"Would your husband be able to help Colin?" she asked.

Mrs Williams promised to try and find him, but she wasn't sure what his commitments were today as she wasn't expecting to see him until late.

Ruth thanked her, sighing as she put the handpiece down on the cradle. There was nothing else for it, she must go up to the woods herself, no matter what Colin felt about her capabilities. She found some buckets, a broom and some disinfectant and put them in the car. She left a note for Mattie on the kitchen table and went to open the garage. She had just backed out and was closing the doors behind her when she saw Greg walking up the steps into the close. She waved at him as she drove past. Their discussion would have to wait for another time.

CHAPTER TWENTY-SEVEN

Ruth was exhausted. It had taken the rest of the day to empty the horse pond, a large, circular basin fed by a piped spring at the entrance to Long Cover, scrub it thoroughly with disinfectant and then rinse it out again. Colin insisted they repeat the process several times as the dead sheep had been dumped several days before and the carcasses were beginning to rot when he found them.

"Who would do such a thing?" he kept repeating but there were no answers.

They worked alone until five o'clock when a truck stopped in the gateway. A man got out and walked towards them, each movement accompanied by a subtle swagger. He was tall and thick set wearing a pale blue overall and jacket, a matching blue cap on his head.

"What does he want?" Colin swore under his breath, knocking the brush he was holding so hard against the brickwork it flew up in the air and would have fallen into the pristine bowl if he hadn't reached out a long arm to catch it.

"Heard you found my dead ewes," the newcomer said, standing by the horse pond and peering into the now gleaming interior. He rubbed his hand over the surface in a sweeping arc, indicating a patch which wasn't quite up to standard.

Ruth glared at him, wiping her filthy hands on a patch of grass.

"How did you find out?" she asked, "it's not exactly common knowledge."

The man tapped the side of his nose and grinned, showing a mouthful of blackened and missing teeth. She felt Colin seething beside her.

"There's no mystery." Colin said, ignoring the man, "After I spoke to George Cooper and Gus at Home Farm, I rang Thompson, the agent at Hollow Barrow. They're the nearest ones with sheep. This is Stanley Clackett, their excuse for a shepherd."

The man's face darkened as he rubbed his hands dry on his overalls. Eventually, he wandered around peering behind Ruth's car. When he couldn't find what he was looking for, he rumbled, "Where are they?"

"Over there," Colin grunted pointing to the heap of bones and wool they'd piled onto a makeshift pole sledge hidden behind a holly bush. The man poked about then came back nodding.

"Mine, all right."

Ruth began to gather up their tools to take back to her car.

"What they die of?" asked Colin.

The man shrugged. "You know sheep, one minute they're roaming the fields eating as much grass as they can find, next minute they're down staring at the sky. Nothing happens to them; they just feel a twinge of pain and turn their faces to the wall. Stupid c…" he saw Ruth watching him and left the last word unsaid.

Colin went to the spring and removed the overflow pipe so water could start to fill the horse pond.

"When did they die?"

"Tuesday, so Ben said. He found them."

Ruth saw Colin's face fill with anger. It scared her. He stood up and took a few steps towards the man. She wanted to jump in the car and escape from the drama. She knew her feelings were ridiculous, no-one was cross with her, no-one was going to hurt her. She needed to break free from Robert's conditioning, but it still made her wary being around any negative emotion.

"Did you tell Ben it would be cheaper to dump them here rather than bury them on your land or pay for their disposal?" Colin asked.

The man took a quick step backwards, almost tripping over a small branch on the ground, his hands out as if in surrender.

"Nothing to do with me, Allon, honest. Ben wanted to call the knacker. I admit I didn't want the expense or the paperwork, so I told him to dig a hole somewhere no-one would notice. I thought he'd taken them to the Copse when they weren't where we left 'em. He said they were gone Wednesday morning when he started work."

Colin picked up the broom he'd been using and came towards the man so quickly, Stanley fell backwards with a shriek. Colin loomed over him, pushing the bristles under his chin so he was pinned on the ground.

"You'd better not be lying, Stanley Clackett. I know you're a lousy shepherd. I don't know why Old Man Kessick keeps you. If I find you had anything to do with trying to poison my horse pond, I'll drag you before the Court myself and let them deal with you."

Ruth saw the man's face blanche. This wasn't the Colin she knew, the easy-going youngster with a ready smile. Now he looked more like an avenging angel, ready to protect his woods under any circumstances. Nothing moved. She found it difficult to take a breath. Around her, leaves began to shiver with a passing breeze and the moment ended.

Colin moved the broom and let Stanley scramble to his feet, dusting off his clothes.

"Don't you worry now, Allon. No harm done. No need to mention the Court." He stopped for a moment, his gaze resting on Ruth, the unwanted witness to his disgrace.

"Who's your little friend," Stanley Clackett pointed at Ruth. She wondered what Colin would say.

"Someone you don't want to cross."

The man gave a forced laugh. "She don't look so scary."

"No?" Ruth smiled at him. "I'm Ruth Taylor, Granny Blackwell's granddaughter. I've inherited her role in keeping our wells and springs clear."

As soon as she mentioned Granny Blackwell's name, she saw fear flickering over his face. A fear she didn't understand but found secretly pleasing. Colin picked up the blue cap which had fallen off while Stanley was on the ground and threw it at him.

"Wrap those carcasses up. Bury them properly where no springs run and deep enough no badgers are going to dig them up again. Take Ben with you and make sure you teach him the words of farewell. If he can't recite them tomorrow in the pub, you'll wish you paid more attention to Anvil's lessons."

Stanley's eyes flicked from Ruth to Colin then back again. She could see he was wondering if he dare have the last word. Something in their stance made him think better of it. He walked briskly to his van and returned with a large tarpaulin. As the two of them stood watching, he wrapped it around the bundle on the travois and then dragged it towards the truck, puffing and blowing at the weight. He made several attempts to hoist it onto the bed of the vehicle, but it soon became obvious he wasn't going to manage on his own. Colin dropped the broom he was still clutching and went to help.

Soon the truck was roaring down the road as fast as Stanley could go.

"What's the Court?" Ruth asked as she loaded the last of the tools in her car and prepared to leave.

"Not my place to tell if you don't know," said Colin. Although he looked relieved to have the horse pond filled again, there was a heaviness about him as if despair were weighing him down. "Ask Granny."

Ruth started the car, wishing it would be as simple to mend his relationship as it had been to clean the trough.

CHAPTER TWENTY-EIGHT

The house was empty when Ruth got home. A note lay on the hall table from Mattie saying she would be back late. Ruth sighed as she went out to shut the hens up, trying to think what to make for tea. Neither she nor Colin had eaten anything for lunch and her stomach was rumbling. Searching through the nest boxes she found three eggs, so an omelette would be possible or maybe a quiche.

Bees were foraging in the pale evening sun, such a hopeful light after the drab morning. She heard buzzing coming from apple trees and could just make out the tiny green swellings of future pears where the blossom faded. It was exciting to think what her harvest might be this year, so different from before when so much was left to rot.

Tomorrow, Henry would be bringing the lambs over. She'd seen them chasing around their pen next to the cowshed. The four were not happy to be left on their own without their other playmates, although Gillian said their complaints were more to do with stopping their last bottle feed rather than lack of companionship. She hoped they would be happy in the orchard.

On the way to the back door she discovered salad leaves growing and stooped to pick them. As she straightened up, she caught sight of a thin tail wagging as it passed the corner of the house.

"Finn?" she wondered aloud. She hoped nothing more untoward

was about to happen. She was looking forward to a peaceful evening on her own in front of the TV.

The quiche was soon in the oven along with potatoes and a tray of vegetables. She knew it was silly cooking so much for one person, but it meant there would be leftovers for the next day.

She was just laying the kitchen table when the doorbell rang. Groaning inwardly, she put down the oven gloves and went to see who it was.

The tall, thin frame of Lord Peter filled the porch. When she opened the front door, he held out a carrier bag towards her.

"Peace offering," he said, looking hopeful. "You didn't come to the library, so I thought I'd bring my great, great, great- grandfather's diaries to you. I hope you don't mind."

Ruth wasn't quite sure what to say as she took the bag and peered inside.

"That's really kind of you." In the bag lay six leather-bound volumes. The sight of them filled her with trepidation. "How did you know which years to bring?"

Lord Peter shifted from one foot to another, seemingly as ill-at-ease as she was. "I cheated. I asked Adrian if he would email me the list of Rectors of Roelswick he's been working on. I remembered some family stories about the feud, so I found out the diaries for the last four years of Isaac Graves and then four years after that when his sons were working in the parish."

"Two different diarists? Lawrence said the Earl died just before Isaac Graves." Ruth said, just as she heard the buzzer go off in the kitchen to say her meal was cooked. She made a decision. "Have you eaten?"

Lord Peter looked surprised then furrowed his brow. "Janet leaves something cold on Saturdays. She's gone to a show with Granny."

Ruth smiled. "Why don't you come in and share my dinner? It's only eggs and veg as my son would say, but it's hot and usually tastes good."

"I don't want to intrude."

"You're not," Ruth assured him. "I'd much rather have company these days and Mattie's not here tonight."

"If you're sure."

As she stood back to let him in, she noticed Finn push past Lord Peter and pad down the hallway into the lounge. On the pretence of leaving the diaries on the coffee table, Ruth followed him in and watched him curl up on the rug in front of the fire. He lifted his head and thumped his tail when he saw her looking at him. She wondered why he was here but didn't have time to ponder any further as dinner needed to be taken out of the oven and served before everything overcooked.

Food worked its usual magic and Lord Peter, as he relaxed, became an astute and entertaining dinner companion. He told her tales of growing up in the village with Granny looking after him before he was sent away to boarding school.

"She used to call me Peter Rabbit," he told her, "because I would never do what I was told; always escaping from the nursery and getting into mischief."

He helped her clear away and wash up before they took their coffee into the lounge.

"I didn't realise you kept wolfhounds," he said, the pleasure in his voice evident as he sat down on the sofa and made a fuss of Finn. "My boy died some time ago. I've really missed him."

Ruth didn't quite know what to say. Lord Peter seemed the last person she would expect to see her ghostly guardian.

"He's not really mine," she said at last. "He seems to have adopted me. I never know when he's going to come for a visit." There was something so poignant seeing Lord Peter sitting back on the sofa, absently scratching the top of Finn's head.

They chatted for a while longer, discussing the possibility of a food festival to be held later in the year before Lord Peter said he needed to get back to the Priory. Ruth was sorry to see him go but she was looking forward to reading the diaries and didn't feel she could study them while he was there. He began to stand up but quickly stopped and Ruth could see his brow was covered in sweat. She went towards him and he gripped her hands so fiercely, it hurt.

"What is it?" she asked, wondering if she was going to have to call an ambulance. He released a long breath and eased himself carefully upright, not able to answer until the wave of pain was fully passed.

"So sorry. Bloody shrapnel's been giving me hell these past few months. Sometimes I wonder if being paralysed would be preferable to all this pain." He released her hands and waited for her to move away from him but she didn't. She wanted to help him, to take away his torment. Something told her she could do this. She had to try.

"Can I touch you?" she whispered. "I promise not to hurt."

He frowned at her but didn't object, so she opened her palms and placed one over the centre of his chest and let the other move slowly up and down his spine until she sensed the spot where she needed to settle. She closed her eyes, feeling a warmth beginning to build in her right hand until it was almost unbearable. She trapped the heat in her fist and flung it behind her then returned it to the original spot. Twice she gathered the heat until the temperature on that portion of his back returned to normal. She smiled as she stepped away from him.

"What was that?" He was staring at her, but she could see from the way he was holding himself he was no longer in pain.

"Not a clue," she admitted, shaking her hands to rid them of any residual tingles. "It seemed like a good idea. Something my grandmother suggested." How could she tell him she began to heal when she was only a small child and had practiced every week with her Grandmother's group until she left for university. Everything she knew had to be hidden and eventually suppressed during her marriage to Robert. Only now did she have the confidence to begin again.

She could see he was about to say something but whatever it would have been was drowned out by the sound of furious barking outside. Ruth looked down but Finn was nowhere to be seen.

"I'd better go," Lord Peter said but Ruth was filled with a sense of foreboding. If Finn was barking, it wasn't safe outside.

"Why don't I make some more coffee?" but Lord Peter was already striding towards the front door only stopping in the porch to thank her again for her hospitality. She followed him out to where his ancient, yellow Landrover was parked on the roadside, looking around to see what might be causing Finn's alarm.

She could see nothing, so she waved goodbye and stood to watch him leave from half way down the path. As he put the key in the ignition, she heard the engine catch. Finn hurtled down the road and in through the open passenger window, pushing Lord Peter out of his seat so hard, the driver's door sprang open, spilling him out onto the pavement. In that same instant, a huge yellow fireball appeared in the cab, tongues of flaming matter shooting through all the windows.

Ruth rushed to Lord Peter, dragging him away from the burning vehicle. They both watched in horror as the Landover became an inferno then, as suddenly as it had started, it was all over. Neighbours appeared from several houses, some armed with buckets of water. They approached the vehicle cautiously then backed away, seemingly unable to believe their eyes. The Landover was cold, with no evidence of burning anywhere they could find.

"I saw flames," protested one man who kept touching the yellow metal expecting it to be hot.

"Very difficult to burn a Landover," said another.

"It's not even scorched," said a third, "better tell the wife to cancel the fire brigade."

"I'll make some tea," said Ruth, shepherding Lord Peter towards the front door, away from the crowd. "You've had a shock." He stopped, clutching the door frame.

"Finn saved me, didn't he?"

Ruth nodded, encouraging him into the lounge. "He's a guardian now, just like he was with you but different." She settled him in the rocking chair with a cup of tea then excused herself for a minute, leaving one of the neighbours who had followed them inside to stay with him.

She went back to the Landrover, trying to stop her hand shaking as she removed the keys from the ignition and closed the driver's door. What was going on? Who could make a fireball appear inside a vehicle only to have it disappear shortly afterwards. The metal might be cold but she could smell something.

"Can you look underneath?" she asked Andrew, one of the Morris men who lived further up the close. "Just in case there's something there that shouldn't be?" She waited while he fetched a flashlight and shone it all around but didn't find anything.

Finn came up and nudged his head under her hand. She scratched his ears, thanking him silently for saving Lord Peter. His tail was upright and his hackles raised as he took her to the top of the flight of steps which led down to the green.

Ruth caught sight of a familiar shadow hiding in the darkness. The sickening laughter was surprisingly absent, but Finn continued to growl.

"What did I tell you," Ruth flung her arm out to point at the shadow. "Not in my house, not on my land will your footsteps pass this day or any day while I have breath to say, 'Be Gone!' Your games will fail, we shall prevail, 'Be Gone!'"

The shadow flickered but Finn was silent so Ruth knew it was no longer there. For a second, she thought she heard footsteps running in the street below but dismissed them as echoes of all the activity going on in the close as a police car arrived.

"What are we going to do with you, Isaac?" she muttered under her breath. "I hope the diaries hold some answers because I'm running out of ideas."

CHAPTER TWENTY-NINE

It was nearly an hour later when the police car finally left. Two bemused constables listened to the neighbours' stories, examined the Landrover and made notes after talking to both Lord Peter and Ruth. She wondered if those notes might disappear when she overheard one of the officers muttering about a full moon and mass hallucinations. The Landrover bore no sign of anything untoward. They checked it thoroughly inside and out, taking the keys from Ruth to start the engine. Everyone held their breath, but nothing happened, no fireball, no shooting flames, just the engine quietly purring in the twilight.

"Doesn't seem to be any problems, Sir," said the first officer, handing the keys back to Lord Peter. "You don't think you could have been dazzled by the sunset, perhaps."

"I don't think so, Constable. I don't usually throw myself out of my Landrover for no reason."

Ruth could see the second policeman doodling on his notepad.

"You don't think it could be a reaction to your time in the Army?" he suggested. An air of satisfaction hovered over his face as if he were secretly pleased to find a plausible explanation for what had happened.

"I do not suffer from PTSD," snapped Lord Peter. Ruth knew he was lying but she wasn't going to be the one to challenge him. He was already stressed, this interrogation needed to stop. She stood up, so did the two neighbours, who had stayed with them throughout.

"Thank you so much for coming," she said, "I'm sorry you've had a wasted journey. I don't think any of us fully understand what happened." There were mutterings from the two police officers, but they didn't prevent themselves from being ushered to the front door, followed closely by the two men.

"Anvil will be here in a minute," Andrew told her as they watched the policeman get into their car. "He didn't want to come while the police were around."

Greg was the last person she wanted to see but she supposed it had to be done. He knew about Finn, so that was one thing in his favour. She nodded to her neighbour and went back to the living room.

Lord Peter was still sitting in the rocking chair, shoulders hunched, with his fingers locked together as if he could stop their shaking by sheer willpower alone. Ruth knelt in front of him, resting her hands over his.

"The police have gone. Is there anything I can do to help?"

His eyes were locked on his hands, the lids almost closed. She wondered if he were trying to shut out the world. He gave a convulsive shudder but she kept her hands where they were, trying to give him a point of stability, some semblance of normality in a world gone crazy.

"Everything's all right," she said softly. "Whatever tried to attack you, failed. Nothing is hurt. The Landrover isn't even singed."

"I must be going mad," Lord Peter said through gritted teeth. "I thought I saw a fireball inside the driver's seat. I felt something push me out. I did. He pushed me out. But he can't have done. He's dead. Anvil helped me bury him. I'm going mad."

Ruth sat back on her heels.

"If you're mad, then so are half the close. They saw the flames. They saw you landing on the ground. I was probably the only one who saw Finn but that doesn't matter. I can see between the worlds. I don't know if it's a gift or a curse but it's real."

Lord Peter lifted his head, meeting her eyes for the first time. She was shocked how bright they were. It was like staring into the depths of a sunlit sky.

"You know Finn?"

Ruth nodded. "I saw him when you arrived. He settled himself in the lounge to wait until after dinner, so he could spend time with you. He's been my guardian here since I moved in, even before he passed over the rainbow bridge. Whenever there was trouble I would hear him barking. Since I lost my job and discovered what my husband was up to, he's been at my side at any sign of danger. I don't know what I'd do without him."

Lord Peter stared at her as if he were trying to make sense of what she was saying.

"How could you be in danger? Has your husband...?" He left the sentence hanging in mid-air as Ruth quickly shook her head. She got up as she heard a knock at the back door and went to let Greg in. If she was going to tell Lord Peter all about Isaac Graves, she might as well tell them both together and save time.

"Lord Peter."

"Anvil."

The two men acknowledged each other then sat in silence as Ruth fetched more tea and brought in the mugs and a plate of biscuits.

"Heard you had a spot of bother," Greg began.

"You could say that." Lord Peter sipped his tea after reaching for a biscuit, biting it into small, precise morsels, chewing methodically until it disappeared.

Although he was sitting with his back straight, Ruth could tell he was no longer in the dark place she found him earlier. She tried to catch Greg's eye, shaking her head imperceptibly to warn him from asking more questions of Lord Peter. Despite his improvement, she could tell he was far from fully recovered. She didn't want to risk any further relapse which might prompt more extreme reactions. She'd seen him explode in anger in his own home, she didn't want him doing it in hers.

"Isaac Graves is back." Ruth didn't mean to blurt out the words, they seemed to jump from her mind into the room without her doing anything in between. Lord Peter stared at her so intently she thought he must be blaming her for something. Not telling him sooner? For being responsible for the ghostly cleric's return? She couldn't tell.

Greg wouldn't look at them. He kept his gaze firmly on the carpet, maybe hoping the pattern would provide him with answers. After a few minutes, he reached for a biscuit then leaned back in his seat, chewing thoughtfully. He took a slurp of the hot tea to wash the biscuit down.

"That explains a lot," he said at last.

Ruth glared at him, willing him to explain himself without her having to ask.

"Granny said you had summat to tell me, I didn't reckon it would be that." He shrugged his shoulders. "No wonder Zeb is chewing bricks."

"Why?" asked Lord Peter. "Zeb has always struck me as the most level-headed man in the village."

"He is," agreed Greg, "except where Isaac Graves is concerned. He never forgave Ernie for asking the evil spirit to help him win his Miriam. He got her all right but the whole village paid the price and keep doing. It's a terrible thing to lose an Anvil, even worse to lose his legacy, whatever that might have been."

Ruth swallowed a gulp of tea the wrong way and spent the next few minutes coughing wildly.

"Not lost forever," she gasped at last.

Greg looked at her, eyes narrowed.

"What you trying to tell us, little hare?"

Ruth cleared her throat and took a careful sip of tea. She hated being under scrutiny like this. Lord Peter was looking at her as if he were expecting her to suddenly grow a second head, even though Henry had already told him the news. She couldn't tell what Greg's reaction was going to be. It was clear Granny hadn't told him or if she had, he was waiting to hear it from her.

"My father was Roger Flint," Ruth said. "He was adopted by Granny Blackwell's sister. The name on his birth certificate, according to Granny, means 'son of Anvil', the Anvil killed by Isaac Graves, Roger Iles. We're cousins, Greg."

For long seconds he continued to stare at her then without saying a word, he shot out of his seat and disappeared. Ruth and Lord Peter exchanged glances as they heard him pacing up and down the hall muttering to himself.

"What do you think?" Ruth asked the question direct, wanting to know if this second declaration meant anything to Lord Peter, who was sitting, staring into space, completely lost in his own thoughts. It exasperated Ruth so much she was almost ready to bid them both goodnight and go to bed. Leave the two of them to sort everything out. "Peter?"

He turned towards her. She wondered if he was going to tell her off for not using his title but instead he was smiling.

"I'm sorry, Ruth. When Henry told me you were Granny Blackwell's granddaughter, I was in such a foul temper, I didn't believe him. If you'd known Granny Blackwell as a small child, you'd have had trouble thinking she knew anything about children. She was such a straight-laced old harridan. She made Granny's life a total misery and that was before she went senile. We all thought Granny was a saint to look after her the way she did for all those years."

Ruth returned the smile, albeit sadly. The tragic events as told her by Mrs Williams were etched in her mind. "Maybe if expectations hadn't been so different all those years ago, Granny Blackwell would have been a different person. Can you imagine losing both your fiancée and your child so close together and never being able to tell anyone what you'd done? It's beyond heart-breaking."

Greg's revelation about Zeb's uncle suddenly hit her. How could anyone live with the person who believed they were responsible for her lover's death. Did she know? How did she find out? If she did, no wonder Granny Blackwell developed such a fearsome reputation.

She must have wanted to punish her husband for what he'd done and everyone else got caught in the crossfire.

They sat together in silence for several minutes before Greg rejoined them. He perched on the edge of the sofa as near to Ruth as he could and took her hands in his, stroking them gently with his thumbs.

"I should've known," he said. "I should've realised when I first saw you. I knew there were sommat but I couldn't get my head around it. You have her build, nothing but a little bird, but your face is Iles. When I look at you, I see my Granda's eyes."

Ruth pulled her hands away from his. She wasn't used to people touching her. It was different with Lord Peter, she felt an overwhelming need to make contact with him, but Greg felt different. There was a wrongness about him she couldn't explain, something she'd not noticed before. His fingers on hers made her feel distinctly uncomfortable. It felt like he was trying to take something from her, something she wasn't willing to give.

She reached for the biscuit plate and offered it to him, but he shook his head. She was so grateful when Lord Peter broke into the moment.

"Do you know why Isaac Graves has returned?"

Greg leaned forward then hunched his shoulders. Ruth thought he was going to speak but something was stopping him.

"I've no idea," she said. "I don't know any of the village dynamics which could have brought him back. All I know is he told me he is tied here. I'm hoping the diaries will give me clues to what he means. What about you, Greg?"

She looked towards him, but he wouldn't meet her gaze. He reeked of guilt, like a small boy accused of something he hadn't done but couldn't clear his name.

"How should I know? I have enough trouble keeping faith with the living, without keeping track of the dead."

Ruth exchanged glances with Lord Peter. She couldn't understand what was going on. Greg was normally so sure of himself, so confident in what to do and how to do it. This wasn't like him at all. Anyone would think he was the one attacked by the fireball by his behaviour.

Lord Peter, on the other hand, was slowly recovering from the shock. Colour had returned to his face and he was moving more easily. The haunted look was gone from his eyes and he seemed much more like the man who had arrived at her cottage only a few hours ago.

"I think it's time I went home." He pushed himself up from the chair, Ruth rose with him.

"Are you sure you're all right to drive? Do you want me to come with you?"

"Really, I'm fine. It was a shock, but I feel better now."

Ruth smiled.

"Amazing, the recuperative power of tea and biscuits."

Lord Peter nodded, his mouth curling upwards in an answering grin. Ruth was surprised by the warmth in his eyes, she didn't think she'd seen him smile like that before.

"Not to mention the support of friends," he said, his hand moving to include both Ruth and Greg but his eyes resting on her.

Greg got to his feet. "I'll come back with you. I need some air." Ruth got the impression he wanted to talk to Lord Peter without her. She didn't care. She was very tired and was glad they would soon be gone and she could go to bed. The diaries would have to wait until tomorrow.

CHAPTER THIRTY

Sometime during the evening, Mattie slipped in and went upstairs without anyone noticing. When Ruth was getting ready for bed, she heard sobbing coming from the girl's room.

"Can I come in?" she asked, knocking softly as she opened the door. Mattie was lying face down on the bed. She raised a tear-streaked face as Ruth came in.

"It hurts so much when you argue with someone you care about," Ruth said, sitting on the edge of the bed and stroking her back. "Have you spoken to Colin yet?"

Mattie sniffed, reaching for a tissue to blow her nose. "Stupid twit," she said, lobbing the tissue into the bin. "I'd have explained, if he hadn't got in such a huff."

"He loves you," Ruth said, "he just didn't know how to tell anyone, especially himself. The thought Anvil might have a claim on you is tearing him apart."

Mattie stared at the headboard. "I thought I wanted Anvil to love me. When I was three, I told Mum I was going to marry him. He fascinated me. I practically lived at the forge until I was eleven. Anvil had to chase me out to go home for meals. I just loved watching him work. He was so gentle with the horses yet so strong when he was working metal or mending machinery."

"What happened when you were eleven?" Ruth asked.

"I don't recall what sparked the conversation, but I told Mum again I wanted Anvil for my husband. She said the strangest thing. 'Don't set your heart on the impossible, Mattie love,' and she had this soft light in her eyes as if she really understood what I was feeling. 'Anvil can't marry, you or anyone. He belongs to the Green Lord; it's his will he serves and through him, he serves us all.' I didn't understand her at all, but I never forgot her words."

"Did things change?"

"Not really. I stopped hanging around the forge so much because I was away at school in town for a lot of the time and then there was homework and they let me join the Thursday Women's Circle, so I really only saw him on high days and holidays. I still wanted him, but I don't suppose he noticed me as more than any other village kid. There was something different when Colin and I joined the village Circle gatherings."

"What happened then?"

"It was the Autumn equinox. I could feel Anvil watching me all through the ritual; like he was seeing me as a person for the first time. I managed to stay close to him when we moved from the Grove to the function room at the Pub for food and dancing. I knew how we would flow during the swings and baskets. In my imagination, I could almost feel the touch of his hand on my waist as we weaved familiar steps and figures together.

"Then the twins erupted into the room with Colin close behind and the moment shattered. Bessie appeared at Anvil's side. She'd just become Maid. She was a year older than me. She was shy, overweight, with black, frizzy hair."

Ruth nodded, "Yes, I met her at the café with Greg."

"I smiled at Anvil, hoping he would ask me, but it was Bessie's hand he held as he moved forward for the first dance. I felt such an idiot. Granny said I needed to get away from the village for a while. 'You can't return and find your proper place and calling iffen you don't leave," she said, mimicking Granny's voice, "so I applied to university as far away as I could find. I thought I'd meet lots of new people, fall desperately in love and set up home with my soul mate in the wilds of Stirling."

Ruth chuckled. "Did you?"

"No," Mattie sat up, hugging her knees. "I met loads of men and not one could hold a candle to Anvil or Colin. So I came home."

"And became the Maid."

"And became the Maid." Mattie's face flushed. "It's been horrible. Anvil's changed; I've changed. I don't feel the same and it's as if I've betrayed him, especially now Beltane's coming up."

"What's so special about Beltane? I thought it was just a fire festival and dancing around the maypole."

Mattie grabbed another tissue. "Beltane is when the Spring Maiden runs through the maze and the men have to chase her to ensure the fertility of the land. The Green Man chooses Anvil for his champion and he's the one who takes the Maid, except I don't think I want Anvil any more. I want Colin but now he's angry with me and he'll never ask me. I've ruined everything." She cried on Ruth's shoulder.

"No, you haven't. You've just grown up. Everyone does. Anvil wouldn't expect anything of you. I bet he told you it was your decision, your gift." Ruth held her close, patting her back gently until she stopped crying.

"That's part of the problem," Mattie hiccupped. "He's been so nice about it. I'd feel better if he shouted and called me a scheming hussy. It's what I was."

Ruth handed her another tissue and waited while she blew her nose. She wondered whether she should say anything but the words came before she could stop herself.

"If you don't feel any attraction to him anymore, don't think about

189

going with him at Beltane just because you think you should. You'd hurt him more than you'd ever know. There is nothing worse than a 'mercy lay', believe me."

Mattie looked at her open-mouthed as Ruth went back to her own bed.

CHAPTER THIRTY-ONE

Two weeks later, Ruth woke to hear Mattie crashing about in the bathroom. A quick glance at the clock told her she was going to be late for church if she didn't hurry. She was thankful the lambs didn't need feeding. The orchard grass was already showing signs of their increasing appetites. She would need to let the hens out before she left.

Today was Palm Sunday, one week left before the Bishop's visit. Adrian was outside the porch with the choir, clutching the halter of an ancient donkey. The children, including two-year-old, Arthur, crowded round him, patting the beast and clamouring to be allowed to ride him into the church.

"Not now, later." Adrian promised, grabbing his son before he disappeared underneath the beast. Ruth felt sorry for the harassed Rector and swiftly took charge of the choir, making sure they were lined up in the correct order.

Although the hymns were joyful, Ruth felt an air of anxiety throughout the service which had nothing to do with the impending crucifixion. Lawrence's playing felt angry, with none of his usual finesse. The donkey, despite his age and placid nature, flinched at every crashing chord, shaking his head when the music reached a sudden crescendo. The rope tying him to the choir stall worked loose.

Discovering he was free, he turned and trotted down the aisle at surprising speed. He would have escaped outside through the open south door if Colin hadn't rushed to catch him.

Ruth saw them after the service. Colin was sitting on a bench at the far end of the graveyard with the donkey peacefully munching grass between the stones. She was about to join him when she heard raised voices just inside the doorway.

"What do you mean the church will be open for silent meditation all Good Friday?" Lawrence shouted. "Friday is the last chance for the choir to rehearse for Easter Sunday. How could you announce such a change without discussing it with me first!"

Arthur was trying to drag his father away by the hand screeching, "Donkey, donkey!" There had been no sign of his mother in the church and Ruth hoped she wasn't ill again.

"This wasn't a problem last year, Lawrence." Adrian said.

"Last year, we didn't have the Bishop coming," Lawrence spat, "or have you forgotten?"

"There's always Saturday," said Adrian, moving step by step towards the porch.

"No there isn't," screamed the choirmaster, "We never rehearse on Saturdays. I don't have time. We rehearse at six o'clock on Fridays. In the church."

"I'm sorry, Lawrence, but six until nine is a really important time for meditation." He let go of Arthur's hand and disappeared outside almost as quickly as the running child.

Lawrence's face was bright red. Ruth didn't want to say anything, but words tumbled out before she could stop them.

"We could always rehearse at my house."

Lawrence blinked, as if he couldn't quite make out who was talking. Instead of thanking her, he began to berate her in the same tone he used on Adrian.

"You shouldn't provide an alternative venue, Ruth. It allows Adrian to win. He should be taught a lesson. He can't go about changing things without my agreement."

Ruth frowned. What was Lawrence thinking? Did he really put the choir ahead of everything else in the church or did his ancestral ties make him believe his needs were more important than anything else?

"Adrian does have a point," she said, clutching her pile of books firmly. "Good Friday evening is the most solemn time of the Christian year. The time of Christ's death."

Lawrence glared at her. "We're not Catholic."

Ruth thought she would much rather be sitting quietly in the church next Friday evening than be subject to any more of Lawrence's vitriol. She smiled, imagining what it might be like to slap Lawrence's face until he turned into a normal human being.

"Even so," she said quietly, "I'll let the others know we'll be rehearsing at mine next Friday. I'll see you then."

She walked away, refusing to give him the opportunity to say any more. She wanted to reassure Adrian the issue about Good Friday was sorted. As she reached the edge of the churchyard, Arthur was jumping up and down on the seat beside Colin shouting, "Baa, baa, baa".

"Donkeys don't say baa, they go hee haw," Colin told him, patting the beast's soft neck with his hand. Arthur wasn't taking any notice, he climbed down from the bench and ran up the path to the wooden stile marking the footpath leading to Glebe Farm still shouting "Baa, baa!". Ruth followed his gaze, her heart sinking as she saw the familiar figure of a lamb with a heart-shaped birthmark on her left flank, calmly grazing amongst the trees on top of the opposite bank.

"Oh no," Ruth groaned. "How did she get out?" The black-faced lamb with overlong ears had been named Moose by Henry and Gillian's children. She acted as leader to the orchard flock. With her great jumping prowess, she was always searching for an escape route from her current location.

Ruth looked down at her shoes, deliberating whether she could attempt to follow the escapologist or return home for more appropriate clothing. As she watched, a figure materialised from behind the tree.

It was Greg. He walked slowly down behind the lamb. It looked to Ruth he was trying to get close enough to grab it. Just as he got near, Moose took off. Ruth thought she was heading down into the valley but at the last moment she veered to the left and leaped towards a huge clump of brambles. There was a terrible crash, followed by the sound of splintering wood then loud bleating.

"Hold this," said Colin, thrusting the donkey's halter into Ruth's hand as he removed Arthur from the stile and ran down the footpath towards the bramble patch.

"Baa gone, baa gone," yelled Arthur, tugging at his father's trouser leg.

"He did, didn't he," agreed his father. "I think we need to go too. Mummy will be wondering where we are." He scooped the protesting toddler up into his arms. Ruth could hear him all the way to the lychgate trying to persuade the child that Mummy wanted to know all about the lamb and the donkey.

Ruth looked down at the animal who was still placidly tearing off chunks of rough grass all around their feet, oblivious to the drama in the field beyond. She could see Colin peering into the bramble patch from this end, while Greg was doing the same from the opposite side. The lamb sounded very distressed, but Ruth was relieved the small troublemaker was still able to make noise.

"What should I do?" Ruth called out.

"Tell Zeb to get the truck here with slashers and some rope." Colin yelled.

Ruth looked around the churchyard but there was no sign of anyone.

"Up you come, donkey, looks like it's just the two of us to find help." She pulled on the halter rein and thankfully the donkey followed obediently behind her all the way to Glebe Cottage.

Granny was standing in her open front door when Ruth arrived.

"What's going on?"

"Moose has escaped. She was grazing in the field behind the church. When Greg tried to catch her, she jumped into a bramble patch and fell through something. Colin asked if Zeb could take some slashers over in the truck. I presume he means a trailer for the lamb?"

Granny swore under her breath before shouting for her husband. The donkey nudged Ruth from behind, reminding her she still needed to get him home.

"Where does the donkey go?" Ruth knew it was a feeble question. It sounded as if she wanted to put him in a box somewhere like a toy being tidied away. It didn't help when Granny ignored her, staring past her as if she wasn't there. The donkey began to nibble the budding rose bush.

"Don't let him do that," Granny shouted, waving the tea towel towards them which the donkey ignored. "Take him back to the Priory. You can put him in the paddock opposite the car park." She shooed them both away and turned back into the house, shutting the door behind her.

Ruth wasn't sure what to make of Granny's behaviour. She was just about to lead the donkey down the lane when they had to stop as Zeb's truck roared out of the driveway down to the gate into the field.

CHAPTER THIRTY-TWO

It took another half hour to walk along the lane as the donkey insisted on stopping to graze whenever he could. As they passed the entrance to Home Farm, she saw Henry hitching up the small trailer to his Landrover. She heard the familiar rumble and clatter as it went down the road behind them.

There were two carthorses and two hunters in the paddock next to the Priory. As he caught sight of them, the donkey kept pushing the gate as Ruth was trying to get it open, anxious to return to his friends.

"Stop that, behave yourself," she said yanking on the halter. To her great surprise, the animal obeyed, standing quietly by her side until she led him through the opening and pulled the halter from behind his ears.

"Go on then." She patted his neck and he trotted off towards the hunters. The two carthorses were coming towards her to see who she was, their enormous hooves thundering on the ground. She always felt intimidated by them when Colin wasn't around. She slipped back through the gate and fastened it firmly, just as they reached her, great plumes of breath escaping from their nostrils. They leaned their heads over the gate towards her.

"Hello Molly, hello Dick," she said, rubbing their long faces. "I don't have anything for you, today."

She wondered what to do with the halter, so, with a final pat, she followed the drive round to the stables. Lord Peter was pushing a load of foul bedding straw along the yard as she approached.

"Where should I put it?" she asked waving the halter at him.

"Just a moment," he said, disappearing behind the buildings. He returned a few moments later wheeling an empty barrow, which he left in front of the open stall.

"Where did you get the halter?" he asked.

She explained about being left with the donkey while everyone else was busy rescuing the lamb.

"Granny said to turn him into the paddock with the others. I hope that was alright."

Lord Peter nodded, taking the halter from her and together they walked to the tack room where he hung it on a hook below a printed name.

"Drago?" Ruth read. "How did he get a name like that?"

"It's all my son, Edward's, fault." Lord Peter chuckled. "He really wanted a dragon for his fourth birthday, so when the donkey arrived, he insisted on the name. I did have to put my foot down when he tried to give him petrol to drink so he'd start producing flames."

Ruth couldn't help but laugh.

"Coffee?" Lord Peter offered as they headed towards the kitchen. She waited for him to remove his boots and decided to leave her muddy shoes at the back door as well. She was still carrying her hymn books and put them down gratefully on the kitchen table. There was no sign of Mrs Williams or Lily.

"I have to fend for myself at weekends when we're not entertaining," Lord Peter explained, spooning coffee and then pouring boiling water into two mugs. He fetched a jug of milk from the fridge and opened a tin of biscuits standing on the shelf.

Ruth helped herself, the scratched picture of lambs on the lid, reminding her of her current predicament.

"Is there a wooden building in the field behind the church?" she asked, "I'm sure I heard smashing wood as Moose jumped into the brambles. It seems so strange."

"I really don't know," said Lord Peter. "It's not a field I'm familiar with. Jack Henson doesn't like anyone walking his land without permission."

"There's a footpath and stile in the churchyard."

"Yes," Lord Peter rubbed his unshaven chin thoughtfully, "But the footpath doesn't go anywhere. You expect it to either go up into the trees and down the other side to Glebe Farm but there's nothing after the bank starts to rise. It's not on the current OS map because Jack had a real go at them for trying to move the real footpath from the top of the hill to behind the church."

Ruth sipped her coffee, accepting another biscuit when Lord Peter tipped the tin towards her.

"Do you have any old maps?" She asked.

With a biscuit in his mouth, Lord Peter led the way to the library and opened one of the long drawers. He took out a sepia map and spread it on the table. It clearly detailed the whole area, showing the village and Priory with woods and fields along with any ancient monuments and boundary stones.

"This is the 1901 OS map," Lord Peter explained, running his finger over the village. "Good heavens! Whoever would have thought! It's there!"

Ruth strained to read the upside-down words. "What's there?"

He turned the map towards her. In clear, italic script were the words, *St John's Holy Well*. "Have you not read the story in the diaries? I thought that was what you were looking for."

For a moment she felt guilty, she had started to read the diaries, but the handwriting was very difficult to decipher in places and once the weather improved, she was out in the garden every moment she could.

"I've only managed to get about half way through the first one," she confessed. "There hasn't been any mention of a well, just comments about the family and the estate."

"Ah." Lord Peter removed his glasses and rubbed his eyes. "The battle over St John's well comes at the end of the second volume. I read that section because it fell open at the page when I was hunting them out for you. It explains quite a few things in a way."

Ruth felt her mouth go dry and a cold chill around her right shoulder made her shiver. Her eyes were drawn to the large painting hanging on the wall above the bookcase. An imposing man in military uniform was sitting astride a large, chestnut horse with a sword hanging from his belt. In the background she could see the Priory and in the foreground was a pair of wolfhounds stretched out either side a dead white stag. The man's eyes were piercing. She almost expected him to speak to her from the painting, but it was the dogs who demanded her attention.

The hound on the left was pure white with striking blue eyes. The one on the right had a sandy coat with deep brown eyes. He was the image of Finn.

"Oscar and Belle," she murmured to herself, remembering one of the long passages from the diaries which had recorded the arrival of the Priory's first breeding pair of wolfhounds.

She had to stop herself from stepping back when she saw both dogs jump down from the painting and walk sedately towards them. She held out her hand for them to sniff. Belle, the white dog, sat down by her side while Oscar walked around the table towards Lord Peter, bumping against his leg until he reached down to pat his head and scratch behind his long ears.

"Good boy," said Lord Peter, continuing to peruse the map. Ruth was sure she heard the dog whine with contentment as he laid his great head on the Earl's lap.

Ruth could hardly believe her eyes, but she knew they were both there and that Lord Peter could see them as well as she could. No wonder he had no trouble communicating with Finn when he visited her.

Two dogs, she thought. *Two dogs protecting the orchard before Finn died.*

Two dogs protecting the village from outside forces, but only where the property is warded. It made sense now. She wondered about the Priory, but Lord Peter interrupted her thoughts.

"Shall I tell you what I remember about the feud between Isaac Graves and the fourteenth Earl of Haverliegh? That's him in the portrait over there." He pointed towards the painting and Ruth realised the dogs were back in their original place.

"From what I can gather, both from the diaries and family stories, it was mainly to do with money." He began. Ruth frowned; she'd always thought it was something to do with religion rather than anything secular.

"St John's well was a very popular healing well. It was on several pilgrim routes. They could get their badge for visiting the saint's relics in the church then take a dip in the holy water. It must have worked too, the income generated from pilgrim's offerings was huge. The priory was an influential force both locally and nationally. The fourth convocation was held here in 1468.

"After the reformation, it was sold to my ancestor, who loaned Henry money for his foreign wars. It was nearly two hundred years later when the trouble started between the village and our family.

"Isaac Graves was appointed by the Bishop to take charge of the well. It was still producing a sizeable income from grateful visitors and the Bishop wanted to make sure it stayed with the church. The fourteenth Earl said the well was on his land, so he should collect any donations."

"Isn't the well on Glebe Farm?" asked Ruth. "I thought anything with Glebe belonged to the Rector."

"Unfortunately, not in this case. The land is part of this estate and it is our discretion whether the farm or income from renting the farm out is tithed to the Rector. Isaac's Graves' predecessor did take us to court, but they ruled in our favour."

"Ouch," said Ruth. "No wonder Isaac Graves wasn't happy."

Lord Peter shrugged. "The fourteenth Earl saw the world in black and white with no grey areas. Isaac Graves was very similar. Neither of them would back down and for twenty years there was open warfare between the church and the Priory with the village caught in the middle. The end was very sudden and tragic for both sides."

"What happened?" asked Ruth, completely enthralled by the story.

Lord Peter stared into the distance; his voice subdued as he continued.

"Isaac Graves decided if the church couldn't have the money, no-one could. He cursed the well and the earl." Ruth gasped. "Within a week, the earl's eldest son had been killed by a falling tree branch in the Abbott's orchard. The earl was so distraught he died a few days later. Isaac himself only lasted another week. The doctor said it was his heart."

Ruth's mind was spinning. "What happened then?"

"The earl's second son took over. He carried out his father's wishes and closed off the Abbott's Orchard. Threatened to hang any villager for poaching if they went near the place. His son was looking to set up in practice as a local doctor. He was finding it difficult to make a living because no-one consulted him, they'd rather visit the well. The new Earl covered the well in a wooden structure and over the years people forgot it was even there."

"They forgot it was there," Ruth said, words tumbling out on a single breath, "they forgot it was there and it's cursed and now it's open and there's no telling what will happen!"

CHAPTER THIRTY-THREE

Ruth leaped to her feet. "Can you drop me at the village? Please, it's really important."

"Of course."

She could see Lord Peter didn't really understand but he strode quickly to where his Landrover was parked while Ruth ran into the kitchen to retrieve her hymn books.

They called at the cottage to collect her boots, then Lord Peter drove back to the field entrance and all the way up the valley to the well. Zeb and Colin were hacking at the brambles with the slashers as if their life depended on it, while Greg was piling all the cuttings and pulling out great hunks of timber. She heard a hollow bleat from inside. She could tell it was not as strong as before and worried the lamb was fading.

"Stop here," she said as the land began to rise in front of them. She didn't want to get too close to the well. Lord Peter put his foot on the break, the gear lever protesting as he pushed it into neutral.

"Don't get out," she said quickly as she saw his hand move towards the ignition. He looked at her, about to protest, "You mustn't risk the curse." She knew he didn't want to go but she could tell from his eyes he was remembering the fireball and was trying hard not to panic.

"What about you," he called after her as she jumped down from the Landrover.

"I'll be ok," she called back, "or I'll sort it out later," she muttered under her breath as she watched the vehicle back up and then turn around and drive off. She remembered her grandmother's advice to visualise herself some protection if she found herself entering a difficult situation and quickly drew the silver cloak around her frame.

Ruth looked up towards the church. A pregnant woman was leaning over the stile.

"Go back," Ruth yelled, recognising Andrea, the Rector's wife. "Don't come down here."

Andrea continued to climb over the stile, but she was finding it difficult. Ruth ran up to her as best she could. The path was steep, and she was out of breath by the time she reached the edge of the footpath.

"You mustn't come over here," she panted.

"Why ever not?" asked Andrea. "Lawrence told me they'd found the lost holy well. I need to see it. It might help me with this everlasting sickness."

Ruth wondered how Lawrence knew where the holy well was situated and how he had managed to tell Andrea in the short time since the end of the service. He normally went straight home to cook dinner for his elderly mother. Had he called in at the Rectory on the way to cause more trouble?

Andrea began to sag against the wall beside the stile. Ruth climbed over and helped her to the bench.

"When did you see Lawrence?"

"He popped in after church with some more Moroccan mint tea he'd made for me. He knows how much I've been suffering. He thought it might help. He's such a sweetie."

Ruth couldn't think of a worse description for the choirmaster but tried not to let her thoughts show. Maybe he did have another side. Andrea must have known him for much longer than she had.

"I don't think it's a good idea for you to go there now," she said. "There's far too many brambles. You'd hurt yourself. You don't look very well. Shall I help you back to the Rectory?"

"Don't worry about me." Andrea pushed herself upright, but as she did, Ruth caught sight of a dark stain on the bench and another on the back of her skirt. Her heart sank. She wrapped her arm around Andrea's waist and slowly they began to walk through the churchyard. They stopped to rest again on the seat under the lychgate. Ruth found her phone in her pocket and dialled Granny's number.

"Could you come up to the Rectory, please, Granny. Andrea's not feeling too good." She heard Granny mutter something under her breath then said she would be there in five minutes.

The slow walk to the Rectory seemed to take forever. Adrian met them at the door and took his wife upstairs to their bedroom. Granny arrived with her basket a few moments later.

"What's the matter? She vomiting again?"

Ruth shook her head. "She's bleeding. Lawrence brought her some mint tea and told her to visit the holy well behind the church. Why would he do that? He must know it's cursed."

Granny's face blanched. "Why would he do that? If she went anywhere near, every child of her womb would be cursed."

Ruth tried to swallow but her mouth was too dry. "I saw her at the stile, but she was too weak to climb over, so I brought her home."

Granny patted her arm. "You did your best. Ally Tulliver will be here in a minute. Put the kettle on, would you? I need to brew her a tea." She pushed the basket at Ruth and hurried up the stairs.

Ruth looked in the lounge and study, but couldn't see Arthur, so presumed he was upstairs having a nap. She took the basket into the kitchen and filled the kettle with water. Dirty plates and cutlery filled the sink and littered the table while the cat was investigating the remains of Arthur's bowl on the floor underneath. Ruth looked around for a dishwasher and when she couldn't find one, gathered everything together and began to fill the sink with hot, soapy water. She really wanted to get back to the well and makes sure Moose was safe but couldn't leave without telling anyone. She heard the front door open and close and footsteps approached.

"You've made yourself at home," Ally said, her cheerful voice preceding her into the kitchen.

"If you can't help, wash up, was my Grandmother's motto," Ruth told her. Ally disappeared upstairs for instructions and soon returned with tears threatening to spill from her eyes.

"Granny said to make the miscarriage mix in her basket." She searched for a handkerchief in her pocket to wipe her eyes as she found the bag of herbs she wanted. Ruth handed her a large china teapot from the dresser and watched as Ally spooned out the mix and poured over the now boiling water. She set the kitchen timer for ten minutes, picking up a tea towel to start the wiping up as Ruth continued to wash.

A small, silver thermos was sitting on the table. When Ruth unscrewed the top, she found herself staring at a light, green liquid. She sniffed then passed it to Ally.

"What do you think that is? Some kind of tea?"

Ally sniffed and frowned. "It's almost like mint but it isn't."

Ruth felt her heart skip a beat. "Andrea told me Lawrence had brought her some Moroccan mint tea to help with her nausea. I've drunk Moroccan mint tea before and it smelt nothing like that."

"Oh, dear Lady, I hope it isn't what I think it is. Granny will know." She screwed the top back on and disappeared up the stairs. Ruth followed her out to the hall where she could hear a hurried, whispered conversation between the two women. Then she heard Granny go back into the bedroom. Her voice was very clear and kind, but Ruth could tell she wanted answers.

"Andrea, dear. Is this the mint tea Lawrence brought for you? Did he give you some to drink? Is this the first time he's brought you mint tea?" She was too far away to hear Andrea's soft replies and thought she'd better return to the kitchen, rather than be caught eavesdropping.

She was wiping the kitchen table when Granny and a weeping Ally came in.

"It's pennyroyal, isn't it?" Ally sobbed.

Granny's face was grim. She nodded.

Placing the thermos on the table, she took out her phone and began to take pictures of the offending object, including the contents.

"What is wrong with the man?" Granny hissed through grinding teeth. "What has Andrea ever done to make him try to get rid of her baby?"

Ruth had a flashback of wildlife programmes she'd watched. Newly conquering chimps and lions would kill any small offspring and terrorise any pregnant females until they aborted, so no trace of the previous breeding males' genes remained. She shuddered.

"Maybe he wants her?" Ruth suggested. Granny stared at her. "His behaviour is so bizarre. He loathes Adrian but can't keep his eyes off Andrea. Andrea, herself, called him a sweetie, so she must like him in some way. "

"She's nice to everyone," Ally sniffled. "It's how she is. She loves Adrian. She'd never do anything to hurt him."

"We all know that," Granny patted Ally's arm absentmindedly. "Lawrence must have misunderstood."

"He thinks because he's a Graves, he's better than anyone." Ruth told them; her voice bitter. "He even had the audacity to call Lord Peter's ancestor a sorcerer, when it was Isaac who cursed the well and caused all the deaths. If anyone was a sorcerer, it's him."

"Now, now," said Granny, shaking her finger at Ruth, "there's no point in name calling. It doesn't help. We have to think."

CHAPTER THIRTY-FOUR

Ruth made her way back to the churchyard with a heavy heart. All they could do now was wait. She heard men's voices as she neared the graveyard boundary but when she looked over the wall, she saw Greg shaking his fist at Colin, who was waving the slasher towards him as if he wanted to cut Greg down rather than the brambles. The moss-covered well house, with its pitched, stone roof and arched doorway could be clearly seen now the wooden frame and woven undergrowth were gone.

"She's got to come and look," Greg shouted.

"No!" Colin thumped the end of the slasher hard into the ground.

"This is part of our history," Ruth had never heard Greg so angry. "She must come and record it; like she did the cheese cave. If we go inside and disturb the archaeology, we'll never here the last of it!"

"No!" screamed Colin. "Can't you get it into your thick skull. You don't get to tell her what to do."

Ruth saw Zeb amble over to the two men but couldn't hear what he was saying as she concentrated on climbing the stile. Just as she began to walk down the hill towards them, Greg and Colin started pushing each other. Zeb moved forwards, trying to break up the tussle but in the sudden blur of moving limbs, something caught him in the stomach and he landed in a heap.

"Stop, stop this at once," Ruth yelled, running to Zeb. She leaned over him, trying to see if he was seriously hurt. He was gasping for air and his face was pale.

"What were you thinking?" she shouted in frustration. Neither men could hear her or were deliberately ignoring her. Like boxers, they traded blow for blow until a particularly vicious jab from Greg's elbow, caught Colin's ribs, pushing him down the hill a few paces. Colin stood, bent over, panting. He reached down for Zeb's discarded slasher, but Ruth darted forward, kicking it out of his reach. The look on Colin's face terrified her.

"Stop it, Colin. Greg, look at yourself!" Blood was pouring out of Greg's nose and running down the front of his jacket.

"I'll not let him claim Mattie. I won't," yelled Colin.

"She's not yours!" Greg shouted. "She deserves to make her own mind up."

"She's not yours either," Colin made a lunge towards the older man, but Ruth grabbed hold of his sleeve, dragging him back.

Laughter echoed from inside the well. Ruth whirled round expecting to see black smoke or at least the ghostly apparition of Isaac Graves but there was nothing except a white shape lying on the grass by the far side of the well house.

"No!" She stumbled over the long, slick meadow grass, tears running down her cheeks unnoticed. The lamb's eyes were open, milky white. Her curled wool was almost yellow and the heart-shaped birthmark on her flank was black. Ruth fell to her knees beside the motionless body, barely conscious of the wet grass seeping through her jeans.

It was all her fault. She had allowed the lamb to escape from the orchard. She had not gone to help when she discovered the lamb was in the field. She had stayed talking to Lord Peter when she could have been another pair of hands removing the brambles. She didn't deserve to be entrusted with the lives of others when she couldn't keep them safe from harm. She should go back where she came from and stay out of things she didn't understand.

As the last suggestion filtered through her mind, she realised the sentiments were not her own. Someone else's thoughts were being projected into her head. She got to her feet, looking around for the elusive flicker on the edge of her vision.

"You don't get me like that, Isaac Graves," she said. She turned towards the men, who were looking at her strangely. At least they had stopped hitting each other.

"Idiots!" she grumbled. "We're all idiots. Letting the well's curse attack us like that." Colin was helping Zeb to his feet.

"You alright, Zeb?" she asked, walking towards them.

"I'll do," he replied. "Just been a while since anyone knocked me down in a fight."

"I didn't mean to," Colin said, trying to brush the dirt off Zeb's clothes. He glared at Greg. "If someone didn't think he had the right to order Mattie around. Just because she's Circle Maid, don't mean he can abuse his position."

Greg stooped to pick up his cap which had fallen off during the fight, shaking it out before returning it to his head.

"I weren't trying to abuse anything or anyone. Mattie's been the one yelling and screaming because folks have gone ahead with uncovering a new discovery without her there to do all the proper recording. I just thought we should invite her over before we went inside."

"No-one's going inside." Ruth said. She pointed towards Moose's body. "Didn't anyone wonder why the lamb died."

Greg shrugged. "Sheep do that. They feel pain or get in a place they think they can't get out of and they just give up." He backed away as Ruth shot him a look.

"If one more person gives me that crappy excuse, I shall beat them to a pulp myself."

"But it's true," Zeb protested.

"I don't care if it's true or not. That lamb was alive before it went into the well housing and now it's dead. Its wool has changed colour or were you so busy trying to prove which of you was the greatest village idiot, you didn't notice?"

One by one they trooped over to the lamb and peered at it.

"I don't remember that colour when we brought it out," said Zeb, "I'd swear it was white."

"Nor me," echoed Colin.

Greg just stared at the well house then back at her. "What are you trying to tell us? Something killed the lamb? There's no marks on it."

"No," she said quietly, "The marks are all on you, by your own hands. It's what Isaac wants. The last thing he ever did during his earthly life was curse this well. His anger and hatred has drawn together every vile and evil thing he could attract. Every time someone acts to hurt another, his power increases."

Zeb and Greg were silent. She could see them both thinking things over, but Colin said, "He's dead. He died hundreds of years ago. What do you mean, his power increases?"

Again, the wellhouse echoed with laughter. This time they all turned towards the sound, even if Colin tried not to react. He looked like he wanted to run down the hill as fast as he could.

"Stay here, all of you!" Ruth held up her hand. "Yes, he cursed the well and yes, his spirit is still tied here. We need to decide what to do next and how to achieve it safely."

"You mean it's not safe!" Colin interjected. He pointed towards the lamb and shuddered.

"I think the lamb was just by chance," Ruth said. "No-one could have known she would fall through into the wellhouse. What I'm more concerned about is the three of you."

Zeb started walking towards his pickup. "We need Amy. She'll know what to do."

"No," said Ruth. "No-one else must be exposed to the curse until we can clean the place out and hallow it again."

"How are we going to do that?" asked Colin.

Ruth was about to say something about the need to burn everything and give the well a good scrub but in her head, she heard someone chanting. The noise was so loud she put her hands up to cover her ears, but it didn't help. The words grew and grew until they consumed her,

"Cursed be the hunter, cursed be the wine
Defiling our water, our relics divine.
If prayers and high praises once more here resound
Then blessings and peace will hallow this ground."

CHAPTER THIRTY-FIVE

"You all right, Ruth?"

She felt the warm touch of Zeb's hand on her arm, bringing her back to the present. The noise in her head was gone and she could feel the warmth of the afternoon sun on her back.

"What happened?" she asked, wondering if she'd imagined everything but the blood on Greg's jacket told her it was all true.

"You started chanting, like you did in the café with me," Greg said. "Something about the curse and removing it. Can you remember?"

Ruth nodded, biting her lip. She didn't want to repeat the words. They'd already been said. Every time strange words came out of her mouth, she knew it was her grandmother speaking; refreshing memories Ruth didn't know she had.

She came to the village an empty, frightened rabbit, but now she felt secure in addressing so many different challenges. She had no idea if they would work, she only knew they had been used successfully in the past. A plan to remove the curse was slowly forming in her mind.

She looked back at the wellhouse. It was taller than she imagined, taller than Colin. It was constructed of stone slabs with a pitched roof going back into the hillside. Although this was the first time in her life she had seen it, she knew if she peered through the broken, wooden door she would find an empty chamber with two stone benches either side where people could sit and wait their turn at the well. Beyond this chamber was another, cut deep into the hillside, with the spring running into a sunken square trough, deep enough and long enough for a grown man to lie.

She knew there were steps from the first chamber to the well, worn in the centre like the ones in the church leading down to the crypt. Built by the same masons, trod by the same pilgrims who came to pray at the staff of John the Baptist before walking to the well to wash away their physical ills and be re-born. In another life, she had been a guardian for the well, tending to visitors who came to take the waters.

"Four hundred years," she breathed. "Four hundred years, travellers came here to be cleansed with prayer and praising. Two hundred more years people continued to seek healing before money caused the rift between church and landowner. Six hundred years of good before Isaac laid his curse. Nearly two hundred and fifty years of evil. Four deaths we know about," she ticked them off on her fingers, "five if you include Moose." She refused to think about the battle for the potential new life being fought in the Rectory. Granny presided over that; this was hers.

"You really think the curse can affect us?" Colin was looking worried.

"Would you have attacked Greg otherwise?" Zeb asked him. They all saw his cheeks begin to flame and he wouldn't look at them.

"We all know how you feel about Mattie," Greg said. Colin jerked as he spoke.

"Then why do you want to claim her at Beltane, like all the others, when I was going to ask. You can have anyone. Mattie means everything to me." The anguish in Colin's voice echoed around the valley. Greg's shoulders slumped.

"That's just it. She's my maid. She's grown up trying to woo me. That's why Granny sent her so far away, to give her time to see things clearly. I didn't know working together at the Abbotts would bind you two so close, so quickly. That's why I came to see her the other week at your place," he nodded towards Ruth, "I needed to find out what she wanted. I've never forced anyone. I could see Mattie was torn between her past and her future. I told her it was up to her. She'd know which way the maiden ran on the night. Who gave chase and who she would allow to claim her was up to her. The Horned One might choose me, but I sense this Spring a younger man with longer legs will run the Beltane maze."

"Why didn't she tell me?" Colin wailed. "I've been so angry; I haven't known what to do."

"Anger and sense never make good bedfellows," Zeb chuckled. "Now, Ruth. What else do we need to do here?"

She looked around. They'd done a good job of clearing all the brambles and wood away from the wellhouse, only stalks were left in the ground.

"Can we make a place for Moose in the middle of the pyre?"

Zeb frowned. "Why do you want to burn her? We could just leave her out for the foxes."

"And risk them spreading the curse all over the village? No, she burns. Your clothes need to go on too."

"You can't ask us to walk around naked!" Colin looked so shocked and scared, Ruth wanted to laugh but knew she couldn't without hurting his feelings. Just at that moment, the phone in her pocket began to buzz. She pulled it out and walked a few paces away from the others, glad of the interruption.

"Is everything ok?" She could hear the worry in Lord Peter's voice through the crackles.

"Not really," she said. "I'll tell you everything later. I need your help. This is what I want you to do." She wondered what he must be thinking as she explained she wanted the four of them to be washed in water from the Nun's well in his garden, then smudged with smoke from a chafing dish, before finishing their drying in the sun.

"You want me to do this too?" She could tell Peter wasn't sure.

"Yes," she said, "after everything Isaac Graves has tried to do with you, I'd feel safer if you joined the cleansing."

217

"Aren't you going to be here? To supervise?" he added quickly.

"Not this time," she felt herself smiling at the thought he wanted her with them. "I'm going home to do something similar at the Blackwell, after we've burned everything here. It's mine and it will be easier for me there."

As she ended the call, she noticed Greg was also on his phone.

"We'll be wanting herbs for the fire and some paper," he explained. "Granny's sending Ally Tulliver to throw them over the stile, so we can pick them up."

Colin started to take off his jacket. "You really want us to burn our clothes?"

Ruth shook her head. "Not you and not Zeb, unless you want to. Greg?" She looked over to where he was standing. Their eyes met and he nodded. "Take everything out of your pockets. Those can be smudged. Don't throw anything on until the fire's going well. Then wait in the truck until the fire can be left. Make your way to the back of the Priory. Lord Peter's waiting for you."

"How do you know all this?" Colin asked. "Mattie said you were a proper city-lady when she first met you. Didn't even know how to make soup."

"She's my cousin, Colin," Greg interjected, "granddaughter to Anvil Iles and Granny Blackwell. I reckon they've been teaching her in her sleep to make up for lost time. Don't you worry about what she knows or doesn't know. Her knowledge is sound enough. Would you have thought to use a sunwise cleansing on a curse?"

Colin shook his head. "Don't have much need to deal with curses, but I'll remember iffen I do."

He picked up his slasher and began to make a hole in the centre of the brambles while Greg and Zeb picked up Moose and carried her as best they could up to the pyre. Ruth saw Ally waving on the other side of the stile. She walked up the hill towards her wondering how many more times she would have to climb up and down the hill today.

Ally passed her a pile of old newspapers, followed by a large bundle of red-topped sticks and a bag of leaves.

"Granny said to put the St John's wort in the fire by the lamb; the mugwort is for smudging." She reached into her pocket and handed over a bag of charcoal discs. "Greg knows how to set these up in a chafing dish but Granny wasn't sure what you were going to do."

"I didn't think it was a good idea to go with them. Being hosed down with cold water with four naked men isn't really my idea of fun anymore." She smiled and Ally laughed with her. "I'm going to wash my clothes with lavender and then have a cold bath down by the Black well. Do you think that will be enough?" She took three charcoal bricks out of the bag and put them in her pocket, giving Ally the mugwort to hold while she transferred a large handful into a clean tissue for her own use.

"Granny was going to suggest something similar. She did say not to forget your hair."

Ruth nodded. "I can put some drops of lavender oil in my shampoo."

Ally passed her some small bottles and a lighter. "Granny made these up for you. You mustn't go into your house until you're cleansed. Go to the well first, then smudge, then go to the house and put everything in the washing machine."

Ruth groaned. "Just what I need on a Sunday afternoon. A cold wash followed by a naked dash through the orchard. Whatever will the hens think!"

Ally laughed and turned back to the Rectory. Ruth wondered if she should have asked how Andrea was doing but she was sure Ally would have told her if anything changed.

Ruth liked Ally. She was always kind and cheerful. Laughing together had lightened her mood, making everything more possible.

Greg was already in the truck when she reached the bonfire. The three of them scrunched up the newspapers and pushed them into spaces near the ground. Zeb made a torch and went round lighting the paper until it was almost burned away and he threw it on top of the pyre. Soon the fire began to roar with flames shooting high into the sky forcing them back with its heat.

So many emotions played across Ruth's mind. She mourned the innocent lamb, then, as the flames soared, so did her anger towards Isaac Graves. If he hadn't cursed the well, none of this would have happened and they wouldn't need to do what had to be done. As the flames died down, she found herself thinking about Isaac the man. She wondered whether he felt trapped. His superior gave him an impossible mission. He knew he couldn't live much longer with his failing heart. Maybe he thought the curse would be his salvation. He'd be able to die in peace, his work done.

But it didn't happen, did it Isaac? The curse trapped you here and weak men have been using you ever since for their own ends. Do you want to leave?

She looked towards the wellhouse and thought she saw a familiar, clerical figure.

"You know nothing of me, Blackwell whore!" The voice was beside her. Fear held her fast. "Just like all the peasants here, wanting something they shouldn't, using me to pursue their evil wishes. Fair words fill no promises. Why should I leave before the Devil claims all your maggot-ridden souls?"

Black smoke swirled, a snaking line along the grass towards the fire. Ruth watched in horror as flames began to run towards her. She screamed. She knew if she ran they would follow. The fire would consume her whatever she did.

"Little hare," she heard Greg's voice in her head. "Hares jump the flames. No harvest fire shall burn thee."

She saw Zeb and Colin trying to beat out the flames with slasher blades but it was just making them worse. Already they were past her, curling back towards the pyre so the three of them were trapped inside its walls.

"Jump!" she screamed. "Jump with me!" She held out her arms, feeling their hands join with hers. "Jump now!"

The heat was intense, then they were rolling down the damp, grassy hillside and everything was cold and wet.

Colin was the first to get to his feet.

"What was that?" he asked, smears of ash on his hands and face.

Zeb sat up groaning. "Whatever it was, I'm too old for all this. I want a nice cup of tea and a nap."

"So do I," agreed Ruth, "but we can't. That was Isaac Graves. He didn't take too kindly to my suggestion he leave."

Zeb's pickup was moving slowly down the hill towards them with Greg at the wheel. He rolled down the window.

"Everyone ok?"

"I think so," Ruth got to her feet slowly. "Thanks for the suggestion about the hare."

"What are you talking about?" Greg's blank expression made her wonder who had been talking to her in her head. It sounded like Greg. Maybe their grandfather had come to the rescue. Whoever it was, she was grateful.

She looked up towards the bonfire. All the brambles were burned down. No-one would believe the inferno they'd just faced. Time to go.

Colin went back up the hill to retrieve the three slashers and threw them in the truck bed before climbing into the cab. Zeb was driving with Greg sandwiched in the middle.

She waved at them as they drove towards the gateway, then trudged after them, ensuring the heavy, oak gate was fastened securely before she made her way home along the bottom road.

CHAPTER THIRTY-SIX

The sound of closing curtains roused her from sleep. In her dream she was trying to herd the lamb across the flames with the help of two wolfhounds. The lamb kept twisting and turning as the flames followed them across the field. She kept calling to the two dogs to follow but although one stuck closely to her side, the other refused to leave the tree line. All the while, the crackle of the fire was coming closer and closer.

Ruth opened her eyes. It took her several moments to realise where she was and why she was lying naked under the living room throw. It wasn't as long as a blanket and her feet stuck out from the bottom.

She remembered the biting cold of the Blackwell water as she scrubbed herself clean underneath the trees. It sapped all her remaining energy and it was all she could do to drag herself onto the sofa after setting throwing her clothes into the washing machine. She remembered pulling the rug over herself, but nothing else.

Lord Peter was tending the fire in the wood burner. It was sparks shooting up the chimney which had woken her. She watched him poking at the logs, thinking what a comforting sight it made.

"What are you doing here?" she asked, pulling the rug around her more securely.

"Did I wake you? You were fast asleep when I arrived." He shut the

223

wood burner doors and turned towards her. "I thought you might be cold and I wasn't sure whether your heating came on automatically, so I took the liberty of lighting the fire. You don't mind, do you?" He stood up; his face seemed suddenly unsure whether he had done the right thing. She held out her hand to draw him closer.

"It was kind of you to think of me, even if the fire did bring some unpleasant dreams."

Lord Peter took her hand in both of his. "I'm sorry if I brought it all back. They said how brave you were, jumping the flames in the field. You must have been terrified!"

"There wasn't time to be scared," she said. "I wouldn't have known what to do if a voice in my head hadn't told me to jump." She smiled at him. "You'll be locking me up if I talk about hearing voices."

"I won't tell anyone," he promised, stroking the back of her hand. "My motto has always been to accept whatever help is offered, especially if you're in a tight place and there seems no way out."

Ruth sat up, making sure the rug was tightly wrapped around her.

"You still haven't told me why you're here."

"I was worried about you. Besides, Granny asked us all to meet here to discuss what to do next."

Just at that moment, Mattie came to the doorway, a tea towel over her arm. "Granny said you missed lunch, so I've cooked a roast dinner for the three of us. I've just got to make the gravy."

Ruth made her excuses and ran upstairs to get dressed. It wouldn't do to meet anyone else wrapped only in a throw. She found her favourite powder blue jeans with a matching blouse and sweater and hoped Peter would appreciate her choice of colours.

Dinner was delicious with Mattie excelling with the Yorkshire pudding surrounding a slab of roast beef followed by rhubarb crumble and custard.

They were drinking a cup of coffee when the front doorbell rang. Ruth went to greet the visitors and ushered them into the living room while Mattie put the kettle on.

"Greg's not coming," Granny told her as she took off her coat. "Henry found the foot and mouth notices to hang on the gates and the stile and they're marking off the top of the well field with old police incident tape in case anyone thinks of wandering off the footpath down to Glebe Farm."

"We need to ward the field." Ruth said, taking Zeb's hat and hanging it on the end of the bannisters.

"Why?" asked Ally Tulliver, who arrived at that moment with Colin. He disappeared into the kitchen, closing the door before anyone could hear what he was saying to Mattie.

"To keep Isaac Graves out of the church when the Bishop arrives and anyone else from seeking his services."

"Seeking his services?" Ally looked bemused but didn't say any more when Granny thrust a mug of tea in her direction.

Ruth waited until everyone was seated and with Granny's permission began to outline her understanding of events.

"I think Isaac Graves is a trapped spirit who has been warped by the evil intentions of those villagers who have sought his help," Ruth began. Ally Tulliver gasped, spilling her tea. Mattie got up to run to the kitchen for a cloth

"Sit down, girl, and let Ruth get on with it." Granny barked.

"He thought cursing the well and the Earl would be the end of everything. He didn't realise that if he died without releasing the curse it would tie him to the well and he wouldn't be able to pass over."

"Poor thing," breathed Ally.

"Don't get feeling too sorry for him," warned Granny, "He was responsible for the death of the fourteenth Earl and his son and because of that the whole village suffered. Don't forget Tom Hastings and Edwin Marlon who were hung for poaching, not to mention Old Mother Jenkins who froze to death because she wasn't allowed to gather fuel in the wood."

Everyone nodded. Colin looked as if he was about to say something to Lord Peter, but Granny hushed him.

"What's done is done. What we need now is a reconciliation of old differences and work together to stop any more harm coming to the village." Again, there was a circle of nods. "Go on, Ruth."

"I believe there have been at least two villagers, who made Isaac kill, maim or attack others they consider as rivals. Zeb, your uncle was one and I think the other is Lawrence Graves."

There was a chorus of gasps and "Really?" and "What makes you think that?" from around the room.

"Why, Ruth? Why Lawrence?" Ally asked.

Ruth chewed her lip. She wasn't certain she had the evidence to accuse Lawrence, but she was sure he was behind the assault on Lord Peter. He had changed so much over the time she had known him. When they first met, he seemed shy and earnest. Now, he was nothing but a petty-minded tyrant.

"Isaac Graves has attempted three recent attacks, two on me and one on Peter." She hesitated for a moment. "I'm sure Lawrence sees me as a threat to his position with the choir and he hates Peter because of his family. He idolises Isaac. He's also tried to kill Andrea's baby."

This time there was a stunned silence, only broken by a sob from Ally Tulliver. Granny patted her hand.

"You're sure about this?" Lord Peter asked.

"He's been giving her pennyroyal," Ruth said. "Granny, Ally and I saw the half-empty flask. It's an abortifactant." Ruth heard her voice rising in anger. She took some deep breaths to try to calm down. Lawrence's actions made her blood boil. "I also heard footsteps running away the night you were attacked with the fireball. I believe it was Lawrence who orchestrated that attempt."

"What do we do now?" asked Colin. "Lock Lawrence up?"

"Not unless you're volunteering to look after his mother," Granny snapped. Ruth saw both Colin and Mattie cringe at the thought.

"As I said earlier," Ruth continued, "we need to contain Isaac until next Sunday, unless anyone feels he should be dealt with earlier?"

"Best we get the Bishop over with," Granny said. "I'll go and secure the field boundary with Greg when we've finished here. At least that will keep him in one place."

"Will you call Oscar and Belle, Peter?" For a moment she thought he was going to ask her what she was talking about but in the end he just sighed and gave a low whistle. A few moments later, they heard a scratching at the door and all three wolfhounds came into the room.

"Good dogs," Lord Peter greeted each one then sent Oscar and Belle to Granny but Finn he kept by his side, scratching him under the ears. Granny held out her hand in front of her, obviously unable to see the dogs themselves. "Just tell them what you want them to do. They're very good at protecting boundaries, especially if they're warded."

"Sit," said Granny firmly and Ruth watched the two of them settle either side of her chair.

"On Easter Monday afternoon, Adrian, Peter, the choir and I will walk the parish boundary, starting at the Priory, down the bridle path to Crabtree Corner, through Long Meadow to Badger's drift then up to the church and back to the Priory along Glebe Farm footpath."

"Why beat the bounds?" asked Ally.

"We'll be casting the largest circle around the whole village. I'm going to teach the choir the monk's blessing chant and maybe they will join us and hold the circle for us later on."

"You want medieval monks to hold a circle?" Ally was not convinced.

"Don't knock it," said Colin, "we need all the help we can get. They like Ruth, they showed her the cheese cave."

"Colin. I need you to build us a yew arch to be secured in the ground by St John's well between north and west. It doesn't need to be in place before 6pm but everything needs to be ready for the final circle by 7pm. You should also prepare some wooden fencing to go around the well to stop any animals getting in. We could do with a new door for the well house but that won't be needed until we do the individual well blessings the following Sunday. Someone might like to warn Jack Henson, I don't really know him well enough."

"You planning two circles or three?" asked Granny.

"Why is Ruth planning anything," asked Mattie suddenly. "I mean, she's not even a full member of our Circle."

Ruth held her breath. She had wondered if anyone was going to challenge her ability to take charge. What Mattie said was true. She'd only attended one ritual and no-one had asked her about initiation into the Grove.

"It's Madron's choice," Granny's voice was firm. Beside her, Ally Tulliver nodded vigorously.

"Poor Andrea can't do anything, the way she is. She asked Ruth to take her place. It's only right, with her being the Wealla Holda, Keeper of Water."

"But you look after the Ladywell," protested Mattie, "why don't you take charge? She's only been here five minutes."

"I keep Ladywell but I can't walk between the worlds like Ruth. I wouldn't know where to start with Isaac Graves. He scares me something terrible."

"Do you have a problem with any of Ruth's actions so far, Matilda?"

"No, Granny."

"Good, then let's continue. I need to get going as soon as possible."

Ruth cleared her throat; conscious Peter was squeezing her hand in support.

"My plan is for two further circles. One around the church and half the well field and the final one, the rescue circle, around the well itself."

"Rescue circle?" asked Lord Peter

"My Grandmother used to perform rescue circles for spirits trapped here on earth. You visualise a bridge or a gateway between this world and the next and invite any lost souls to make their way over. You also call helpers from the other side to come and support them during the crossing. I used to help her as a child until I left home. They're always very grateful."

"I don't reckon Isaac Graves is going to be grateful," said Colin. "Look what he did to you the last time you asked him to leave."

"We hadn't prepared properly. Next time will be different."

"It better be," muttered Colin. "I don't want to go through that again!".

Granny stood up. "Right, that's that, then. Everyone knows what we're doing. We'll pass the message along to everyone else on Tuesday and Thursday if not before." Calling the dogs to her, she and Zeb grabbed their coats and disappeared into the night. Ally followed. Colin helped Mattie clear away, leaving Ruth and Peter alone in the living room.

"Are you sure this will work?" he asked.

"How can we ever be sure of anything," she said, allowing herself to be drawn into his hug. "All we can do is hope."

CHAPTER THIRTY-SEVEN

It was Monday evening before Ruth managed to catch up with Greg. Balancing movement orders for Henry's new calves and yet another choir rehearsal kept her away from the forge.

She was surprised how amiable Lawrence was with everyone but her. She wondered if the presence of several parents listening from the nave was keeping his temper in check when it came to the choir members, but it didn't stop him pointing out every minor error she made. He gloated in every wrong note she struck. There was something very strange about his mood. When Ruth caught glimpses of him through the organ mirror, he seemed excited, bouncing up and down on the balls of his feet as he conducted.

She asked Mattie's brother to take her books home for her, saying she needed a walk to clear her head. She decided to go up to Long Cover to see if any of the bluebells were out in the woodlands. A faint blue haze was starting to emerge all along the copse in front of the mill leat.

The forge was silent, its doors shut tight and when she peered through the dirty windows, it looked as if the fire was banked up for the night. She turned away to go through the over the stile into Long Meadow and found Greg sitting on a bench set up behind the hedge. He scooted over to offer her a seat.

"How are you? Did Granny get everything done last night?" she asked, brushing his upper arm in greeting. She couldn't feel the slimy sensation which so repelled her before.

"We did what we could. We used wand and rattle to mark the area we wanted kept safe. Zeb brought a basket of hag stones left over when they cleared Granny Blackwell's cottage and we buried those to strengthen the boundaries."

"Hag stones?" Ruth wondered what they were. Greg felt in his jacket pocket and brought out a piece of flint with a hole in it. He dropped it into her hand with a deep sigh.

"You take this one. You'll need it to keep Isaac away from you. I'm not sure how much help I'll be when you take him on."

Ruth held the stone up in front of her. She couldn't see any signs of tooling, so the hole must be natural. When she turned to ask Greg how such a stone was made, the words caught in her throat. He looked so sad; she could see pain reflecting in his eyes.

"Didn't the cleansing help?" she asked as another deep sigh escaped from him.

"It did what it was supposed to outside. It's inside he's got me, dragging me back to those trees every day to sap my strength."

"Why did you go there? The playgroup?"

A sob shuddered through his body. He crouched forward with his head in his hands rocking backwards and forwards in a silent litany of despair. Ruth knelt in front of him, trying to comfort him. She felt him shake with each tortured breath.

"Whatever it is, you can tell me. You can't keep it locked inside forever if it's causing you so much pain."

His answering howl swept along the valley like a wounded animal.

"I can't. It's not my secret," he wept. "It hurts so much."

She held him tight, offering what support she could until the sobs began to slow and he relaxed against her. He pushed her away, pulling a grubby handkerchief from his pocket and blowing his nose loudly.

Ruth returned to her seat on the bench and they sat in silence watching the sun set behind the opposite hill. She could hear blackbirds singing their evening songs in the hedge behind while a pair of buzzards quartered the fields beyond.

"I know there's a secret you've given your word never to reveal," she said at last, "but I can't see it tearing you apart like this. You put yourself in danger because of your pain. You didn't know what the cursed well would do to you. I wouldn't be surprised if half the dead horses you've been flogging weren't provided by Isaac Graves, just for the joy of watching you suffer."

She felt Greg stiffen beside her as if he were going to protest but after a moment or two he slumped down again.

"You may have something," he said, "I've not been able to think straight for months."

"Ever since you started watching the playgroup kids from above the well."

"Sommat like that."

"How many of those children are yours?"

"Only one." He turned quickly to face her. "How did you know?"

"I watched you watching Arthur after church on Sunday. I saw the hunger on your face. Hunger for your son, who can never know his father."

"It wasn't like you think," he said quickly. "Our Anvil has always offered if a couple can't conceive. Adrian caught mumps when he was a teenager. They both asked me. Andrea didn't come on her own."

"Is the baby she's carrying yours, too?" Greg nodded. "Has Lawrence Graves found out?"

"I don't see how. Why do you ask?"

"He's been giving Andrea pennyroyal. He told her it was Moroccan mint and Andrea was too sick to notice. Granny thinks it started her bleeding yesterday."

Greg shot up from the bench. "I'll kill him. I'll bury him so deep no-one will find the body!"

"You and several others," said Ruth pulling him down to sit again.

"Granny said he has to answer in Court. No-one is to challenge him alone. It's too dangerous. The only trouble is, I can't see a judge finding against him when Andrea drank it willingly. He'll say she should have known what it was. He'll plead he was only trying to help."

"It's not a court like you have in the city," Greg said. "It's our Court."

"Colin threatened Stanley Clackett with Court when someone put sheep in his horse pond. Stanley was really scared, couldn't get away fast enough. What is this Court?"

"You'll see. Lawrence can't run anywhere until we've had justice. He always was a lying, snivelling, little toe-rag. He'll pay for what he's done."

CHAPTER THIRTY-EIGHT

The following morning, Ruth was finishing her breakfast when she heard sirens coming down the road past the church. Mattie's mobile rang upstairs then feet thundered down the stairs. The breathless girl crashed into the kitchen door, her face ashen.

"It's terrible. We have to go. Now."

"What's happened?"

"Colin found Mrs Graves floating in the river. The police have brought frogmen to pull her out. I need to go to him."

Ruth was too shocked for words. Mattie was pulling on her coat and boots and disappeared down through the orchard. Ruth followed, almost forgetting to pull the back door shut in her haste. After crossing the road, they took the short cut over the fence at the back of the Post Office, following the badger track down the steep hill to the clapper bridge over Roelswick Brook into Mill Lane. The path brought them out opposite the Lodge gates.

Four police cars were parked at the end of the lane, the coroner's black ambulance was moving slowly towards the edge of the river.

"They'll get stuck!" Granny said, meeting them in front of the gates. "Not safe driving that close to the bank."

Two policemen were standing near the water with Colin. His horse was grazing on the opposite bank near to the bridleway, her leading rein tied to a willow tree some way back from the river. They could see two dark figures in the water, trying to free something caught where withy branches cascaded over the bank just before the bridge.

People in white coveralls were erecting a tent in front of the ambulance. Two others were crouched by the water waiting to pull the body onto land once it had been retrieved by their wet-suited colleagues. It took a long time to bring the floating shape back through the fast-flowing water to this side of the river. The bank beside the bridge to too steep for anyone to attempt it there.

Mattie had her hand over her mouth, turning away as the corpse was lifted out.

"It's horrible," she moaned.

"It's just a body," said Granny. "Joyce Graves is gone. May she rest in peace."

Ruth noticed the body was clothed in a night dress and bright pink quilted robe. The outer garment was unfastened, the nightie pulled up to her knees, purple varicose veins on her calves standing out against the white of her skin. Ruth couldn't look any longer, it reminded her too much of when her grandfather died.

Colin stumbled over to a bush and was vomiting onto the grass. Mattie gave a cry and ran to him, despite a police officer trying to prevent her.

"Where's Lawrence?" asked Ruth, looking around for the red mini cooper.

"Must have gone to work," said Granny.

"I thought he didn't start until the afternoon on Tuesdays," Ruth told her. "I see him going up the hill when I come back from Home Farm."

As she finished speaking, they saw the red car approaching along the lane and moved out of the way as it screeched to a halt and Lawrence jumped out.

"What's going on? Why are the police here?"

"I'm afraid it's your mother," said Granny.

"Mother? What's wrong with mother? She was fast asleep in bed when I left." Lawrence's face was white.

"Mr Graves?" A plain clothed policeman came towards them flashing a warrant card. "Could we have a word? I'm afraid there's been an accident. If you would just come with me." He led Lawrence around the back of the Lodge towards the tent. Ruth and Granny tried to follow but blue incident tape had been put up around the area and a uniformed officer was standing in front of it to deter visitors.

"No!" They heard Lawrence scream then he came running out and collapsed against the stone wall which bordered the Lodge.

"It's all my fault," they heard him moan.

"Why do you say that, Sir?" asked the detective.

"We were talking about the otters last night. I told her I'd seen the babies out for their first swim yesterday. She must have come out to look for them after I went shopping, slipped on the mud and fell in." He began to cry. The detective motioned to a constable standing close by and she led Lawrence into the house.

"Nothing more to do here," Granny announced. She motioned for Mattie to join them and Colin followed. "I'll ask Henry to send Gus to take Molly back to Home Farm. You can pick her up when you've had a cup of tea. Come on."

She didn't look to see if they were following as she set off down the lane back to her cottage.

Gillian dropped by on the way home from taking Harry to playgroup. She was surprised to see the four of them sitting around Granny's table staring at their empty mugs.

"I'm so sorry, Gill," Ruth said. "I didn't realise what the time was. I'll make it up this afternoon."

"What's going on?" Gillian asked, "You look as if somebody's died."

Mattie burst into tears and Colin put his arm around her.

"Colin found Joyce Graves in the river this morning. The police recovered her body not an hour ago," Granny told her.

Gillian caught hold of the sink to steady herself. "Whatever was she doing by the riverbank? I didn't think she went outside by herself since she had that bad fall last year."

"Lawrence told the police she must have gone to look at the new otter kits while he was out shopping." Ruth said.

Granny was unnaturally silent, her mouth a thin, straight line. They heard Zeb come in the back door, banging his boots against the wall as he took them off.

"Dolly was right then," he called as he came in, stopping short as he caught Granny's expression.

"Can you do without Ruth for a while?" Granny asked Gillian. "There's a few things we need to discuss."

Ruth's heart sank. She would much rather go to work and try to imagine this was a normal day but when Granny mentioned "discussing things", no-one argued.

"Yes, of course." Gillian looked at her watch. "I'd better get back, the tanker's supposed to delivering oil around ten o'clock."

"Mattie, Colin, get yourselves up to the Priory and let them know what's happened. Can you ring Mark and ask him to call me?"

"Yes, Granny." There was a loud scraping of chairs against the flagstones as the kitchen emptied, leaving the three of them.

"It's better those three don't know just yet." Granny said, getting up to turn the kettle on.

"Don't know what?" Granny's grim expression and Zeb's strange comment was unsettling Ruth. She was sad Joyce Graves was dead, but she'd never met the woman face to face. The only time she encountered her was the night she went to ask for a replacement Benedicite and that was weeks ago.

"Lawrence may not be telling the truth."

Ruth felt a cold shiver run down her spine. She heard the kettle boiling and felt someone remove the empty mug from her fingers. She hadn't realised how tightly she had been holding it.

"How could you think that?"

Granny took down another mug from the dresser. "Dolly told us."

Ruth heard the skitter of claws on flagstones as the spaniel dashed into the room from the garden, wagging her tail wildly.

"Daft dog, sit." Zeb placed the teapot on the table and sat down, rubbing his hand along Dolly's soft flank.

"What do you mean, Dolly told you?" Ruth looked from one to the other. Zeb was nodding and Granny expression softened a little.

"I don't know how she does it, but Dolly always knows when someone dies in the village. It doesn't matter where she is, she comes to Zeb and whimpers until he comforts her." The dog came over and licked her hand then settled herself on the floor beside Zeb.

"I don't understand how Dolly's actions make you think Lawrence is lying about his mother's death," Ruth said.

Granny sighed as she pulled the three mugs towards her and poured them each more tea. She sat for a moment blowing the steam away to cool it before taking a long sip.

"I want to believe Lawrence. Truly I do, but as Gillian said, how did she manage to walk to the riverbank by herself? There was no sign of her walker or stick anywhere. Besides, Dolly told us she died at four o'clock this morning. Lawrence said she was asleep when he went out shopping."

"He might have thought she was asleep and not wanted to bother her." Ruth didn't know why she was trying to defend Lawrence. The alternative was just too dreadful to contemplate. "You know she used to abuse him."

Zeb seemed surprised, but Granny shook her head. "I think she hoped Lawrence would grow up to be the man his father wasn't. Lawrence was always a disappointment to her. I've seen her beat him black and blue as a child but there was nothing I could do back then. I hoped it had stopped. What makes you say it didn't?"

Ruth told them about losing her music and going down to Mill Lodge to ask for another copy.

"I realised Lawrence's mother was very deaf because he had to repeat everything several times, very loudly. The front door was open. I could hear every word. She started grumbling about him not having a wife and children to keep the family name going. There was a noise. I'm sure she was hitting something as she spoke. I know she hurt Lawrence because he shouted in pain." She hesitated then went on. "I was going to tell you, but it brought back horrible memories. Memories I try not to think about, so I forgot. I'm sorry."

"Nothing to be sorry about." Granny said. "You couldn't know for sure what was going on. No-one did. Now it's too late."

Zeb got up and disappeared into the front room. When he returned, he was holding a white piece of paper with a blue cross above some gothic print. He put it down on the table in front of Ruth. She stared at the Benedicite, the one which had gone missing from her first choir practice.

"Where did you get this?"

"Found it tucked under one of the wooden roof pieces we took off St John's Well. It wasn't damaged in any way. Just seemed a strange thing to find so I brought it back. I'd forgotten all about it until you mentioned it."

"Lawrence must have taken it and put it there, but why?"

"Maybe he thought your copy was better than his."

"That makes no sense." Ruth felt herself getting angry. Everyone was playing games. Why didn't people just tell the truth.

"I think he wanted to give Isaac something of yours, so the Rev would know how to find you," said Granny. "It's easy enough for Isaac to move between the well and the church. Any further, he'd have to have help finding his way around the village, it's all so different from when he was alive."

"That's sick!" Ruth put down her mug on the table so hard, tea splashed onto the cloth. "What have I ever done to hurt him?"

"Isaac thinks you're Miriam. Maybe he thinks she had the power to send him away, even though she never used it. Maybe Lawrence doesn't want you to try. I don't know." She shrugged her shoulders and got up to put her mug in the sink.

"Are you going to tell the police?"

Zeb laughed. "Do you think they'd believe us?"

"It all depends how soon they start to ask questions," said Granny. "Until then we need to be extra vigilant. If Lawrence has started to take things into his own hands, we need to do what we can to keep everyone safe."

CHAPTER THIRTY-NINE

The rest of the day passed in a blur. Ruth didn't manage to work at Home Farm until Wednesday morning. Even then, she was hardly able to get anything done because of the constant stream of visitors and phone calls, most of them wanting to know about the goings on at Mill Lodge.

Henry was worried about the new calves he'd bought. Two of them had a bad case of scours and they were all losing condition.

"If I didn't know better, I'd think someone cursed them."

Ruth knew he was trying to joke, but it was in poor taste, especially as she was still worried about what was needed to cleanse St John's Holy Well.

When the surgery rang to say the vet was going to be an hour late due to a difficult foaling out at Hollow Barrow Farm, she went to give Henry the message herself, taking the opportunity to visit the cowshed where the calves were penned up. They were all lying down when she went inside, not even bothering to greet her. She knew they weren't right.

She stared into the six water buckets. Through murky water she could see green slime covering the bottom. Tom was next door in the milking parlour. She called him over and showed him the buckets. He scratched his head.

"They were clean when I filled them up yesterday. Almost looks as if someone has swapped these two for the pig swill buckets." He took them away. As Ruth followed him outside, she noticed the elder tree which usually covered the doorway had been hacked almost down to the ground.

"Did Henry do this?" she asked.

Tom turned off the water where he was scrubbing the dirty buckets and stared at the damage. It was obvious he'd not seen it before from his shocked face.

"Why would he do such a thing?" Tom said, "That tree's been there before Zeb brought Granny home after their wedding; it weren't doing any harm. Granny always said it produced the best flowers for her elderflower champagne. She said it were there to protect the cattle."

Now someone's destroyed it and we've got sick calves. Ruth kept her thoughts to herself. She couldn't think who might have chopped it down. There was no sign of the branches anywhere in the yard but when she looked over the wall into the pig pen, pieces of wood lay scattered all around. The leaves had been eaten and she could see teeth marks everywhere.

She went back to remaining gnarled roots sticking up beside the door. She ran her hands over the limbs. The cuts were smooth, not ragged as they would have been from a saw. She looked at the wall of the cowshed and saw white marks on the stone. An axe maybe? Who would be skilled with an axe? Anyone who chopped wood for a fire. Anyone could have done this, but why and why hadn't anyone noticed it sooner?

She thought about the door. It was the original entrance to the cowshed. This was the first time she'd seen the top of the stable door open, letting light in for the calves. Most people came and went through the milking parlour. Apart from feeding the calves twice a day, they wouldn't go into the building and when they did it would be through the other entrance. She'd only noticed the tree's absence because she could see it from her office across the yard.

She touched the cuts again, wondering how long ago this happened. It couldn't have been in broad daylight and if a stranger had come during the night why didn't Tess bark? She looked over to where the short-haired collie was lying asleep in a patch of sunlight. Of course, Tess liked to go hunting when she was let loose at night, she probably wasn't even around when the perpetrator was in the yard. She felt sick to think anyone would use such violence to a healthy, living tree for no reason.

He must have a reason. She reached the bottom of the stairs leading to her office. A thought struck her, making her grip the banister to stop herself from swaying. What if this were another act inspired by Isaac? Was Lawrence mad enough to go out in the middle of the night to chop down the witches' tree?

If he was trying to frighten them, he was succeeding but Ruth refused to give in without a fight. She didn't know what to do to protect them against such evil, but she guessed the women of the circle would know. Sitting back at her desk, she rang Mattie.

"What would people use to protect animals and children in the old days?"

"Rowan," said Mattie. "Rowan crosses tied with red ribbon. They were hung on cradles to stop the fairy folk from snatching a child and exchanging it for one of their own."

"I need seven. Six to hang above the stalls, another, larger one to nail on the cowshed door. Someone's trying to hurt our new calves."

When Ruth went home, she found the kitchen table piled high with sticks and lengths of red ribbon. Mattie, her mother, Lizzie Ackerley and Colin's youngest sister, Carly, were all busy putting crosses together.

"It were a good job we had that storm the other week. Found lots of rowan the other side of the Abbotts." Lizzie said, passing two sticks for Carly to hold while she wound the ribbon around the centre. "Strikes me, if you've noticed a need for a Rowan cross at Home Farm, we all need them. Something's not right in this village, so we all need to be vigilant."

Hearing Colin's usually cheerful mother talk in such a way, made the sick feeling of dread she'd experienced earlier in the day return in full force. Ruth fled out into the orchard, seeking a hidden place where she could think. The remaining lambs were resting under the roadside hedge. She tried to ignore the hens' appeals for more food as she could see the feeder was full.

She walked down to the hazel guarding her well, coming to a sudden stop as she saw the shadow of a figure on the other side of the tree. When she gathered the courage to peer around the branches, she found Greg bending over an iron structure, tightening a bolt. He straightened up as she gasped and turned to face her holding a large spanner.

"Don't scare me like that!" she cried, clutching the tree trunk for support.

He stepped away from her towards the road gate, revealing a beautiful, wrought iron bench set into the ground.

"Who's chasing you now, little hare?" He held out his hand, guiding her down onto the bench." "I'd never set out to frighten you. You know that." She nodded, not trusting herself to speak. His appearance was so unexpected, for a split second she had seen Lawrence standing over her well, his axe in his hand. It took some time before the calming trickle of the Blackwell and the warmth of Greg's hand stopped her shaking. She released her grip and ran her fingers over the delicate tracery of the bench ends.

"You made this for me?" She couldn't understand why he would bring her such a beautiful object.

"I've watched you, since you called me to you, that first night," he said. "You've been alone a long time, well before you moved to this village. You're used to hiding in shadows. Granny believes everyone prefers to be part of a crowd. She tends to jump in with both feet no matter where she is.

"She has a good heart and she's usually right, but I remember your face that first morning you came downstairs into your kitchen and found us all eating breakfast at your table without asking you if you minded us being there."

"I know you were trying to help and I really did need help." Ruth spoke quickly, trying to cover up the rawness of her feelings and her acknowledgement of how perceptive he was, this strange cousin of hers.

"When I first saw this little glade, I thought what a perfect place it would be for you to hide away by yourself with just the water for company. Specially as you've been given the role of water-keeper. It takes time to understand what's being asked of you. You'll be safe here"

She looked away, trying not to cry. She wasn't used to people understanding her perspective, let alone her needs.

"What do you think?" His face seemed troubled by her silence. "Don't you like it?"

When her voice still refused to work, she wrapped her arms around his chest and hugged him tightly before dropping a kiss against his cheek.

"It's perfect. Thank you so much. You know me better than I do myself."

He grinned at her as she released him, then bent down to pick up his spanner from the soil, dropping it back into his tool bag.

"I set the bench here against that old walnut. Walnut's good for blocking energy from other people, especially if they want to stop you doing summat. I reckon between the walnut and the hazel you'll be able to sit here and forge your own path, whatever that might be."

Ruth shook her head, smiling at him in wonder. "How did you get to be so wise about trees and people?"

"Can't help it, growing up here." He grinned at her. "Of course, there is one more thing we have to do before the Blackwell is back to its original form."

Ruth frowned. His words filled her with a sense of unease but at the same time it piqued her curiosity. "What do you mean?"

He pointed to a triangular stone sticking out of the bank. "The Blackwell always had two basins, one for folk to ask questions and the lower one for animals. It was the lower one you unearthed, which is why no-one questioned the lambs drinking here. I'm guessing you never noticed this capstone."

Something began to niggle at the back of her mind. Something she'd been reading in the Earl's diaries. When they boarded over St John's well, he mentioned two wells. At the time it didn't make any sense as she was only interested in the well in the field.

"You mean this is the well of false oracles?"

"Not so sure they were false," Greg said, pulling a small shovel from his bag. "Unless you didn't like the answer to your question. Granny Blackwell said her grandmother told her you could ask the well if your relative far away were alive or dead, also what had happened to any cattle or other stolen goods."

Ruth sat down on the bench. She wasn't sure her knees were going to hold her up for much longer. "He wrote about it in the diaries Lord Peter leant me," she said. "The earl who built over St John's well. His son was a doctor and he made it impossible for the villagers to seek healing from the Holy Well. He put a capstone over the Blackwell and buried it at the same time."

"'Bout time the true well saw the light of day again, don't you think?" He began to stab the spade into the bank above the stone, tossing the earth aside until the huge slab of stone was revealed. After stopping to get his breath back, Greg motioned Ruth to grab hold of the other side. Together, they slid the stone aside until another, narrower stone trough was revealed.

The stone was heavy. Ruth was relieved when it was safely stored behind the seat where it couldn't fall and hurt anyone.

She stared into the well, amazed there was no build-up of silt over the centuries. The water pipe had been diverted to feed only the lower tank, but once Greg moved it back to its original position, the trough began to fill, the water sparkling in the dappled light. There was a lip in the right wall, so once the top container was full, water began to cascade into the lower one. The added movement and sound made the little clearing feel completely different.

"How do you know the answers to any questions?" Ruth asked as Greg replaced his shovel inside the tool bag. He stood for a moment watching the water.

"It's not really my place to say," he began, "I'm not the water guardian. I do remember something about watching the bubbles. If bubbles rise, then all is well. If the water clouds, then the person is either severely ill or died. Haven't got a clue about anything lost. You're going to need the well to teach you."

Ruth hugged him again. "Thank you," she whispered, feeling him stiffen as though her touch were not welcome. As soon as she released him, he gripped the tool bag tightly and was gone through the gate before she could say another word. She heard him whistling as he walked up the road towards the forge. She sat back on the bench, letting her head rest against the cool walnut bark.

All she could hear was a gentle rustling of nut leaves in the afternoon breeze and a blackbird singing somewhere out in the orchard. Beside her, the spring continued its journey from the earth into the two stone troughs, then down the overflow to disappear amongst the trees on its way to the brook. She felt her fears drift away with the water. She had strength now to face the future.

CHAPTER FORTY

Ruth spent the evening practicing for the Easter Sunday service. No matter what happened with Lawrence, she wanted the choir to do their best. When she finished, she felt restless. She heard a lamb bleat and stood out by the orchard gate wondering what could have disturbed them. For a moment she thought she saw a light flicker inside the church but put it down to moonlight reflecting on one of the windows. The moon was almost full, but clouds kept the silver light to a fleeting haze.

In the middle of the night, barking woke her. This time it was the howling alarm from the well field. She pulled on some clothes and picked up the torch from her bedside table.

Mattie stood rubbing her eyes at the top of the stairs while Ruth put on her coat and unlocked the front door.

"What's happening?"

"I don't know. If I'm not back in fifteen minutes, get Colin dressed and tell Greg to meet me at the church." Granny insisted Colin stay with them after the events of Tuesday morning. It didn't bother Ruth which bedroom he slept in as long as it wasn't hers.

"I'm awake." Colin peered at her over the banisters. "I'll come with you."

"I'm only going to check. It's probably nothing. I'll be back before you find your boots."

Ruth opened the front door and found Finn waiting for her at the roadside gate. He was whining and trotted off towards the steps as soon as he knew she was following. She walked quickly up the road to the church. There was light inside but not electric. The porch gates were both flung back against the wall and when she shone her flashlight towards the door, that too was wide open.

She hesitated, trying to guess what she might find inside. She didn't feel nauseous, so it wasn't anything to do with Isaac Graves. Perhaps Adrian had come in for some special prayers. Why hadn't he put the lights on? Why leave the door open? Was it someone trying to steal the collection box?

Footsteps came running up the street towards her. She turned off her torch and slipped inside the porch.

"Ruth? Ruth, where are you?" It was Greg. She was so relieved, she wanted to hug him.

"Here." She stepped out into his torch beam. "I was too scared to go in. Stupid of me."

"Not stupid, sensible."

They walked in together, Greg reaching around the door post to put on the nave lights. The carnage in front of them stopped them where they stood. The lectern with its huge, golden eagle was on its side. The chancel floor was strewn with debris from a smashed table. The metal cross from the high altar was lying against the communion rail. The candles were burned down to a stub but still flickering. It was their light she must have seen as she approached.

They walked slowly up the nave. As she reached the chancel steps, Ruth gasped and grabbed Greg's arm.

"There's blood on the cross. Look!"

"And on the carpet. Someone's been attacked!" He pointed to blood spatters on the chancel tiles and Ruth saw spots on the choir stalls. There were others on the steps and larger smears on the carpet in the nave. They followed them down to the bell tower door, which was also standing open. They stood for a moment looking at the empty space underneath the neatly tied ropes; silence dragging on their ears.

"We're missing something," Greg said, his words making Ruth wince.

"There!" She pointed to the empty corner where the elderly wooden bier usually stood. It always reminded her of an overgrown wheel barrow with its long black handles. Had someone used it to take a body out of the church?

A scream came from behind the church followed by furious barking. They rushed out into the graveyard, their feet crunching along the gravel path and saw the bier resting beside the stile. Mattie was running up the road pointing towards the well field. As they reached the stile, the sky was lit by a huge ball of fire arcing from the well house towards a dark lump on the grass. As it reached the ground, they realised the lump was a body.

Shock planted their feet until Mattie rushed up to them. "Andrea's there!" she gasped. When they followed her pointing finger, they saw another figure slumped halfway down the field wall.

"No!" Greg yelled, jumping over the stile and running down the hill towards her. Just before he got there, another fireball struck exactly where she lay. Her whole body convulsed, then lay still. Greg threw himself on the ground to protect her. Ruth couldn't watch any longer, she scrambled over the stile and ran towards the other body. A fireball struck in front of her, forcing her to throw her arm up to defend her eyes from the blinding light. Like the attack on Lord Peter, these burning spheres had no scorching flames, just ice.

She fell to her knees as she reached the small mound.

"Who is it?" screamed Mattie behind her. After the fireball's brilliance, it was impossible to see. Ruth reached into her coat pocket and brought out the torch. In front of her lay Adrian, his body tossed onto the ground like a rag doll.

The back of his head and his shoulder were dark and muddy as if he'd been dragged across the field by his feet then dumped where he lay.

"Is he dead?" Mattie whispered Ruth leaned over to check his pulse. Adrian groaned.

"No," Ruth felt giddy with relief. "Call an ambulance. Someone did this to them."

Colin lurched to a halt beside them. "Granny said to wrap them up but not move them. She'll be here in a minute."

She glared at him, furious with Granny for thinking she could look after everyone.

"Call the ambulance, Colin. Now. Adrian has been attacked. There's no telling how badly he's hurt. He could need surgery. We have to get him to hospital." She heard Mattie get to her feet behind her and start talking into her phone.

Another fireball whistled towards them. Instinctively, Ruth threw up her arm while Colin pulled Mattie out of the way. She heard the fireball fizzle and plop to the ground in a wet hiss.

"No more," she yelled, scrambling to her feet. "Enough!"

She saw a dark shape flicker in front of the well house and felt familiar nausea pulling at her stomach. Light flared again as Isaac Graves stood rubbing his hands then drawing them back to throw again.

"I said, enough!" Ruth screamed, running down the field towards him. She heard him laugh.

"Enough when imposters leave, and bastards die." The words crawled in the air around her then fell against her skin in a sticky slime. The sky flashed again but he was gone.

CHAPTER FORTY-ONE

Ruth pulled the blanket around her and took another sip of cocoa. She couldn't stop shivering, even though she was sitting against the Rayburn. It was still dark outside, but no-one wanted to go to bed. The ambulance took an age to arrive but eventually took Adrian and Andrea to Chalmsbury Hospital; Granny and Zeb following. Everyone feared Andrea would lose the baby.

"Why were they both in the field?" Mattie said, handing another mug of cocoa to Colin. "There was no reason."

"This may tell us." Greg entered the kitchen and threw a thin book on the kitchen table. He was taking Arthur to Home Farm when a patrol car arrived in the village, alerted by the emergency operator. He was angry to see outsiders intruding in village business, so he sent everyone else back to Pear Tree Cottage. That was over an hour ago and he had just returned.

Greg pulled another chair near the stove, his body hunched over the mug Mattie gave him. She went upstairs to find him another rug. All those who had been in the well field were suffering with bone-aching chill.

"What is it?" Ruth asked pointing to the book.

"Why couldn't he have waited? We had it all planned. Why did he have to try it on his own? Stupid! Stupid! Stupid!" He thumped his fist on the top of the stove so hard, his drink spilled all over his trousers.

Ruth got up to find a cloth. She went to pick up the book as she passed the table. It had a brown, mock-leather cover on it with the title embossed in black, gothic letters.

"Don't touch it," Greg growled at her. "It may have his fingerprints on it."

"Whose?"

"Lawrence's"

"Why would Lawrence have a book called 'Delivering us from evil'?"

"It's not a song book. It's about possession. Evil spirits. It belongs to Adrian. His name is inside the front cover."

Ruth's exhausted brain finally began to make connections.

"This was in the church?"

"Wedged underneath the front choir stall."

"Why didn't you leave it for the police?" She had visions of Greg being dragged into the local police station for tampering with evidence and perverting the course of justice and began to shake again. Greg held out his hand and she let him draw her back to the stove.

"I'll take it back," he promised. "I wanted you to see it first. It's the only thing which makes sense of this mess."

Colin was slumped over the kitchen table, snoring lightly. When Mattie came back with Greg's blanket, she woke Colin up and lead him upstairs. Ruth wished she could follow them, but she knew she wouldn't sleep if she did. Her mind was going round in ever-decreasing circles, trying to make sense of what they knew.

"You think Adrian was trying to get rid of Isaac Graves? I didn't know he even knew about him."

"Maybe Isaac has been taunting him, the same as you."

"I thought I was the only one who could see him."

"We won't know anything until Adrian can talk." Greg sighed deeply, "Who knows when that will be." He drained his cup, ignoring the cloth Ruth was holding out to him to mop up his trousers.

"Isaac left once we arrived," Ruth said, thinking back to when she confronted him. One minute he was standing in front of the well lobbing fire balls at them and the next he was gone. "If only we'd reached the field earlier, maybe we could have stopped him attacking Andrea."

"Can't think like that." Greg gave another deep sigh. "May bees don't fly in September. If I'd come to the church earlier, maybe I'd have stopped the attack on Adrian or maybe I'd be lying there with my head caved in. He never mentioned being part of the Church's Deliverance Ministry. What worries me is if he borrowed this book from someone else and was trying out the prayers for the first time on his own."

Ruth thought back to the mayhem they'd found inside the church. "It can't have been Isaac who attacked Adrian. I thought he couldn't get into the church any more after you and Granny put the wards around the field."

"He can't. Isaac can throw fireballs, but he can't pick up heavy objects. No, there was someone else in the church with Adrian. My guess is he came down to the church sometime this evening intending to go through the deliverance prayers and somehow Lawrence got wind of what he was doing and attacked him."

"But why drag him all the way into the field? Why would you do something like that?" Ruth rubbed her temples, trying to get rid of the headache which threatened to overwhelm her. She noticed Greg staring at one of the fire handles, his eyes glistening. When she tried to put out a hand to comfort him, he pushed her away.

"It must be the baby," he said at last, blowing his nose loudly. "You stopped the pennyroyal. He needed another way of getting rid of it. We made it so Isaac couldn't leave the field, so Lawrence had to bring Andrea down to the well. What wife wouldn't leave her sick bed if her husband was injured."

"You think Lawrence went and fetched her? How? Why didn't Ally wake up?"

Greg shook his head slowly. "I don't know. She was still asleep when I went to see how Arthur was faring. The back door was wide open;

the little man was standing in the doorway, trying to get his wellies on when I got there. She said she heard nothing, nothing at all."

"She must have been beside herself."

"She was. It was the reason I took Arthur over to Home Farm. She wasn't in a fit state to look after him and he'll be better there with the other kiddies. Ally said she'd stay at the Rectory until the morning in case either of them were sent home."

In her mind, Ruth saw the fireball sent from Isaac Graves' hand landing on Andrea and how she convulsed in the blaze of light. She couldn't stop the sob which tore through her.

"Why?" she cried. "Why is he doing this? It's madness."

Greg took her hands and leaned forwards, so their foreheads touched.

"No point in torturing ourselves with whys, lass, we just got to stop him doing anything else." He yawned loudly. "Get yourself to bed now. I'll lock up. We need what rest we can get."

"Do you want the spare bed?" Ruth found herself yawning in return, her body suddenly admitting the great weariness it had been keeping at bay.

Greg shook his head, pointing towards the lounge where he'd slept before. Ruth wanted to suggest he join her upstairs even though she knew it would send out the wrong message. She had forgotten what it was like to share the same sleeping space with another body, to find comfort in another's arms or curl up against a warm, strong back.

Robert always fell asleep the moment his head touched the pillow. His loud snores kept her awake and if he reached for her in the night, she soon learned it wasn't her body he sought but whichever woman he was hunting at the time. In the end it was easier to sleep on the chaise longue in the window, slipping downstairs to make his breakfast well before he woke.

She rolled over in bed, wrapping a pillow inside her empty arms, weeping for Andrea's lost baby, her own estranged child and the sheer helplessness she felt about the whole situation. At one point she thought she heard the stairs creak. A pang of hope shot through her. Maybe Greg was coming to save her from this misery. Silence. Her bedroom door stayed firmly closed but at last she slept.

CHAPTER FORTY-TWO

Ruth dreamed Lawrence was ringing the church bells to call the village to hear his ancestor preach the Easter message. Isaac was banging his fist on the pulpit in a curious rhythm, more like someone knocking on a front door. Ruth opened her eyes. Someone was knocking on the front door. She looked at the clock. Ten am. Where was everyone? She pulled her dressing gown around her and stuffed her feet into slippers.

She heard Mattie yawning as she reached the bottom of the stairs. She opened the door and found two men standing in the porch. She recognised the man in a dishevelled suit as the detective from Mill Lodge two days before. The other was younger, wearing a smart jacket and dark trousers.

"Mrs Turner? Mrs Ruth Turner? I'm Detective Inspector Ross and this is my colleague, Detective Sergeant Cullen."

Ruth stared at them. Why were they here? Surely Robert hadn't implicated her in Mrs Graves murder.

"Please don't say you've come to tell me they're both dead."

The two detectives shared puzzled glances.

"No, who are you talking about?

"Rev and Mrs Hope. They were attacked last night and taken to hospital."

"May we come in?" said the Inspector. "We won't keep you long."

Ruth showed them into the lounge, her mind tying itself up in loops. Did they want to arrest someone? Did they think Colin murdered Mrs Graves? There was no sign of Greg, only a pile of cushions and a folded rug showed where he'd been. She couldn't hear what they were saying to her, the noise of her heart thumping was too loud.

The shriek of the hall telephone stopped her thoughts. Ruth hesitated to answer it, hearing the thunder of Mattie's footsteps before she picked up the receiver. Ruth heard sniffing. When she stepped into the hallway, she could see tears running down Mattie's face.

"Granny said she'll be up this afternoon. Greg's going to the hospital in case Andrea wants to come home." Ruth nodded. There was nothing to say. "I'll put the kettle on."

"The police are here, make coffee," Ruth told her. "Lots of coffee."

Both faces turned towards her as she went back into the lounge.

"Bad news?" asked Inspector Ross.

"As I said, our Rector and his wife were both attacked last night. She was five months pregnant. Now she isn't. I presume that's why you're here? To take our statements?" She could hear the harshness of her voice. It wasn't their fault. It wasn't anyone's fault except Lawrence and Isaac Graves. How did you bring a ghost to justice?

"We heard there was an attempted burglary in the church but that's not why we're here."

"Why not?" Ruth wanted to scream. Couldn't they see the two events were linked? Did they need everything spelling out for them? She thought detectives were supposed to be intelligent; what was the matter with these people?

"If not for the assault, why are you here?" Ruth sat down in the rocking chair, letting the slight movement calm her.

"We understand Colin Ackerley might be here?" The lilt in his voice made him sound almost apologetic for asking the question.

"He's probably still asleep," she said. "We didn't get to bed much before dawn." As she finished speaking, Colin appeared in the doorway.

He was still in pyjamas.

"I smelled coffee," he said, rubbing his eyes. "I heard my name mentioned as I was coming downstairs. Oh it's you."

"It's just a minor thing, Mr Ackerley" said Detective Ross, "nothing to worry about. We're taking casts of all the footwear everyone was wearing on Monday morning. You don't happen to have them here, do you?"

Colin frowned, propping his long frame against the doorpost.

"You don't want to take them away, do you?" he said, "I've only got the one pair and I need them for work." He went to fetch them from the conservatory.

"Tell me more about last night." Inspector Ross retrieved a notebook and pen from inside his jacket. Ruth closed her eyes, letting the aroma of the coffee seep inside her nostrils.

"Greg told the officers who came last night everything we know." She didn't want to tell anyone else; it was too painful. They wouldn't believe her even if she did. Ghosts don't exist. Ghosts don't attack people with icy fireballs. Unless you see them. Unless you felt the chill hit your skin. She rocked back and forth, clutching the mug of coffee tight in her hands, hardly feeling the heat.

Inspector Ross leaned back in his seat.

"You see, we have a slight problem. The officers who attended the scene last night swore they put the usual tape on the church doors to stop anyone going inside until SOCO arrived this morning but when they turned up, there was no tape and no sign of anything amiss. Can you think why that might be?"

Silence filled the room as Ruth and Mattie exchanged glances.

"What do you mean?" asked Ruth.

Inspector Ross shook his head. "If we didn't have the report from the night shift, you'd never believe anything happened in the church."

"You're saying we imagined it?" Mattie was on her feet, eyes blazing. "I know what I saw and heard."

"We're not saying anything." Inspector Ross kept his voice calm, but Ruth could tell he wanted to take charge of the situation and she wasn't going to let that happen, there was too much at stake.

"Oh dear," said Ruth. "I'm sorry we can't help you any further. I'm afraid there are things we need to do. Animals to attend to. Mattie will show you out."

Once the policemen were safely out of the way "Do any of you have any ideas who might have tidied up?"

Mattie's hand shot to her mouth. The same idea had just come to Ruth.

"Phone your mother, Mattie." She and Colin listened to the one-sided conversation until Mattie returned, ashen-faced.

"I've asked her to come over," she told them. "She says Lawrence phoned her around seven this morning and said the choir boys had been fighting in the church with muddy boots. He asked her to bring the carpet cleaner, so it would all be nice for the Bishop." She collapsed onto the sofa, sobbing. Colin went to comfort her.

Ruth was weeding in the front garden later that afternoon when she heard the church clock strike the half hour. She found it soothing to clear the earth around her plants. This was the first chance she'd had to be alone and think about the events of the past few days. So much had happened and none of it made sense. She felt as if someone had strapped her into a roller coaster at the top of the ride and all she wanted to do was get off and stop the world spinning around her. She wondered what Peter was doing and wished they had a chance to talk.

Footsteps coming along the road interrupted her train of thought, then Granny rushed through the front gate.

"You don't have time for that now, Ruth. Go and get changed. You need to play for the service tonight."

Ruth stared at her.

"I thought everything was cancelled because Adrian's still in hospital."

"Lawrence is taking the service. You need to play the organ."

She stood up, shaking the kneeling mat. "He can't do that. It's a communion service. He's not ordained."

"Unfortunately, he is. Now come on!" She led Ruth into the house, fussing all the time.

"Why did you agree?" Ruth asked, dropping her trowel and fork into the conservatory.

"Give him enough rope and he might just hang himself," Granny muttered, shooing her upstairs to get changed. She pulled on some cleaner trousers and a thick jumper. The church was always cold unless it was the middle of summer. She was in the bathroom filling a hot water bottle when Granny called up the stairs to see if she was ready.

Someone was ringing the sacristy bell as they reached the lychgate. Ruth looked at her watch. It was 5.45pm and the bell was only supposed to be rung five minutes before the service started. Up and down the road, she could see figures walking quickly towards them. Others were coming to see what was going on.

Inside the church, there was a deathly hush apart from the bell. Usually she could hear voices from the vestry and whispering from the choir members already in their stalls but not today.

Various parents and spouses of choir members were dotted about the pews. No-one sat together. It looked like they had been told where to sit to provide the impression of a full church. She tried to greet some of them as she walked past but they refused to look at her or even return her smile. What was going on?

The organ was locked. She had to search for the key in its hiding place behind the stone figure set in the wall. She wondered why Lawrence hadn't opened it when he first arrived. Everything was very strange tonight. At least the hymns were listed. She put the first one ready then pulled out her book of voluntaries and began to play on the softest setting. Every so often, she glanced through the squint into the nave, noticing just how many people were now sitting in the pews.

There was a rustle beside her and she heard everyone stand up. She brought the piece she was playing to a swift close and put the book aside, preparing to start the first hymn. She heard someone walk from the vestry and come to kneel at the altar, offering up the initial prayer of the Holy Communion service.

When he finished, he stood and turned to face the congregation. She heard a muffled gasp. The clergyman standing in front of the altar was dressed in the full Lenten robes, black cassock, white surplus and a purple stole. It wasn't until he began to speak, Ruth realised it was Lawrence. She almost fell off the organ stool in surprise. He looked so different, so calm and self-assured. He looked at home. From the buzz of whispers emanating from the nave she was sure someone was going to challenge him. Then she saw Granny shaking her head. Lawrence smirked. He could do what he liked now.

"Hymn number one hundred and thirty, An Upper Room did our Lord prepare."

Ruth stared at the music. She could feel Lawrence's gaze boring into her back, but she wasn't going to look in the mirror or turn around. She put her foot on the swell to increase the volume and started to play.

The tune surprised her, a forgotten favourite from her school days. The choir and congregation began the hymn, but in her head, she heard a deep voice singing *"I leaned my back against an oak, thinking it was a trusty tree, but first it bent and then it broke, and so my true love proved false to me."*

Tears began to well up, threatening to obscure her sight. She was such a failure, thinking she could stay here and be happy. She blinked rapidly, listening hard for phrases everyone else was singing, determined to recover her place without making a mistake.

The service continued. Lawrence preached a sermon which could have come straight from Isaac's pen. Everyone was weighed down by their sins and would burn in hell unless they woke up and started living a new and wholesome life.

His words made Ruth angry. Each time he banged his fist on the pulpit to emphasise a point she saw choir members flinch. It was all so different from Adrian's gentle jokes. She longed to hear laughter echo once more around the nave and whispered a short prayer for the Rector's safe return.

She clutched the hot water bottle on her lap, thankful for the warmth so her fingers remained supple enough to play. She heard shuffles coming from the nave and wondered if anyone had the courage to walk out during his diatribe. She thought she heard the church door open but then it was time for the next hymn, so she couldn't look.

She stayed resolutely on the organ seat while everyone filed up for communion. She wondered why Lawrence had stayed in the village instead of seeking his own parish. She closed her eyes, trying to clear her thoughts.

When she peered down the nave, she saw the detective standing beside the south door. Lawrence's intonation faltered momentarily when he saw the outsider, but he soon recovered, placing his hand on a child's head and intoning a blessing.

The service ended with a final hymn and benediction. Lawrence covered the cross and snuffed out the candles, walking quickly into the vestry. The congregation filed out of church in silence as the choir made their way into the vestry followed by Inspector Ross.

Ruth gathered her books and slid off the high, narrow seat. She couldn't work out why she felt so miserable. She was glad to get out into the fresh spring air. The brilliant blue of wild forget-me-nots danced for her in the breeze. Granny was standing just inside the lychgate, talking to some men. Ruth recognised several of the Morris side. They broke off as she came towards them, one group wandering down the road towards the pub while the others loitered in twos and threes chatting about the May Day dances.

"Hungry?" Granny asked as she reached the lychgate. Ruth nodded, realising she couldn't remember eating lunch.

"Colin and Mattie are having dinner with his family, so you'd best come home with me. There's a bacon joint needs eating up."

"How could Lawrence…" began Ruth but Granny shot her such a fierce look she couldn't complete her sentence. Inspector Ross was walking briskly towards them.

"Have you seen Mr Graves?" Both Ruth and Granny shook their heads. "I wanted to talk to him but there's no sign of him in the church. He seems to have vanished."

Granny frowned at the Inspector. "You must have missed him. He goes to the cinema on Thursday evenings"

"I'll try again tomorrow," sighed the detective, making his way back to his car.

Ruth was beginning to get a bad feeling about this. It wasn't enough for Lawrence to take over Adrian's position without challenge from the congregation. Now, he was disappearing without trace. Why?

A cold shiver began to run down her back as she remembered the conversation between Lawrence and his mother all those months before, coupled with the final outburst from Isaac the previous night. Lawrence was courting an unknown woman. A woman, who was now childless, therefore free to bear Lawrence's child.

She felt sick. Would Lawrence try to claim Andrea now she was back home?

"Is anyone with Andrea at the moment?" she asked Granny, feeling a catch in her throat.

"Greg's staying with her. She wanted to go back to the hospital to see Adrian this evening, but she's not fit to travel. His parents were going today."

"Do you think we should check she's all right?"

Granny pulled out her mobile. "No point in bothering her, she needs all the rest she can get. I'll ring Greg." They stood waiting but there was no reply.

"Strange," said Granny, setting off at a fast pace towards the Rectory. She went straight to the front door, but it was locked. The back door was the same. Ruth rang the doorbell. They waited for Greg to answer the door, but nothing happened. She lifted the heavy black door knocker and let it fall, in case the doorbell wasn't working but still no-one came. They walked all-round the house, trying to peer through the windows but all the curtains were drawn even though it was still light outside.

"Something's not right," said Granny. "The kitchen blinds are never drawn. Someone has closed the curtains in Arthur's bedroom and he's not there."

Granny tried the knocker again and called through the letter slit in the door.

"Andrea, are you all right? Can you come to the door?"

They heard footsteps coming down the stairs, then an angry voice.

"My wife is asleep. She's not well. Will you please go away?"

The two of them looked at each other. Surely Adrian hadn't been discharged from hospital without anyone knowing.

"Could you open the door, please."

"Go away! I told you, my wife is asleep."

Ruth shut her eyes. She knew that voice. She hated that voice. She began to shake.

"What is it?" Granny whispered, clutching Ruth's arm roughly.

"Isaac," Ruth muttered.

Granny beckoned them far enough away from the door where they couldn't be overheard.

"You think Lawrence is in there?" she asked. Ruth nodded.

She went back to the front door and banged on it again. "Lawrence, we know you're in there. Open this door and let us in. We want to check Andrea is all right."

"Be gone from this place, sinner that you are. The Lord keeps this house. Off with you!"

Ruth looked round for a window she might be able to force. She was terrified Lawrence might hurt Andrea. If Isaac was controlling him, there was no telling what he might think to do to his "wife", especially if she refused to co-operate.

"Ruth, here, quickly." She heard Granny call. She dashed towards the woodshed, tucked against the garden wall. Granny was standing by the doorway. Ruth peered through the crack between the door and its warped frame. On the floor was a long shape, tied around with thick rope, squirming like a caterpillar amongst the wood shavings. It must be Greg. Granny called to him softly but there was no response, only a muffled moan.

Granny turned to Ruth. "I've rung home but Zeb's not answering. You need to go to the pub and get someone up here with a pair of bolt cutters to remove this padlock. Run."

Ruth dropped her hymn books and ran down the road as fast as she could. She tried to think where Zeb might be. As she pushed open the door to the main bar, she could see three men, including Nigel, playing darts on the far wall.

"Please," she said, grabbing Nigel's arm just as he was about to throw. "Lawrence has gone mad. He's locked himself in the Rectory with Andrea. Greg's tied up in the woodshed. The door's got a padlock. Granny said we need Zeb's bolt cutters. Is he here?"

The three men stared at her, then shook their heads.

"I saw Zeb going to Glebe Farm earlier. Something to do with new calves?" said George, the pub landlord.

"Is there anything here that would open the door?"

Nigel was on his phone to Gillian while George disappeared from the bar, returning with a large iron crow bar.

"Try this," he said, passing it towards her but Mark took it off him and was gone up the street towards the Rectory before she could thank him properly. She followed with Nigel and Andrew. She had to stop and catch her breath, halfway up the hill. She hoped the others had managed to release Greg. She couldn't bear the thought of him tied up on the floor, helpless.

When she reached the Rectory, she heard voices arguing near the woodshed. The door was open and Greg was propped up against a wall.

"We need a knife," said Nigel, pulling at the rope which still curled around Greg's body.

"You can't cut that," Andrew protested. "It's a brand-new bell rope. It cost us nearly two hundred pounds."

Ruth wasn't in any mood to let them squabble like school children.

"Get some light over here." When Nigel turned on his phone torch, she pulled his arm, so the beam shone directly on the knot. "My father always told me to push knots when you want to untie them, pulling only makes them tighter." She grabbed one of the men's hand and showed him where to grasp the rope nearest the knot while she held another. Together they pushed towards each other, gradually easing the knot until they were able to prise it loose and unwind it from around Greg's body.

There was a collective sigh of relief, especially from Andrew, who coiled up the rope and held it protectively under his arm.

Greg was swaying on his feet. Mark was trying to ask him what happened, but Granny waved him away.

"Let's get him home and he can answer questions there."

Nigel offered to fetch his car, but Granny said he would be better walking to get his circulation going. The two men steadied him between them, while Andrew volunteered to watch the house in case Lawrence tried to leave.

"What are we going to do now?" Ruth wanted to know. "Andrea could be dead if we don't do anything. We can't leave her in the house with a madman!" She noticed the crowbar still lying by the woodshed door where Nigel had dropped it. She went to pick it up, but Andrew got there first.

Ruth glared at him. "We've got to do something!"

"I agree." Before she could speak again, he pushed the crowbar against the back-door lock and was levering it open. Metal screeched as wood began to splinter. The door swung open. Andrew dropped the crowbar on the floor and stepped carefully into the kitchen.

"Stay there!" he hissed to Ruth. He disappeared into the Rectory and she heard him start to climb the stairs. She picked up the crowbar, holding it tightly in case she needed to protect herself.

She heard shouts and sounds of a scuffle then footsteps came dashing down the stairs. Ruth shouted at Granny, who was watching the front door but there was no reply. She didn't know whether she should go and look for him or stay where she was. Just as she moved around the corner of the house, she saw struggling figures in the driveway then one fell to the ground and the other ran off towards the church.

"Down here," Ruth shouted as Andrew appeared at the front door. He started to follow the figure into the churchyard, shining his torch and bellowing for Lawrence to stop.

Ruth knelt beside Granny, who was moving with care. "You all right?" Ruth helped her get up, brushing debris from her clothes.

"I never thought Lawrence would touch me," Granny wheezed. "He pushed me away me before I had a chance to do anything. Stop fussing, girl, I need to get home to Greg."

Reluctantly, Ruth watched her walk down the road, then dashed up the stairs to Andrea's room. The Rector's wife was sitting up in bed, sobbing. She flinched as Ruth entered the room, then relaxed as she saw who it was.

"Is he gone?" she whispered, wiping her eyes with the back of her hand.

"He ran down into the churchyard," Ruth told her. "Andrew went after him, he can't go far."

"I swear, I never did anything to make him think...," Andrea's voice broke as Ruth sat on the bed and put an arm around her. She couldn't imagine what the poor woman must have gone through.

"Did he hurt you?" Ruth could hardly bear to ask the question, but she needed to know. It was a relief when Andrea's eyes widened in understanding before she shook her head vigorously.

"No, he didn't touch me the whole time he was here. I was so frightened. I tried to pretend I was asleep. He kept muttering to himself about one last thing he needed to do, then everything would be all right."

"Did he say what it was?"

Andrea started to shake her head, then her whole body stilled. Ruth wondered what she was remembering, holding the silence until she began to speak.

"The Priory. He wants to set fire to the Priory. He talked about cleansing the village from popish filth. At the time, I thought he was talking gibberish, but now I think he means to kill Lord Peter as well." Andrea turned towards Ruth, her face a mask of terror as she tried to throw back the bedclothes. "We must go and tell Granny. Warn Lord Peter."

"I'll go." Ruth stiffened as she heard footsteps and heavy breathing on the stairs. She looked around the room for a weapon, but nothing was within reach. She stood up, meaning to put herself between Andrea and the intruder. She felt a flash of relief as Ally Tulliver rushed into the room.

"We lost him," Ally wheezed. "Can't jump walls at my age."

Ruth knew she had to get to Glebe Cottage. She pulled out her house keys and thrust them into Ally's hand.

"Andrea needs somewhere safe. Take her to my house. I'll be there shortly." They started to protest but Ruth ignored them. She knew Ally would sort it all out. She had more important things to do.

For the second time that evening, Ruth ran down the road. Granny's back door was open when she reached Glebe Cottage. She found Greg installed on the settle beside the fire in the living room being forced to drink one of Granny's foul concoctions while Zeb and Colin watched from the other side of the room.

"I was a fool. Never thought to check for danger," Greg said, touching the back of his head gingerly. "I saw the wood box was empty in the kitchen. While I was filling the bucket with logs from the wood store, someone hit me. I don't remember anything else until I came to, in the dark, trussed up like a roll of carpet sent out for cleaning."

"Just be thankful Lawrence didn't do anything more serious,"

Granny said, turning as Ruth came into the room. "Any news?"

"He's escaped. Andrew lost him in the churchyard," she told them. "Ally arrived as I left. Andrea's ok. She heard Lawrence say he wants to torch the Priory. We need to find him." She sank into a chair to catch her breath. Greg put his head into his hands and groaned but Granny stood like a statue. Ruth could almost hear her mind making plans.

"Colin, go to Hollow Barrow Farm and get the bloodhounds." She thought for a moment, "How do we provide a scent for them?"

"The vestments he wore during the service. Dan should be able to point them out." Ruth said.

"Call Mattie and her mother and tell them to go to Pear Tree Cottage with food and stay until Lawrence is found."

"Why there instead of the Rectory?" Greg asked.

"The Rectory has too many tunnel entrances. How else do you think he got there from the church without anyone noticing?" Granny snapped.

"Ruth, I want you to get your car and pick up Gus from Home Farm Cottage. The most important thing is to get all the animals out of the stables and take them down to Home Farm.

"Colin, where are your horses?"

"Already there. Gus took them on Monday. I've been too busy with other things to take them back."

"Zeb, tell Henry to set a watch on the rickyard and barns, just in case. It might be wise if Gillian takes all the children to stay with Emily in town, if she'll go."

Zeb grinned, "Gillian's not going to leave the village, she's as stubborn as you." His expression suddenly changed, the colour draining from his face, "You don't think he'll use the barrels of flying juice hidden under the Old Squire's Summer House, do you?"

Granny closed her eyes, Ruth wondered if she were offering a quick prayer.

"Gods preserve us, I'll bet my last fruitcake that's where he's headed.

I know he used to play around there when he was a child. Let's hope he doesn't know about the tunnel leading to the big house."

"Or that it's fallen in. I'll tell Mark to go there first, just in case," Zeb said as he followed Colin out of the room.

Ruth stood up, "What are you and Greg going to do, Granny?"

Granny frowned, "If Greg's up to it, we'll be preparing Court in the Priory church. Rev Graves must be brought to justice. We don't have time to send his spirit across a rescue bridge."

"You're going to try a ghost?" Ruth couldn't help it, the words jumped out of her mouth.

"If needs be," Granny replied. "You can't attack your own village without expecting consequences. Lawrence Graves has tried one trick too far. It's got to stop."

CHAPTER FORTY-THREE

Ruth's heart was thudding as she went into the house to collect her car keys. Lights were on and she could hear voices coming from the kitchen. She was glad to see Ally coming downstairs to fetch a drink for Andrea, now safely ensconced in the spare room.

Mattie and her mother were standing around the kitchen table with Colin's mother and eldest sister, going through a huge box of bandages and other first aid equipment. A large kettle and a pot of stew were heating on the stove, the aroma reminding her she hadn't eaten; Granny's promise of a meal long forgotten. She grabbed a banana from the fruit bowl and put a chunk in her mouth to stop her stomach rumbling.

The sight of their industry made her feel even more apprehensive about unfolding events.

"Looks like you're preparing for disaster," she said, trying to lighten her words with a smile.

"Just precautions," Colin's mother said. "It'll be all right, you'll see."

"Where are the children?" Ruth asked, thinking of Colin's youngest sister and the twins, who were always causing mayhem. They weren't old enough to be left in the cottage on their own.

"The boys have all gone on the hunt for Mr Graves and the youngsters are camping out at Home Farm." Mattie's mother said, "Gillian called around to say she she'd host a sleepover for anyone who needed to be elsewhere."

"Let's hope they find him before he does anything stupid." Ruth grabbed a warmer coat and hat and set off for the Priory. Gus and Bessie were waiting for her at the end of their lane. Ruth wondered if they'd been asleep, given their dishevelled appearance.

"What's going on?" Gus asked as he folded himself into the front seat. "Tom woke us up banging on the front door. Said we better get ourselves here and wait for you." Bessie clambered into the back seat, slumping against the head rest.

"Lawrence Graves has threatened to torch the Priory. He's already attacked Anvil at the Rectory this evening. Granny wants you to take all the animals in the stables down to Home Farm. Can you do that?" Ruth drove round to the back of the house,. Everywhere was dark. She couldn't see any lights in the kitchen and wondered where Lord Peter was.

"Is Anvil all right?" Bessie's voice from the back was trembling. Ruth remembered she had been Anvil's Circle Maid and companion for several years before she started going out with Gus.

"He's ok. Just a sore head. He's with Granny." Ruth stopped the car and got out, waiting for her companions to emerge before locking it and shoving the keys in her pocket. "Will you be able to take them all?"

Gus was already running towards the tack room with Bessie lumbering behind. "Don't you worry. We'll be back to help with anything else once we get 'em settled."

As lights went on in the stables, Ruth tried the back door of the Priory, praying it would still be open. The handle turned, and she pushed against the old wooden door. *It wouldn't take much to break it down*, she thought, wondering what could be used as a barricade.

"Peter? Peter, where are you?" she called, opening the kitchen door and finding the light switch on the wall. She half expected to see Lord Peter's body lying in front of the range, but the room was empty, the quiet hum of the kettle grating against her already-frazzled nerves.

She went down the corridor, opening doors and setting lights blazing where she could. She was determined not to leave any dark places where Lawrence could hide and surprise them later yet for every light switch which worked, another clicked on and off but seemed to be missing a bulb. She knew Peter was trying to economise, but this was ridiculous!

"Peter, Peter, I need to talk to you." The library was empty, and she realised she didn't know the layout of most of the rooms. Her recent visits had been limited to the kitchen and servants' quarters; she'd never been taken to the family rooms. What if he was upstairs? Would she have to investigate every nook and cranny before she found him?

The Great Hall was a sea of darkness. She couldn't tell if the curtains were drawn or there was no moon or starlight to filter through the windows. It was so cold. She pushed her hands inside her pockets, thankful for her coat and hat. Her fingers wrapped around a small torch, left there after checking the hencoop one night. She breathed a sigh of relief and let the beam of light play across the wooden panelling to her left. She thought she saw a crack of yellow around a doorway and rushed towards it.

As she pushed, the door swung open, revealing a snug sitting room, filled with comfortable chairs and small tables. A fire was burning in the grate, a single standard lamp the only illumination. Lord Peter was slumped in an armchair with his eyes closed, headphones over his ears.

Ruth froze. Had Lawrence been here already? Her eyes scanned his face and eventually noticed the gentle rise and fall of his chest. He was breathing. She let out a long sigh of relief and moved forward.

"Peter?" No response. She placed her hand lightly on his arm. "Peter," a little louder this time. Still no response. "Peter, wake up!" This time she shook his arm then carefully removed the headphones, placing them on the table.

Lord Peter's eyes flew open.

"What the hell?" he cried, making Ruth take a step back in alarm. For a moment he gripped the arms of the chair so hard, Ruth wondered if he were going to leap up and attack her, so wild was the look in his eyes. She stopped, uncertain what to do next.

"What are you doing here, Ruth?" She saw he recognised her and relaxed.

"I'm sorry," she said. "I've been calling you ever since I got here. Didn't you get Granny's message?"

"Message?" Peter rubbed his eyes and yawned. "I've been sawing logs all afternoon. Janet made my favourite steak and kidney pie for dinner. I came in here after I'd eaten and lit the fire. I must have fallen asleep. Is something wrong?"

"Just a little," Ruth knew her relief at finding him unharmed was making her sarcastic, but she couldn't help it. She'd wondered why Granny sent her to the Priory rather than one of the men. The tingle which rushed through her the moment she touched him, made her realise she needed to be at his side, working with him to save the past and protect their future.

"Lawrence Graves is coming to burn down the Priory and, he hopes, you with it."

Peter was obviously having trouble both waking up and believing her.

"Lawrence, our organist? Wants to burn down the Priory?
How? Why?"

Ruth wanted to shake him.

"Zeb said something about a hidden store of kerosene in the summer house?" She didn't understand where this mythical summer house might be or why someone would hide aviation fuel there, but her words certainly had the desired effect on Lord Peter. He shot to his feet, suddenly returning to his military bearing.

"Shit! Why now?"

"He thinks he's Rector of Roelswick and has possession of the Rector's wife. Destroying you and the Priory removes the only thorn left in his perfect story."

Peter was already striding towards the Library as Ruth spoke. She followed closely, determined not to let him out of her sight again.

"He's mad."

"We know that."

Peter flung open the library door and soon the room was the centre of operations. The map of the village was still laid out on the central table. He pulled open a drawer and searched through until he found a plan of the Priory, which he unrolled while Ruth found various paper weights to hold it down. She wasn't quite sure what Peter was searching for.

"There!" he said, jabbing his finger on the west wing. "That's where the tunnel comes out."

"Tunnel?" Ruth was confused. Granny had mentioned the Rectory having too many tunnels to make it safe. Lawrence was seen leaving the Rectory, so he wasn't using a tunnel now, as far as they knew.

"One of my ancestors dug a tunnel from here to the summerhouse so he could entertain his mistress without the family knowing. During the war, the RAF built a small airfield nearby and one of the workers at Hollow Barrow Farm used to "borrow" fuel for their vehicles. His boss was part of the black market. He discovered the underground room below the summerhouse and stashed the drums there. He stored so much, there was some leftover after the war and we never got around to moving it."

"What are we going to do?" Ruth asked as Peter took his mobile phone from his pocket.

"Ring the fire brigade." He pointed towards the telephone on one of the side tables.

"Can we phone them before a fire happens?" Ruth wasn't sure. What if they captured Lawrence before he could do anything and someone else was put at risk?

"Tell them whatever you like but get them here," Peter snapped at her. "It will take at least half an hour for an engine to reach us, probably an hour by the time they get lost twice. Do you want to wait and have the whole house go up?"

Ruth shook her head and began to dial. Lord Peter was already punching numbers on his mobile and when someone answered all she heard was a single word, "Red". The operator was asking which emergency service she required and when the fire officer asked for more details, she was busy trying to convince them the aviation fuel was already burning and the whole village was at risk.

"They'll be here as soon as they can," Ruth sighed. Peter was opening the large iron safe in the corner of the room. She wasn't sure what he was retrieving until she saw the box of ammunition he placed on the table.

"No guns, Peter, please," she screamed at him. "If you kill Lawrence, you could go to jail and I'll never see you again!" Her words seemed to stun Peter. He stood quite still staring at her.

"He needs stopping," he said at last.

"I don't care. We're not Americans. If he's killed, he can't stand trial. He must be brought to justice!" Ruth felt something twisting in her chest and gripped the table.

Peter narrowed his eyes. "What do you mean, brought to justice?"

"Granny and Anvil are preparing the Court." As she spoke the words, Ruth realised she had no idea what they meant but Lord Peter did. He swept the pistol in its holster and the box of ammunition back into the safe and swung the heavy door closed, turning the lock.

"Have it your way, then. Poor sod, he'll wish I'd shot him and ended it all before the Court sentences him."

CHAPTER FORTY-FOUR

Lights flickered against the library windows, followed by the sound of two cars driving towards the stables.

"Come on," said Peter, picking up a thick walking stick with a large, carved lump on the end which was lying against the far wall. "No guns, but I'm not meeting this madman without some means of protection."

They ran to the back door, only to find Ralph Williams and Greg walking towards them with Granny and Janet Williams just behind.

"Come with us, Ruth," Granny said. "Let the men do the heavy stuff. We need to prepare the Court."

"But." Ruth looked from Granny to Peter. She didn't want to leave him. What if something happened and she never saw him again? She couldn't bear it.

Peter smiled at her, pulling her into a brief hug.

"I know you want to help, Ruth, but I'd feel much happier if you were somewhere safe. Thank you for warning me. I'd have been a sitting duck if you hadn't. Now, we've got time to prepare."

"What are you going to do?" She had to ask, although she could see he was anxious to be off.

"Barricade the tunnel entrance in the west wing cellar. Then we'll go over to the summerhouse and see what's going on there. Hopefully we'll be back with Lawrence before you know it." He turned away, pulling a bulky key ring from his trouser pocket. The other two men followed him into the house, leaving the three women standing outside in the wind.

The stable block was once more in darkness, all the looseboxes empty. The silence was earie. Ruth could feel a sense of apprehension emanating from the Priory building. She was sure if she turned her head, she would see dark-robed figures standing around them. The thought comforted her. The monks always protected her. There was no need to be frightened.

"What do we have to do?"

"What we always have to do," Granny said. "Get everything clean and tidy." Mrs Williams disappeared into the house, returning with three large torches which she handed out.

"No point in tripping up or losing our way," she said cheerfully, turning on her powerful beam and leading the way past the stables towards the church. Ruth wished it was light enough to see the ancient building. She knew this was the original Priory Church dedicated to Our Lady and guessed it was as large as the village church, if not larger.

Just as they reached the great west door, the moon came out from behind the clouds, throwing shadows on the flying buttresses. They looked like huge spiders' legs protruding from the body of the church.

"Not here," Granny said, pulling her away from the doorway. "We'll go in the Nuns' Door, next to the garden. It's kept unlocked for anyone seeking sanctuary."

Is that what we're doing? wondered Ruth. *Seeking sanctuary from the madness of the world, to pray for the safety of our loved ones and compassion for the darkness in hearts of wounded men?*

"All in good time," said Granny. "First we need to clear and cleanse."

Ruth didn't know whether she'd spoken out loud or if Granny really could read minds. She followed the two women through a narrow wooden door hidden behind a screen of ivy not far from the Nun's well. A carved stone stairway led down to a large space behind the main altar. Granny went down more steps and returned with an armful of long, thick candles. Two she gave to Janet to set on the High Altar, one she stood in the east window, where it shone to give light both inside and out. The other three were placed in the south, west and north windows, showing the large, empty space in the body of the church.

"We'll fill the ceiling rings later," Granny said. "No point in wasting candle light before its needed."

Mrs Williams emerged from a room to the left of the altar carrying three brooms.

"Sweep first, then we'll wash to settle the dust."

Ruth took her broom, thinking this was the last thing she thought she'd be doing so late in the evening.

"Why are we cleaning now?" she asked. "Isn't there something more important we should be doing."

Granny gave her a long, hard stare. "You know we always clear a ritual space beforehand. You remember the lengths you forced the men to go through when they were contaminated by Isaac's curse. Imagine the mayhem if Isaac's ghost were let loose in here without removing all the old energies first, then making sure the boundaries were secure? Our job is just as important as anything the men are doing. Never think any different!"

Ruth gripped her broom more tightly. Granny's explanation did make more sense. It was hard dealing with both the seen and the unseen, but she set about the job in hand with renewed vigour.

Just as they finished clearing the debris, Bessie appeared with buckets of water in both hands.

"I thought you'd need this," she said as Granny thanked her. "We heard the bloodhounds baying just as we put the last horse in the paddock. Tom and Zeb are keeping watch at Home Farm, so Gus said we'd better come back here and see what needed to be done."

"Which direction were they heading?" Granny asked, while Janet went to fetch the mops and buckets. Bessie pointed towards the west door. "Where's Gus now?"

"He's down with Mr Williams in the cellar. Lord Peter said to tell you he's taken the Landover. He and Anvil have gone to the Old Squire's summer house. We're to keep a lookout for the fire engine."

In silence, Mrs Williams and Granny poured water into four buckets and they all began to mop the floor. As Bessie entered the Lady Chapel in the south aisle, she started to hum and then sing. Ruth was cleaning by the west door and couldn't make out the words but found herself singing along. Soon the whole church was alive with melody, echoing into the rafters until their task was complete and the song died away.

Ruth went to the undercroft to put her mop and bucket away. Built into one of the arches she found a huge wooden cupboard. The key was in one of the doors and it opened to her touch revealing sets of different coloured clothing. These weren't normal church vestments. Colourful costumes hung on padded hangers. From each one hung a bird or animal headdress made from papier mache with a cloth back.

"What are these?" she asked Granny, who was putting her equipment back into the cleaning alcove.

"You've found them, then," Granny said, searching through the collection until she came across a green robe with a frog's head. "This is yours. You'll need it for Court tomorrow." She pulled it out and hung the clothing on a nearby coat stand.

"Why do we wear costumes? Those masks," Ruth shuddered, "They must be terribly claustrophobic, and you'd never be able to see properly."

"Justice is blind," Granny said. "You see and hear what is needed. The costumes take us out of this world and into a place within. They connect us with the land, our land, our village, our community. It's not us as individuals who judge the deeds, it's the whole. We all have a part to play."

"Why me?" Ruth said, her fingers stroking the rich material of the robe. She could feel the frog staring back at her and she was sure it would leap forward and implant itself on her face if she didn't move away. "Why do I have to be part of the Court? I don't mind being a witness, but will I be called to pass judgement on Lawrence as well?"

"Wake up, Ruth!" Granny wagged her finger in front of Ruth's face, making her jump. "Without you, we can't hold Court. You're the only one who can see the shadow world clearly. You've proved it again and again. Isaac talks to you. The monks talk to you. You can follow them in their world. You move between the worlds of now and then without fear or effort. We need you. How else are we going to deal with Isaac?"

Ruth gulped. "Surely someone else must see them?" She didn't want to see Granny shake her head.

"In the old days, such abilities were a curse. The church called it witchcraft and drowned those who mentioned what they saw. Eventually, the Blackwell women were the only ones with Sight. Granny Blackwell bore no children, so we thought, but something brought you back to us, offered a final opportunity to rid the village of Isaac's darkness once and for all."

Ruth stepped back; the full weight of responsibility thrust upon her making her stumble. "I'm not sure I can do this," she mumbled, her voice refusing to work properly.

Janet Williams came forward out of the shadows and put her arm around her, holding her steady.

"Don't worry, Ruth. Despite what Amy says, we know we're asking a lot of you. All you can do is try your best. We're not trying to frighten you, just prepare you for what might come."

They closed the cupboard doors and walked back up into the nave. With every step away from the costumes, Ruth felt her strength returning. As they neared the West door, Granny took a torch out of her pocket and gave it to Ruth.

"Take this and climb up onto the balcony." Granny pointed to the walkway running all the way around the walls. "You'll find the stairs beside the left door. Wipe your shoes, so you don't slip on the stone. Go to the corner. There are arrow slits looking out towards the Priory and over the fields to the summerhouse. Shout if you see anything."

To Ruth's surprise, there was a large mat on the floor next to the

287

west door. She dutifully rubbed grit from the soles of her shoes while swinging the torch across the walls until she located the narrow staircase.

I'll never get up there, it's too steep, Ruth thought, her fear of heights threatening to overwhelm her.

"It's quite safe," came a voice beside her. "Let me go first and I'll show you." Once more the smiling lay brother was coming to her aid. He pointed to each step with his foot and waited until she was behind him before moving on to the next one. It wasn't as arduous as Ruth feared and she soon found herself sitting on a carved stone seat in the corner beside the arrow slit.

"Thank you for showing me the way," she said to the brown figure beside her.

"Ic ðe fylste a. I'm always here to help you," she heard his reply but lost sight of him in the surrounding darkness as she gazed out into the night.

She could hear the hounds calling, their cry changing as they lost the scent for a short while, then found it again. At the far end of the valley she could see the road leading into town, white car lights appearing and disappearing amongst the trees.

She heard chains rattling in the body of the church as Granny let down the two large iron crowns for Janet and Bessie to fill with candles. They were left lowered, so they could be lit quickly when needed.

When she turned back to the slit, she saw blue flashing lights heading towards the village. It would be five minutes before the fire engine came to Abbotts Orchard. Ruth knew they couldn't take the bridle path which would lead them straight here. It would be another ten minutes to drive into the village and then out again towards the Priory. The Satnav would take them to Glebe Farm. She hoped they'd listened to her instructions on what to do at the end of their journey.

The ancient, yellow Landrover bounced and rattled over wet, muddy fields. *It was quite the most uncomfortable heap he'd ever owned,* thought Peter. Even the army vehicles he'd driven had better suspension than this. At least his back didn't hurt. He couldn't believe the miracle of life without pain. All thanks to Ruth. He owed her so much and still hadn't thanked her. Was he afraid she would disappear if he said anything? He treated her so badly when they first met. He wouldn't have blamed her for ignoring him. Instead she healed him and yelled at him for thinking about using a gun. Shouted at him because she couldn't bear the thought of him away from her in prison if something went wrong.

She must care for him a little. He could still feel her softness when he hugged her. Still catch the scent of her. God, he could have killed her, waking him up like that from such a deep sleep. His hands could have been round her neck instead of the chair arms. The thought of inadvertently harming her scared him far more than the current danger.

He swerved to avoid a tree root, causing Greg to clutch on to the door and only just managed to steer through the gateway with enough speed to avoid becoming stuck in the mud.

"Sorry, mate, not far now," Peter muttered.

The Old Squire's summerhouse loomed up in front of them on the far side of the field. It was built in the shape of a ruined castle, the half-finished tower leaning against the crenellated body of the folly. It had been a favourite place for all the village children to play. A meeting place of equals far away from the rigid demarcation of the village of Lord and vassals.

He remembered lighting a fire with Greg in the huge, ornate fireplace, only to have the gamekeeper rush in and dowse it with a bucket of water before it could get going enough to cook the sausages Greg had brought.

"Never, ever light a fire here again!" the gamekeeper loomed above them. "You'll set us all aflame!" They didn't understand until he took them through a hidden doorway in the panelled wall and down into the cellar where large drums labelled 'kerosene' were stacked against a wall. He tried to remember if Lawrence was with them that day. He was such a scrawny, little kid, sneaking around the edges of their games, running off crying if they shouted at him.

He stopped the Landrover in front of the summerhouse just as the search party came to a halt in front of the building. The two blood hounds were baying and pulling on their leads, trying to get into the building.

The eldest Cooper boy from Glebe Farm came running down the steps crying, "He's here, he's here, Lawrence is here. Nigel's gone after him into the tunnel."

"Should I release the dogs, Sir?" asked their handler. It took Peter a few seconds to recognise the speaker.

"Let's see what's going on first, shall we?" He looked around at the group of men and boys armed with torches and various sticks and staves. He noticed Jack Ackerley was carrying his broken twelve bore across his arm and remembered Ruth's plea for no guns to be involved. "You stay here, Jack, but don't shoot. We don't want the police arresting the wrong person, do we?"

"No, Sir." Jack didn't look pleased, "You know I always take my gun when we're hunting vermin."

Lord Peter turned to Greg, "I suppose you won't listen if I ask you to stay here."

Greg grinned and shook his head carefully. "He's hurt too many I care for."

"Listen, everyone," Lord Peter stood on the second step, shouting to be heard above the baying of the dogs. "Anvil and I are going down into the tunnel to try and find Lawrence Graves and Nigel. Steven and Mark, you come with us but stay inside the summerhouse in case we need help. The rest of you, spread out around the summerhouse so if Lawrence comes out, you can capture him. If he runs, set the dogs on him, Clackett. We can't let him get away, but we need him alive."

Inside the summerhouse, the dust-covered furniture was pushed out of the way, the door to the cellar wide open. Lord Peter gripped his stick and crept cautiously down the stairs, stopping every few steps to listen for any noises, the smell of fuel getting stronger the closer they came. The cellar was deserted with storage drums scattered around and when they moved them, two were empty.

"Looks like he's poured kerosene in the tunnel already," said Greg. They both turned towards the entrance as muffled shouts and the sounds of metal bouncing off brickwork could be heard.

They exchanged glances, then entered the tunnel together, arcs of light from their torches revealing the wide, circular passageway stretching in front of them. They splashed through puddles, never sure if they were rain water seeping through the bricks from the fields above or aeroplane propellant.

After several minutes they came towards two figures wrestling on the ground. They were too far away to see who was who but as they came closer it was obvious that Nigel was failing to keep hold of Lawrence, who was fighting like a madman, punching and kicking.

Nigel fell to the ground, groaning.

"Keep back," shouted Lawrence, holding a fuel can over the motionless body. "One more step and he becomes a human candle."

Peter and Greg froze. Peter fingered his walking stick. The movement knocked it against the brickwork.

"Drop it," Lawrence screamed. "Don't try anything or I torch this place now." Peter opened his fingers and the stick clattered to the ground.

"There's no need to do anything foolish, Lawrence. Come with us and everyone can be safe," said Peter, clutching Greg's arm to stop him rushing forward. "It's going to take two of us to carry Nigel, if we want everyone alive," he whispered.

"Can't we leave the little shit here?" muttered Greg.

"You want his death on your soul?" Peter countered through gritted teeth. "Nigel's more important. Think of Hilary."

They inched forward, keeping their backs to the wall until they reached Nigel's body. Lawrence watched them, dancing from one foot to the other, his eyes wild and staring. As they bent down, he dropped the can and began to run towards the tunnel entrance, chanting, "I've won, I've won!"

"We need to run," Peter said, "it could go up at any second. They called Nigel's name but there was no response. Holding him under one arm, they started to jog as fast as they could, hoping someone else would be able to capture Lawrence.

Although they were less than half way along the tunnel, the journey back seemed to last forever. With every step they took, Nigel's body seemed to weigh more, until Peter's arms felt as if they were being dragged out of their sockets. His lungs hurt from breathing in the fetid air mixed with fumes. He knew they were both wondering if they would be faced by a wall of flame at any moment.

There was no time to change their grip on Nigel, no time to shout a warning to the two men waiting in the summerhouse.

"No good," panted Greg beside him. "Stop. Fireman's Lift. You or me?"

Greg's face was sickly white. Peter leaned down and together they hoisted Nigel onto Peter's shoulder and set off again without another word. It was easier now and Peter could see the opening up ahead.

"Help!" he wheezed.

"Help us!" shouted Greg, his voice carrying further. They heard footsteps on the stairs and mercifully the weight was lifted from Peter as Mark and Steven took Nigel up the stairs between them. Greg followed them, hanging on to the rope banister.

Peter was about to close the tunnel door when Lawrence leaped from behind it, pushing him back inside.

"Not you, not you," Lawrence chanted. "You started everything; you will be cleansed by the flames."

Peter twisted and turned, pushing against the heavy, wooden door. He couldn't believe how strong Lawrence was. He could hounds baying outside, the noise coming nearer with every second. Lawrence let go of the door, shouting at the dogs as they attacked him. Peter gave a final push and fell into the dark cellar. He felt a cold nose against his hand, a cold, wiry body he was able to lean against as he got to his feet. He felt absurdly comforted to know Fynn was still around.

"Away," he shouted at the bloodhounds. "Come away now!" The dogs fell silent, drool slipping off their tongues onto the ground. They stood watching him as he hauled Lawrence to his feet, his clothes torn and muddy, with blood beginning to swell from one of the bites. "Out," he ordered and they walked up the stairs, claws tapping on the wooden slats.

"Come on," Peter said, pushing Lawrence in front of him up the stairs. He didn't realise what Lawrence was doing until it was too late. The crazed organist pulled something out of his pocket. He heard flint striking and Lawrence threw the flame behind him onto the cellar floor.

"Run! Fire!" Peter screamed, pulling the panel across the opening. Lawrence was trying to get out of his grip but Peter wouldn't let him go. Together they ran down the stairs towards the group half way down the field. Willing hands took Lawrence away. Peter hardly noticed when they tied Lawrence's hands and feet and tossed him in the back of the Landrover. His lungs were sucking in long gulps of cold, damp air but they felt wonderful.

For a moment, Peter wondered if everything would be all right, that the spark hadn't ignited. He heard a tremendous bang and found himself on muddy ground as the door in the panelling exploded and flames began to shoot out of the summerhouse door and up into the night sky. He could hear Lawrence crowing from the Landrover until he saw Greg take an old rag from his pocket and walk purposefully towards the vehicle. Silence followed.

Peter shivered. Did this mean the end? He looked around at the men and boys watching the flames. No, Lawrence might try to destroy a building, but the people were safe. They didn't want Lawrence, but they believed in the village. It wasn't the end of anything, just a chance to begin something new, something better.

He picked himself up and walked towards the Landrover. Nigel was sitting hunched up in the front seat, wrapped in a coat.

"You alright?" Peter asked.

"Think so," Nigel coughed. "Thanks for getting me out."

Greg came towards them with the Cooper boy.

"You take them back to the Priory," said Peter, indicating the driver's seat. "Make sure he's secure in the church cell before I get there." Greg grunted. "Try to keep him alive enough for the court." Greg gave a hoarse laugh. Peter could see in his eyes Greg would rather deliver his own justice. Unfortunately, now was not the time.

CHAPTER FORTY-FIVE

Mayhem followed the return of the Landrover and the incarceration of Lawrence in a tiny cell underneath the chapter house next to the church.

"Thank goodness we finished when we did," said Bessie, pouring water into a huge teapot. "I were that worried Isaac Graves might be loosed on us all if Granny hadn't finished securing the etheric boundaries. We don't want him chucking any more fireballs on us while we sleep!"

"Couldn't we just hold Court now and get it all over with?" Ruth wondered, making herself a cup of coffee.

"You can't do anything on Good Friday," said Bessie, "wouldn't be proper. Besides, Anvil needs to rest if he's going to hold the circle tomorrow. Granny told me Nigel's lungs must heal for as long as possible before he starts the 'Speaking of the Wrongs'. It wouldn't do for him not to be heard."

Ruth looked around the kitchen to ask Granny to explain what her own role was going to be during the Court when she remembered Granny was down in the cell tending to Lawrence's wounds.

She didn't have time for any further thought because the search party returned; everyone streaming into the kitchen to be fed stew and mugs of tea and share stories of their part in the rescue. Peter disappeared. Granny said he was organising guard duty with the Morris team but when Ruth went over to take food for Lawrence and the guards, he was nowhere to be found.

Mark Lowtham, the Morris Team Leader, was sitting at the top of the stairs leading down to the single cell, carved out of the rock. When he opened the door so Ruth could take in the tray, Lawrence was lying on a thin mattress on the floor, covered with a blanket; a harsh, white light coming from a lamp in a niche, high up on the wall.

Although his eyes were closed, his mouth was moving continuously. Ruth couldn't be sure if he were praying or singing.

"I've brought you some food, Lawrence," she said but he ignored her so she left him alone, wondering what the Court would decide to do with him.

She could hear the tawny owls calling to each other as she walked back to the Priory. She always heard them herald the early hours of the morning if she couldn't get to sleep. It was comforting to think life was continuing as normal in the fields despite the excitement going on around them.

Ruth stood outside Peter's bedroom door trying to decide whether to knock or turn the handle and go in. The Priory was quiet now the fire engines were gone and most people had returned to their own homes. Granny was keeping watch over Greg and Nigel in the nursery, dosing them with a tonic designed to counteract the effects of their ordeals.

Ruth expected to follow Mattie and Colin back to Pear Tree Cottage, but Granny insisted she stay.

"You must go to him tonight," Granny said. "He needs your strength." Ruth knew her surprise must have shown in her face because Granny added. "Your heart needs loving too," before she strode off towards the back stairs.

Janet Williams found her a spare nightdress and showed her to a guest room in the private wing. Ruth suspected Janet didn't believe she would be sleeping in the bed from the knowing smile Janet gave her as she closed the door. Ruth took one look at the four-poster bed and decided she would never sleep a wink until she knew how Peter was.

A cold draught played around her bare ankles. She turned the handle.

"Peter, are you asleep?" she whispered as she opened the door and crept inside.

The far bedside lamp cast a soft pool of yellow light onto the red, tartan rug on top of the bed. Peter was propped up against the pillows, a book on his lap and glasses dangling from one ear. His eyes were closed and from the regular rise and fall of his chest, Ruth could tell he was sleeping. She stood for a moment, drinking in the scene.

"Here lies the Earl of Roelswick", she thought to herself, *"a man born to privilege and status yet who has offered much and lost more, continually hiding his suffering behind a mask. I don't really know him, but I love him."* Her admission surprised her so much, she didn't realise Peter's eyes were open and he was speaking to her.

"Ruth? What are you doing here? Is something wrong?" He pulled off his glasses and retrieved the book, placing them both on the bedside table.

"Nothing's wrong. I just wanted to see you. Make sure you were all right." She fidgeted from one foot to the other, feeling a fool for invading his privacy. What if he didn't return her feelings. What if he thought she was being too forward and would revert to his icy treatment of her again?

"You'll freeze to death if you stand there all night," Peter said, throwing open the bedclothes. "I'm convinced the landing is connected to a Siberian wind tunnel."

Ruth ran to the bed and scrambled in beside him before she could have second thoughts. "Are you sure it's Siberian? I was thinking Arctic. Maybe a long lost Samian reindeer trackway?"

Peter laughed, wincing as she tucked her cold feet against his. When she felt his reaction, she moved away but he drew her closer with his arm.

"Don't move," he said, "I'd forgotten what a shock cold feet could be, that's all."

"Was your wife blessed with warm feet?" Ruth asked, kicking herself as the words left her mouth.

"I don't know," Peter shrugged. "Susannah didn't believe in sharing a bed for anything other than sex. She had her own suite of rooms in the West Wing. This has been my room since I left the nursery. She said it was too gloomy and full of dead ancestors." Ruth giggled. "What?"

"I can't sense any dead ancestors. There are no monks around, so I don't think this was part of their sleeping quarters."

Peter began to laugh so much, he was doubled over the counterpane. When he finally recovered, he hugged Ruth fiercely and kissed her forehead.

"You," he said, trying to draw breath while still chuckling, "are amazing!"

She grinned, settling herself in the crook of his arm and rubbing her cheek against the softness of his jacket. She could smell the scent of his clean pyjamas mingled with a mixture of aftershave and soap. He must have showered before coming to bed but not shaved because she could feel bristles as she touched his cheek.

The tingle she associated with touching him was gone, replaced by the certainty she was where she should be. His body welcomed her, sheltered her, protected her, had regard for her welfare. It was such a different shape from Robert's, long, thin, angular, she could feel every bone, yet she fitted him perfectly. She never wanted to leave.

They lay for several moments in companionable silence. She loved the way he held her, stroking her arm and down her back in gentle, smooth strokes.

"I've never thanked you," he said at last, hugging her tightly.

"What for?" Ruth wondered what she'd done.

"For taking the pain away in my back."

"Oh." It seemed such a long time ago since he came to dinner. The first night Isaac attacked anyone with his fireballs.

"The healing helped more than you could ever imagine." He shifted in the bed, reaching for a small bottle which he held in front of them. He shook it and she could see tiny fragments of metal glinting in the light. "You made this possible." He shook them again.

"This was the shrapnel embedded in my spine. The shrapnel all the surgeons told me was impossible to remove without the danger of making me a cripple. They gave me the choice of either living in a wheelchair for the rest of my life or existing with the pain but still able to walk."

Ruth held him tightly across his chest. She didn't know what to say. The thought of Peter in a wheelchair was terrible, but she knew what the pain had done to him, almost destroying his personality, turning him into the puritanical introvert she'd first met.

"I don't know what you did," Peter continued, kissing her hair gently. "The next few days after you gave me healing, I started to get tiny lumps appearing just under the skin of my back. It felt like I'd rubbed myself against an old piece of wood and been left with splinters everywhere. I wasn't sure what was going on, so I asked Janet to take a look."

"What did she say?"

"She wasn't sure either but she plastered me with plantain poultices and they did the job of pulling the metal fragments through the skin. Amazing really. Are you sure you're not a witch?"

Ruth pulled away and looked at him. "What would you do with me if I were?"

Peter returned the jar to the table before leaning back against the pillows with his finger against his chin, giving all the appearance of deep thought.

"I think," he said, his voice deep and slow but Ruth could see his eyes were twinkling, "as the nineteenth Earl of Haverliegh, I have a responsibility to the people under my immediate care to keep you constantly by my side to ensure you harm none."

"As if I would," Ruth protested. "That's a terrible thing to contemplate."

"Being forever by my side?"

"Dreadful," she said, bouncing towards him to kiss the end of his nose. "I might just have to tickle you to make you reconsider." She began to make good her threat until he retaliated, and the bed became a heaving mass of struggling bodies. Eventually they fell apart, giggling and panting like naughty children. She lay on her front, exhausted, while Peter flopped back onto the pillows with an enormous sigh,

"Have I ever told you how much I love you, Ruth?" he said at last, pushing a strand of hair back from her face.

"No," she said, "but the feeling is entirely mutual."

"Good," he said, drawing her back to snuggle against him. "I'm so glad you feel the same. With you by my side I believe I can face anything."

CHAPTER FORTY-SIX

Ruth looked at herself in the bedroom mirror the following morning, wondering what she was letting herself in for. The green robe fitted perfectly; the embroidery exquisite but the mask scared her silly.

"I know all this is new," Granny said, as she helped Ruth dress. "The Court is not about individuals, it's the village protecting its own. You are the Water Keeper, so the frog is your emblem. The ancients knew wherever they saw a frog, water would be close by."

Ruth wondered what Granny would represent but she lacked the courage to ask her. She would know soon enough when they took their places in the body of the church.

"What about Lawrence?" she asked, "do you make him wear something?" She tried to imagine what creature the organist might find affinity with, but nothing came to mind, only darkness. To cast him as a carrion crow seemed to do the bird a disservice.

Granny sighed. "His father wore the magpie. He said it reminded him of a preacher's black and white, but Lawrence won't get that chance. He comes as he is; with Isaac or without, he must make his own amends."

Ruth fiddled with her watch, trying to push it underneath her sleeve. She stole a quick look at Granny, thinking how tired the older woman looked, not just from the lack of sleep. The whole business was dragging her down, dragging them all down.

"Bessie said Nigel would be 'Speaking the List of Wrongs'," said Ruth. "Is Lawrence facing the music alone? Does anyone support him? If Isaac possessed him, should Lawrence be held responsible? Should he take the blame for everything? If Isaac forced him against his will, how do you punish a ghost?"

Ruth closed her mouth, knowing she was letting nerves control her tongue. She didn't mean to upset Granny. Goodness knows, she didn't like Lawrence, didn't really know him apart from his temper but she did feel he shouldn't face the Court alone; it wasn't fair.

"I'm supporting Lawrence."

Both women turned towards the partly opened door. It was Peter's voice but the figure standing there bore the mask of a huge hound.

The look Granny gave him could have sawn through concrete.

"When was this decided?" her voice icy as she pulled the door wide open.

"As I put on the robe. It didn't seem right for him not to have a voice in circle. I doubt he's heard his own voice in his head for months now if Isaac's been controlling him. We, I mean my family, are as much to blame for Isaac laying the curse on the village as he is. It's about time we did something to make amends."

Ruth shivered. She didn't like the idea of Peter being so close to the mad cleric's ghost. What if he tried to kill him again? She opened her mouth to protest but as she looked towards him, she saw determination in his eyes and the tiny shake of his head which told her not to try and dissuade him. He had made his decision and that was that.

"Well," humphed Granny, "I can't stand here all day, I've got my own robes to wear. Put your cloaks on before you go across to church and make sure you've both been. I doubt we'll get any comfort breaks before it's all over."

The Priory church was filled with light as they entered, both from the morning sun streaming through the south windows and the two rings of lit candles suspended from the nave ceiling. Morris men, their faces blackened, stood at every entrance, pointing them towards the Nun's concealed doorway. They weren't the only ones walking along the path. There were several groups milling around inside the nave clad in woollen cloaks, their faces covered by different masks. She didn't like not knowing who was who.

The church felt different seen from inside her mask, she couldn't smell the stone or incense burning in the sensor. Peter squeezed her hand.

"I need to go down to the cell," he said. "Don't be scared. It's going to be fine. You'll see."

"How do you know?" she protested. "How many Courts have you attended?"

Peter laughed. "I wasn't born when the last one was held. My father wore the hound. He made me read his account from his diary. He said I needed to be prepared if we held another."

"What happened?"

"Nothing. Nothing could be resolved. Miriam Blackwell was gone and there was no-one else who could see beyond. Isaac ran rings around them. Fireballs everywhere." He stopped and stroked Ruth's cheek with his fingers. "You're here now. It makes all the difference. Isaac can't play games with you around."

She wanted to disagree, to tell him she wasn't as strong as everyone thought. How could she achieve anything when Isaac made her physically sick?

"What would have happened if Miriam had been there?" she asked. "What's the worst punishment the Court can deliver? Why is everyone so scared?"

Peter's expression was bleak. "Roelswick Court never rescinded the death sentence. It's considered the ultimate deterrent." He squeezed her hands, but she felt her world turned to stone. "I need to go," he said, "If the Court reaches a verdict this time, I'll need to plead on his behalf and on my own. Our families are tied in this." He strode briskly away, not waiting for her response.

No wonder everyone was so frightened of the Court. When she complained about him taking a gun, Peter said Lawrence would prefer a clean death, rather than have judgement passed by the Court. Albert Clackett, the ghastly shepherd, was genuinely terrified when Colin threatened him with the Court. If so long had passed since the last gathering, village memories must be running riot. She wondered who was stoking them and whose responsibility would it be to carry out the sentence? Greg? The Morris Men? She doubted anyone would tell her if she asked.

"Come and stand with me in the West," Ruth felt a hand on her arm and looked around to see the mask of an otter. The voice was Ally Tulliver's. She was wearing a beautiful robe with the Ladywell embroidered on the back. They went to stand in front of the great west door

"How's Andrea?"

Ally reached under her mask to rub her eye. "She's improving. I brought her over this morning. She's with Granny. All the Leaders will come in together before Lawrence is brought up and they close the circle."

Ruth glanced around, trying to recognise anyone she knew but it was hard with so many people milling around.

"It's going to be a full ritual?" she asked, "Like the one I attended for Spring Equinox by the mill?"

Ally blew her nose and deposited her handkerchief back into the depths of a hidden cloak pocket.

"Not exactly, you'll see. Look, here they come now."

Ruth watched as a small group emerged from the chapter house entrance through the transept, stopping at the centre of the chancel steps until there was total silence. She counted six people, realising the usual ritual leaders were also responsible for leading this Court.

The wolf must be Greg, the slightly taller Badger beside him, Zeb. The holly tree could only be Colin. She recognised Granny in the beautiful feathered cloak of a barn owl. Andrea must be the fallow deer hind and Mattie the tortoiseshell cat.

"Let Roelswick Court be formed." Greg's voice boomed around the ancient church. Ruth realised he was in the perfect position for sound to carry. Those who had not yet found their place moved towards their chosen spot until a huge circle formed with a gap towards the north east.

"Bring up the accused."

Ruth heard muffled shouts which became clearer as they reached the body of the church. Lawrence emerged; half dragged along the floor by two burly Morris men.

"I won't go. I won't play your games. I demand you release me, you loathsome creatures."

"Where do you want him?" asked one of the Morris men. Greg pointed to spot in the middle of the circle. Lawrence was deposited in a heap, the two men standing over him.

Ruth was surprised there were no handcuffs or shackles. Lawrence was free to move as he wished. He crouched on the floor with his arms around his head as if he feared blows would start raining down on him. Nothing happened, except the space in the outer circle disappeared.

Two figures, the barn owl and the badger, began to travel around the circle, one either side, wooden shakers in their hands. Three times they walked around before the badger came inside. One by one, the four directions were invoked by the four associated creatures, eagle in the east, stag in the south, salmon in the west and bear in the north. A bay horse walked towards the smoking brazier in the centre of the circle and threw a handful of dried herbs on the coals. As smoke curled towards rafters, she invoked the ancestors, asking their support and wisdom to guide proceedings. Ruth breathed a sigh of relief as she recognised another friend in Janet Williams.

As Janet's words died away, Ruth stood transfixed watching two lines of monks appear from the chapter house and walk around the circle, each monk standing behind a villager, providing a secondary circle.

"The monks are all here," she whispered to Ally, wishing she could tell Granny. Then she realised a message was being passed along the circle. Granny must have primed Ally to pass on anything she said. Her sight was their secret weapon.

The owl brought her staff crashing down on the stone floor.

"This circle is now closed," Granny intoned. "Let all within dedicate themselves to matters ahead. Let our ears be open, our minds clear and our hearts free. Blind justice will decide our fate."

No-one spoke. Ruth wondered why Lawrence didn't move. Defeat and despair didn't sit comfortably with him. Ruth could see it in his eyes, which were glaring at her. She shook herself. It wasn't Lawrence who looked at her, it was Isaac. She felt sick. An open palm touched her back.

"We're here," she heard a whisper inside her head. "He cannot harm you or anyone else. Stay strong." She knew if she turned around, the lay brother would be behind her. The nausea passed.

"The time has come." Granny said, "Herald, come forward. Let everyone hear the List of Wrongs performed by villager, Lawrence Graves. Make the accused stand."

The two guards went to haul Lawrence to his feet, but he moved first, standing defiantly towards the main altar, his back towards Ruth.

"Nothing you say means anything to me, vile hypocrites," he spat. "The Lord is my witness; you are all spawn of Satan. You defile the sanctity of this once proud church, though it is but a popish relic."

Nigel stepped forward, unrolling a large scroll from under his arm. He bowed to Granny and the rest of the group she stood with and then acknowledged the rest of the circle.

"Hear me, citizens of Roelswick. Under our ancient custom, I stand before you to list the actions of this villager, Lawrence Emmanuel Graves. Actions which have caused harm to his family, friends and neighbours. Until he speaks, we cannot know his intentions in performing these acts but they are listed as they happened.

"First, that he did let out a young sheep from her pasture, who then strayed into the curse laid upon St John's well and subsequently died.

"Second, that he did poison the unborn child of Andrea Hope, causing her to miscarry.

"Third, that he did cause the death of his mother, Joyce Graves, through drowning in the river.

"Fourth, that he did attack our rector, Adrian Hope, causing serious bodily harm and inveigle Andrea Hope to attend her husband in the well field so both could be attacked by his pernicious ancestor, Isaac Graves.

"Fifth, that he did imprison Andrea Hope in her own home for several hours, at the same time attacking both Gregory Iles and Andrew Turton, causing bodily harm.

"Sixth, that he did set fire to the Old Squire's summer house, property of Lord Peter, Earl of Haverliegh, causing it to be burned to the ground, making unsafe the tunnel leading from the summerhouse to the Priory and causing damage to the cellar under the West wing.

"What say you to these accusations, Lawrence Graves?"

Silence. Ruth watched Lawrence. She wondered what it must be like to have so many eyes fixed on a single person. Slowly, he turned around, his face a contorted grimace.

She knew he was staring at everyone in the circle, sweeping them with his baleful glare. She heard several gasps as someone's gaze met his and the sound of several half steps backwards which were quickly recovered so the circle did not break.

"You are all damned!" he shouted. "All of you will burn in the fires of hell! This is the devils' work and I have no part in it. I will not answer your questions. They will not touch me. I am God's representative here in Roelswick, ordained by the Bishop. You will forget these foolish words and beg my forgiveness."

Ruth looked around the circle. She wondered why no-one was

reacting any more. Was she the only one who could hear what was being said?

"It's Isaac talking, not Lawrence," she whispered to Ally, but the other woman didn't stir. Ruth felt stifled underneath the robe and headdress. Moving her arms felt like swimming through treacle. Was everyone feeling like this?

"Ally!" she hissed but there was no response at all. The Ladywell Keeper either couldn't or wouldn't hear her. The headdress was giving her claustrophobia. She tried to pull it off but nothing happened. Isaac began to laugh.

"Foolish woman!" he taunted her. "You think you have skills but they are nothing. No-one can stop me! This village is cursed. You will all live out your days in miserable torment until you turn from your wickedness."

Ruth frowned. Something was touching her nostrils through the headdress. Something she remembered. She breathed in the scent of floral incense. Incense which led her to the song of the wells, incense which came every time she saw the monks. She wasn't alone with Isaac.

She took a deep breath, allowing her irritation to give her strength instead of sapping it. Her body moved more freely. Isaac's hellfire and brimstone was getting old. She stepped forward.

"Enough, Isaac." she said. "Let your puppet rest. Don't damage him more than you already have. This has gone on too long. Today it ends."

"Whore!" Lawrence roared; lunging towards her. She was grateful the two Morris men grabbed his arms before he could reach her. A dark haze trickled up from Lawrence's body until the ghostly cleric himself was standing in the centre of the circle.

"You can't escape me," Isaac said, his hands working to form a sickening ball of flame. Her feet were rooted to the ground. She knew he was going to throw the fireball straight at her. She could hear Lawrence screaming at Isaac, begging him not to hurt anyone else.

She closed her eyes, waiting for flames to engulf her. The screams and shouts began to fade. She let her thoughts wander back to the orchard. She had no staff to protect herself, her only weapon the cool flow of water from her spring into the bubble tank. She saw it gushing over the rim into the stone trough below, imagined she was underneath the flow of water, the droplets cleansing Isaac's fire, taking it deep into the ground where it could harm none.

His cry of frustration roused her. She opened her eyes to see him standing before her, his black cloak dripping onto the stone floor.

"Your time here is done," she said. "You need to let go of darkness and walk towards the light."

"There is no light," Isaac raged.

Four monks moved into the circle, their dark habits shining brighter with every step they took.

"Come with us, brother," said one. "We all serve the Lamb. We will guide you onwards now you have agreed to move."

"I can't see the way, I will not go," Isaac screamed, his body fighting an unseen foe as they came closer. Two monks placed their hands under his, their light passing through his shadowy frame. Still he struggled to free himself, to remain where he was but the monks could not be stopped.

"This way, brother." Step by inexorable step, the group went forwards towards the altar, passing through the Roelswick beast circle without anyone noticing. A pool of sunlight shone in front of the carved altar steps. Ruth watched, mesmerised, as the group progressed slowly up the chancel. Each figure began to shimmer as sunlight touched them. The light hurt Ruth's eyes and she blinked. They were gone.

Lawrence was on the floor, sobbing. Ruth went towards him, pulling off her mask so he would know who she was. She knelt down so she could touch him aware Peter joined her on the floor.

"He's gone, Lawrence. Isaac's gone. You don't have to do anything he tells you ever again."

"I'm sorry," he mumbled. "I never meant to hurt anyone. He said the baby was already dead. I could see how ill Andrea was. He said the tea would make everything well. He showed me which plants to pick.

"Isaac told me the Rector was standing where I should be. He told me to bring him outside into the well field and he would do the rest."

"Couldn't you have brought him without hitting him over the head with the cross?" muttered Nigel, standing above them but Ruth shook her finger at him. Lawrence wanted to talk. He didn't need to be interrupted.

"I didn't kill Mother. I wasn't there when it happened, I swear. Not that she didn't deserve it." He wiped his eyes with the back of his hand. "She murdered my father. He didn't leave us, she murdered him!"

"How do you know?" Ruth hoped her surprise didn't show in her voice.

"She told me. The night before she drowned. She was hitting me with her stick. She said I was useless, just like my father. She said she should have killed me when she killed him. All these years thinking he left me alone to her fury, when it wasn't his fault. He couldn't protect me from her because he was dead!

"I didn't know what to do. I locked myself in my room. When I got up the next morning, she was asleep. I went shopping. When I came back the police told me she'd fallen in the river. I did not push her. I didn't. I wanted to, but I didn't have the courage. I'm useless, just like she said."

"You did set fire to the summerhouse. Was that you or Isaac?"

Lawrence slumped back onto the floor. "He said he'd take care of everything. If I followed his instructions, I'd have everything I ever wanted. I knew it was wrong, but I was past caring by then." He looked up at Peter. "Are you going to kill me?"

"It's not my decision," Peter said. "I can tell the others what you said but the final judgement is up to them."

Peter stood up, waiting until everyone fell quiet before beginning his speech.

"Hear me, villagers of Roelswick. I, Peter, nineteenth Earl of Haverliegh, speak on behalf of Lawrence Graves."

"Why should we listen?" someone called out. "He's confessed. Let us vote."

"No," thundered Peter. "This is no simple matter. It began with greed and avarice. The church wanted pilgrim's money and so did my family. Neither would agree to any compromise. Isaac Graves cursed the well. He died before he could revoke it. His shade was tied to the well house. The curse killed my ancestor and his eldest son. His second son took revenge on the village, casting everyone into darkness. This darkness spread. Some villagers sought to use Isaac's power for their own gain, drawing the darkness closer and giving power to Isaac's ghost.

"Lawrence was weak. He was brought up in fear and conflict. His mother beat him; while the village stood by and let it happen. We all share his blame. His mother confessed to killing his father. Did anyone else know this? Did anyone suspect?" He paused and looked around the circle. Most people shook their heads; a couple could not meet his gaze and turned away.

"We failed both child and father." Peter took a breath before continuing.

"Lawrence knows what he has done. He mourns the loss of the child as do we all. He swears he did not kill his mother. I believe him, though some of you may have a different view. The truth and judgement for her death lies with Joyce Graves. Her soul will testify, we can never know."

Ruth shivered. If her role within the village was to talk to those beyond the veil, she didn't relish the thought of a conversation with Joyce Graves any time in the future.

"I say to you all, villagers of Roelswick, Lawrence Graves did not act alone, of his own volition. He sought help of Isaac Graves and the darkness of Isaac's twisted shade blackened Lawrence's will. Lawrence accepts the harm he caused but I say to you, he was not of sound mind when he performed those terrible deeds. For that, alone, I ask you to show mercy, to seek in your hearts for forgiveness and consider a judgement which will enable Lawrence to both atone and move forward from this terrible time."

Ruth moved beside him, tucking her hand into his and squeezing it. A flickering smile sped across Peter's face. All around them people looked at each other; some whispering together without moving from their designated place.

After a few minutes, Granny raised her arms. Greg crashed his staff onto the stone floor, the noise thundering around the church.

"The village will now vote."

Zeb brought out two empty bowls, one black and one white. Janet Williams stepped forward holding a bowl full of conkers. They stood before the village elders while they picked a conker and placed it in one of the bowls. The pair went around the circle allowing everyone present to cast their vote. The bowls were presented to Granny and Andrea, who counted how many were in each. The six elders conferred, with a great deal of impassioned whispers, arm waving and head shaking.

Eventually there was agreement. Granny indicated to the two Morris men and they hauled Lawrence to his feet. Ruth could see he was shaking, his eyes red-rimmed and sunken. Peter put his arm around him to hold him steady.

"Rise, Lawrence Graves," said Granny, her words echoing into the rafters and around the outer circle of monks. Ruth found herself listening not to one voice but to a multitude of different timbres. The whole village was speaking at the same time. "Rise and be thankful. For all your acts, your life is not forfeit. You will face our wrath, for your deeds were terrible. This village is no longer yours. You are exiled from this land, never to return."

Silence, only broken by Lawrence's sobs, a murmur of comments and nodding heads around the circle.

"Not now." Ruth heard the quiet words inside her head. "The judgement is not questioned but there must be time before the execution. The man must go before the bishop."

"Wait!" Ruth held up her hand as the Morris men prepared to move

Lawrence back to the cell.

"Ruth, what is it?" Granny's voice was frosted.

"The monks," Ruth said. "The monks say Lawrence has to appear before the Bishop."

"He has to play tomorrow," the voice prompted.

"They believe it important he plays the organ tomorrow for the service."

"Surely you can do it," Granny protested.

"I don't think I should. I think he should be allowed to finish what he started. I'll help, but he should play for his last service here."

Granny conferred with Greg and Andrea.

"You're sure this is what the monks want?" Greg asked her.

Ruth nodded. "They've never asked us to do anything before. They've taken Isaac into the light for us. He can't harm anyone. I think we should agree to their suggestion."

"As you wish." Granny said. Ruth stole a glance towards Lawrence. He was staring at her with a strange expression on his face, but he had stopped crying.

Ruth hardly heard the closing phrases of proceedings. She kept hoping she had acted correctly, and it wasn't going to cause more problems.

"Stop worrying." She looked up and saw the smiling face of the lay brother as the monks processed towards the Chapter House door. "All will be well, you will see."

CHAPTER FORTY-SEVEN

"Have I done something terrible?" Ruth wailed. She was sitting in the Priory kitchen drinking coffee with Peter.

Janet Williams and other women in the village were busy sorting all the ritual robes in the drawing room. Zeb was taking Andrea to the hospital to collect Adrian and Granny went off with Greg, muttering that she had to make sure he went straight to bed as his head was still aching.

She ignored Ruth, even when asked a direct question; too busy giving instructions to Mark and other Morris Men responsible for guarding Lawrence at his home, rather than the church cell.

"I didn't ask the monks to change the judgement."

Peter gave her a sad smile. "They didn't change it, just postponed it by one day. He still has to leave after the service. He seems resigned, relieved almost, to get away."

Ruth felt her heart go cold. "Before the circle, you said you'd have to share his judgement. Are you going to leave as well?"

Peter looked away, setting his mug down on the work surface next to the dish washer. His shoulders were hunched.

"I know what he faces. Being in the army felt like exile. Other people controlling how I lived, what I thought. I wanted to come home when my father became ill. There was no love lost between the two of us, but

315

the land was crying out for someone to end the neglect. So much red tape before I could leave. So many plans buzzing around in my head, I've not been able to think clearly. Until you arrived."

Ruth closed her eyes, feeling her nails cut into her palm as she clenched her fists under the table. She didn't want him to go, they'd only just found each other.

"Would it make any difference if I asked you to stay? If I told you I want to help bring your plans to fruition?" He opened his arms and she slid inside their warmth. "Don't go."

"Who's going?" asked Janet Williams, detouring around the table to get to the kettle.

Ruth sat up, embarrassed the housekeeper should see them like this. "Peter told me this morning he would share any judgement passed on Lawrence because of his family's actions."

Janet poured boiling water into a teapot, her brow furrowed. "I don't think that's fair on anyone. Granny doesn't either, she told me. You've suffered enough. It's about time you brought stability to the estate and the village. Who else is going to manage everything? Young Eddie won't want to dig himself into the depths of beyond just yet, besides, he's only just been accepted into officer training. Do you want another manager like Grainger here for the next twenty years?"

Peter groaned. "I don't want to go anywhere, there's too much to do."

"Is there any news about the missing estate rents?" asked Ruth, wanting to change the subject before she could worry any more. Peter shook his head.

"The police are trying to get him extradited from Australia, but his lawyers keep finding excuses to delay the process. The accountants are supposed to be dealing with it. I've left it to them."

"It's a shame your Blackwell couldn't tell us where he hid the money," Janet Williams said as she collected their coffee cups and put them in the dishwasher. Ruth pushed her chair away from the kitchen table.

"You know, that might not be a bad idea. To ask the well." She grabbed her coat from the hook outside the kitchen door. She didn't want to stay here any longer, the events of the past two days were crowding in on her, making her long for the relative peace and quiet of her own home.

Peter looked confused. "You're going?"

"You need to come too, I can't ask the question for you, it wouldn't be the same."

"What question?"

"Where your money is."

Janet Williams went to the line of coat hooks and took down her employer's coat and hat, offering it to him with an amused expression on her face. He shrugged it on and went to find his boots from the rack by the back door.

"He'll be fine," Janet whispered to Ruth as she went out the door. "You both need some fresh air and time not to think."

Ruth led the way to her car, steering Peter away from the old, yellow Landrover. Every time she saw it, she remembered Isaac's fireballs. She didn't want to think about Isaac any more. She waited while Peter squeezed himself into the passenger area until she thought to suggest he pushed the seat back. She wondered how long it had been since anyone had driven him anywhere.

The drive home seemed short compared with the frantic journey of the previous night. She could see the new calves cavorting around the paddock next to Home Farmhouse. Tom must have let them out of their pens for the first time. They were certainly enjoying the spring sunshine.

She parked the car in the drive and led the way into the orchard. Just before they reached the gate, she stopped.

"Do you have a pen and paper?" she asked. Lord Peter patted his various pockets and eventually pulled out a small notebook and worn-down pencil.

"Will this do?" She nodded, pushing open the gate. The hens were busy scratching around under the far hedge and ignored them. The lambs looked up from grazing as they came into the orchard but decided they weren't a threat and carried on eating.

"Why do I need something to write on?" Peter asked as they walked down towards the spring.

"To make notes. We might not be able to remember the answer otherwise. I don't know about you, but my brain feels like scrambled egg. I wouldn't want to risk giving you the wrong message."

Peter was quiet for a few more steps.

"You're expecting the spring to talk to you?"

Ruth tried to suppress a giggle, but it didn't work. "No, the spring doesn't talk. It sends clear and cloudy water and bubbles, and I have to interpret them."

"Bubbles," Peter looked up at the sky. "You're intending to find my missing rents with bubbles."

They both stopped beside the hazel bush, admiring the yellow carpet of primroses adorning the glade. Dark spears were pushing up between the plants and Ruth was sure there would be bluebells flowering in the next few weeks. She took Peter's hand and led him to stand directly in front of the upper trough.

"Ask your question."

Peter shuffled his feet and cleared his throat, showing his discomfort. Ruth waited, feeling the peace of the glade seep into her bones.

"I'd like to know where my missing rent money is."

Ruth thought for a moment he was going to say more but he closed his mouth and shoved his hands deep into his pockets.

She gazed into the water. For a long while nothing happened. Then she caught sight of bubbles appearing from the silt.

"Three," she said while Peter scrambled to find the notebook and write down the number

More bubbles. Ruth counted as each burst onto the surface. "Twelve"

"Thirteen"

"Four"

"Ten"

The water clouded over and Ruth thought the answer was complete but as she watched it cleared again and more bubbles rose and popped.

"Five"

"Seven"

"Eight"

"Two"

An oak leaf floated on the surface of the water. Ruth blinked. It hadn't been there a minute ago. There weren't any oak trees nearby. She looked up into the branches above, wondering if a bird or squirrel had dropped it but there was nothing, not even the ubiquitous robin peering at them from his usual branch.

"That's strange."

"What?" Peter stood with his pencil poised.

"There's an oak leaf on the water." Ruth leaned over the tank to retrieve the leaf but it wasn't there. She felt the hair rise on the back of her neck. "Write down oak leaf." Peter scribbled then looked at her.

"That's it?" He squinted at the paper. "You know, if you'd just handed me a paper with those numbers on it, I'd have assumed they were co-ordinates for buried treasure."

Ruth shrugged. "I don't have any suggestions; I'm only just learning how to interpret what I see. Do you think it might be helpful?"

Peter pulled her to him and hugged her. "You are the most helpful thing which has happened to me in a long time. Now," he said, returning the paper and pencil to his pocket. "I need to get back before my children arrive. They left a message two days ago to expect them sometime this afternoon." He released her with a soft kiss on her forehead. "Go and get some rest. I'll walk back to the Priory."

Ruth watched him open the gate and disappear up the hill towards the bridle path with mixed emotions. What would his family think of her? Would they try to prevent the relationship developing? She was too tired to fight any more battles. She trudged up the slope towards the house, hoping no-one else would be there.

CHAPTER FORTY-EIGHT

The sun was shining as Ruth walked down to church on Easter Sunday morning. The whole village pulsed with new light and breezes spiced with blossom from flowers and trees. A family of ducklings were taking their first swim on the village pond in front of Granny's cottage accompanied by anxious quacks from the two parents.

The well field was full of sheep, peacefully grazing the spring grass. Ruth could see a fence had been hastily erected around the holy well. She was determined to scrub the entire structure during the week and had spent most of yesterday afternoon potting up primroses from her garden to plant around the enclosure to bring colour into the drabness.

She stopped as she came to the lychgate. The last time she walked along this path was Thursday night when Lawrence took over the service, then imprisoned Andrea. Four days ago, yet it seemed like another world. A world she did not wish to re-enter. A child's infectious laughter broke into her reverie, making her breath again. Harry, Granny's youngest at Home Farm, was running up the hill with his sisters, their mother behind them trying to keep up.

Ruth studied the daffodils and pheasant eye narcissi lining the borders. She noticed a strange car parked by the village hall, wondering who it might belong to. The church door was open and she could see

Nigel inside gathering hymn books ready to hand out to those who were coming for the service.

"Bishop's here," Nigel said as she smiled in greeting. "Adrian's in the vestry."

"How is he?"

Nigel shrugged. "He said he'll cope. The Bishop will be taking most of the service. George said he'll keep an eye on him"

Ruth remembered Mattie's father sat next to the Rector in the choir stalls so was best placed to offer any support. She was about to ask where Lawrence might be when she heard air rushing into the organ pipes and soft tunes being sent around the empty pews.

"We told him to make the most of his time here," Nigel said. "Who knows when he'll get the chance to play again."

"What if he escapes?" Ruth still didn't trust the organist not to disappear again.

"He won't. We've locked all the known tunnel entrances, two men are in the crypt, Sidesmen have a door to watch inside and Andrew is staying in the Rectory kitchen, just in case."

Ruth nodded. She was just about to ask what was going to happen after the service when she caught sight of a tall figure in a brown monk's habit standing in the north aisle. She looked around the rest of the church, but she couldn't see any other ghostly figure, nor could she hear any singing or smell incense. Nigel turned away to gather up more hymn books as Gill and the children came towards them.

Ruth went towards the north door.

"Oswin?" she whispered. The figure turned towards her, pushing off his hood. He was much older and taller than the lay brother, with iron grey hair cut short and steel-rimmed glasses. She almost stepped backwards when he strode towards her holding out his hand.

"Good morning, I'm Joseph from the Priory of Our Lady and St Kenelm in Gilchester. I'm standing in for my brother, Bishop John, he's not well, I'm afraid."

His handshake was warm and firm. His eyes crinkled when he

smiled.

"You're a monk," Ruth blurted.

"This is true." Father Joseph looked amused "I am also a bishop."

"But you're wearing a lay brother's belt." Ruth wished she could stop herself speaking her thoughts out loud. Father Joseph's gaze became more intense.

"Am I?"

Ruth looked away. "I'm sorry. I really don't know anything about modern monks. I didn't mean to be rude."

"Nonsense," Father Joseph assured her. "I'm intrigued. You mentioned the name, Oswin, was he a lay brother? A friend of yours?"

Ruth nodded. She wasn't sure how such an elevated cleric would think of a friendship with a twelfth century ghost.

"You see I woke from a very strange dream this morning." Father Joseph continued. "A monk from my order before the dissolution told me I was coming home today. He said his name was Oswin. I've been looking for signs in this church."

"There's nothing here," Ruth said. "This isn't your church, it was built for the village and dedicated to St John the Baptist." She heard Lawrence begin a new voluntary, one he often used before the choir and Rector entered the nave. A strange idea was running through her head and time was running out.

"Does your order still offer sanctuary to those in need?" she asked, shaking her head at the puzzled expression on Father Joseph's face. "Not for me. Our organist must leave the village immediately the service finishes today. Could you take him?"

"Why does he need to leave?"

Ruth thought for a moment, wondering how much of the truth she dared to share with this stranger.

"His mother abused him until she drowned last week. He asked for help from an unfortunate source and got himself into a spot of bother with both the Rector and some of the villagers. He really needs to get away somewhere he'll be safe and can recover from his ordeal."

She could feel Father Joseph looking at her more closely.

"Why are you asking this for him? Why can't he ask himself? Are you in a relationship?"

"No!" She heard the sudden silence from other parishioners nearby but steeled herself not to turn around. "It's partly my fault he's being sent away. I dealt with the influence."

"I see." Father Joseph steepled his fingers together under his chin. "Let me consider your request during the service."

"Thank you." Someone touched her arm. She looked up into Peter's face and breathed a sigh of relief. Three young people were standing behind him, eyeing her with curiosity.

"Ruth, I'd like you to meet my children, Edward and Frankie and Edward's girlfriend, Annabelle. They arrived yesterday afternoon for Easter."

They exchanged greetings. Edward seemed friendly, but Ruth felt an undercurrent of hostility from Frankie. Nigel hovered in the background, glancing pointedly towards the door where the choir was soon to emerge.

"Peter, I'm so glad you're here. This is Father Joseph from Gilchester. His order originated here. He's come to find his roots. Father, may I introduce the Earl of Haverliegh, current custodian of Roelswick Priory."

"Peter, please," The two men shook hands before Father Joseph excused himself to return to the vestry. Ruth was glad to let Nigel usher them towards the family pew. She was going to go in first, but Peter held her back, making the others go before them. She sat at the end, in case she needed to help the choir.

As soon as they were seated, the organ voluntary came to an end. The vestry door opened with a rustle of vestments. A triumphal chord sounded before the choir began to process singing the opening Easter Hymn.

It was a surprisingly joyful service. Father Joseph seemed infected with Adrian's propensity for telling jokes during his sermon. The Choir sang beautifully, never putting a note wrong, even during the most difficult solos. Lawrence even smiled when he finished conducting the anthem as he returned to the organ stool. Ruth felt her tension drain away with the last hymn; she had done all she could.

The congregation went downstairs for coffee after the service, Frankie dragging her father off with her despite his protests. Ruth lingered beside the lectern, wondering what was going to happen, now Lawrence's duties were ended. She watched him lock the organ for the last time, placing the key in its hiding place behind the stone memorial to the sixteenth earl. George Cooper, now devoid of his robes, was slowly collecting hymn books, keeping an eye on Lawrence as he did so. Three other Morris men were standing with Nigel in front of the font.

"I trust you won't let my standards slip, Ruth. It's your responsibility now."

Lawrence's words startled her.

"I'll do my best." She was going to say more, to wish him well, but she never got the chance. Father Joseph came striding up the nave.

"My dear Mr Graves," he boomed. "Such wonderful talent you have here in Roelswick. Who would have thought such a tiny village could boast such amazing music. I don't know if you've ever thought of leaving here but I have a proposition for you. We need a new choir master and I feel you would be perfect for the position. You could live at the Priory with us. What do you say?"

Ruth saw Lawrence looking wildly between Nigel and his other guards.

"Would it be possible," his voice squeaked then he coughed and started again. "I'm very flattered, my Lord Bishop. I have been looking for a new position. My mother died last week and now she's gone, I feel it would be a good time to seek something new in a different environment." There was a general murmur of condolence from the monk. "Would it be possible," Lawrence continued, "for me to come to the Priory today?"

"Not a problem," Father Joseph grasped Lawrence's hand, pumping it up and down. "Our guest rooms are open to everyone. I could show you the way now."

"Are you not staying for dinner?" asked Adrian, walking slowly towards them. "They tell me there's a veritable feast for us in the village hall."

Father Joseph declined, asking for his apologies to be given. He needed to return to Gilchester as soon as possible. With a smile at Ruth, he put his arm around Lawrence and before any more could be said they were walking down the road talking animatedly with two Morris men behind them "to help with the packing".

Ruth didn't know what to do until Gill told her Granny was expecting her help at the village hall. Together they loaded each table with piles of steaming vegetables while Zeb and Henry carved joints of lamb until there was meat enough for everyone. She saw Peter looking for her as everyone took their place but there were no spaces left near his family. Granny pulled her into a seat near them.

"Let them be for now," she said, "they need time to talk. You can meet them properly later. That way, you'll see how much mud needs cleaning up."

Ruth wished she hadn't accepted the second piece of rhubarb tart. The food was delicious and very filling: she could have cheerfully fallen asleep. Instead there was work to be done. Dirty dishes didn't wash themselves. Peter came to help with the drying-up, apologising for not saving her place.

"It's fine, "Ruth assured him. "Your children must be surprised to learn about me."

"Everything's happened so quickly," Peter admitted. "It's difficult to know what to say."

"We're friends?" suggested Ruth, handing him another water jug to dry.

Peter smiled, possibly the happiest smile she'd ever seen on his face, which gave her a warm glow inside. It was impossible to say any more with so many others milling around and once they finished, Frankie and Edward insisted he return to the Priory with them, so they could take Annabelle for a ride around the estate.

"Come up for tea tomorrow," Peter said, leaning down to kiss her cheek. "We can chat properly before the kids have to go back to London."

Ruth smiled to herself as she entered the close, still feeling the touch of his lips on her skin. What she saw next stopped her in her tracks. Robert's black Porsche was parked in front of Pear Tree Cottage. He was banging on her front door with his fist, calling her name.

Not so many months ago she would have turned around and run away before he saw her, but now the sight of him made her angry. This was her home, her cottage, her village, her friends. He had no place here.

She walked closer, noticing how untidy he looked. His clothes were stained and crumpled and he could not have shaved for days. Very unlike the Robert she knew.

She stopped at the gate, wondering how long it would be before he noticed her.

"There's no-one home, Robert," she said quietly. He whirled around to face her, rubbing his hand.

"Where were you? I've been calling for hours." He sounded more petulant than angry, too tired to cast his usual venom. His skin was so pale, she wondered if he were ill.

"Why are you here?" she asked.

He tried to smile but his mouth wouldn't co-operate. "I've brought you a present," he said, brushing past her to reach the car. "You always said you wanted more children. I've brought you one. It's yours. You can keep it. I don't want it anymore."

His words tugged at Ruth's heart. In their first few years of marriage she had imagined a family with many children. Only after Simon's birth had she realised he expected no part of raising their son. While she wept after her miscarriage, he poured scorn on her grief, constantly reminding her how relieved he was to be spared the expense of another screaming brat.

Now she watched him, mouth open, as he struggled with the seatbelt, pulling at a baby's car seat.

"Robert, what are you doing?" she protested. "You can't just turn up and dump a child here. I'm not going to look after it. I'm not your servant."

Robert stopped what he was doing, his shoulders slumped.

"Where's the mother?" she demanded. "What have you done with her?"

"Done with her?" Robert whined. "I haven't done anything. She flew back to China two days ago leaving this behind. She said her parents wouldn't accept a mongrel, especially not a girl. As it was my child, I could do what I liked with her. So I am. I don't want it. You're my wife. That's what wives do. You must take her."

Ruth was so angry, she wanted to shake him. The baby must have felt her emotions because she began to cry.

"Don't be so stupid, Robert. I'm not your wife. You can't tell me what to do any more."

Greg and Nigel came into the close from the steps.

"Everything all right, Ruth?" Nigel asked. "One of the neighbours said you had a visitor." Greg said nothing but came to stand beside her, alternately gazing at the baby and glaring at Robert. His presence made her wonder if there might be a simple solution.

"Is Andrea home?" Ruth asked.

"Yes, she and Granny were arguing about something," Greg said, stroking the baby's fist with one of his fingers. "I was glad to come away. Adrian's playing with Arthur's train set."

"Good." When she looked, Robert was slumped against the car with Nigel standing over him.

"I'm going to the Rectory," she told them. "Greg can come with me. Nigel, can you drive Robert's car? He doesn't look fit to do anything."

She backed out of the drive and was parking behind Adrian's car a few minutes later.

"Do you think I'm doing the right thing, offering the baby like this?" she asked Greg. "I know how much Andrea is hurting, Adrian too."

"What about me?" Greg muttered. Ruth squeezed his arm. "You need to find someone who can give you children you can acknowledge. You can't keep doing what you've done. It's not helping. You deserve more. So do I."

Greg got out and went to fetch the carrier from Robert's car which was pulling up beside them.

"When did you get so wise?" he grinned at her, hooking it onto his arm.

"When you rescued me from the thorns and brought me home." She locked the car and together they walked into the Rectory.

EPILOGUE

A circle of people gathered in front of St John the Baptist's Holy Well,. The newly scrubbed stones of the well house sparkled in warm May sunshine, the air perfumed by spring flowers festooned around the entrance. In the centre of the circle stood a marble bowl filled with water resting on an ornate wrought iron stand.

"Who gives this child for adoption by the village?" asked Granny.

"I do," said Robert, looking out of place in his dark blue pinstriped suit when everyone else wore robes and cloaks, awkwardly holding the baby in his hands. The little girl was looking up at him, her face moving as she prepared to yell. He thrust the shawl-clad bundle towards Andrea, who nestled her in her arm and rocked her until she calmed.

"Do you give up your rights, your hopes and your dreams as her father from this day forward?" said Granny.

"I do." He looked around the circle. Ruth could see he was trying to meet a friendly gaze, to find someone who understood what he was doing and not condemn him. She knew there were mixed feelings in the village. From talk in the pub or over tea cups in the past few weeks, no-one could comprehend how a man would willingly give up his own child but they did not criticise him as much as they might because he was giving his child to them.

As Robert stepped back into the circle, Andrea walked forward with Adrian to the marble bowl. She ran her hand through the water, forming a small wave.

"Ailsa Lian Zhen, I will be your mother. I promise to love, cherish and nurture you as long as we both shall live." She touched her wet hand to the baby's heart before passing her to Adrian.

"Ailsa Lian Zhen, I will be your father. I promise to love, cherish, support and protect you as long as we both shall live." Again, he pushed his hand into the bowl to form the blessing wave, then gently touched his new daughter's heart.

Arthur was watching his parents closely. When Andrea picked him up, he stuck both his hands into the water, swishing them to and fro at great speed. Then he dripped them carefully onto the baby's shawl, shouting, "I'm your big brovver. We're going to have fun togevver." The baby's eye's opened wider with the noise but there was no mistaking the happy chuckle she gave him as she waved her arms.

Ruth saw smiles breaking out all over the circle. It was hard to be solemn in the face of a child's exuberance. Arthur was very excited by his new playmate.

Mattie and Colin were next. Mattie brought the blessings of the east, of winds and new beginnings. Colin promised to teach her woodland lore, to understand the cycles of the sun and its effects on all growing things. Greg followed, pledging to teach her about fire, metal and the wonder of transformation.

Ruth and Ally Tulliver stepped forward together, Ally offering her knowledge of the Ladywell and to watch over her as sunset moved into night. Ruth felt her heart beat faster as she stood beside the tiny bundle. She still carried a twinge of guilt for rejecting Robert's offer of another child but she knew she had done the right thing. She couldn't go back to a world of nappies and sleepless nights. This provided a better outcome for everyone, especially for baby Ailsa. Ruth would still be here to watch over her, to be part of her family and her friend.

She slipped her fingers into the water and felt her worries disappear. She noticed their circle had been surrounded by a group in grey habits, their heads covered with black and white wimples. Were they here to provide protection from another threat from beyond? She felt no danger. The nuns looked happy and she could hear the haunting melody of the well song she learned from the monks. She must teach this to the choir before they toured the parish boundary for Rogationtide next week.

She swirled her hand around the bowl, carefully shaking off drops of water before touching the baby.

"I promise to teach you the ways of water, of life, of health and healing. I promise to bring you stories to remember your heritage and your community."

She stepped back to her place in the west of the circle.

"How can you do that when you know so little?" The voice came from an old woman, standing in front of her dressed completely in black apart from the colourful paisley scarf around her shoulders.

"I'll do my best," Ruth protested. "Who are you?"

The old woman cackled. "So full of confidence, Ruth Blackwell, just like your Grandad. He never admitted any shortcomings either."

Ruth stared at the apparition. Granny had promised to find her a picture of Miriam Blackwell, but events had overtaken them. Was this the wizened crone who made Granny's life hell? She sensed no threat from this new arrival, merely honest amusement.

"I know my knowledge is sketchy," she said at last, "but I'm sure you and Amy will help me out."

She felt, rather than saw her grandmother's smile. It spread over her like a warm blanket.

"I'll do what I can, young Ruth, but your journey is just beginning. You've found one cousin but there's still another who needs your help and guidance and only a short time to make them see sense."

"Another cousin?" Ruth felt her head swirling with questions, but the woman was gone. Granny had finished the ritual and everyone was heading towards the village hall for tea.

GLOSSARY

Aga – An AGA is a type of range cooker combining heat storage, stove and cooker. It works on the principle that a heavy frame made of cast iron can absorb heat from a relatively low-intensity but continuously burning source, and the accumulated heat can then be used for cooking. It is particularly good for all kinds of slow cooking such as stews, custards and double infused oils.

Allon – The man responsible for all the trees within the parish. As Colin Ackerley is under thirty and hasn't yet fathered a child he takes the role as the young God during rituals.

Anvil – the senior male position within the village, responsible for iron and all its mysteries. Takes the role of the mature God within the Circle rituals. Usually partners the Maid at Beltane or other rituals which require fertility magic.

Bather – when birds, especially hens and game fowl, take dust baths to help deal with insects on their feathers. This is known as bathering.

Beltane – fire and fertility festival held around Mayday. Historically this was the time when animals would return to summer pastures after being inside all winter, passing through two large fires to remove insects/parasites. A May Queen was chosen to represent the Young Goddess, who would often be chased and bedded by the representative of the Young God. Any children born out of wedlock from this day were often given the surname of "Robinson" as they were considered to be the offspring of Robin Godfellow. Common practices on this day was the Maypole dances and outdoor decorations of hawthorn blossom/May.

Benedictine Double House – Although many of the original Saxon monasteries were formed of both men and women, presided over by an Abbess, after the Norman conquest, it was unusual for religious establishments to be built for both sexes. Such "double houses" were few. Roelswick Priory is based on the Benedictine double house in Nuneaton, which was founded in 1155 by Robert Bossu, Earl of Leicester, as an alien house dependent on Fontevrault Abbey in France. It was taken back into English control by 1442 and was dissolved in 1539.

Billhook – curved agricultural knife with a short handle used, single-handedly for cutting wood, stone weeds etc. The name, bil, is Anglo-Saxon.

Blackwell – the name of this well comes from two Old English words "blaec" meaning black or dark and "wella" meaning spring or well. It gives the surname "Blackwell" to people who lived in close proximity. The Roelswick Blackwell is a "scrying well" based on the now extant Gulval Holy Well in Cornwall, which was known in the 19th century for being able to tell enquirers if their absent loved ones were living or dead, in health or sickness and the location of lost goods and cattle.

"Bob" as in "a bob or two" is an English slang expression for a shilling which became 10 new pence after decimalisation.

Clapper bridge a construction made from large stones resting on stone piers. Name comes from the Anglo-Saxon word "claeca" meaning "bridging the stepping stones".

Court – the Roelswick Circle of Justice where serious crimes are judged by the whole village.

Flying buttress – a stone arch used during the 12th to 16th centuries, usually in churches, to ground the lateral forces that push a wall outwards. Such forces usually arise from a vaulted stone ceilings or wind-loading on roofs.

Granny (Crone) – the most senior female elder in the village. Holds the position of north in the ritual circle. Granny is a senior druid and herbalist.

Hagstone – a naturally occurring stone with a central hole in it, usually flint or other hard stone. A hagstone is usually buried in the ground before an entrance to keep away evil/unwanted spirits or people. It can also be used as a boundary marker or to protect people or property.

Keep (v) – to guard, look after, be responsible for.

Ladywell – Holy well on the outskirts of Roelswick village dedicated to "Our Lady". Such a dedication usually implies the spring feeding the well was used as a water source since prehistoric times and would have been owned by a female water nymph/spirit. After Pope Gregory's edict to baptise every well with their own saint to prevent the worship of the water spirit, a well chapel was built, served by the Priory monks and nuns. This chapel was restored at the beginning of the 20th century by the Earl of Haverliegh as a memorial to his son, Cedric, who died in the Boer War. The water was associated with healing skin conditions.

Maid – the youngest female position within the village circle. The Maid keeps the East quarter, sweeps the circle free from any negative energy before rituals and is Granny's assistant/apprentice, carrying out whatever tasks are necessary.

Madron (Mother) – the position held by a woman of childbearing age, usually leads the circle rituals.

Morris Men – folk dancing teams of men who help to celebrate local festivals wearing a costume which includes rows of bells attached to legs and shoes. The first mention of Morris was in 15th century in the Tudor court and 16th century amongst lower classes. Four villages, including Chipping Campden in Gloucestershire, claim an unbroken Morris legacy. For most villages, Morris was revived on Boxing Day,

1899. Cotswold Morris is a particular dancing style carried out in Gloucestershire and Oxfordshire. Border Morris have a history of blackening their faces to prevent those in authority from recognising the dancers. Roelswick Morris Side use sticks and handkerchiefs in their dances but also serve as an unofficial police/security force for the village.

Nun's Door – the door in the side of the nave where the Benedictine nuns of Roelswick Priory would enter the church from their living quarters.

Nun's well – this well provided the drinking water supply for the nun's side of the priory (the water for the lavatoriums and for washing would have come from the river). Although not dedicated to a particular saint, it was considered holy by local people and pilgrims because of the location within a sacred enclosure.

Plainsong – the earliest form of sung music developed in monasteries as liturgical chants. It has a single unaccompanied tune and fairly free rhythm.

Processional Crypt – Churches which housed popular relics which attracted a large number of visiting pilgrims often built two staircases down into the crypt so there was a clear entrance and exit which reduced the chance of accidents. Roelswick Church is based on an amalgam of St John's, Berkswell (Warwickshire) and St Peter's Upper Slaughter (Gloucestershire). Most churches which bear the name of St John the Baptist had connections with the Knights Templars. St John's, Roelswick, housed a reliquary containing the Baptist's staff. The Village Men's Group sing a rowdy song called "John's Staff" sung to the Swedish folk tune, "Paul's Little Hen".

Rayburn – a smaller version of the Aga cooker which acts more as a heat source than the Aga.

Rector – a parish priest funded by tithes and rent from any Glebe lands (lands held by the church).

Rectory – the tied home of the rector and his family/servants.

Slasher - a long-handled knife-like farm implement used for cutting brambles and hedges. Used with two hands.

St John's Holy Well – this Roelswick healing well was part of the medieval pilgrim's route from St Frideswide well in Oxford to St Winifrede's well in Flintshire. Invalids were best served by immersing themselves in the well basin for several hours. The water was particularly associated with diseases of the bones, eyes and infertility, both male and female.

Swings and baskets – moves in English folk dances. A swing involves two people, a basket four (two couples). If the basket moves fast enough the women's feet fly outwards due to centrifugal force.

Tied (adj.) – a building which can only be used by the incumbent during the duration of their job. Ownership remains with the landholder.

Waella Holda – person (usually female) who is responsible for all waterways, rivers, springs and wells within the parish boundary. Must be consulted by anyone managing water within the village e.g. miller, waterboard.

Vicar – a parish priest usually lesser in status than a rector funded by lesser tithes. In medieval times, vicars were under the jurisdiction of the local monastery while a rector was chosen by the Lord of Manor. Prior to the Norman invasion, vicars were often married and started to pass their assets down to their offspring. This loss of assets forced the church to insist on priest and monks being celibate. In modern times, the terms vicar and rector are interchangeable.

Vicarage – the tied home of the vicar and his family/servants.

DRAMATIS PERSONAE IN THE YEAR 2014

Characters grouped according to their location, together with their age, office held in the parish and occupation (if appropriate). Residents who do not appear in the book are not listed.

ROELSWICK

High Street

The Rectory
Adrian Hope (36) Rector
Andrea Hope (32) (Madron) Rector's wife
Arthur Hope (2)

The Plough Inn
George Freeman (58), Landlord

The Crescent

No 12
Andrew Green (43) Surveyor, bell ringer and member of the Morris side

No 15
Mark Lowtham (51), Abattoir Manager and Morris Side Leader

No 19 Pear Tree Cottage
Ruth Turner neé Flint (52)

No 27
Nigel Milson (55), Solicitor, Chalmsbury and member of the Morris side,
Hilary Milson, his wife

Chapel Hill

    Roelswick Forge Cottage

    Gregory Iles (Greg) (52) (Anvil), village blacksmith

    Post Office

    John Richards (62) Postmaster and member of the Morris side

Mill Lane

    Glebe Cottage

    Amy Compson (65) (Granny)

    Zebadiah Compson (Zeb) (66) Retired farmer of Home Farm

    The Dingle

    Steven Trowbridge (50), Antique Dealer, Special Constable, member
    of the Morris side

    Mill Lodge

    Lawrence Graves (42), organist and choir master at St John
    the Baptist

    Joyce Graves (74), Lawrence's mother

    Roelswick Mill

    Karl Clayton (36) (Non-resident owner and restorer)

Priory Road

    Home Farm

    Henry Compson (35), Farmer,

    Gillian Compson (30) (Gill), his wife,

    Joe Compson (9)

    Sophie Compson (6)

    Harry Compson (3)

Home Farm Cottages
No1
Tom Tulliver, (53) Cowman, Home Farm
Allison Tulliver (48) (Ally) his wife, Ladywell Guardian,

No2
Gus Fletcher, (34) Assistant Cowman at Home Farm, member of
the Morris side
Trevor Fletcher (70) his father, retired, member of the Morris side

Keeper's Cottage
Jack Ackerley (56), Gamekeeper for the estate,
Lizzie Ackerley (50), his wife
Colin Ackerley (25), (Allon), Keeper of the parish trees
Lucy Ackerley (16)
John & James Ackerley (14)
Carly Ackerley (8)

The Lodge
Ralph Williams (58) Priory Gardener
Janet Williams (60) Priory Housekeeper
Lily Williams, (19) their daughter/ day release catering student in
Chalmsbury

The Priory
Lord Peter Brazington, 19th Earl of Haverliegh,
Viscount Edward Brazington (28) (Officer Training at Sandhurst)
Lady Francesca (Frankie) Brazington (24) (Assistant Marketing
Manager, London)

Hossington Lane

Flinder's End

George Cooper (58) shepherd at Glebe Farm

Eleanor Cooper (Ellie) (53), his wife

Matilda Cooper (Mattie) (26), Maid and PhD archaeology student

Roger Cooper (20) apprentice blacksmith

William Cooper (16),

Gerald Cooper (14),

Dan Cooper (11) Choir soloist

Glebe Farm

Jack Henson (74), Farmer,

Pippa Henson (70) Farmer's wife

Others living in the Parish

Geordie Brown (22) part-time labourer under informal Adult Special Needs Support Scheme

Patrick Hunt (25) part-time labourer under informal Adult Special Needs Support Scheme

Dogs

Dolly, spaniel – Zeb

Jet, wire-haired terrier cross - Greg

Gracie, Golden Retriever, - Colin Ackerley

Russ, Jack Russell, - Jack Ackerley

Tess, short-haired collie – Henry

Horses

Molly – Shire – Colin

Dick – Clydesdale – Colin

Drago – Donkey – Lord Peter

Flash – pony – Zeb

Sheep

Moose – pet lamb living in Ruth's orchard

LOWER MEYFORD

Bridge Road

Hollow Barrow Farm

Old Man Kessick (86), Farmer

Bruce Thompson, (48) agent/farm manager

Hollow Barrow Cottages

No1

Stanley Clackett, (55) Shepherd

No2

Ben Smith, (35) Farm Labourer

Bessie Smith (32), his sister, Waitress and former Maid, fiancée to Gus Fletcher

CHALMSBURY

Police

Chief Inspector Ross

Inspector Cullen

Police Constable Brown (F)

Police Constable Pullman (M)

Emily Treadwell, Midwifery sister, Chalmsbury Hospital, daughter of Amy and Zeb

Gerard Moulton, Accountant to Lord Peter's estate

Rachel Ackerley (21), Colin's sister, veterinary nurse

Metchley

> Robert Turner (53), Ruth's husband, Senior Partner, Crippendales
> Solicitors
> Sadie, his secretary.
> Clara, Ruth's best friend from secondary school.

Gilchester (Bishop's seat)

> Derek Carmody (50), Businessman, Lawrence's cousin
> Father Joseph (62) Bishop and monk from the Priory of Our Lady
> and St Kenelm

London

> Dowager Countess Georgiana Brazington, nee Moorcroft (74)
> Lady Caroline Enderby nee Brazington (46), Peter's younger sister.

Abroad

> Charles Grainger, Farm Manager (embezzler) at The Priory,
> Australia
> Simon Turner, Ruth and Robert's son (26) Engineer, Zurich

Deceased

> Lieutenant Cedric Brazington (1879 -1899), Peter's great-uncle,
> died during one of the initial battles of the Boer War in South Africa.
> (The Ladywell chapel was completely rebuilt in his memory.)
> Countess Susannah Brazington (1960-2004) wife to Lord Peter
> Miriam Compson (1909-1985) nee Blackwell, former Granny
> Ernest Compson, (1897-1973) Priory Gamekeeper, Miriam's
> husband, uncle to Zeb
> Roger Iles, (1899-1925) Farrier, former Anvil
> Geoffrey Graves (1939 – 1979) Lawrence's father
> Aunt Izzy (1936 – 2011) Ruth's godmother

Ghosts

Fred Anderton, ghostly resident of Ruth's grandmother's house

Isaac Graves, Rector of St John's 1724-1767

Monks and Nuns from Roelswick Priory Including Lay Brother Oswin

Wolfhounds: Finn, Oscar, Belle

ABOUT THE AUTHOR

Born in a small North Cotswold village, Sarah grew up listening to stories while helping her family around their arable farm. As a small child she climbed the steps of the medieval water cross, singing hymns in the 11th century Norman church while her grandmother played the harmonium.

Her landscape was steeped in history, from Neolithic henge through Roman roads to the second Civil War. Living halfway between two villages on their new farm and sent away to secondary school, isolated holidays left plenty of time for dreaming about the people who lived before.

After studying social policy at university, she made a career supporting NHS patients in many different forms. She has kept in touch with her Cotswold roots, providing relief organ duties to several villages for many years, like her mother and grandmother before her. Writing inspired her to study the medicinal use of plants and become a spiritual healer. Now, she teaches herbwifery on the family farm and music in the town where she lives with her husband. She enjoys exploring different parts of the UK to discover ancient sites and healing wells. *A Necessary Blessing* is her first published novel.

Original music composed by Sarah Head, arranged and produced by Johnny Yates accompanies the audiobook.

Find out more about Sarah and her work at heresypublishing .co.uk and SarahHeadAuthor.co.uk

Printed in Great Britain
by Amazon